Elizabeth L. Silver is a graduate of the MA programme in Creative Writing at the University of East Anglia. In addition, she holds degrees in English from the University of Pennsylvania and Law from Temple University, both in Philadelphia in the United States. After graduating from law school, where she studied capital punishment, she spent two years as a research attorney at the Texas Court of Criminal Appeals. She has also taught ESL in Costa Rica and English Literature and writing at several universities in the US. Born in New Orleans, she currently lives in Los Angeles. *The Execution of Noa P. Singleton* is her first novel.

'Elizabeth L. Silver is a writer to watch out for, one of great scope and passion. Here she tackles a bold topic with skill, compassion and verve'

Jill Dawson, author of *Lucky Bunny*

'Haunting, thought-provoking and beautifully written, *The Execution of Noa P. Singleton* is both a compelling psychological thriller and a meditation on the nature of justice. I was gripped'

Jessica Ruston, author of *The Lies You Told Me*

'A searing debut . . . Th[...]ands less as a polemic against [...] eartbreaking brief for [...]ers Weekly

THE
EXECUTION
OF NOA P.
SINGLETON

A NOVEL

ELIZABETH L. SILVER

headline
review

First published in Great Britain in 2013
by HEADLINE REVIEW
an imprint of HEADLINE PUBLISHING GROUP

First published in paperback in Great Britain in 2014
by HEADLINE REVIEW

1

Cataloguing in Publication Data is available from the British Library

ISBN 978 0 7553 9953 6

Typeset in Adobe Caslon by
Palimpsest Book Production Ltd, Falkirk, Stirlingshire

Printed and bound in Great Britain by Clays Ltd, St Ives plc

HEADLINE PUBLISHING GROUP
An Hachette UK Company
338 Euston Road
London NW1 3BH

www.headline.co.uk
www.hachette.co.uk

For Amir

Injustice is relatively easy to bear; what stings is justice.

H. L. MENCKEN

IN THIS WORLD, YOU ARE EITHER GOOD OR EVIL. IF NOT, then a court or a teacher or a parent is bound to tag your identity before you've had a chance to figure it out on your own. The gray middle ground, that mucous-thin terrain where most of life resides, is really only a temporary annex, like gestation or purgatory. It shadows over everyone in its vacuous and insipid cape, flying across the sky, making smoke letters out of your fears. You always know it's up there, but you never quite know how to get rid of it. It waits for you, patiently, until the day it wraps you in its cyclone and you can no longer vacillate between black and white, artist or scientist, teacher or student. It is this point at which you must choose one way of life or the other. Victor or victim. And when you do, the fear drips away as seamlessly as a river drains into an ocean. For me, it happened on January 1, 2003.

*   *   *

My name is Noa P. Singleton. I am thirty-five years old and I reside in the Pennsylvania Institute for Women. My identification number is 10271978. I am the only child of Miss Teenage California 1970 and a weeklong sperm donor whose name my mother claimed she couldn't recall. I was salutatorian for my high school, where I ran varsity track and wrote for the school newspaper, investigating the illicit and often extensive use and sale of drugs on campus. I studied biochemistry and engineering at the University of Pennsylvania and have worked as a restaurant hostess, roller rink waitress, substitute teacher, math tutor, and laboratory research assistant. I can recall with faint hyperbole the moment I took my first steps. I've had one serious boyfriend. The trial that led me to you lasted only five days, though the jury deliberated for another four. It took only a handful of additional jury pools to select the twelve individuals who were to sentence me to death five short months following my trial. Their names are now embossed in my memory, along with my grandmother's scent (mothballs and jewelry cleaner), my first boyfriend's habitual postcoital cigarette, and the feeling of the Latin letters from my high school diploma raised against my thumb.

Sadly though, my memories are starting to fade in here. Events slip off their shelves into the wrong year, and I'm not always sure that I'm putting them back in their proper home. I know the loneliness and the lack of human contact is the ostensible culprit for my memory loss, so it would be nice to talk to other inmates at least. There are so few of us.

When I arrived, there were fifty-one women on death row in the United States. All we needed was to drop one to have a proper beauty pageant, or add one if you wanted to include Puerto Rico and Guam. Now they tell me there are fifty-eight. And, of course, of these fifty-one, fifty-eight, fifty-something women, half claim to be innocent. They're always trying to blame their crime on a phantom. The phantom perpetrator who framed them, the phantom DNA evidence that vanished from the evidence locker, the phantom accomplice who was truly the megalomaniacal brains behind the operation. But the reality is there is really only one phantom who matters. The state of Pennsylvania, madam landlord to one of the most copious apparitional populations in the country. She bubble wraps humans onto death row, rolling us out on the conveyer belt of justice as if we were nothing more than bobble heads, only to let us sit forever in our single cells, with our heads wobbling to and fro, to and fro, to and fro, to fucking eternity, never allowing the stifling, nauseating shrill of motion to stop. It's almost as if that death sentence sucked the stability out of our minds, ripping out our vestibular anchors, and now everything around us, for all intents and purposes (and pardon the pun), wobbles.

I can see the five silver bars three feet beyond my arms' reach. They shift into double vision as ten lines of coil, prison garments, a staff of music. I hold out my hand to observe the intersecting life lines on my inner palm, and they morph into the unknown streets of a town map. A town I barely recognize anymore. The outer sheaths of my dry hands slough away in crepelike film before my eyes. And my five shaky fingers become ten, and twenty, and sometimes forty. This wobbliness never ceases, no matter what they do to us, no matter how many appeals our lawyers feign to promise us, no matter how many visitors we get, or how many journalists and television producers suckle on the teat of our fascinating life histories. Pennsylvania rarely kills us, almost as if she is trying to mimic my sovereign California home in a perpetual state of circumventing mediocrity. We just stay here until we die of natural causes – old age camouflaged by a potpourri of breast cancer, ovarian cancer, pulmonary emboli, cirrhosis, lupus, diabetes, suicide.

So here I sit, attempting to relive the flaws of my own past with ineffectual fortitude. I know I did it. The state knows I did it, though they never really cared why. Even my lawyers knew I did it from the moment I liquidated my metallic savings bank hoarded in the bloated gut of a pink pig to pay their bills. I was lucid, attentive, mentally sound, and pumped with a single cup of decaffeinated Lemon Zinger tea when I pulled the trigger. Post-conviction, I never contested that once.

SIX MONTHS

BEFORE

X-DAY

Chapter 1

IT ALL STARTED SIX MONTHS BEFORE X-DAY WHEN Oliver Stansted and Marlene Dixon visited the Pennsylvania Institute for Women in Muncy. Oliver trotted eagerly in first, like a wet surfer trying so desperately not to miss his second wave. He had thin brown hair that hung limply around the cherry contour of his face in a style that was probably at least a decade behind the times. (I know this because it was the hairstyle of choice when I was arrested.) A lone dimple nicked the center of his chin in a clean gunshot.

I was in the diminutive holding cell with the telephone receivers where they dragged me whenever I had a visitor. Visitors weren't rare – a story for the local newspaper? a feature for a news magazine television series? a book deal? – but when Oliver Stansted came up for his first breath, firm but anxious, steady but nervous, twenty, maybe twenty-five, I realized that my expectations would quickly need readjustment.

'Noa, is it?' he said, speaking impossibly close to the receiver. 'Noa Singleton?'

The aristocratic *Noa is it?* British phrasing of his greeting skipped upward at the end of the statement as if it were a posh question in one syllable. Confidence and naïveté burst in the same hyperenunciated greeting.

'My name is Oliver Stansted and I'm a lawyer in Philadelphia,' he said, looking down to his little script. His was handwritten in red ink. 'I work for a nonprofit organization that represents inmates on death row and at various other points of the appeals process, and I've just recently been appointed to your case.'

'Okay,' I said, staring at him.

He was not the first wide-eyed advocate to use me as a bullet point on his climb to success. I was used to these unexpected visits: the local news reporters shortly after I was arrested, the national ones after my conviction, the appointed appellate lawyers year after begrudging year as I was drafted into the futile cycle of appeals without anyone truly listening to me explain that I had no interest in pursuing further legal action, that I just wanted to get to November 7 as quickly as possible. They, like this new one, had no concern for my choices.

'So what do you want with me?' I asked. 'I'm out of appeals. They're killing me in November. "First woman to fry in years." You read the news, don't you?'

Mr. Oliver Stansted forced another smile to replicate the

one that had deflated while I spoke. He ran his fingers through his hair, pulling it out of the clean part on the side, all in order to appear the very image of a public interest lawyer; a die-hard anti–death penalty advocate who chose to marry the alleged system of justice instead of entering a legal union of his own. And, like all the others who came to me before the middle-age conversion of Republicanism set in, even his voice was typecast to match his hairstyle and choice of wardrobe: docile as a prostrated ocean, as if he had slipped from his mother's womb begging for a nonprofit position and studio apartment to match. I hated him instantly.

'Well, despite the fact that you're out of appeals, I've been chatting with some of your lawyers, and—'

'—which ones?' I jumped. 'Stewart Harris? Madison McCall?'

I'd been sitting in this cubicle for nearly a decade listening to a veritable rainbow of lawyers talk at me about the lowly little trial attorneys they thought screwed me over.

'Tell me this, Mr. Oliver Stansted. Why am I supposed to sit here and destroy their careers just so you can feel like you're doing the right thing?'

He smiled again as if I had just complimented him.

'Well, I have spoken with Mr. Harris about some of the things that happened at your trial.'

'Harris is useless. What about McCall?'

He nodded and I could tell he'd prepared for this visit.

'Unfortunately, he's since passed.'

'Passed?' I laughed. 'No euphemisms here, Oliver. Ollie. Look around. I don't think any one of us deserves a gentler explanation. What was it? Cancer? AIDS? I knew he slept around. Maybe it was syphilis.'

'There was a fire at his office,' he conceded. 'He wasn't able to get out in time. He died from smoke inhalation.'

My head nodded three short times. Things like this weren't supposed to impact people like me.

'I see,' I finally said.

'I've also spoken to some of your appellate lawyers,' he added, moving on. 'The habeas ones.'

'What did they tell you? That I was abused by my uncle? That I'm mentally unstable? That I didn't mean to do it? That there's something in my past that should give the court cause to spare me?'

I waited for a comeback. They always have one. It's like law school trains these junkies to masticate language as if it's gum. Stick a slice in your mouth, chew on it, blow it full of hot air, and then spit it on the ground when it no longer tastes good.

'No,' he said. 'Not exactly.'

'So why are you here, then? I've come to terms. It's over.' He followed my lips as I spoke, as if the Plexiglas between us stifled his voice. 'And if I'm okay with it, you should be okay with it. You don't even know me.'

'The thing is, we really do believe that you could be a good case for clemency.'

'We?' I asked.

'Yes, we think you're in a remarkably unique position that could make a strong case for filing a clemency petition.'

And there we had it, the perennial reason for the visit. A deep-seated desire to right a wrong. Or wrong a right. Or right a wrong that was done rightly for someone who did something wrong. But there was nothing more to hear. He might as well have handed over another stack of appeals, new evidence on my behalf – all futile attempts of desperation that nearly every other person with a JD who's met me has already tried.

'You think I'm wrongly convicted, don't you?' I smiled. 'You want to start your career off with a bowl of karma so big you'll be set for all the nasty stuff you'll do in the future when you work for a multinational bank or reinsurance company or something like that. Am I right?'

He didn't reply at first.

'I'm right, right?'

Again, no reply.

I sighed. 'Please.'

He looked around cautiously. 'Innocence is always a factor to discuss, especially when dealing with executions.' He almost whispered, placing extra emphasis on the word *innocence*, as if it actually meant something to him alone.

The truth is, at one point, I did contemplate my innocence, but it was short lived, like adolescent lust or a craving for chocolate.

'Did you know, Ollie, that there are, like, five thousand lonely women in Europe who are dying to marry all the men in prison?' He didn't respond. I don't think he was amused. 'You're British, right?'

'Technically yes.' He nodded, not realizing I was barely listening. 'I'm actually Welsh. I was born in Cardiff.'

'Well then. Guess how many Welsh Romeos we women have?'

Mute. He was mute.

I lifted my hand to my mouth as a whisper cone. 'I'll give you a clue. It's the same amount as the Russian ones.'

Still nothing. His reticence wasn't much of a surprise. Silence in retaliation did have its roots in proper places. After all, he walked in trying to act like Atticus Finch but didn't realize that smug complacence on the body of a pale-skinned soccer player from Wales wasn't exactly the most effective legal tactic.

'Ollie, you've got to be quick on your toes if you want to make it with the likes of these other defense attorneys,' I said, snapping my fingers. 'They come in here semiannually, begging for my free hour a day, you know. Come on, you can do better.'

When he didn't kick the ball back my way, I figured that was that for this umpteenth self-righteous solicitor.

'Fair enough,' I said, and then put the phone down. 'Guard!'

'Noa, please listen,' he finally said, faintly. I could barely hear his words leaking from the receiver in my resting hand. 'Please pick up the phone.'

He held out a hand to the division. Four of his fingers kissed the Plexiglas wall so that I could see their blueprints, little lines curved within the cushion of his surprisingly meaty fingertips. Their heat fogged the glass.

'We very much would like to talk to you.'

I waited for him to follow that statement with a name, but not one materialized. I almost turned away when he knocked again on the Plexiglas wall, imploring me to listen. A name drifted faintly through the noise. Hands pantomimed, beseeching me to pick up the receiver. *Place it near your ear*, I heard. Almost ten years after my incarceration, staring at that mismatched set of Welsh teeth, I could have sworn that Ollie Stansted was saying Sarah's mother's name.

'We?' I asked, eventually picking up the receiver.

He smiled, relieved.

'I've recently had the pleasure of meeting Mrs. Marlene Dixon, and she believes that you should live. That is why we believe – the both of us – that you're a viable candidate for clemency. It usually is a routine, dead-end last option, but because of her relationship with both . . .'

I stopped listening at 'viable'. The last of his imprints had faded on the Plexiglas, and all that was left was a greasy translucent wall. It was the only thing I could focus on at that moment. The thick manufactured division between those who live and those who, well, live another way.

'Really,' I finally replied. 'Marlene . . . ?'

The polysyllabic connection of letters that spelled out

Mahrrrr-leeen Dihhhck-sunn brought me to nauseous self-flagellation every time I heard it, so for the last ten years, I've tried never to think of those sounds together. Ollie, clearly trying to think on his toes to compete no doubt with the likes of people just like Marlene Dixon, didn't stop to listen to what I was saying, or not saying, or intimating, or, I don't know, protesting in unrepentant silence. He was a quick learner – at least that's one thing to admire about him on first impression.

'Mrs. Dixon has recently started a nonprofit organization called Mothers Against Death and doesn't feel that even the cruelest of killers deserves to be murdered by the state. I'm one of the attorneys volunteering with MAD.'

The four syllables of her name continued reverberating in the telephone wire between us like a plucked string on a guitar.

'Mothers Against Death?' I said, forcing a laugh.

'Uh-huh,' he said.

'Mothers Against Death?' I said again, this time, actually feeling the humor flush through my voice. 'You're kidding? MAD? Mad, like, you mean, like, angry?'

Oliver Stansted swallowed and looked back down to his lonely feet before pulling out a stack of papers. 'Well, yes, M-A-D.' He spelled out the acronym, pausing between each letter with perfect diction. It must have been that trusty Oxbridgian education. Pygmalionesque right down to the pronunciation of the English language.

'Isn't that a drunk driving group? Has she been sued yet for copyright infringement?' I laughed. 'Oh, wouldn't that be poetic.'

'That's Mothers Against Drunk Driving. MADD,' he corrected, punctuating the extra *D* with discernible effort.

'MADD,' I recited, enunciating the monosyllabic word as clearly as possible. 'MAD,' I tried again in the same inflection, as if articulating the difference between *their* and *they're*. 'They sound the same to me.'

'Please,' he said, rather impatiently.

'So what is it that the formidable Mrs. Dixon wants with me?' I finally asked. 'Last I checked, I'm fairly certain she wanted to witness the execution. She testified at my penalty hearing, you know.'

I couldn't tell if he already knew this or if he was still waiting on that memo to arrive at his desk.

'I believe she said that she thought the death penalty was the single most profound form of punishment to grace our nation's system of justice, and one that should be reserved for only the most egregious of crimes and the most horrific of people who could be stopped by no other means than deactivating their path of terror.' I paused, flipping through the library of scenes in my mind. 'And, if I remember correctly, she declared that, quote, "no person more suitably fit into the suit of a deserving body of that precious designer as did Noa P. Singleton". Closed quote,' I dictated.

Oliver Stansted pulled out a legal pad, clicked the top of a ballpoint pen, and placed them both on the table.

'Did she tell you that?' I asked.

'Well, things have changed for her since then.'

'Have they?'

'Like I said, she formed this organization—'

'—right, you said. Mothers Against Drunk Driving—'

'—and she no longer believes, as you say, that the death penalty is the most profound form of punishment.'

Mr. Stansted, refusing to acknowledge me, continued as if he had planned this speech for days and would get through it no matter the cost.

'She now believes it to be archaic, barbaric, and contrary to any goal that can be found in your country's history and purpose.' Oliver stopped speaking for a full fifteen seconds before he continued. 'Are you following?'

'Oh yes. Perfectly. But what if I believe in the death penalty? What if I actually believe in "an eye for an eye"?'

He stared directly back at me as if he believed I was lying. As if his beliefs were superior to mine, merely because he had an accent and, once upon a time, I had a tan.

'You don't really believe that, do you, Noa?' He folded his arms, the right on top of his left. 'I know you don't actually believe that.'

'Mr. Stansted, come on. I'm not looking for sympathy.'

'There are so few statistics from appeals for executions that have been turned down at this level – at the point of clemency, the absolute last moment to save a life,' he pleaded. 'We have to do it. We need to do it. Whether it works or not, we need to know the pattern of the governor at this point in the process. If groups like MAD and others can't see and document patterns – the patterns of the judges and juries for sending inmates to death row, the patterns for the appellate courts for affirming those sentences, and now this final pattern of governors who deny final requests for clemency – it will be harder to present a proper image to the public of how egregious this system is. Without those statistics, the government is never going to realize what sort of laws it perpetuates. This barbarism, this ancient form of punishment that offers no deterrence whatsoever to . . .'

Once more, I stopped listening. Sadly, it seemed as though I was turning away just at the point at which Oliver Stansted was, in fact, hopping into the pages of Harper Lee; but my head ached, and I couldn't listen to another speech. My mind scorched from words pronounced more properly than I'd heard for a decade. It seethed from blind ambition, from unrequited hope. And again, my head began to wobble, the heavy weight jiggling on my neck like the old throwaway toy that it was. I wanted to say something life changing to stop his proselytizing, but he was going so fast that he seemed to stumble over his words on his own until he eventually just stopped himself.

'So what do you say to all of this?' he asked. 'If not for yourself, then for the system. For other inmates.'

He didn't know any other inmates, and if he did, he certainly would want to do anything but help them.

'Look, Mr. Stansted, do you really think this is the first time I've thought about clemency or another wad of appeals? I've been through this before. Are you in here to torture me? Give me some additional hope when I'm nearly done?' I tried not to chuckle when I said the word *hope*. It's so melo-dramatic. So *Shawshank*. 'Whether it works or not – no thank you.'

'Oliver,' he said softly, unaffected. 'Call me Oliver.'

'No "Ollie"?'

He didn't reply.

'Fine, Oliver,' I said. 'You do realize that clemency's pretty much reserved for retards or those who really are—'

'—well, those who are *actually* innocent hopefully won't still be in prison six months before their execution date, and those who are impaired mentally are not even death eligible.'

'Spare me your legal sermon.'

'The reality is that I've only just begun to look at your case, and I think that we have something. The victims, the weapon, the evidence, the motive. It is all so bloody unclear.'

'Let me get this straight. You want to get my hopes up for what? A statistic?'

He shook his head. 'No.'

'You don't want to get my hopes up?'

'No, that's not what I said.'

'You want to use me for other inmates? Is that it?'

'No, Ms. Singleton,' he said, elevating his hand to his brow.

'Relax,' I smiled. 'It's fine. It's fine.'

'We just believe that, with Mrs. Dixon's new position on the death penalty, the governor might actually look at your case differently.'

'Why?' I laughed. 'Because Marlene Dixon is going to, let me make sure I understand you, plead for my life?'

As Oliver continued to lecture, my eyes drifted just beyond his mouth to a veiled backstage door from which only echoed sounds emerged. From my muffled chambers, I heard it as a high-heeled shoe tap-tap-tapping against the floor, visceral and stentorian, like listening to thunderous hail hit the surface from under water. It appeared to be a low navy-blue pump, pygmylike and broad around the heel; the type that middle-aged women wear once they no longer care about the sensual curve of their calf.

'Oliver,' I said, trying to stop him. 'I'm sorry. I know why I'm here. I don't need to recount the stages of my guilt, yet again, for another ambitious attorney who gets his kicks off of visiting convicts like me.'

'If we could just talk about what happened,' he said, overpowered by the metronomic clicking of thick old-lady shoes behind him. Her gait was so loud, I could hear it in the background through the receiver. Ollie bounced with each step, as if dancing along with the beat until she arrived in full view at the visitor's booth. Through the Plexiglas divider, I saw her say something inaudible to Ollie, but caught enough of a reaction that my soon-to-be-mulish-boy-attorney stood instantly to greet her in an obedient bow of respect. Just as Ollie was developing a twinge of fortitude, down he came in doglike hierarchical surrender. There it was. I almost lost my appetite.

'Hello, Marlene,' I whispered, tapping my receiver against the glass partition. I made sure that I spoke first, and with pinpoint precision. I didn't mean for it to sound creepy, but I suppose there's no way around that. Maybe I just want to give people what they want when they come here. I don't think that's such a horrible thing to do.

I said it again, this time with theatrical elocution.

'Hello, Marlene. I didn't realize you needed to send in an opening act.'

A subtle tic flew through her face, and she flinched. Mute before me, she removed a clean tissue from her pocketbook and wiped the mouth of the receiver. Only then did she lift it to her ear.

'Hello, Noa,' she said, clearly struggling to say my name.

That wasn't so hard, I wanted to say. Instead, I told her that she looked well, and she did look well. She had dyed her hair again, a formal practice she'd abandoned during the trial for obvious reasons. It was now a pleasant deep blonde; that same luminescent color that most over-fifties take to in lieu of allowing the gray to broadcast reality. I have to say, though, it did look good on her.

I glanced over at Ollie, who was holding Marlene's

briefcase as she settled into her seat. Then he sat down beside her and picked up the extra receiver so he could eavesdrop on our sacred reunion. The more I think about it, he really wasn't so terrible a palate cleanser. Then again, perhaps that's just the illusion of incarceration.

'So, I hear you have a new execution date,' she finally said. Her long bony fingers brushed through her bangs, and she tossed them like a teenager.

'Yup, November seventh.' I switched the receiver to my other ear. 'What are you really here for, Marlene? You can't actually be in favor of keeping me alive.'

Marlene glanced at Oliver once again and then clutched her heart with the same bony hand. She cleared her throat, dancing the waltz of hypocrisy through her lilting, nuanced tilt of the head, tender and decisive placement of her hands, and preprogrammed vocal strum.

'Well, yes I am, actually.'

My eyes narrowed at their edges, pulled upward by invisible strings until my face settled into one of those allegedly humble smiles. God, my timing was perfect. I mean, it wasn't like she was looking for happiness or mirth or gratitude or remorse, or who knows what else, but she seemed genuinely overjoyed – of course in subdued discomfort – that I seemed happy. I could never tell her that my response was actually more from humor than hope.

'Why?' I finally said. 'Why do you suddenly want to help me?'

'Oliver discussed this with you, did he not?'

I nodded.

'Still . . .'

'I have my reasons, Noa. You above all people should understand that.'

'Come on, Marlene.'

She straightened her chair to face me and pressed her lips against each other as if she was smoothing out her lipstick. It must have been blood red when she initially applied it, probably hours earlier, and now was faded into a rustic mud. No doubt she ached from the inability to reapply inside these walls.

'You really won't tell me why you want a do-over?'

Marlene ignored me. Instead of answering, she momentarily put away the receiver so that she could lean down to pull out a stack of folders from her monogrammed leather briefcase. As soon as she came up for air, she dropped the folders on the table with a loud percussion. She wasn't going to answer me. Fair enough.

'So, what's the deal with MAD?' I asked, playing along. 'You couldn't come up with a better name? You were bored? You were kicked out of Mothers Against Drunk Driving after you were cuffed with a DWI?'

She picked up the receiver again, still searching through her files.

'I'm going to presume your ignorance is a direct result of your confinement, Noa, and I will no further entertain your curiosity about my participation in your clemency petition as I will discuss the details of my daughter's funeral with you.' She finally looked up to me. 'Is that clear?' She was the first visitor outside Ollie S. not to offer me candy or refreshments from the vending machines.

'Sure,' I sighed. 'I don't get it, though. What can your coming here even do?'

'Oliver should have explained this to you,' she said, without turning her head a quarter of an inch to her right where he was still sitting motionless. 'I explicitly told him to tell you about this. Besides, haven't we already gone through this?'

'He did, he did,' I said, forcing an empathetic smile toward Oliver. 'And yes, we sort of went through this. Still, I don't understand the sudden change of heart.'

'It's not a change of heart, Noa,' she said, staring directly through the partition. 'It's owning up to the one I've always had.'

I had never known Marlene to possess even a quarter of a heart, let alone a full one.

'What? Now you're speechless,' she half-laughed. 'That's never been your problem, Noa.'

'I'm sorry, Marlene. I don't mean to offend.'

'You didn't offend me, Noa,' she said. 'You just still haven't grown up. After all these years. You've bled through all of your appeals at the state and federal level without so much as lifting a finger to help your attorneys. And yet,' she stalled. 'And yet . . .'

She never finished her sentence. Not then. Not over the next six months.

'I suppose I deserved that,' I said, looking over to Oliver. He quickly turned away.

'Look, I want to help you, Noa,' she said, her voice slipping. 'I want to talk to the governor about you. But if I'm going to use my influence to speak with the governor and tell him that, as the victim's mother, I cannot live with this execution, I need something – anything – from you that tells me that you have changed. That you are a good person now. That you never meant to do what you did. That you are a worthwhile asset to this earth. So just talk to me, prove it to me.' Her lips were dry. She wet them with her tongue before continuing. 'Life is not my choice or the state's choice to end. I believe that wholeheartedly now. But with even greater urgency, on a personal level, I want to believe it to be true with you.' She patted the sagging skin under her eyes with a single index finger. 'Does any of this make sense to you?'

'You have changed, but I don't think that there is anything I can tell you that will make you change your mind about me.'

'Do not insult me,' she commanded, and with that tone, I could tell just exactly how she'd become so successful. Before the trial and, even more so, after. 'Do *not* waste my time, Noa.' It was still monotonous and shiveringly potent, but now so calm. Calm like the eye of a tornado calm. Calm like a millionaire who walks by a street bum calm. Just confident calm, you know? So with that, my muzzle finally unclipped, and without her suave coercion, I was finally able to say it.

'I'm . . . I'm sorry.'

It wasn't even that hard. That was the most surprising part about all of it. I couldn't say those words for the duration of the trial, and here, they slipped out, like extra change falling through a hole in your pocket.

She exhaled and her flattened chest puffed outward.

'I just want to know you. I want to understand.'

Oliver and I shared a glance when she stopped speaking.

'Why did your parents call you Noa?' she asked. 'What is your favorite food? What colors do you like? Do you,' she paused. 'Excuse me, did you listen to any specific types of music?'

No acknowledgment to my apology. But again, I played along.

'Okay,' I said. 'I used to like sushi, really, before it became so popular. I have a thing for show tunes, Broadway musicals, especially *Cabaret, Carousel, Chicago* – the one-word *C* ones, not necessarily the prison ones. And, well, I guess it's not even that I liked them, just, I listen to them mainly because of my mom,' I quickly corrected. 'Sorry. Listened.' I stalled. 'Hmmm, what else? I like green, pretty much any shade of green. Forest green, lime green, plain old green-green, grass green, hunter green. I did actually complete a half marathon once.' I looked at her attentive eyes. 'My name,' I asked. 'Really?'

'Don't feel compelled to talk about only those sorts of things, though,' Oliver interjected.

Marlene twisted her neck like the top of a soda bottle opening and stared Ollie down so much so that his chair pushed away – almost on its own – and squeaked like a subway mouse. The chair actually did the job for him, both verbally and physically. He dropped his receiver and quickly picked it back up again as to not miss anything. I had almost forgotten he was even there. That's the kind of person Marlene Dixon was – pre-radiation and post. She just sort of eclipsed everyone else in her presence. Perhaps that's why she never liked me. I didn't allow her that narcissistic luxury.

'Really,' she nodded. 'I want to know.' She paused again, forcing concern. 'Why *Noa*?'

She made no pretenses about anything, really: her desire, her pleas, her appearance. Dressed extravagantly in that tailored suit, pitch-black and flowing loosely over her widening hips, she was the complete opposite of every other woman in my life. Ruby studs poked through each of her sagging earlobes right at their heart. A long golden chain hung over her blazer, sinking down between what would have been her breasts if they hadn't been removed in the publicized double mastectomy that ran concurrently with my trial. (I know that my verdict had nothing to do with that, but I can't help but wonder – even now – what would have happened if the jury members never knew about her health problems.) At the bottom of the chain was a stout locket, approximately two inches long, that I'm sure housed a portrait of Sarah at birth, and of course, college graduation.

'Fair enough,' I said. 'I can't really explain what my mother was thinking, but I was fairly certain she wanted a boy, so she gave me the boy's name of Noah. It's pretty much that simple.'

'But you spell it *N-O-A*,' Marlene continued.

'Are we back to spelling words out now? It's not an acronym for anything.'

Still she persisted.

'Look,' I said, 'when I got to high school, I dropped the *h* because I thought it sounded cooler. More original.'

Ollie perked up. 'They gave you a middle name.'

'No middle name.'

'But the record.'

'I gave myself a middle name, Ollie,' I said, raising my voice. 'Imagine getting bored with parenthood before you even finished naming your own kid.'

Ollie didn't respond. Marlene did not look pleased.

'It's fine,' I said, lowering my voice. I cleared my throat before continuing. 'It's just that you can't do anything original or memorable if you've got a boring name. That's all. Middle name, hyphenated name, polysyllabic ethnic name or not, know what I mean?'

'Well,' he said, thinking to himself. 'What about Bill Clinton? Or Jane Austen? Or Jimmy Carter?'

'Flukes,' I concluded. 'They slipped through the cosmic cracks.'

Marlene finally spoke up again. Ollie had taken a few too many lines for her taste. 'The thing is, the way you spell your name,' she said, 'it's a Hebrew name. A beautiful Hebrew name for women.'

'Hebrew, eh?' I inquired, as if I didn't already know. People are always coming in here telling me things as if they're the first to bestow the obvious on the incarcerated, as if they like to feel like they are telling me something I don't already know. A stamp of righteous superiority by virtue of prison seat selection.

'Really?' Oliver asked, like I had just told her that Michelangelo painted the Sistine Chapel or that Jesus was a Jew. Really, Marlene. This was the best you could find?

But while I was talking and Oliver was taking notes, I could tell that something was changing. A sudden drop in temperature in the visitor's room. A slowing of the clock. A stalling of a pulse.

'I wanted to name my daughter Noa,' Marlene confessed, 'but my husband didn't like it.'

'I didn't know,' I said after giving her time to mourn this farce of a loss.

She lifted the stack of folders in her hands, placed them upright, and tapped them until they fell into alignment. 'Well, things don't always turn out the way we plan them, now do they?' She then leaned back down to her briefcase and put away the folders. 'Thank you for your time, Noa. We'll be in touch.'

After Marlene and Oliver abruptly left, just as abruptly as they came, Nancy Rae (my sometimes favorite prison guard – she works only three days a week) cuffed me and walked me back to my cell in my own version of the correctional institute Walk of Shame (or, in our case, Walk of Fame).

It never takes long, particularly because, in recent years, I've come to be a model citizen on the Row. When they shout 'Hands' immediately after finishing a visit, I walk backward to the door like the queen of England is before my personal Plexiglas court, cross my arms behind my back, and slip them through the opening in the door, where Nancy Rae (or someone slightly less resembling an institutionalized caricature) cuffs my wrists. They don't apply them with care, and for about three months into my incarceration, I would often return to my cell postvisitations with a scattered sanguinary design, not too dissimilar to those bangle bracelets I used to wear in the '80s or my favorite diamond tennis bracelet anteincarceration.

(One of my former neighbors, Janice Dukowski, who was convicted and sentenced to death for paying someone to kill her husband, used to try to kill herself at least once a month by slitting her wrists with her fungal toenails, and you could never pick out the scars because her bloody bangles always covered them up. But I digress.)

I, of course, am nothing like that now. I always allow my arms to be locked and always hold my head high during the Walk of Fame until arriving back at my cell, where I sit for another twenty-three hours for a single hour of recreation or until another journalist or lawyer wants to come and speak with me. Really, it's that simple.

I lie down so much in my bed that my body can't always handle the mere act of standing upright. Sometimes, when a guard comes to my door and lets me know that I have a visitor, like with Oliver and Marlene, I stand from my bed, and instead of walking toward the bars, I fall to the floor instantly, my muscles atrophied, my limbs bereft from activity, my bones hollow and echoed. Once, I gave up my daily hour of recreation because I was so upset with my mother after she stopped calling and writing for two weeks that I lived within that six-by-nine-foot cell by myself for upwards of five additional weeks, only standing up to urinate and defecate. I found out later that she was on a Baltic cruise with a fireman named Renato, whom she met while at a support group – not for parents of the incarcerated – but for single mothers slash actors sans equity cards. By the time she got in touch with me again, the five weeks were over, and I had to spend another ten trying to redevelop my muscle mass by pushing up from the cold floor forty times an hour.

Now, though, I take advantage of my recreation hour (often sprinting for fifteen feet at a time, watching television, or selecting new reading material), and I sashay with correctional humility when I'm walked between the visitation booth and the cell as if my handcuffs are actually diamond bracelets, Nancy Rae is my secret service officer, and my cocoa-brown prison scrubs are cashmere shawls.

At least once an hour, I'm woken up in my cell. Most people wake up midslumber because of nightmares or to quash their dreams or to use the bathroom. I wake up because my current neighbor screams hourly for her lover. She killed him in Harrisburg, allegedly in self-defense, but the truth is quite contrary. I remember it vividly because it happened before I got here. She was robbing a convenience store when she shot him in the head. 'Him,' of course, was not, in fact, her boyfriend or lover or husband or friend, but a guy named Pat Jeremiah, who was the owner of a local sports bar she frequented. He had gone out to pick up some cigarettes when she followed him inside the convenience store to get the cigs for him – of course free of charge. She pulled out a gun when the convenience store clerk wouldn't oblige but, not knowing how to use it, accidentally set it off toward the door where her stalkee was exiting. She was so fraught with fear and heartbreak that she shot the convenience store clerk as well and ran away. All of this was caught on surveillance camera and played on the news at the time I met Sarah, so she has a special place in my heart. But the point of the story is that she screams at twenty-one past each hour, the time of death for her beloved 'Pat' of 'Pat's Pub'. It keeps me aware, at the very least, though. I don't have a clock, and the only way I know the time is by my neighbor screaming, 'Pat, I love you, Pat! I need you, Pat. I miss you, Pat!' in triplicates. In truth, I don't know that she even has a clock in her cell. Presumably not. Maybe it's not actually twenty-one past the hour each day when the conductor taps her baton. But something tells me her internal hour stings at that moment daily, so I trust it as much as I'd trust a sundial. She's reliable and omnipresent. I like to call her Patsmith in homage to the olden days when your name indicated your vocation, like a blacksmith or silversmith. In this case, she was a lover-killer, a Pat-killer, a Patsmith.

The other fifty-five minutes of each hour are occupied by contemplation of my past, of my crime, of the spiders that build their homes in the corners of my cell. I can't speak with any counterfeit personalities that purportedly live in the cell with me, and I don't think that anyone wants to hear my singing voice. My neighbors speak with themselves rather than through the wall to me. And I'd rather remain silent than confess, yet again, through a wall with bars and eyes and ears and microphones.

I'm in prison, for Christ's sake. It's literally a vacuum into which people are sucked to clean up the outside. I live inside this vacuum that is my own universe, and I think about me (and Sarah and Sarah's child, and occasionally Marlene and my father and my childhood friends). That's why, when I get a visitor, all I can do is talk. Talk and take in what the visitor is wearing or saying or not saying. Observation is my only remaining skill. If they or anyone else (be it Oliver or even Marlene) want to claim that I was self-absorbed before I got here – fine. But not now. Now I obsess over image because that is what people obsess over with me. What I look like, what I say, what I did. I obsess over the fact that I'll never become middle-aged. I obsess over the fact that I'll never be able to change my hair color to cover my experience. Or counsel younger versions of myself.

Then again, every once in a while, a person will come into the vacuum to bring me something new to ponder. Oliver certainly didn't. At least not yet. But there was something seductive in his innocence. For hours after he and Marlene left, I pictured him looking at me through the Plexiglas divider, smiling a smile stretching from Alcatraz to Sing Sing. In that hour, he was a politician, a TV game show host, a weatherman, selling me on his authenticity and his reliability. He was also a fifteen-year-old boy who had just graduated from middle school and this was his first assignment. No, he was a twenty-four-year-old young man who had just graduated from law school, and this was his first appointed case – the case, in fact, that he felt could inform the rest of his pathetic career. But he was too young to do anything. Too untested. Too unsure of who he was going to become to devote his time to anyone like me.

Then he came back alone the day after Marlene gifted me with her presence and brought with him an empty pad of yellow legal paper. He pushed a loose strand of hair behind his ears (where an unexpected tuft of gray sat like a bird's nest) and pleaded to me, just like Stewart Harris and Madison McCall and all those lawyers pleaded to the jury so many years ago when they convinced me to fight the charges in court.

'Let's look at you as a person,' he said. 'Let's look at Marlene and what she has to say. Victim impact testimony is precisely what makes this case different from others. And because of Marlene, we can approach clemency from the inside out. We can allow her to spearhead everything. A clemency petition, a declaration from the victim's family, an affidavit with her signature and with her plea for you to live, all directed to the governor's desk for his immediate review. Let's see what the governor thinks. Does he really want to let you go to the gurney without a fighting chance?' Oliver said to me, as if begging me to grant him clemency. 'People are what matters now. It isn't the facts. It isn't the law. It's compassion. It's people.'

It was clear that I was Oliver's first client in here. And who doesn't want to be somebody's first anything?

Still, even though the taste of being someone's first something (even while incarcerated) seemed delectably irresistible, I did resist. He wasn't offering anything new for me. It was the other way around, and quite frankly, I was exhausted from giving. Then he reminded me about Marlene.

'She doesn't believe in the death penalty anymore?' I asked. 'Truly?'

Oliver shook his head.

Clearly there had to be more to it than just that, but in an instant, my head dropped to my chest in defeat. To Oliver Stansted, though, my acquiescence was a vigorous nod of compliance. And almost on cue, he picked up his legal pad in his right hand and pushed on the head of the ballpoint pen with his left.

'Do you mind if I take notes?' he asked. It was his first moment of willful determination, and I couldn't help myself. I wanted to spend my final days with Atticus Finch. I wanted to be charmed by Mark Darcy before I ate my final meal. I wanted to speak with Clarence Darrow. Instead, I settled on Ollie Stansted.

'No, I don't mind.'

I'm sorry for agreeing. In retrospect, I wish I never had. I'm saying it out loud so it's quite clear: I wish we had never started this.

Chapter 2

MY MOTHER DROPPED ME ON MY HEAD RIGHT AFTER I was born.

It happened in the hospital, just moments after bequeathing my first sound (a rough high-pitched scream reminiscent of a mezzo-soprano). The doctors handed me to her, and slimy and laminated with blood and amniotic fluid, I just slipped through her fingers and fell right onto that sweet spot of softness crowning my skull. Preempting a double lawsuit, one of the nurses gathered me from the ground and pumped me with drugs while the doctors attended to my mother. I never even had a chance.

Okay, it didn't exactly happen that way. And clearly, it's not exactly a memory per se, but it's a story that I like to think captures my early days. Take it or leave it.

It is true, though, that my mother dropped me when I was

a baby. As the story goes, I actually did fall out of her hands from the top of a stairway when I was ten months old, landing on my right side where the shoulder meets the arm. My mother screamed at the top of her lungs after it happened and rushed down the stairs until she grabbed me from the floor.

'Noa!' she cried, scooping me up into her bosom, kissing my ears, my forehead, my shoulders. 'I'm so sorry, I'm so sorry.' Kiss, kiss, kiss. 'I'm so, so, so, so sorry,' she continued, as if any ten-month-old could understand her muffled apoplectic utterances. But perhaps I did, because, as the story goes, I stopped crying at that point, which did anything but calm her.

'Noa?' my mother stuttered. 'No . . . Noa?'

Needless to say, she was afraid I was dead.

'Noa?' she screamed, running to the phone to dial 9-1-1. 'Please be okay, please be okay, sweetheart.'

No doubt not only the idea of my death or paralysis tackled her fears, but perhaps also the news that a year earlier, her best friend's boss's older sister's cousin's next-door neighbor accidently fell in her kitchen, rather unfortunately causing a burning skillet to fly off the range of the stove and land on the soft head of her two-week-old newborn, killing him instantly. This woman was immediately arrested for capital murder and had since been in jail in some nameless state in middle America awaiting trial for something over two years. I'd like to think that my mother was more concerned about my continued life, but somehow I'm fairly certain her fears were slightly more focused on the urban legend *du jour*. That's what I take from her semiannual mythological reprisal of the day that changed our lives forever. (At first, she seemed almost proud of her ability to cover up for her immortal maternal deficiencies. Then I was arrested, and oh-so-conveniently, she decided to publicly blame herself and this incident in particular for how I turned out.)

'Noa, sweetheart,' my mother screamed. 'Cry for me, baby. Cry!'

At that exact point in time, I apparently issued a guttural sound, a choke that sounded like I was releasing a gulp of seawater.

'Noa!' my mother cried. 'You're okay. You're gonna be okay. You're gonna be okay. You have to be okay.'

She reached for the phone. She still used a rotary and struggled to insert her red-tipped index finger into the pea-sized holes.

'You have to be . . .' she mumbled. 'You have to be.'

She called the police.

'Nine-one-one operator. What is your emergency?'

My mother picked me up and patted the pillow of my arm as she spoke.

'Yes, please, send someone right away. My daughter, she's ten months old.'

'And?'

'And there's been an accident!' she continued.

'What happened, ma'am?'

My mother froze, words unable to both form and swim from her. 'My daughter—'

'What happened, ma'am?' the operator persisted. 'I need to know what happened.'

'My . . . my daughter has been injured!' she cried.

'How was she injured?'

My mother kissed the windshield of my forehead with her two wide lips and continued to smother me with them, creating a path of saliva all the way down my arm, from the injured shoulder to the elbow.

'Hello?' the operator asked. 'Ma'am, are you still there? Is this a crank call?'

She held my arm between her thumb and index finger, feeling the heat of the injury beneath.

'Ma'am?' the operator asked, raising her voice.

'There was an intruder,' my mother blurted, spontaneously spouting language. Any language. 'I don't know who it was, but he came in and took some of my jewelry and then left.' My mother paused. 'And . . . and . . . and when he was here – he was wearing a black ski mask, so I didn't catch his face – my baby girl started screaming. He ran . . . he ran . . . he ran upstairs to stop her, and, and then . . . when he got there, somehow, she . . . she had crawled off the top of the stairs. And . . . then . . . that was when it happened!'

'When what happened, ma'am?' the operator asked, her voice still calm.

'That was . . . that was when she fell.' My mother paused

again, gasping and punctuating her tears. 'She fell down from the second story. Oh my God, please come quickly with an ambulance. Hurry, please!'

An unnatural pause dangled between them.

'What is your address, ma'am?'

'I don't even know how she got out of her crib,' my mother added. Each syllable was laced with emphatic tension.

'We can worry about that later, but let's get your daughter the attention she needs,' the operator added in a soothing voice. 'I need your address now, though.'

'It's 1804 Pin Oak Drive,' she sputtered. 'Hurry!'

'We'll have an ambulance there right away, ma'am. And please try to stay calm until it gets there.'

'Uh-huh . . .'

My mother hung up the phone before the operator could complete her warnings, ran back upstairs with me in her shaky grip, and placed me on a rocking chair. Then, she leaned over and kissed me again, this time on the tip of my nose.

'I'm so sorry, sweetheart. I can't lose you. Not this way.'

People might wonder how much of this story is true. But every other year when she got a part in the local theater or when she met someone new, there it was like the goddamned quality of mercy, polished in iambic pentameter. I don't know. Perhaps I piece together bits and pieces of the legendary story in a way that makes me comfortable. It doesn't really matter. The only thing that matters is the truth, and the truth is, I'll never forget the sound I next heard.

'I love you, sweetheart,' my mother whispered, before lacing up a long black boot, sticking it out from her body like a martial artist, and pirouetting it to kick the wooden bars of my crib with so much power so that they broke into dozens of splintery pieces. I began to cry again.

'Shhh, shhh, sweetheart,' my mother continued to say, looking over her shoulder to make sure I was still safe. 'I have to do this. I have to do this.'

She tore apart one side of my crib so that an exit route was simple, even for my underdeveloped ten-month-old mind. She picked me up and then ran downstairs, grabbed a butcher's knife and launched it into the cushions on the couch. Dragging it horizontally, a single stab carried across the flat surface, resembling a fault in the earth's crust. Puffs of polyester shifted beneath.

My mother knew that in order for the break-in to appear authentic, there had to be collateral damage. She picked up her trophy from the Los Angeles County Beauty Pageant of 1970, and with the strength of an Olympic shot-putter, tossed it directly into the television. An explosion of colorful wires, seizing and scorched with clouds of smoke, culminated. My mother dropped the trophy on the serrated sofa and fell onto it; I was placed on the neighboring love seat. And then we waited. She, sweaty with feathers of polyester floating across her chest, and me on my back, upturned like an exterminated cockroach.

As soon as the ambulance arrived, my mother was finally

able to dry her tears. She sat in the back of the van, along with the two paramedics who arrived on the scene a cool seven minutes after the television exploded. No police arrived, even though my mother's call expressly suggested illegal activity. No report was filed about a break-in, and nobody ever called to follow up. I'm not sure how she managed to avoid that, but then again, she was an expert actress. It never brought her the success she dreamed of, but it came in handy at times like this.

'She's going to be fine, Mrs. Singleton,' a paramedic said. He had blond hair and a long Corinthian neck.

My mother was strangled by tears. Her left hand, naked as the day I was born, caressed my right arm.

'It's a good thing your little tot has so much baby fat. It really protected her fall,' another paramedic added. 'It looks like it's just going to be a bad bruise.'

My mother's voice croaked through her hysterics. 'A bruise?'

The first paramedic put his arm around her, covering her shoulders with one of the red blankets in the back reserved for flood survivors. 'Yes, Mrs. Singleton, we've just got to check her out at the hospital, but it looks like she's going to be okay.'

She shrugged, pulling the blanket a little closer to her chest. 'It's only Ms. Singleton. There's no mister.'

Three months later, my mother married Paramedic One in a little white chapel in Las Vegas. She was pregnant again and determined not to lose this one to another woman five years her junior. It was June in the late seventies. My mom wore a miniskirt, long auburn hair, flat and singed at the tips by an iron, and gold-plated hoops. I was her bouquet, dressed in a ballerina costume painted with lilies. My mom even sprayed my dress with perfume so that I would smell like flowers. She walked down the aisle to 'Bridge Over Troubled Water' when Paramedic One took her as his one and only wife. And then, he proudly slept by her side for another fourteen months.

Regardless of what transpired during my first year, my arm never properly healed. Although the ER doctors disagreed with Paramedic One's initial diagnosis of 'just a bruise, ma'am,' my mother refused to accept anything but his advice and treatment. In fact, my arm was broken in three places and, considering the early stages of bone development of a ten-month-old, required a great deal of care. After we arrived at the hospital that night, my mother stopped paying attention to me. She was flirting with Paramedic One throughout the drive, the examination, and the treatment plan, with which, of course, she and Paramedic One disagreed. She was supposed to wrap my arm every few hours for ten days, changing the dressing and keeping the arm tightly wound to my torso, but over the next month, she was too busy making baby #2 to wrap and rewrap the arm, so needless to say, it healed improperly.

The baby fat that protected me from the initial fall slowly evaporated, and my arm atrophied into a pencil-like spike for a short portion of my toddlerhood. I was briefly left with only three working limbs, which, at the time, wasn't as horrid as it sounds. I learned to walk earlier than most toddlers because I needed my feet to take me places that my arms never would. I learned to talk early, too, because I couldn't point to what I wanted. This is not to say that one look at me, and I appeared like Kevin Spacey migrating between Verbal and Keyser Söze. My right arm was fine – it fell parallel to my left, enabled me to grasp a pen, write on a chalkboard, hold a flute, that sort of thing. By the time my little brother came around, it was as if my mother had never dropped me in the first place. Had she not felt the need to habitually remind me of that day, memorializing jolts of electricity up my right arm with each retelling, I would have forgotten it even happened.

But this was not enough for Ollie's first day out.

'The more we speak, the more I can know you,' he pleaded to me when I told him I was done for the day. 'The more I can try and find people who can write in to support you. It will help us produce the best clemency petition possible. Marlene's endorsement is essential, but if you have any other people in your past who might write in to help commute your sentence, it can only help.'

Like Paramedic One was going to sign an affidavit in favor of keeping me alive.

I actually lived a decent, middle-class suburban life with a single working mother, stereotypical tagalong baby brother, and a rotating set of stand-in fathers, each one sporting a different style mustache. One was a wormlike Clark Gable do, another an oily blond handlebar, another an ebony Dalí, and sadly, I'm embarrassed to report, my mother slept with a man sporting a Hitler 'stache. (I know it was peculiar, to say the least, but I didn't know better at the time.)

I must have been seven when my mother stuck me in speech therapy, thinking it would help eradicate my minor speech impediment, thanks to an incident with one of the 'stache men. She had been sleeping with a man with a cater-pillar mustache and thick wiry spectacles who worked as an accountant for the restaurant where she waited tables. (I saw him at our house for breakfast one morning. He was wearing blue pin-striped boxer shorts and a V-necked white under-shirt with mustard stains across the chest. I remember feeling his shifty eyes scanning my body like a Xerox machine, from top to bottom, slowly, a light flashing behind his eyes when he reached my end.) One morning, he made fun of the way I asked for my cereal ('Mommy, can you pwease pass the fwoot woops?'), and the next thing you know, I was stuck in speech therapy two afternoons a week.

The speech therapy continued for two years, bleeding into my mother's theatrical antics, and led to advice by my therapist to propel my newfound freedom of speech into professional public speaking. So, when I was nine years old, my mother dragged me and my brother to some forty rehearsals for her one and only starring role in a musical.

She was playing Annie Oakley in *Annie Get Your Gun*, and dressed to the nines in colorful anachronistic country western flair, she belted out those ridiculous songs from the stage as if singing directly to me.

Anything you can do, I can do better. I can do anything better than you, she sang, as the pathetic twelve-person orchestra below her cranked the final notes of the obnoxious song. At the time, I might not have known what they were singing about; but what I did know was that my mother and this actor (who, because he had a mustache, I'm pretty sure she was sleeping with at the time) sang that they could do random acts of attrition better than the other, thirteen times in three minutes without any evidence backing it up other than playful romps that only slightly humored the audience. I was on the crux of double digits, and even then the music seeped under my skin with irritation. Here was a woman who could do nothing right in life singing before thirty or forty people about how great she was, and they all believed her because of painted-on freckles and a fake wooden rifle. On opening night, right after she finished the song, I remember her tilting her head ever so slightly to my direction and winking. It was the last time she would break character.

When I was ten years old, my mother's facial hair fetish gave way to an athletic addiction. By that, I mean, she only dated runners. And by runners, I mean competitive speed walkers. I don't mean to pass judgment or anything, but approximately half of the speed walkers my mother took home sported a mustache across their upper lips, so she can claim she got over the 'stache fetish, but she didn't. Not really.

I'll never forget walking home from school one day and seeing my mother and a mustachioed speed walker sashaying up to the front door after a whopping three-mile jaunt, their hips shifting from left to right, their arms staggered in pendulous rhythm, and their feet tenderly touching the ground from heel to toe, heel to toe, like developmentally challenged salsa dancers. I was with Andy Hoskins, the most popular boy in school, and Persephone Riga, the most popular girl in school. My mother's feet picked up movement along with her boyfriend's, all the while as she placed the key in the door's keyhole, and then within moments, their rotating hips almost swayed in syncopation, his mixed with hers, like vodka and cranberry juice, like rum with coke. Right there in public. On our front door. For the entire neighborhood and Andy Hoskins and Persephone Riga to observe.

Despite this nefarious production, Persephone later became my closest friend, my constant companion, and my confidante, until the middle of seventh grade, when her parents moved the family away from the school district to a neighborhood where having a tennis court in your backyard was not considered excessive or 'affluent. It was just considered normal, like having an indoor bathroom and doggie door was considered normal in my neighborhood.

At first, I didn't see a lot of Persephone after she moved,

but after about a month or so, she started to invite me over to her house and teach me how to serve and volley on the backyard tennis court, or smash down a lob so that nobody could possibly return it. After only two or three weeks, it was as if she had never left.

I still remember the first time I visited her small palace on the other side of town. Her parents were pleased that she was still comingling with her former classmates, as she was having a rather clumsy time acclimating to her new school. They invited me in, gracefully, almost as if they were the servants to a new manor, and served me lemonade in a crystal wine glass and Girl Scout cookies on a crystal cheese platter.

'Thin Mints, Noa?'

I nodded, eloquently, the way I thought someone in her home would reply. 'Yes, ma'am, Mrs. Riga. Thank you very much, Mrs. Riga.'

'Freshly squeezed lemonade or pulpless, Noa?'

'No pulp, Mrs. Riga. Thank you so much, Mrs. Riga.'

Persephone laughed when she heard me talking to her mother as if she were royalty.

'Come!' she cheered, 'I want to show you something.'

She grabbed my hand and pulled me over to her parents' dining room, where dozens of porcelain dishes were displayed behind glass so thick you'd think it was protecting the Mona Lisa from itinerant fingerprints and bullets.

'Check it out,' she told me. 'My mom says they're worth like twenty thousand dollars.'

The china had fleurs-de-lis hand-painted on each bowl and dessert dish. How did I know they were hand-painted? Persephone told me.

'They're hand-painted,' she said proudly. 'My mom told me they're hand-painted. That's what makes them worth so much. We got them with the house after my grandpa died. Isn't it cool?'

I wasn't sure which part of it was cool, but I was pretty sure that I didn't fit in with people who spoke about china patterns and fleurs-de-lis, and even less so with people who had tennis courts in their backyards. I understand now that Persephone and the Rigas didn't fit in with them, either. Susan and Georg Riga didn't paint those fleurs-de-lis by hand. They didn't build that tennis court by choice. They were merely inhabiting new imperial robes, almost like I have with the color cocoa brown.

For months, Persephone proceeded to invite me over after school on days when she didn't have a tennis lesson or a French lesson or dance practice, to show me some extravagant new relic of inheritance that her mother or father deemed too priceless to display. The Rigas were always placing their beloved items behind glass or behind a closet or behind a wooden cabinet or in a safe. It was as if they never felt comfortable in their new station, like they never unpacked from their old life. Clothing that Persephone and I had purchased together when we were neighbors lay dormant in old suitcases, never opened. Mrs. Riga started picking up extra lines around her eyes and lips every time someone called, because she didn't quite know how to answer the phone. And sticky plastic skins cloaked all their furniture, as if they were too nervous to soil it with their old routine. They woke up one day with someone handing them a new life without their choosing, and they were unsure of how to conform, like someone who has recently been relegated to a wheelchair.

It took me over twenty years, but I finally could relate.

My mother told me years later that if someone hands you a new life that has been watermarked as enviable and emerald, you take it – regardless the cost. I thought of Persephone's transformation away from me for years, never quite grasping her need to step into that new life, until it was time for me to do the same.

When I was seventeen years old, I was salutatorian of my high school class. I was chosen to give the oration at graduation. I had earned a scholarship to the University of Pennsylvania and was sharing postcoital cigarettes with the cutest boy in school (yes, Andy Hoskins) on a triweekly basis. To top it off, I had no father to tell me I was doing it all wrong.

Andy Hoskins ran track for our school and was going to Cal State Bakersfield on a full athletic scholarship in the fall. The night before graduation, he slept in my bed along with a box of cigarettes, a matchbook, and an empty notepad. He kept urging me to work on the speech, finish the speech, practice the speech, trying to frighten me with such comments like: 'Do you know how many people are going to be watching you tomorrow?' 'These words will be your epitaph!' 'This is the most important thing you've done up until now'. And so forth. Perhaps he knew how prophetic those comments would be, fast-forward a few years into the future. Perhaps not. It's not my job to dwell on these things.

I remember looking into his blue eyes that night, wanting to throw away the pencils and the pens and the yellow lined legal pads and just stay in bed. I didn't care about my speech. I was sure that my impediment, asleep as it may have been, would come out in public, despite the years of therapy. All I wanted at that point was Andy. He was all I could think about. I can remember, even now, the windmill of air-conditioning cooling my moist back on that night in May. I still smell his olive-hued skin next to mine as I urged him to spend graduation in bed together. It would have been the first time we'd go to sleep together and wake up together. I didn't want robes or mortarboards anymore; I didn't want clapping parents and grandparents. I just wanted us.

My legs crawled around him. 'We can skip the ceremony. It's not that important,' I told him, closing my legs about his chest. Back then, my legs were smooth and sculpted, and my calves swung out as little tennis balls each time I flexed.

His jaw dropped at my proposition. 'People like you aren't supposed to speak that way.' Andy's heart was pounding, probably without him even knowing it. 'You don't even realize what an opportunity you have,' he said, standing up from the bed.

Instinctively I rose and stood next to him. Our eyes met. I was just as tall as he, just as fit, just as tan. He probably never got over that, the equality between us. Then again, I suppose since I was salutatorian and I was going to Penn and he was about to be an ex-jock going to a state school, then we weren't exactly equal, per se, now were we.

'Look, I barely study,' I finally said. 'This stuff – school – just comes easy to me. Why does it even bother you?'

He sat back from me. 'I can't be with someone who doesn't take herself seriously.'

'I take myself plenty seriously.'

He locked eyes with me. 'No, you don't.'

Then he found his shorts and slid them on one leg at a time. His calves, his thighs, his forearms were all so tan; and the hairs on that bronze skin were bleached nearly blond from the hours he spent running outside, jumping over hurdles, slipping on the rust-colored track. 'I gotta go,' he mumbled. 'I have to actually prepare for tomorrow.'

He grabbed his shirt and started draping it over his top just like they do in movies: all those fuming men who can't remember where they put their pants, even though they know the room well, and rush outside half-naked, teeming with an anger that can't be contained inside four walls. That's pretty much how Andy looked when he walked out on me the night after we slept together for the second to last time.

I watched him storm away from the upstairs window of my mom's bedroom. I wanted to scream, 'What the hell do you have to prepare? You walk across the stage, pick up a piece of paper, shake some old freak's hand, and move on. Real tough, Andy!' But I didn't say it. I let him have the last word, and for that, he forgave me the night before I moved to Philadelphia.

At graduation, my salutatorian speech failed to impress. I stole a load of Shakespeare quotes and sandwiched them with Bobby Frost to create the most clichéd 'Go Forth and Prosper' homily my high school ever heard. No doubt, had Persephone not transferred, she would have been salutatorian and postulated more eloquently in front of all those people than I did.

Andy collected his diploma with subdued panache. I heard he went on to train for the Olympics in track and field but couldn't compete due to an Achilles tendon injury. Now he's married to a dental hygienist, is a commercial real estate agent, and lives somewhere in the San Fernando Valley with his litter of five-point-whatever kids.

Three days after my high school graduation, I received a letter in the mail from my father. Not one of the baker's dozen of men rotating through my mom's bed in the '80s. Nor Paramedic One (or was it Two?). No, I'm talking about the sperm donor, the one she'd always called a one-night stand, the ex. My Real Father.

It was a postcard from somewhere just outside Philadelphia. The front of it was a large picture of the cracked Liberty Bell with a little red heart painted on top of it. 'The City of Brotherly Love', it said in white cursive bubble letters. When I turned the postcard over, it said, 'Congradulations! Love from, Caleb'. There was absolutely nothing else on the postcard but the word *congratulations*, spelled with a *d*, and his name and address.

'How do you know this is from my father?' I asked my mom.

She sifted through the mail, picking up a hefty envelope from Publishers Clearing House and tearing it in half, then in fourths, and eighths, and so on until a confetti mug shot of Ed McMahon sprinkled the table. She did not, however, dignify my query with a response of any sort – visual or audible.

'Mom?'

'What?' she asked, without looking my way. She was sweeping the confetti into her palm.

'How do you know this is my father? Is this his name? I thought you didn't remember who he was?'

When she didn't respond, I understood everything. I grabbed the postcard, stuck it in my purse, and took it as an open invitation for contact. My mother disagreed.

'If he wanted to be a father, he would have been a father,' she later said.

And that was the end of the discussion.

Chapter 3

Everyone is so fascinated with the accursed 'why' of my crime. They are obsessed with the organic origin of my hate as if it were born in some petri dish, fused together by the toxic roots of my genetic tree.

If I were to offer an explanation of why I did what I did, half of the public wouldn't believe it, and the other half wouldn't think it changed a thing. The only people who would be transformed by a revelation are related to Sarah, and this so-called revelation isn't going to bring her back. So why does anyone really need to know?

Back when my trial began, I thought about doling out various 'whys' to the press. A new story per printing.

One: I was suffering from posttraumatic stress disorder after having spent that night in the hospital all those years earlier. The Psychologist-Approved Theory.

Two: I was drugged at a New Year's Eve party and didn't

know what I was doing. The Victim Theory. (The public eats this one up, expecting me to ultimately own up to actually knowing what I did.)

Three: I hated Sarah and didn't want her to be happy. The Cain and Abel Theory.

Four: If I couldn't have what I wanted, then nobody could. The Cain and Abel Theory, part deux.

Five: She was rich and I was poor. The Marxist Theory.

Six: She wanted me to do it. She wanted the easy way out. Only not necessarily the way I did it. The Jack Kevorkian Theory.

Seven: I had daddy issues that bled into every part of my motivation. This one is neither logical nor boring, most certainly never gets old, and doesn't even merit a label.

Of course, explanations three, four, five, and seven were heavily developed by the prosecution and ultimately became the reason the public needed to put me in here. Though, deep down, I'm fairly certain nobody truly believed any of it. When I told Stewart Harris of my creative role as press secretary for the prosecution, he quickly got a gag order until the trial was over. By the time it was, I didn't care enough to answer the question of 'why' to the remaining press who were actually interested enough in my life to even cover the story for local periodicals with circulations of less than one thousand.

When you try to find the answer and explanation for a law, a scientific discovery, a tumor, and you can't identify its reasons, then you just cut it out. Surgically remove anything potentially cantankerous. Cauterize society around it so that we'll never know the real answer.

For example, two months after I moved to Philadelphia and began my freshman year of college, my first semester was cut short by an emergency abortion and partial hysterectomy. I was in Van Pelt Library gathering some books for a paper I was writing on the French Revolution when I fell down into a crumpled ball. A quiet librarian found me in the stacks (somewhere in the *N*s of History) and took me to the overpopulated waiting room of the emergency room at HUP. I really can't tell you much else, other than the fact that I left a nasty pool of blood in that spot in the library, and I'm told you can still see a stain.

By the end of the week, I was no longer able to have children. Evidently, the child that Andy and I had conceived three months earlier was growing in my overrun uterus. A handful of fibroids had also decided to take up residence and refused to share the space. The child we conceived had, no sooner than it developed a heartbeat, lost that heartbeat in the *N*s of the library and then later was cleaned out at the HUP Center for Women's Health with another two letters I grew to hate. It would almost have been predestined had the miscarriage brought me to my feet in the *D*s and *E*s of History. That way, when people trace my life history back to this point in time, they could look at books about the Diaspora, Evolution, or Ethiopia instead of Napoleon or Nefertiti or even an edited survey of North Korea.

People always look at that moment in my life as the colorful influence that painted the following five canvassed years. The whispers, the articles, the prosecution's theory, the voices that sit above my cell like poisonous gas. *Can I have children? Can't I have children? Did I blame men forever? Do I blame myself? Whose fault is it? Were the doctors to blame? Did they need to remove her uterus? Maybe she could still have had children if she tried harder. If she wanted it more. If she wanted it badly enough. Really, can she not have children anymore? Really? Did Sarah know about it?*

The prosecution dubbed it the Van Pelt Incident. The origin of my downward spiral, the egg to my angry chicken . . . you see where I'm going. But the truth is, it was simply the worst physical pain I'd ever experienced. Nothing more.

After the Van Pelt Incident, I spent four days in the hospital and was visited by only one person – the librarian who stumbled upon me in the stacks that day. She hand-delivered the book I was researching at the time so I could finish my report on the French Revolution, and also brought me a book on nuclear energy from the *N* section that no longer had any use to the library. I finished the history paper but decided not to turn it in. I remained a student at Penn until the end of the semester but didn't return after the Christmas break.

The bottom line is that I've never sweated through another night worrying I might be bringing a little Noa into the world. Most important, no matter what they say, I've never really cared.

Besides, I know that's what Oliver's really doing here. He's another paid marionette trying to get an answer to Mama Marlene so she can get that interminable 'why' out of her system and finally move on with her life. X-day is certainly not going to help. She's stuck there in that 'why' scratch on her record repeating *ad infinitum* until I pluck the disc from its player, clean off the scratch with a simple puff of my lips, and hand it back to her to hear the music properly. She hasn't a clue that records have been replaced with newer technology. That's the problem.

Of course, Marlene's other problem is that she already knows why her daughter died – she just doesn't want to believe it.

June

Dearest Sarah,

I hope I'm doing the right thing. God, I hope I'm doing the right thing. My thoughts are so jumbled together now that I sometimes lose track. You have to know that whatever happens at the end of all of this, I am doing it all for you. I did it all for you. It's just that these things take so much time. The system works so slowly that you can't always predict the outcome. I know I can't, no matter how meticulous I've been, no matter how many appeals I have filed, and how many friends I make and lose. Life, just like death, is as unpredictable as a jury.

I suppose I'm sort of asking your permission for what I'm about to do. God, even when I type this, I feel conflicted. But I'll just come out and say it. I visited her. I visited her at the Pennsylvania Institute for Women, and she hasn't changed. Not a bit in ten years of incarceration. Not in nearly a decade of solitary confinement. She's had all this time to think about the past, and yet the lies and haughtiness keep spilling from her as if prison doled out credit for good behavior for each and every fabrication, each and every glimmer of contempt.

As you can imagine, it pains me to use that name. Noa. All I can see when I look at her is a cold-blooded, borderline personality-plagued, folie de grandeur double murderer. But her name, sweetheart. Not Noa Singleton. Noa P. Singleton, she declares.

Noa

Noa

<u>*Noa*</u>

It means motion and movement, though she's not doing much of that on the Row.

Noa.

It falls so smoothly from my lips when I say it. I wish you could try it with me.

I'm sorry for all of this, but to whom else can I talk but to you? Sweetheart, I thought I owed it to you to tell you about my visit. It's taken me so many years to get to this place. I've tried to move on, just like I know you would have wanted. I've dealt with the loss of your father. (Thank goodness you didn't have to watch him waste away.) I've tried to make friends, but I think people are still afraid of me so my Rolodex is fairly slim. It's funny, because I don't know if people are afraid of me now because of what happened, or if they've always been afraid of me and I've only just realized it.

Sarah, in all honesty, I wish I knew how you'd feel about Mothers Against Death. You've been with me this entire time, from the moment I testified at her hearing, to the moment I began MAD, until even this week on my visit to the prison. You were so close to motherhood. New to motherhood, really. I know you would have understood this instinct. You understand — as someone who has created life — how it is not in our hands to take it away. It simply isn't.

I'm so sorry it took me this long to get here, but at least I'm here now.

I haven't talked much about the visit to the prison (and I will, I promise – I'm just having trouble focusing right now). I'm now working with a first-year associate at my firm named Oliver Stansted. From day one, he demonstrated an interest in pro bono work – in particular, criminal defense. No other First Years wanted to soil their new suits with prison work, and Oliver walked into my office more eager than he really should have been, almost as if he had planned this all along. At first, it took me off guard. He is a Cambridge graduate. He graduated with a Double First, spent quite a bit of time traveling around America, and also skirted offers from most of the major firms in New York for his summer internships. He chose our firm in Philadelphia for his first permanent job. I actually remember his original application over the summer several years ago. (I always remember the foreign applicants. Their résumés are usually printed on A-4 paper, and they never bother to Americanize the spellings to fit. He did, though.) Right now it's just the two of us. I set up Mothers Against Death shortly after he came into my office with his mammoth smile and perfectly tailored suit. You probably would have had a crush on him. I'm fairly certain Noa already does.

So, I'll just come out and say it and hope that you approve. Through Mothers Against Death, Oliver and I are putting together a clemency petition for Noa. It really is almost a formality, a futile plea to deliver to our trusty executive, and is more than likely to be turned down.

Before you worry, though, make no mistake – Noa will never see the light of day. We are just trying to get the governor to commute her death sentence into a life sentence, where she'll spend the last of her too many remaining decades behind bars. She will still be in maximum security, still a convicted murderer, and will still continue to agonize over what she's done, turning her arrogant, self-centered, self-righteous mind into mulch. But she will be alive while she does all of this. It's not really our place to kill her, just like it wasn't her place to kill you. I believe that now. It took me nearly ten years to get here, but I believe it. You understand, sweetheart, don't you? I know you do. She deserves this. It's a far worse punishment for taking you away than getting to leave this life before me.

I have to go now. I probably shouldn't have written you, but I had a few minutes to spare and there was nobody else with whom I wanted to spend it.

Forever yours,
Mom

FIVE MONTHS

BEFORE

X-DAY

Chapter 4

I THINK THE THING I ACTUALLY MISS THE MOST IS watching a sun sit still on a solid evening hour, its talons skewering the clouds beneath. That elongated stretch through the clouds; that beam downward, pointing like a strict schoolteacher, informing everyone around that, yes, there is a higher purpose. I'm not saying I found religion in here just because I can't watch a sunset anymore. God, that would be cliché, and I'd rather die than pass on that impression. But I do sit alone, sometimes, wondering whether the clouds are gathering together, communing like a collection of cotton balls in a tightly sealed ziplock bag, or whether they've been flattened out like a stack of pancakes. Or if they've been vaccinated with a syringe of rainy dye so that only a select few darken into grays, blacks, and charcoals.

It's funny how most things come in threes. Cumulus, nimbus, stratus. Three times a charm. Three strikes and you're out. Hickory, dickory, fucking dock. I suppose, then, that it would only make sense that I'm going to die in a trio of poisons. Sodium thiopental, pancuronium bromide, potassium chloride. A three-drug cocktail designed first to anesthetize, second to paralyze, and third to exterminate. This, my lawyers told me, was a far more humanitarian way to finish the job than its predecessors, which included all but not limited to public executions of any and all forms, a firing squad, hangings, gas chambers, electrocutions, and, of course, our very own lethal injection. For some reason, people still like to call it The Chair, as if they're holding on to the good old days. But nobody fries from the needle. They know this as well as they know the instrument of death that brought them here. No. They just experience botched anesthesia, welcoming the paralysis that precludes them from informing a single living being that the potassium chloride stings. It stings so much that the volcano at the vein has erupted prematurely, and as a result, molten lava is slowly rolling through the body, incinerating and smoldering arteries and organs in its track, like being burned alive without the ability to scream.

I've read up about it. I have articles from those habeas lawyers and from Madison McCall. It's supposed to be painless, and might actually be. But how can that be tested? Honestly, is someone really going to care about any pain we feel on our twenty-sixth mile? They're going to do it anyway, no matter how many veins they have to test to find the right one, no matter how many people divide up the task, no matter how late in the night they proceed. They're going to do it anyway.

In the '40s, they tried to fry some kid for murder and failed twice. They charged his body full of electricity – the metal cap tickling his brain, the straps wound tightly around his arms – but they couldn't do it. It wasn't his fault that the incompetent executioners messed up twice. Still, they tried it a third time to make sure the boy was dead, taking pleasure as his body shook in a lightning bolt of momentary seizure until, like the sizzling flicker of a fading lightbulb, he finally turned off.

Like I said, everything has a way of coming out in threes.

'I know that your father left before you were born,' Oliver said to me before 'Hello', 'G'day', or any number of greetings he could have mustered this early in our fledgling relationship. It was only a handful of weeks in, and already he was storming into the visitor's booth toting a rolling briefcase behind him looking like Marlene Dixon's fiendish protégé. Part of me wanted to slap him, and the other part wanted, well, the other part wanted the contrary, as I listened to him rambling off an enumerated register of alleged facts from my past that he, no doubt, was proud to uncover.

'I also know that your mother hasn't visited you in five years. Your brother has visited you only once, as he lives paycheck to paycheck in Encino as a production assistant for a small independent film company. You never met your maternal grandfather, and your maternal grandmother suffered a fatal heart attack when you were arrested. You were never able to go to her funeral. Your paternal grandparents' absence needs no explanation. I know that you were accepted to Princeton but decided on Penn instead. I know that you wanted to become a doctor and scored exceptionally high on your SATs but never followed through on that goal. You didn't even attempt to get back into college. You never took driver's education, once took a flight lesson, are nearsighted and lactose-intolerant.'

A smirk seeped out between my lips like an unsuspecting belch. As if he were the first person to take an academic interest in my life from January 1, 2003, onward.

'All that is in my trial record?'

Amused, I unfolded my arms.

'Shall I go on?' he continued.

'If you must.'

'I know that you chose to sleep through your trial and refused to offer any mitigating evidence at the penalty phase. And of course, that is primarily why we are here in the first place, isn't it?'

'If you insist.'

'You didn't help your attorneys at trial or on appeal, and you certainly aren't helping me to piece together anything that can spare your life now. We have five months remaining, and you've done nothing but tell me about your mother's mustache fetish.'

I sat back in my chair and placed my hands together, slapping them hard in slow motion at Oliver's Academy Award–winning speech. It was very melodramatic, if I say so myself. The actress who will play me in the future cinematic depiction of my life will be thrilled to have such rich and hackneyed material from which to base her rendition.

'Well done,' I said. 'You've reread my record and run a ninety-nine-dollar background check. But before you applaud yourself too earnestly, know that I only have a *half* brother, and he works in the exciting but respectable-ish industry of adult film. I actually attended Penn for slightly less than one semester and dropped out, you're right, because I couldn't shake the Van Pelt Incident. But good job there reminding me of the biggest failure of my life. My flight lesson was in a rickety old biplane in La Jolla when I was too young to even see over the dashboard of a car, which is why I *did* take driver's ed. My grandmother died on the day of my *conviction* – not my arrest. And I'm farsighted.'

This was actually quite fun.

'You're not inhuman and fearless,' he said to me, after a long pause. A strand of hair dropped between his eyes. 'I know you think you are, but you're not.'

Across the room, I noticed that Patsmith was getting seated in her telephone booth, awaiting another visitor for the umpteenth time this week. She wasn't looking at me, though. She was staring at Ollie, as if he was another Pat Jeremiah of the ephemeral Pat's Pub.

'We have five months to put together a narrative that might spare your life,' Ollie finally said. 'If you don't open up to me about who you are, about why you're here, I can't help you. And I want to help you, Noa. I really do.'

Beyond Ollie, beyond the multiplying layers of glass, chairs, linoleum, visitors, guards, space, Patsmith was turning away to someone new. I couldn't help myself from watching her, but throughout it, Ollie's gaze never left mine.

'Don't get all serious on me now, Ollie. Come on,' I teased. 'It's the least you can do for me. It's not like you're actually my real lawyer. We both know it's Marlene. You and I are just another one of her little projects.'

He shook his head no with a smile – the universal sign that he knew his place but wasn't about to challenge the one person who could alter it. Maybe he didn't believe me. Maybe he did, and that's why he grew reticent.

'Tell me this, Ollie, did you always want to come to Filthadelphia, America, to work for one of the last remaining Queen Bees of the women's lib generation so that she could make you feel guilty about everything you've ever done? Is that why you hopped over?'

A nervous grin bled through his face. 'She's not that bad.'

'You'll see.'

'And, yes, I did want to come back here.'

'Back?' I said, lifting my legs to the chair. 'Now I'm listening.'

He smiled downwardly again, signaling to everyone around him that he was approaching distinguished-hood prematurely but hadn't quite realized it.

'Noa, please focus.'

'I am,' I said.

He looked behind to Patsmith and Nancy Rae and the surplus of empty chairs before slumping into his chair like a derailed child.

'I spent a summer traveling cross-country on a bus before university, and I loved it here.' He smiled, his cheeks spackled with dark-red spots. 'I always knew I wanted to come back.'

I laughed. 'You spent your summer on a bus?'

'A Greyhound bus,' he said proudly, as if reliving the vile memory.

'You're kidding, right?'

'What?'

'What do you mean . . . what?' I asked. 'Nobody takes the bus cross-country in America. You do realize that.'

He sat up. 'I hate flying – that's why I took the bus. That's all.'

'Oh, Jesus Christ,' I sighed. 'You're one of them. You're afraid to fly.'

'No I'm not,' he said.

'Come on.'

'I'm not. Really,' he said lowering his voice. 'I was actually conceived on a plane.'

I folded my arms, one on top of the other. 'I'm listening,' I said, though in hindsight, I don't think I really was.

My eyes were drifting slightly beyond him to Patsmith, who was now glaring over at us from behind her visitor (a priest? a grandfather?). But Ollie's lips were moving in animation, his eyes jumping about his face. Somewhere between Ollie's throat-clearing anxiety and nail-biting interrogation, he had slipped into the role of enchanting storyteller, far better than Madison McCall, who never told me so much as his wife's name, or Stewart Harris, who claimed he lived in Philadelphia, but I knew really lived in the Delaware Valley on the weekends, where his estranged ex had full custody of his children. Ollie, one month in, was already sharing the files from his life without my prying so much as a birth date or alma mater from him. It takes a certain amount of self-awareness to confide so much in a near stranger this early on. It takes an even greater amount of resilience to proffer it to a double murderer.

'My dad was a pilot, my mom a flight hostess,' he continued, 'and, yes, it's terribly charming—'

'—I was going to say cheesy, cliché, nauseating, but go on.' I smiled, looking directly at him.

'I was conceived on a weekend flight somewhere in either Morocco, Algiers, or Gibraltar, but no one can be sure exactly where.'

'Please tell me your father was not flying the plane that weekend.'

Oliver laughed, briefly. 'No, he was just flying with my mum that weekend as a passenger.'

'I see.' I smiled. 'Cute.'

'He's very important to me,' he added. 'My father.'

He clutched his hands together into a ball but didn't

elaborate. Instead, he gazed at me, looking up, sort of. He was short – I could tell that even when he was sitting down – and blessed or cursed with a mug of babyface magnitude. But his words were so elegantly articulated – even silently – that I was getting lost in his damned gaze. It bothered me.

'You're not very subtle, are you, Ollie?'

Again, the uplifted shoulders.

'How do you know that what you're reading in your record is actually the truth?' I asked.

'Perjury, Noa,' he declared. 'That's how.'

'And nobody lies on the stand? Really, Ollie. You're foreign, but you're not that foreign.'

'You never took the stand.'

'You have a point there,' I said, 'but that's not the reason I didn't testify. Ask Marlene.'

'What do you mean?'

'Nothing.' I sighed, looking beyond him again. Patsmith was still in her booth speaking at someone, while staring over at Ollie. Ollie was my visitor, though. Not Patsmith's. She wasn't about to change her name to Olliesmith days (or was it years?) prior to her execution.

'Noa?'

I looked back to him.

'Nothing,' I said. 'You know, you're not going to find anything new in that record of yours. You think I haven't read it from cover to cover?'

'I spoke with your father yesterday on the phone.'

From their fans of lashes, average brown eyes stared back at me with urgency and precision. It was like he wanted a medal for picking up a telephone.

'Guard!' I called. It was instinct at this point. I stood and looked out from the divider. Out of the corner of my eye, I noticed Nancy Rae putting her Dr Pepper can down on a chair to walk over to me.

'Why won't you tell me about him?' Oliver pleaded. 'I was really starting to like you.'

'He was very concerned about you,' Ollie replied.

'I haven't heard from him in years,' I said, looking back to Nancy Rae. 'I heard he was in Costa Rica.'

'Canada.'

'Canada,' I said, still looking for Nancy Rae. 'Okay. Fine, then. Did Marlene put you two in touch?'

'Marlene?' He laughed, shaking his head no. 'No. She doesn't know where he is.'

'Right.' My head nodded, and I sat. 'How would she?'

'I just felt that there was something missing when I read the transcript,' he said. 'So I tracked him down.'

It was almost as if he were looking for validation. Pride in his job well done far beyond the call of pro bono law firm duty. I was about to hand him a dozen roses and a tiara when Nancy Rae arrived outside my door.

'Noa, please,' he said, almost pleading with me. 'How often have you spoken with him?'

I said nothing.

'Noa?'

'Three times,' I said. 'I've spoken with him three times since.'

'Three times?' he echoed. 'Try again.'

God, he was relentless. I thought the English were supposed to be slightly more passive than us. Meanwhile, Nancy Rae's ring of keys jingled off her belt like a corporate janitress. Metal clanking echoed into my booth as she searched for the proper key.

'Look, I knew my father only briefly before the trial, and honestly, that is the real reason that Sarah died, okay?'

'Excuse me?'

'Forget it, Ollie. You'll never get in touch with that man again. Trust me.'

'What do you mean, that's the real reason that Sarah died?'

'Hands,' Nancy Rae requested, rather timely, as soon as she found her key. She opened the four-by-ten-inch window on the door. It was the size of a mail slot. I stood, backed up to the door, and like a wounded bird, poked my bony fingers through the opening from behind, and the metal cuffs once again adorned my wrists. Oliver stared at me during the whole spectacle without budging.

'Noa, please answer me.'

'There's no need. Clearly you already know everything you need to know.'

Chapter 5

IT WAS AN ANOMALOUS TUESDAY NIGHT IN 2002 WHEN the phone calls started. For over a week (at precisely 6 p.m. on Tuesday, Wednesday, and Thursday nights), my apartment became a torrent of moral decay. His moans lubricated the phone lines like a sexually transmitted disease. Whirls of tornadic subjugation seeped through the little holes of the telephone receiver, which, within seconds, was marred by a rapid dial tone. I would answer, and before having a moment to ask who it was – (Paramedic One? Andy Hoskins? the Rigas? my baby brother joking around?) – was hung up on as soon as I spoke.

I didn't think much of it after the first call. Or even the second, really. It was only after the third that I started to get a little concerned. I believed, even after everything that preceded my incarceration, in honor and in trust, two virtues that belie my current rank. Whoever was calling me was looking for someone and didn't realize he or she had the wrong number. He'll stop when he's ready to stop, I thought. She must have a reason for this. It's not exactly stalking per se; he's just looking for someone, and I've got that someone's phone number. His ex-wife might be terrorizing him, and this is his way of getting even. It's a wrong number. She's an angry student who got a B on her last biology test. And so on. But Bobby McManahan, the police officer trainee with whom I was sleeping at the time, did not have the same patience. So after five calls, I figured I'd ask him for some vaguely professional advice.

At 6:05 p.m. on that Thursday in February, Bobby was waiting with me for the call before heading back to his night shift. He was working the general street patrol on South Street that month, watching street bums attempt to chat with overstimulated, overprivileged college kids just moments after they pierced their gonads or some other brilliant idea of the like. (The resulting interactions were always humorous for at least one party – and I won't say which one.) Meanwhile, the phone call was five minutes late.

'See,' I said to Bobby, smiling at the clock. 'No need to tell the police.'

His face dropped. 'I *am* the police.'

'Oh, Bobby.' I grinned, cupping his face with my palms. His cheeks were pocked with what appeared to be year-old acne that had since cleared in part, and his dusty blond hair was parted down the side a little too carefully for my taste.

But he was fairly benign and easy enough to manipulate, which didn't exactly bode well for his professional ambitions, which wasn't my problem, but that's irrelevant at the moment. 'You're far too gullible to carry a gun.'

He bit his lip. 'It's just a taser.'

'Well, then, I stand corrected.'

I looked over at the clock and again at the phone. He was late. It was after six o'clock. There was nothing to cause concern at that point. He was never five minutes late. He was never two minutes late.

'Go,' I insisted, looking back to Bobby. He wore his nerves like stage makeup. 'You don't want to be late. They'll stick you at a desk if you're late another time.'

He grabbed his cap.

'I worry about you, Noa P.,' he said.

I walked him toward the door and inspected the clock.

'To be honest, I'm a little worried about you,' I said, refocusing. It had been a handful of months since we were sleeping together, and we only did that since he couldn't sleep alone at night because of what they were telling him at work. It was early 2002 and they had just been trained to follow up on every possible threat with urgency – be it a confusing phone call, a white envelope with no return address, a one-way plane ticket, that sort of thing. It's not that they believed that a crank call was exactly the sign of a terrorist-run sleeper cell with operations throughout the continental United States. But it's not like they believed it wasn't either.

'Look, it's 6:07 now,' I smiled. 'We should have put money on this. Would have helped me pay the rent this month,' I said, again looking back to the clock.

'How much do you need?'

'I don't need anything, Bobby. I'm fine. Relax.' Again, I held those prickly cheeks in my hands. 'Nothing to worry about. Go! Go protect our streets.'

He hesitated, holding his hand out to me.

'Seriously, go,' I teased.

'Fine, I'll go. I'm going.' He kissed me on the forehead before leaving. 'Promise to call me if you get another call. Really, we can't be too certain who has access to our phone lines these days.'

'Go!'

'Okay, okay.'

He closed the door on his way out. I looked up to the clock. It now read 6:10, and, of course, no sooner than Bobby disappeared from my line of vision, the phone rang. Part of me knew the caller wasn't quite finished with me, and the other part of me was actually sort of excited that he hadn't given up. Perhaps Bobby knew that. Had he been a better police officer, he probably never would have left me alone. Then again, had he been a better police officer, he never would have gotten involved with me.

I let it ring two or three times before walking over to it. The nameless caller was wading through moments of anticipation, no doubt, and part of me took pride in inflicting that anxiety. I answered it on ring five. At six, it would have gone to voice mail.

'I don't know who you think you are,' I said, 'but you're damn lucky I haven't called the police yet. How do you know this line isn't being tapped as we speak?' I paused, trying to keep a straight face.

Seemingly on cue, the heaving breathing began.

'Your MO is pathetic, you know,' I continued. 'Same time, same voice. Who exactly are you trying to reach? Haven't you figured it out by now? Pick up the white pages, go online, find the right number already. I'm bored with this.'

There was no response. Perhaps Bobby was right.

'What? You have no voice now that we're actually talking?'

He cleared his throat. It was definitely a man. An older man.

'Hello?'

'Noa?' he finally said.

The voice was tender, almost as if he were recovering from surgery.

'Who is this?' I demanded.

'Noa Singleton?' he asked again, coughing through my name.

'Who the hell is this?'

He didn't respond, but I could swear to this date that I heard a glass drop in the background.

'I said, who the hell is this?'

'It's . . . it's your father.'

Chapter 6

WE MET THE FOLLOWING DAY AT A BAR IN NORTH Philly, not far from Temple University. It was sandwiched between a corner store selling lottery tickets and fried sausages and what appeared to be the long-standing rental residence of an out-of-work horticulturist. Shoestrings tied around a telephone wire ten feet above my head dangled a pair of pristine sneakers, which swayed over me like poisonous mistletoe. I stood beneath them looking from right to left, right to left, and back again, ensuring that I had the correct location. One hundred yards in one direction and college kids were learning the Rule Against Perpetuities and the Theory of Relativity. One hundred yards in the other, and some poor teenager would find a knife in his carotid artery because he failed to deliver the proper ounces of cocaine to a guy named Biff. BAR DIVE was painted in yellow letters on the marquee. You didn't have to squint too hard to see remnants of the previous bar underneath in red, also called BAR DIVE, only in reverse – DIVE BAR. Ten feet above me, the sneakers twisted and turned in the spring breeze. A camera was resting under the shade of the awning that welcomed patrons inside. I barely noticed it, but as soon as I crossed the threshold, its lens closed in on me like a furtive spectator.

I walked in at precisely five thirty. Sun still painted the early evening sky and would for at least another hour. That was all the time I gave myself. One hour. After an hour, I would be back on the Broad Street Line to Center City before anyone could mistake me for either (a) a state school student, or (b) the culprit behind the missing drugs that the boy with the knife in his carotid artery would be hiding in his boxers.

The bar was dark, so it took a moment or two for my eyes to adjust. By the time they did, I recognized him instantly – not because he was the only white guy in the bar, but because he looked like me in the way I had always wanted to look like my mother. He was standing behind the bar, wiping the lip of a pint clean with a striped towel. I used to look at my mother's face, studying each pore, each brow crescent, each unattached earlobe, and question my relation. No part of me was sculpted in her features. When I walked into Bar Dive, I realized why.

My father was probably a lot younger than he looked. Lines curved their way into his forehead, haphazardly, as if even Mother Nature wasn't sure how to age him. In the dark room of the pub, the green of his eyes glowed. And just above, where his seemingly once-thick hair was starting to thin, I noticed the faint imprint of my hairline. Jagged and confused, a zigzag of hair traced the top of both of our heads from one ear to the other. I can't explain why, but I never thought it was an attractive feature until that point.

'Noa?' he asked, looking up.

I nodded.

He wiped his hands on the same cloth that had dried the beer glasses, wineglasses, shot glasses, and wooden countertops moments earlier, and stalled, hesitating in his stance. An embrace would have been too much, to be sure, but a handshake, well, that would connote iciness, which I was sure he wanted to avoid. The door opened and closed with the ringing of a bell, and then, almost as if a director had slapped a clapboard, he turned and faced me.

'I'm so glad you came,' he said.

I sighed. 'So, here I came.'

'Want something more private? Just for us, maybe?' he asked, sort of declarative, sort of inquisitive. Without awaiting a response, he walked down the bar, pulled up the wooden flap, pushed through it, dropped it, and then led me to a small table in the rear of the room, holding on to a bottle of water along the way.

'Is this okay?'

I nodded, hesitant.

'You sure?' he asked. His voice was gentle, almost as though he knew he wouldn't have a lot of time with me. It hung on my body language with protection so that each time he validated my nerves, he was attractive, appealing, even.

'Uh-huh,' I said, agreeing. 'It's fine.'

It was darker in the back and substantially more private. There was a small window, cut into a tic-tac-toe panel just behind it. We would still be visible, if necessary. I could still be seen from outside, so I acquiesced.

'Can I get you a drink?'

I forced a smile to make him feel better, though I don't know why. He was chasing me, after all. He had abandoned me. Not the other way round.

I shook my head. 'No.'

'Something to eat?'

Again, no.

He ran his hands through his hair violently, shoving his scalp along with it. There was nothing else to offer. His breath was heavy, and I recognized it, not from the phone calls days before, but from my own chest when I was nervous, leaking out from my mouth every night before I fell asleep.

He held his hand to mine and opened himself outward for me to sit. It seemed as though he was still trying to remember the rules of chivalry – or whatever the rules of chivalry have been made to be when making amends with your long-lost progeny. It looked both exhausting and somewhat endearing on him at the same time. He tried to put his hand over mine. I flinched upon contact.

'So why the hang-ups?' I finally asked, getting comfortable. 'You do realize that each and every phone call was an opening scene to *Law & Order*, don't you?'

'Oh my god, Noa,' he said, looking down, embarrassed. 'It wasn't like that. It wasn't like that at all.'

'I'm not joking. I was this close to calling the police.' My fingers pinched a millimeter of space so that, from a certain angle, it looked like I was crushing his maudlin face, feigned abashed revelation or not. 'People are freaked out about crossing the street next to someone strange, and you think it's a good idea to pop into my life via anonymous telephone hang-up?'

Spills of nervous laughter trickled out in runs, in syncopation with the cadence of my voice. His face jumped in and out of view, and when he moved, for an instant, the light from the window highlighted the skin above his mouth. A thick scar, almost the size of a pea pod, rested over his upper lip.

'So?' I asked. 'Are you going to answer my question?'

'I just wanted to meet you,' he said before taking a sip of water.

'Like that? It's creepy,' I said. 'Like, disturbingly creepy. You couldn't have just sent me a letter? An e-mail? Had my mom warn me? Even just have said hello on the first call, at least?'

'I didn't mean to sound creepy,' he said, defensively. 'I really just wanted to meet you. Is that so hard to believe?'

I looked to the window and then back to him.

'A little, yeah. Especially like that.'

'I was nervous,' he said with a crooked smile that expropriated ninety-eight percent of my attention. Had I met him in a library or a coffeehouse, no doubt he would have appeared distinguished, perhaps even approachable, but in the putrid light of Bar Dive, his awkward smile was becoming distracting. 'I was just nervous,' he said again. 'That's all.'

'It's been twenty-three years,' I said. My voice was my mother's when she discovered that pack of cigarettes under my pillow on my fourteenth birthday. 'Why now?'

He cleared his throat in little couplets. Sitting across from me, he looked more hopeful than I could have imagined, given the circumstances.

'I don't know,' he said, shrugging off the suggestion.

'Really?' I laughed. 'That's what you've been calling me to say? "I don't know?" Come on, Caleb. You can do better than that.'

'I just,' he stumbled again. He drank from his bottle of water and squinted, as if he didn't know what words to put together next. 'You know, Noa, there are things that happen in this world that make you really, really want to make things right.'

'Oh, Jesus. Not another one.' I sighed. 'If I hear one more person talk about how life is precious right now, I'm gonna walk out of here.'

Of course, I didn't. It's not like I was spending that much time with people rethinking their lives in the last few months. It's not like I missed out on his presence. My mother's Lazy Susan of stand-ins did just fine. I rarely sat in bed pondering the missing half of my genetic tree, but perhaps, in hindsight, I was curious. And he was offering. And I was there.

'Everyone goes through a time when he realizes how much he screwed up. I guess, for me . . .' He paused, looking at his water bottle, contemplating his next string of words. 'I guess for me it was my time in prison.'

My chest tightened. I don't know why I was surprised. I don't know why I was even upset. It wasn't like I had fantasized about meeting him or idealized him into a corporate CEO or famous painter or doctor even. His story wasn't even original, for Christ's sake: absent father, alcoholic, no doubt, if his water habit was any indication.

'I'm gonna be straight with you. I owe you that. I made a lot of mistakes in my life. A lot. And they didn't even start with you, if I'm really gonna be honest.'

'Fair enough,' I said, feeling like I'd read this before, seen it somewhere – on-screen, in self-help books on my mother's shelf. 'I don't need to know everything.'

'All that matters now is that I've changed,' he said, as if he were trying to remember my name. 'I've changed my life, Noa. I'm a different person now, and I want you to be a part of it.'

The door to the bar opened and closed, losing a handful

of patrons. He looked over, a bit melancholic, as if losing them were somehow as painful as losing me.

'Do you know the owner?' I asked. 'We're practically the only ones here. Did you plan it that way?'

He grinned with undulating pride. 'You're looking at him. And of course not.'

'Okay.'

Nothing else came out, despite his necessitous expectations. Nothing else was planned. He was the one who called this little meeting. My life's goal up until that point was far from tracking down a missing parent. It's not like I walked around blaming the world for my problems merely because a one-night stand with my mother twenty-three years earlier resulted in my sitting at this wooden booth in North Philadelphia across from a man with a water bottle on his side like a colostomy bag, clearly on his Twelfth Step toward making sure that water bottle remained a water bottle. Still, he needed some sort of recognition for his evolution. That ridiculous scar over his lip was starting to dance into a pitiful expression of desperation and didn't seem to stop no matter how many expressions of acknowledged understanding I tossed his way.

'Well done, then, Caleb,' I said. 'Is that the proper response? You turned your life around . . . then what? You called me? Congratulations. You did it. You're, what, a businessman now or just an alcoholic who owns a bar? Because that's an effective strategy for reform.'

His brows swam together, constructing a moat of protective lines. Sarcasm clearly hadn't made its way down the evolutionary track just yet in Dive Bar, Bar Dive. I wanted to say I was sorry, but I wasn't.

'I just want to know you,' he said. 'That's why I called. That's all. I want to know my daughter. I made a lot of mistakes, and now I want to fix them. It's not a unique story. It's just mine.'

'You've had twenty-three years to know me.'

'I fucked up all twenty-three of those, I know,' he pleaded. 'But maybe the next twenty-three can be better? The next fifty, even.'

I swallowed the nerves at the base of my throat to make a clear pathway. 'Fuck you.'

'I deserve that,' he said, almost hinting for salvation.

'Yes, you do.'

I sort of felt better after it came out, like it was waiting for the right time to arrive. Profanity can be that way – either gratuitous or magical. For me, at that moment, it was probably a combination of both, and I know my father felt the same way.

'Good,' he replied. 'Now that that's over, can we just spend time together? Get to know each other.'

I didn't reply. I didn't stay still, but I didn't stand, either, trying to contemplate my next step, when he leaned forward in submission, chest first, his two hands placed together in prayer.

'Thank you, Noa.'

I squinted my eyes. 'I'm sorry?'

He smiled and again softened his voice. 'Thank you.'

'For—?'

'For coming here,' he said. 'For not hanging up on me the way I hung up on you. For not leaving yet.'

'Don't thank me yet for that one. My right leg here is just about to lead the way from this table.'

He swallowed a smile that was just beginning to take form. 'You know what I mean.'

I hate to attribute charm to my father, but there was no other word at the moment that fit. He smiled, and the scar stretched along with it like a flattened rainbow.

I looked back to the lone patron, but it was just my father and me. The light was no longer piercing the window and instead was glimmering against the cement outside, reminding me that it was dangerously close to fifty-five minutes inside the bar.

'I really have to go,' I told him. I was actually a bit proud of myself for completing the task under time.

'Look Noa,' he said, changing the subject. His voice cracked. 'You should know it's not completely my fault that I wasn't around for you.'

'I find that a little hard to believe.'

He focused, curious. 'I can't blame your mother for not talking about me, if she didn't talk about me. Did she?'

I didn't respond.

'I mean, who would want to raise her daughter knowing that the father was an alcoholic and would always be an ex-con?' he laughed to himself. 'At that time, I'd probably keep me away from my child, too.'

A coarse tip to his shaky forefinger ran around the lip of the water bottle. He was nervous, true; that was not something to be debated, but it was almost an hour that I'd spent inside the bar, and at that point in my life, I followed my own dictum, despite my father's superficial lament. I stood from the table. He rose to meet me.

'Please, Noa,' he pleaded. 'Stay a little bit longer. Let me get you something to drink. To eat.' He smiled. 'To punch?'

A half grin slipped from my chest, but I was already on my feet with my bag over my shoulder, and I could feel the second hand of my watch pulling me toward the door. I would not stay past one hour.

'Another time,' I said.

Chapter 7

At first, we met bimonthly: once at his dive bar, Bar Dive, in North Philadelphia, and the next at a restaurant of his choosing in Center City. Having consumed most of his meals at Bar Dive, the prospect of even tasting the hors d'oeuvres on Restaurant Row brought him to Center City more than I would have liked. Usually when it was my turn to visit, I took the subway in the daytime to him, but only when a faint hint of daylight still skimmed the sky in ornaments of coral and indigo, and only the bus in the evening once those ornaments were no longer. Over those few early visits when we were just starting to learn each other's habits, I grew accustomed to riding the bus home late at night. The crack addicts, prostitutes, and night students from Temple were the only people riding anyway. We quickly grew to recognize one another's scent. We knew to stay away from one another, to clump together when a new face boarded, when the local multiple personality jumped in, throwing punches in the air as she walked by. (Her name was Clara. And other times Claude.) Sometimes my father would be waiting for me near the bus stop. Sometimes he wouldn't. Sometimes he was early. And sometimes we talked until the only recourse was the bus home.

I refused to invite him up to my apartment when he came my way. My studio on Fortieth and Baltimore was becoming more and more colonized with rodents and I could actually hear my neighbor's orgasm at precisely 11:35 in the evening every Friday night. My father didn't need his long-lost child's veneer of prosperity to become such a pauperized image, so I continued to insist upon innocuous safe havens in Center City, Rittenhouse Square, and more culinary hideouts on Restaurant Row. I knew he wouldn't complain, at least not at first. We ended up limited to a small section of Philadelphia, since he specifically insisted upon rummaging around the golden entrails of Rittenhouse.

After two months, our bimonthly meetings soon evolved into weekly meetings, still split evenly between our respective home grounds and still revolving around his cathartic dumps. One week we were in his neck of the woods and the next in mine. *Tit for tat*, he would say. I told him that's not exactly what tit for tat means, but he didn't care.

His past gushed toward me in words and waves of anecdotes. Some I believed; others came across as too strange to be real. Mostly, he seemed less interested in getting to know me than in preserving his own history within the vaulted memory of another.

My father, I soon learned, was born in the City of Brotherly Love in 1960 to an alcoholic father and a hardworking cliché of a secretary mother. Addiction begets addiction, my father said to me, repeatedly, so by the time he was seventeen, he was driving down the Pacific Coast Highway in California, looking for an outlet from his father's pattern of abuse. No sooner than a month after he arrived, he was arrested for lifting a button-down shirt he took a fancy to at a Macy's in Santa Barbara a week after his eighteenth birthday. He didn't have money for it, and at the time, he was able to talk the DA down to probation (without the aid of a lawyer) with the exclusive employment of one Jean Valjean justification, switching up the basic human need for sustenance with the basic human need for clothes – name brand and chromatic, with animal insignia and upturned collars. Pretty soon, the shirt turned into sports cars, jewelry, and even a monthlong flirtation with the illegal transport of Mexicans in large windowless vans across the border.

It was during his year in Los Angeles after the Santa Barbara incident that he met and knocked up my mother and shortly thereafter was caught stealing a Jaguar off a used car lot. This, of course, led to the first of many charges of grand theft auto, thus beginning his polygamist marriage with a handful of state penal codes.

Once she found out about his first prison sentence, his

mother never welcomed him home to Philadelphia. Unfazed by her apathy, on he traipsed, driving from state to state, occasionally getting locked up along the way, sometimes for short jail stints when the local police department didn't look beyond the instant arrest (Kansas, I'm speaking to you) and other times for longer sentences for something as simple as a bar brawl, purely because of his storied rap sheet (Ohio, for example).

Between his sentences in California, Kansas, and Kentucky, a court-ordered stint in rehab in West Virginia, and after the final leg in Ohio, he was on the road to recovery, self-discovery, and sobriety in Philadelphia. Somewhere in that time, his mother died, and he inherited enough money that he could break his father's pattern of dependence, and it was around that time he learned about me. Or rather, he remembered that he left my teenaged mother, alone and pregnant, seventeen or eighteen years earlier.

From photos, from handcrafted letters, from Internet searches, he felt born again. Literally, the undertow of a religious conversion penetrated him like a reverse exorcism, and for him, all his mistakes were suddenly nil. He had a purpose in life. Righting a wrong, correcting a former injustice of paternity, placing all chance of finally finishing Steps Eight, Nine, Ten, Eleven, and Twelve in the body and soul of one Noa P. Singleton and becoming her confidant, her friend, her father. But he wasn't ready yet. He needed to make something of himself first, so he purchased Dive Bar, shortly thereafter quasi-palindroming it, and spent the next few years becoming the ex-alcoholic businessman he was the day I met him. Always with a bottle of water, a sweaty upper lip, and a palatable desperation for forgiveness.

His revisionist candor was remarkable, and for that, I carried a modicum of respect for him. It wasn't like he was hiding behind his record. Instead, he owned it, waving it proudly as his coat of arms to hang in front of Bar Dive. He would tell me in his bar with a handful of customers around that he won the Winfield Correctional Facility's boxing tournament of 1993 by a fierce left hook. And he would never try to whisper – even in five-star restaurants on Walnut Street – that he had suffered from alcoholism for over a decade. And that he had dropped out of high school to explore the country. And that he felt a quadrant of remorse for leaving his own mother alone while he found himself exploring these great united states on the defendant's side of the table in Kansas City, Missouri; Cincinnati, Ohio; Abilene, Texas; Louisville, Kentucky; and, of course, Los Angeles, California. I was fairly certain that he was dropping a few cities off the list and even more certain that there had to be additional charges in there beyond what he'd told me, but it didn't bother me. If he was able to recount the embarrassment of leaving his mother, I was certainly far from a lone victim in his biography. What matters now, he told me one day, is that I've found you.

And I actually started to agree.

Quite clearly, though, our playing fields weren't exactly even. For two people attempting reconciliation after a lifetime of absence, our arrangement was centered around his need to purge errors of his own past, as if doing so would make us a rehabilitated nuclear family. He knew nothing about me, apart from the fact that I was a substitute science teacher for the Philadelphia Public School System and ran three miles twice, sometimes three times, a week, and, after a handful of months, it was no longer working for him.

We were strolling through Rittenhouse Square eating ice cream on one of the visits allegedly on my home turf, when he chose to bring this flaw to my attention. A string quartet from the Curtis Institute of Music was playing Bach in the gazebo. He was licking a chocolate waffle cone of Cookies 'N Cream, and it was dripping all over his hands and sticking to the corners of his mouth rather humorously, given the context. A sooty drop of vanilla fell to his chin and he removed it with his tongue, long and lean as an amusement park slide, cleaning off the frozen remains. He first looked up to the high-rise apartment buildings surrounding us, almost with longing, before returning his gaze to me.

'Are you embarrassed by me?' he finally asked.

Of course I was.

'No,' I said, biting my cheeks. I threw away the bottom inch of my wafer cone in a nearby trashcan.

'It's okay,' he said sweetly. 'I know you are. You don't have to pretend.' He folded his arms together on his chest. 'It's just that I'm the one talking all the time.'

'I'm glad you noticed that, at least,' I said.

'That's not how it's supposed to work, though,' he urged. 'We're both supposed to talk.'

'I hate to tell you, Caleb, but you sort of set a precedent I can't really change now. Rules are rules.'

'Noa . . .'

I walked toward the fountain.

'I want to be a part of your life,' he said, quickly following.

I forced a laugh. 'What exactly do you think this is?'

We both sat on the ledge. It was wet, I remember that much, but I also remember that it didn't bother me sitting on the lip of the fountain, with a baby's breath of water spraying us from behind. I actually enjoyed the dainty massage soaking into the small of my back.

My father placed an arm around me. After twenty-three years, there was no need for him to walk into my life with the same oeuvre as, say, Marlene Dixon would a few months down the line. But I also realized he wouldn't relent. Silent in the current that was his verbal catharsis, part of me knew it was bound to change directions at some point.

'Okay.' I surrendered, looking over toward the quartet strumming in the wooden gazebo. One tornado and they'd all be gone – instruments, wooden platform, people. 'I'll tell you more about me if you first tell me two little factoids about yourself that have nothing to do with Bar Dive or

Dive Bar or your petty thievery across the continental United States or your six hundred and thirteen steps toward self improvement or boxing or Kentucky,' I said, waving two little fingers of peace. The Curtis Institute students were still playing Bach in the background. 'Two things for one. Tit for tat,' I added. '*That's* how it works.'

The string quartet nearly drowned us. The apparition of those four different instruments still sits above me in my cell today. Their wooden limbs and ebony slopes, their horse-haired manes and rosined strings somehow, put together with calm and order and calculation, made music. Nowhere else can four disparate sounds live together in such delicacy of balance. It is the loudest thing I can remember about that conversation. Invisible streams of remorse and regret drip from my dry eyes when I think about it and when I think about him. I fold my hands over my heart, feeling the beat of those four musicians, tapping the floor to keep the beat, making their own metronome of quarter notes, eighth notes, half notes.

He placed his hand before me. 'Tit for tat,' he agreed. And we shook.

Chapter 8

ONE OF THE QUICKEST CHANGES YOU EXPERIENCE WHEN entering prison isn't the compulsory adjustment to the food or square footage, or the privacy you lack during your odd-numbered days in the showers. It's not even the rapid loss of the former friends and family of your life. Rather, it's the internal acceptance that finally you have become the person you were meant to be. When you enter, true, you are given a new number, new residence, and new wardrobe; but it is only when you place those garments upon your limbs that you realize that they were designed for no one but you. No former splinters of your personality carry over into prison life. No relationships, fictional or otherwise, accompany them either. Any superficial intimacy you claim to have experienced with another (whether consanguineous or not) when you wore any color other than cocoa brown fades as quickly as a puff of cigar smoke. You are now the person everyone knows you to be.

People on the outside can never understand this, and it takes more than a phone call or a short month of visitation by an outsider – be he lawyer, clergy, or journalist – to revisit that solicitude. Oliver certainly doesn't understand, no matter how much he tries. He can't. He enters Muncy with his hands swimming through his pockets, meandering through the visitor's booth with increasing familiarity, feeling as though he knows everything about me merely because he's read my life's paper trail and once spoke with my father. He strolls in here, sometimes in a full suit, other times in jeans, holding his legal pad like a novelist's first manuscript, and mentions my father's name to me every single time. 'I still can't reach him, but I'm going to keep trying,' he says as an indefatigable mantra through the telephone.

Ollie will never speak with him again, that much I know, that much I tried to tell him on his second visit, and yet he continues calling that same number only to be met with disconnected phone lines and irreverent telephone operators serving as scapegoats for flighty refugees, or, in my case, fathers. He needs to accept his shortcomings on his own, though. That is not my responsibility. Failure is not something you can impress upon another. It is something earned, something realized with piquant reward. Were he Japanese, I'd spare him the misery and provide him a tantō sword for his flaws.

Yet, no matter the futility, no matter the reiteration, I don't have the heart to confirm this for him. He'll come around to it on his own. He's still visiting Muncy, after all. He's still visiting me. And he still wants to learn more about my father, as if the past will somehow echo the vacant telephone line in Canadian Barre Dive, where my father no longer resides, and allow him to suddenly hear me.

The slender arms of the Philadelphia summer gathered and dropped me off at Bar Dive more frequently than planned in the summer of 2002. I grew accustomed to the predictable synchronicity of the relationship so much so that it loosely became a scheduled passing of the days, like cars drifting into each other's lanes, like ornery spouses on their thirtieth anniversary. No spontaneity, no variation. Just planned order, chess pieces regularly lined up to slide across squares until we collided, either on his turf or mine.

My father decided that his way of repairing twenty-three years without allowance was to have me count a few ledgers and clean a few tables in my spare time. In exchange, he helped me pay part of my rent. Substitute teaching over the summer in a walking city didn't exactly boast the highest income potential. Plus, I didn't have air-conditioning. Bar Dive did. Period.

People came to Philadelphia for the history, for the art, for the food, but were left with the humidity, a possible mugging, and a thin coat of grime on their skin each time they stepped outside. While tourists leaked into Philadelphia to take their pictures with the Liberty Bell or inside

Independence Hall, hopped in the back of a hansom cab to be chauffeured around the cobbly streets of the miniature radius that is Old City, I spent my spare time at a bar.

Things, however, changed for us shortly after the Fourth of July. We were sitting together in Bar Dive in the middle of a particularly vacant day, sharing a pitcher of water, as the odor of summer drifted inside. I dunked the same striped cloth from day one into a bucket of soapy water and then spread it over a small table. I don't know if it was the dirty water or the heat, but it just sort of came out.

'I was arrested once,' I said, almost as an addendum to filling out the Sunday crossword puzzle.

Looking back, I don't know if I was telling him or just pontificating, though he didn't waste a second in return. Not with shock, nor empathy, nor pride even. Just plain inquisitiveness.

'What was it for?' he asked, continuing to clean the tables.

'Nothing,' I sighed. 'Just something stupid.'

'An arrest isn't stupid, Noa,' he said, looking up.

'This was.'

'What was it for?' he asked, matter-of-factly. I couldn't tell if he was more excited and proud than saddened and ashamed.

'Nothing, like I said. Just shoplifting. A teeny tiny misdemeanor three weeks after my eighteenth birthday. It's on my permanent record, and because it's so small, I never even have to put it on applications or whatever. But there it is – a fucking abscess on my past.'

That was another thing that changed after I started spending time with my father. I said 'fuck' a lot more than I ever had in the past.

'Okay,' he said, turning away.

'You're smiling? I just told you about this embarrassing smear on my record, and you're, what?' I paused. 'Feeling solidarity?'

He laughed.

'What?'

'What *what*?'

A sunset flushed across his cheeks, rising at the center.

'You honored the tat,' he said, and for a brief moment, I could see how someone somewhere could possibly find him relatively magnetic.

'Oh, Jesus, Caleb, really?' I picked up the dishrag and moved on to another table.

'Really,' he said, standing up. 'I believe I owe you two facts now. Any facts. Anything at all.'

I turned back to him. 'I'm not doing this.'

'Ask me,' he insisted. 'Ask me anything.'

'I think I know all I need.'

I sat down below the air-conditioning vent, exhausted.

'First movie in a movie theater?' he asked me, without hesitation.

'This isn't how it works.'

'First movie in a movie theater?' he insisted.

I yawned, ignoring him.

'I'm just going to keep asking, you know,' he said. 'First

movie in a movie theater. It's not a taste question. It's a fact one. You can at least do that, right? It must have happened at some point, with a friend, with your mother, at a mall or—'

'—*Scarface*,' I blurted, giving up, unsuccessfully camouflaging a slight smile with disgust. I tossed the rag to Caleb. 'Okay?'

He grinned, childishly, as if he had just won at tug of war.

'Yours?' I asked.

'*The Sting*. Paul Newman.'

Predictable, but nonetheless—

'—first record purchased?' he continued.

'Soundtrack to the movie *Cocktail*,' I replied, hiding my face. 'And you?'

'Bob Dylan. *Shelter from the Storm*,' he said, tossing me the wet rag.

'Favorite food?'

'Burgers and fries.'

'Favorite burger and fries?' I added, tossing the dishrag back.

'In-N-Out.'

He crunched the rag into a ball as he thought of his next question.

'Favorite city?'

'Why, the City of Brotherly Love.' I smiled. 'Country you most want to visit?'

'Antarctica,' he answered, thinking.

'*Country*,' I asked, as he pitched the wet baseball my way. I caught it with my right hand.

'Antarctica,' he insisted, without hesitation. Or an atlas.

'Favorite word?' I asked, holding onto the rag.

He thought briefly. A fly zipped around his face while he considered a response. He didn't even try to shoo it away. 'I think I'm gonna have to say *freedom*. What about you?'

Home. Crystal. Xylophone, I thought to myself.

'Maybe the same as yours, actually,' I replied.

Half of his mouth opened, and he started wiping his hands together, contemplating his next move. 'Let's get to the good stuff now. First kiss?'

'Fair enough,' I said. 'Andy Hoskins. Sixth grade. Tennis courts, out in the doubles margin.'

I tossed the rag up in the air like I was opening a set, and it fell to his hands like a perfectly angled serve.

'Connie Anastasia. Fifth grade. Soccer field,' he said, quickly volleying it back my way. 'First love?'

'None yet,' I said, catching it. 'You?'

He wiped his hands on his jeans. 'Your mother.'

I threw the rag back to him. 'Well, I guess you were more like a one-month stand, then.' He didn't reply. Or catch the rag. Instead, it just fell on the ground in a single thump, like a water balloon that failed to detonate. 'All right. I can detect nonresponsiveness when it's before me.' I sat down at a table and tried to remove the sticky residue on the edge, but it wouldn't budge. My father sat next to me. 'So, is there anyone now?'

He shook his head. 'No, not really.'

'Not really?' I asked. 'Or no?'

'No,' he said. 'What about you, dollface?'

'Dollface?' I laughed. 'I didn't realize we were there already.'

'What about you?' he repeated.

'Nah,' I said, noting his sudden change of mood. 'No one special. Just a handful of guys here and there. There's a police officer trainee and the guy down at Lorenzo's, but he's only for free pizza on Tuesdays. Maybe if you're lucky . . .' I winked. '. . . I'll get you a slice one day.'

'And here I thought I needed to impress you.'

'Addiction begets addiction, Caleb. You said it first.' I held up my bottle. 'Worst thing you've ever done?'

'You mean besides abandoning you?'

'Well played.' I smiled, bowing my head to stare at his scar. I watched it jump around as he spoke, connecting each hemisphere of his face like a lock holding the two sides together. He seemed impressed with himself for his last response, and the scar kept tagging along with his healthy grin. 'The scar,' I asked, pointing to his upper lip. 'Where'd you get it?'

'That'll take more than fifteen seconds.'

'You have fifteen.' I looked at my watch, waiting for the second hand to arrive at the twelve. 'And . . . go.'

'Seriously? You're timing me on this?'

'Fourteen now.'

'Fuck, fuck,' he laughed, massaging it.

'Thirteen,' I said, still traveling along with the watch.

'Fuck!'

'Twelve.'

'Shit,' he cried. 'Okay.'

'Eleven. Ten.'

'Okay,' he called, one hand up. 'Okay, I can do this, here goes: Your mother. Me. 1977. A razor. A bathtub. A slip. A fall. Taa-dah,' he said, hands out in a bow.

'I'll follow up later on that.'

'Worst thing you've ever done?' he asked, changing the subject.

'You mean apart from meeting you here in February?'

He leaned down to pick up the dishrag eroding the cheap carpet beneath us. 'Come on, dollface, answer the question.'

'The arrest,' I said, matter of fact. 'And probably dropping out of school.' I sighed. 'I've got two. Lovely.'

He clutched the dishrag tighter. Wrinkles of dark water dripped out from it, over his hands.

'You know I wasn't just a one-night stand with your mother. You know that, right?'

I couldn't take my eyes off of his hands. They were squeezing tightly, as if he needed to inflict pain on himself.

'If you say so.'

'Your mom and me were living together,' he said, sinking into nostalgia. 'You can't actually believe everything she tells you. We were young and in love. What else do you need?'

'I don't know,' I said bluntly. 'Maybe food, a job. Money. Contraception.'

He massaged the scar again.

'You know, I had twelve stitches from that bathtub

incident. For weeks, I could barely eat. I had to drink everything with a straw, eat soup and shit like that. I couldn't even kiss.'

It was difficult to hold in my laughter, but to this day, I'm impressed with my restraint. 'I can't imagine you would have wanted to after that little production.'

My father relaxed beside me, stretching out his legs so far that they reached my own. I winced when one of them touched my calf, but don't think he noticed. Drops of perspiration materialized over his scar, and I pictured them burnt with anguish, sitting alone in a wet tub while he left my mother or my mother left him for . . . well, Paramedic One? Bruce, the speed walker?

I stood from the table and walked to the one remaining unwashed table. The previous patrons had crushed peanuts into a spilled bottle of beer, leaving nothing less than La Brea tar pits on the table to excavate. I looked down and waxed over and over to remove the sticky residue on top, but it wouldn't budge.

My father walked over to me. 'Here, try this,' he added, noticing my grip. 'You want to clean in circles,' he demonstrated. 'See?'

'You're right,' I agreed, watching as the rag in his hand swallowed the crushed peanuts superficially glued to the table. He continued, though, even after the table was spotless, pushing the dishcloth on the glass and pulling specs of moisture off, the rag always in his grip as if it were a crutch. We were silent there for at least another minute, his hands continuously moving clockwise, and up and down, side to side, cleaning tables as if in an unconscious chant – tables, which had already been wiped at least three times, being wiped and rewiped by my father's calloused fingers and palms coated with scars and remnants from a past I'd never truly know. Each of those nicks and swollen joints got him here; each of those marks brought him to me in Bar Dive, in the humidity of summer, and at that moment, I realized that even though he shared their origins, that even though he'd repeat his stories weekly to me with caricature embellishment, I'd never really know how they appeared. From one of his drives over the border? From the prison boxing ring? From my mother, who had probably attempted to replace my father for the next ten years with varying mustachioed lovers? Without witnessing history, everything that follows is pure perspective.

Eventually he realized what he was doing and stopped, placing the rag in a corner. He wiped his hands on his jeans, took my hand, and sat me down. A brown slither of leather appeared from his right back pocket, and in it, a water-soaked photograph of me from my high school graduation. My mother must have sent it to him after the postcard delivery. *If he wanted to be a father, he would have been a father*, I heard her say. Then he peeled an old photograph stuck to its back, and handed it to me.

'This was your grandmother. My mother. Her name was Dorothy,' he said. 'Dot. She went by Dot to her friends.'

Caverns of air pushed in and out of his chest before he continued. 'She would have been seventy-one years old.'

I took the photograph and held it between my fingers, trying not to leave my prints all over it. She was alone in the photo, spread out on a beach in a polka-dotted swimsuit, thick red lipstick, and a white scarf tied around her hair. She couldn't have been more than twenty-five in the photo, maybe thirty, at most, and commanded that lens like Audrey Hepburn's less attractive sister. I couldn't quite tell where she was, but it looked balmy and tropical.

'You know how I told you that it was because of her that I wanted to find you?'

'Sort of,' I said. 'It kind of got lost in there a bit, somewhere in the illegal coyote phase and knocking up my mom.'

He smiled, penitent. 'Right. Well, it's a bit more complicated than that.' I was a child when her parent is handed news of an illness. The more he tried to talk, the faster the disease spread. 'I was with some buddies in Cincinnati and they wanted to do a bank robbery,' he continued, struggling. 'I was just the driver. I didn't go into the bank. I didn't do anything. To be honest, I barely even knew the guys. But I did agree to it and we got caught, and even though I just drove the car, I got five years for it. And I had to serve every goddamn one because of my history. They knew about everything, from Macy's to Tijuana, and at that point, probation became laughable. I had about two months left on my sentence when my mom got sick. Really sick. The warden actually came and delivered the news himself. He handed me a letter, and just said, "I'm sorry".'

'She died?' I asked, nervously, holding my hand out to him. He didn't take it.

'No. Not at that point.' He rubbed her photo between his fingers. 'She had written a letter asking the warden if I could be released early. She knew she was going to die. She knew where I was. She had been keeping tabs on me from Kentucky to Ohio and everywhere in between. She knew exactly where I was even when she cut me out of her life decades earlier.'

'I'm so sorry,' I said to him.

He looked up to me and tried to smile in appreciation, but what came out was a sort of Picasso rendering of mixed grief.

'She wrote in her letter that she wanted me to come home to Philadelphia no matter what. She was begging the warden for my release, but—'

I shook my head, no.

'Claimed it would be a break in procedure or a fucking floodgate or something,' he continued. 'So I sat in that cell for another two months knowing that my mother was ready to speak with me, regardless of where I was. I just sat there and thought.' He laughed, and the Picasso expression scattered like a cluster of pins dropped on the floor. 'I know it's sort of dumb. I mean, I'd been in jail. I'd been in prison before for a really long time, but I never really spent any time thinking in there, you know? There's weight lifting, there's TV, there's chores. I guess I could have spent a lot more time over the years sitting and thinking about my mom. Or about you,' he said, looking my way. 'But I didn't.'

'You never know what you'll do in a situation like that,' I said. It was the only phrase I could muster – a vacant platitude just like my salutatorian speech. 'Nobody does.'

'I suppose,' he said, unmoved. 'By the time I got out and came to Philly, she had already died. She left her house to me, and with it, a box with a handful of letters from your mom and some pictures of you growing up.'

My chest pinched.

'I sent you a postcard pretty soon after I came home, and when I never heard back, I realized that it was pretty clear you were going places and I was not. So I sold the house, bought the bar, and . . .'

I nodded in acquiescence. Of what, I'm not sure, but there was something about the way he smiled back at me that confirmed that he wasn't lying. I didn't even think he needed to hear a story in riposte, but the pressure was too strong, and I just couldn't keep it inside any longer. My hand reached out to his and he accepted.

'. . . and,' I said.

It was now my turn. I know he wasn't asking. He didn't even need anything more, but it was my turn, and I was finally ready.

Chapter 9

ON MY PENULTIMATE VISIT TO BAR DIVE, I STUMBLED in at nearly one in the morning unannounced, just as the bar was closing. It was pitch dark when I deboarded the bus, avoiding a dead rat and a homeless man (who smelled curiously like tulips) on my way. Before I could start walking the few short blocks to the bar, I noticed a shadow lurking on the corner, a diffident amalgamation of restraint and might all in the same amorphous splotch. When I looked over to him, instantly he glanced the other way.

He is not real, I thought, and continued walking the two blocks remaining toward Bar Dive. The more I walked, though, the more the elongated smudge of his feet followed. The more I shifted my gait, the more his dirty trim shifted, so much so that the head of his confused shadow connected to the shadow of my moving feet, and when they first touched, a tender shiver swept down my spine. I felt dirty from our shadows' intercourse. I couldn't tell where mine ended and his began, but I walked faster, our shaded unit traveling as one, until it split when I ambled in front of the bar, just below the dangling tennis shoes still suspended from the sky, still perched over the wire, still providing notice to drug addicts of where to get their fix; only now, they were drenched with darkened exhaust from car engines, cigarette ash floating out from open windows on third-floor apartments, and acid rain. I stood under them, prayerlike, my hands placed together as if I were in church. Grant me this one wish, I thought. Grant me just this one. When I turned around, he was no longer there. My hands were still touching in prayer and I was still standing directly beneath the dangling shoes.

I rushed to the door and jiggled the locked handle with my left hand, looking up into the camera, hoping my father would see me and the handsome set of lines squatting between my eyes.

It took less than a minute for him to open the door and pull me inside. I think he asked me what was wrong. I think he asked me why I was calling for help. But I can't remember calling for help. All I can remember is telling my father that someone was following me. A man in all black with brown cowboy boots and glasses.

'Stay where you are,' he instructed.

There was a loud jingle of bells, a creak of a door opening, and then nothing. Blackness of a dreamless night. A vacuum of all of my fears in one. And without hesitation, without sensation of any sort, my father vanished. Everything happened quickly from that point. I ran my hands across my arms, tenderly, inspecting them for injury. No spheres of pain erupted anywhere on my body. No mounds of future bruises forecasting a night sky on my temple or my chin or my back or my thighs or anywhere else. Just a beat inside the bar and nobody else beside me.

'Dad?' I called out, quietly.

I looked out front, but nobody was there. I looked in the back room, but he wasn't there, either. Finally, I ran to the back door leading to an alley, scattered with trash bags and metal cans, opened the door and saw my father, hunched over the shadowman, breathing laboriously, as he was on the evening we first met.

'Dad?' I called again, screaming toward him. (In retrospect, I know that my voice carried barely a decibel of volume, but in my head it was so much louder.)

He didn't respond. He didn't hear me. He was too busy fighting off the shadowman who had abandoned his trail on me, or who had used me to get to him, or had mistook me for someone else or—

'—look out!' I called, as he pounced onto my father. On cue, my father mulled his fist into a ball of friction and began pounding the shadowman's right temple until he retreated.

I hobbled toward him, and as I got closer, I saw that although the shadowman didn't seem to be fighting back anymore, my father was still punching him on his right temple with his fist, once, twice, three times, dislodging the man's eyelid from its home. I counted as he thrust. Five. Six. Seven. The man's face twisted toward me in the most grotesque, disfiguring motion I'd ever seen, before falling flat on the concrete. It was at this point that I noticed how young the shadow was – perhaps not much older than me.

I didn't know what I should do, but I couldn't stand where I was, inches from my father, and watch as he put this man in the hospital and himself back in prison. In an instant, a thick pulse traveled from my feet all the way up to my heart and lips. I had never seen such precise fighting. I never told my father that, although I was scared of the thump in my heart, it was one of the most intoxicating moments of my life.

The shadowman pleaded for my father to stop, but he didn't care. My father's left hand, clean and untouched from the previous beating, lifted magically from his body and pounced into the thin shadowman's gut, eight, nine, ten more times, until he bent in half, perched on the ground like a folded shirt.

'Stop!' I cried. 'That's enough!'

My father looked up at me and speared me with anger, with love, with devotion. His hands were twisted and torn. Spores of skin peeled from his knuckles.

Now, someone might think that I should have stopped him earlier. That I should have prevented another aggravated assault charge for my father or an ER visit with forty stitches and a concussive monthlong headache for the shadowman. But I didn't. Nobody knows what she'll do when she feels her life threatened. Or how he'll react if he feels his family in danger. And my father was attacking him to save me. A man twice his age, using both right and left hands in self-defense, saving my life. It was one of the few times I saw any part of myself in my father. In anyone, for that matter. Perhaps I really did have the same gift of instinct, of self-defense, of violent protection: a present wrapped ineloquently with the two violent hands of my father, but a gift no less.

'Is he okay?' I asked.

My father didn't reply. As soon as he caught his breath, he pulled me back to the bar with one hand. I nearly tripped over the cracks in the sidewalks. Had he not dragged me inside so forcefully, I might have fled in the opposite direction. I think about that moment in here at least once a week. What would have been had I not gone back into the bar with my father?

'What the hell was that?' I cried, just as my father locked the door behind us.

Inside, he bent over to catch his breath, and for a brief moment, it was strangely smooth. Like molasses, even, it spilled in thick globules, each richer than the previous drop. No coarseness, no coughing. A trail of dark blood formed in the corner of his mouth.

'How did you—?'

'—come with me,' he insisted, pulling me into his office in the back of the bar. He wiped his mouth with his bloody shirt and pulled out a small box from his desk. In it was a Smith & Wesson .357 Magnum revolver. Had I not been in North Philadelphia, had I not been with my long-lost father, had I not just been nearly attacked, had I not been sleeping with Bobby McManahan, had a lot of things not happened in my life, I would have thought that it was a toy. A sort of silver and metallic utensil with thick grooves where your fingers rest. Pillows for your hands designed with comfort and purpose in mind. It was relatively small and compact and sat in his hands like a remote control.

'Where did you get that?'

He placed the gun in my hands and they fell instantly onto the desk from the shock of it.

'Take it, Noa,' he whispered. 'Be very careful. It's not loaded now, but—'

'—who was that?' I asked, pulling my hands out of the grip of the revolver.

He didn't respond.

'Take it, Noa. Please.'

My chest ached from the top down.

'Who the hell was that? Why did you do that? Are you some sort of secret spy? Do you work for the FBI and this is your cover?' I gasped. 'Oh my god, are you . . . are you an assassin?'

He tried not to smile, which fueled me even more.

'Take the gun, Noa,' he urged, dropping the grin in an instant. 'You need it for protection.'

'From what? From whom?'

'It doesn't matter.'

'I'm not taking your contraband,' I told him.

'It's not about me,' he insisted. 'It's for your own good. It's for your own protection.'

'Stop saying "protection". Protection from what?' I cried. 'From whom? I don't think that guy will be following you around anymore. Or was he following me?'

Silence.

'Tell me. Tell me exactly what you're involved in.'

'I'm not involved with anything.'

'If you want me in your life at all, then you'll tell me.'

He shook his head and dropped to the chair in disbelief.

'How can you sit there in the same body and tell me how much you want to be a part of my life with gentility and kindness, and change, and then beat a man to a pulp in the same breath?'

He refused to speak. He refused to change his expression out of concern. He refused to take the gun back. I turned away to open the door, but he had locked it when we came into his office. I looked back to him. Instead of explaining things to me, he walked around his desk, took my hand, and pulled me back to the chair.

'I don't know who that man was, Noa, but I've spent

enough time around men like that to know that you can never be too prepared.'

'You know that's not true,' I said to him, pulling my hands away.

'Please just take this.'

He was sweating heavily through his shirt, almost all of which was drenched in his own moisture, with just a few quarter-sized spots left dry as doubloons.

'I don't know what I would do if something happened to you.'

'I'm not taking a gun, Caleb. You know this. I'm not carrying a gun. I'm not shooting a gun. That's final.'

His head drifted downward. He was disappointed. If this had been ten years earlier and I had broken curfew, he would have sent me to my room. I would have probably spent years in therapy trying to overcome that paternal disappointment.

'I'm sorry,' I said. 'I can't.'

He held out his hand to me again, and this time, I didn't meet it. Instead, I just turned around and jogged the doorknob of his office.

'Can you please unlock this?'

My hands were sweating over the metal knob. My right arm burned at the shoulder in a way it hadn't in years, so I tried my left hand, but the doorknob would not budge. His breath closed in behind me, and I could feel its exhaust on my neck. With one violent hand pushing down on my shoulder and the other unzipping my bag, I knew exactly what he was doing, and I didn't stop him. After a long enough pause, he reached behind me and placed his hand over mine, twisting the knob to the right until it clicked open. With my weighty backpack sealed to my body, I left without turning around.

When I got home that night, I locked my door and took a long shower. Waves of tears came forth in series and rounds. Perhaps, to this day, I never truly washed that night or my father off of me. When I got out, I walked over to my backpack and took out the little napkin from our first meeting at Bar Dive with my father's name and number written on it, signed with a small heart below the signature, as if written by an adolescent girl. It waved between my fingers, the old paper starting to harden at the edges, before crumbling in my hand into even little pieces that I could scatter outside my window. A ceremonial disposition of my father's ashes.

I opened my backpack to remove my wallet, cell phone, and key, and found the revolver sitting there awkwardly like an adult in a kindergarten class. A box of .38 caliber bullets was resting beside it, heavy with ammunition. Next, I scrambled around inside the canvas bag to find the postcard, but it was missing. I carried it around with me for the better part of the last decade and now it was gone.

July

Dearest Sarah,

There are some numbers I'd like to share with you: Two hundred and ninety-seven. Seventeen. Thirteen.

Two hundred and ninety-seven is the number of innocent people who have been exonerated post-conviction, due to newly tested and retested DNA evidence. If you took two hundred and ninety-seven books and put them together, it could cover the circumference of my house. With two hundred and ninety-seven dollars, you could fly from New York to Los Angeles, you could visit Las Vegas for the first time, you could buy a business suit, take a handful of night classes at your local university. I don't know what you'd do with that amount, but I know you wouldn't squander it. You'd give it away. One dollar for each homeless man waiting by City Hall, for each beaten woman in asylum at a local shelter.

Seventeen is the number of individuals freed from death row, exonerated, and let go to return to their lives. Seventeen, Sarah. A number you'd recall most fondly, no doubt, as the magazine dictating how to wear lip gloss or flirt with a boy. Now that number is exclusively devoted to the seventeen souls who are lost somewhere between anger and joy, between gratitude and thanklessness, resolve and resentment. They walk among us as living bodies unable to cope with the duplicate death sentence newly handed them upon exiting their cells.

Thirteen, the average number of years served by innocent inmates for a crime they didn't commit. A life. A coming of age. I simply cannot fathom this amount. I cannot. Sarah, I return home each night and review the narratives behind these sobering statistics. Sometimes I sleep thirteen hours a night, dreaming you are still with me. Sometimes I sleep thirteen minutes. The coroner said you were alive for approximately thirteen minutes after the bullet hit you.

Boxes of evidence cloak the storage walls in Philadelphia, and will at least for another four months or so, after which point they will be destroyed by bureaucratic incineration. And then, we'll never know whether it was thirteen or fourteen or twelve.

You understand what I'm saying, sweetheart. Don't you? I know you do. The jury has as limited a view of what happened that day as do I, and yet they were the ones to determine guilt and death. Not me. I am not a jury, despite the fact that I'm the only jury. That's the real reason Oliver is on this case. I know that she will open up to someone like him. I just need to know what happened. I need to have all the facts before me. Right now, it's the only thing left keeping me connected to you.

Besides, I don't think I could think of all the ways I failed you. But I'm not going to fail you anymore. I promise you. I promise you. I promise you. I promise . . .

With all my love, always,
Mom

FOUR MONTHS

BEFORE

X-DAY

Chapter 10

TRUTH BE TOLD, AMERICA IS NOT AGAINST THE DEATH penalty. And to be honest, I'm not entirely certain I am, either.

Historically, people have never held their morals high enough above their brows to follow through on their firm, yet pliable, beliefs. Rather, we are a species of voyeurs, eager to witness the demise and destruction of one of our own. To claim that groups like MAD are part of a new movement is insulting to our progress. I've done my research. Half are admittedly in favor of the death penalty, while that other so-called noble half says with an air of superiority that they are against it. Then, through their yellowing brittle teeth, they close in on you to whisper that it might be okay, you know, if the person was truly evil. Evil-evil, like Hitler or Milošević or bin Laden. Yes, then, they confess, it would be okay.

I think it's better to admit our weakness (or strength as you might see it) and just accept who we are: animals whose pulses race and eyes devour the spilled blood of another. (As long as it's not actual spilled blood anymore and, of course, so long as we did not do the cutting ourselves.) Let's take a quick look back.

Ancient Rome: gladiators draped in metal garments, arms swollen with bulbous flesh, hands grasping a lampoon, a lance, or a shield. Surrounding them: thousands of cheering fans, screaming as their veins pulse through their temples and their necks, eager to watch one body fall prey to another. Two human beings fighting before fans until one of them drops dead.

The Crusades: medieval fundamentalist Christians making pilgrimage in chain mail and swords, exterminating those who got in their way to the Holy City, roaring crowds on the side, cheering them on.

The French Revolution: guillotines, aristocracy, a teeming crowd of peasants ready to drop the slice of metal that beheads one Marie Antoinette or Louis XVI. Humans screaming with all their might that it must be done, she deserves it, get rid of that, off with her head.

The noble English, our sovereign forefathers, Oliver's beloved home: the Tower of London, King Henry VIII, Anne Boleyn. Murdering the enemy and chopping off its head to place as the tip of a life-sized effigy for all to see and loathe. An example so that no other soul would repeat such errors.

Indigenous tribes. Shrinking heads. Thai prisons. Fuck it, modern-day boxing, wrestling matches, cockfighting.

So then, how about this? Pay-per-view.

The United States of America. Present day: Americans are glued to their handheld computers, digital television systems that hang on walls like great portraits, satellite radios and cell phones, and any other technological advancements that evolved during my incarceration. People are living solitary lives, their brains controlled by what they see on TV. So why not just stick my gurney in the center of a boxing ring with multiple video cameras, a trained movie producer and sports commentator, and let everyone watch me die? Nobody has to watch, just as nobody had to attend the public quartering of William Wallace. All the proceeds can go (a) to those who want to raise money for some lost child or aging parent or grandparent, (b) to pay back all those legal fees, or (c) for whatever reason they choose: better prison food, cancer research, a new public school. This way, people who take pleasure in this sort of extermination can pay a mere ten bucks, all proceeds going to the little child or even (and I'm trying to write this without laughing) MAD. Clearly, it wouldn't come on too often. It would probably only air during political campaigns or summer recesses from situation comedies and prime-time soap operas. American capitalism at its height. It's not that crazy a thought.

Look, I'm not about to use this little idea to protest that I can't be executed on November 7 because I can't understand what I did or why I'm going to die. I know what I did. I know what I didn't do. I said that from the beginning of this manuscript. But my death – my public death – would give some people pleasure, and it would bring others quite a well-deserved windfall. If you ask me, it's unadulterated altruism that has yet to be exploited.

I first met Marlene Dixon approximately one month after the Bar Dive incident. She called my cell just as I was walking across the Market Street Bridge on my way home from an eighth-grade science fair.

'Is this Noa Singleton?' she asked.

Instantly I could tell she was a lawyer. That confident tone bordered on aggression, and it didn't take long for me to realize that the tone veered closer to the arrogant slant of the scale than mere confidence.

I cleared my throat.

'This is she.'

'I think you and I have something in common that I'd like to discuss with you.'

I bit the nail of my index finger and tore it from its bed.

'Who is this really? Did Bobby put you up to this?'

'This is not a joke,' she insisted. 'Do you have a father who owns a bar called Dive Bar off of Girard Avenue?'

I cleared my throat again.

'Bar Dive?'

'Dive Bar,' she corrected without pause. 'It is called Dive Bar according to city records.'

I walked to the edge of the bridge and looked down over the filthy water of the Schuylkill. Wind crescents carved themselves into the flow. I spit out the papery nail and watched as it floated downward like a feather.

'Ms. Singleton?'

'Who is this really?' I asked.

Nobody knew about my relationship with my father, save for Bobby, and only he knew about it loosely as far as the fact that he was an anonymous telephone caller. I never told anyone, including Bobby, that I actually met him. But Marlene didn't answer me. Instead, she began to do what she did best. Delegate. Order. Manipulate.

'Meet me at the diner on Fitzwater and Seventh tomorrow at noon. Can you do that?'

I cleared my throat again.

'I . . . uh . . .'

'Is that a yes or a no?' she demanded. 'I don't have all day.'

'No ma'am.' I stumbled, looking around the bridge. There were only teenagers walking by in flip-flops and sunglasses. 'I mean yes ma'am. That's a yes. I'll meet you.'

Chapter 11

MARLENE WAS SITTING AT THE RESTAURANT ALONE AT a corner table by a tall bay window, dressed in a black pantsuit with a colorful French scarf tied around her neck three times. She was flipping through the pages of a yellow legal pad when I walked in. She didn't even bother to look up. Instead, she placed a fancy black ink pen carefully at the edge of the legal pad, pushed it away, and only then looked up to me.

'Marlene Dixon?' I asked, shoving my hand out to greet her. 'Hi, I'm Noa P. Singleton.'

'Noa,' she said, after an uncomfortable two or three seconds in which she examined every crease in my clothing, every hair out of place in my ponytail, every blemish on my cheeks. She placed an elegant hand on the table as if to push herself up to greet me, but decided against it. Now I understand why, but at the time, her utter disregard for my name and presence felt like acute disapproval.

'Good. Please sit, Noa.'

My name almost popped out of every sentence the way an English word splices the fluid Spanish of a Telemundo newscaster.

'Weren't we meeting at noon?'

I shrugged. 'Yeah, I think so.'

'Well, it's twelve twenty now. I have a meeting at one. That doesn't give us much time, does it?'

She pulled up her sleeve to reveal a platinum watch framed with hundreds of miniature diamonds. It was the type of watch that a powerful woman wears only after purchasing it herself – not a token of courtship.

'I have to admit, I'm a bit nervous right now,' I said, sitting down.

She didn't respond. A woman like that didn't need to. Instead, she leaned over to her briefcase and pulled out a yellow folder that contained several photographs.

'Take a look at these.'

'No drink first?'

Again, she didn't reply. Almost as if I had no choice over my actions even then, reluctantly, I took the folder and opened it. Inside, a colorful photograph, documentary-style, peered out at me from the table. At first, it was a bit hard to tell who he was, but upon closer glance, the pixilated image settled in my line of vision and its clustered dots of oranges and blacks, reds, blues, and browns formed an image I'd been trying to forget for weeks.

'What is this?'

'I believe you know exactly what this is,' she said, glancing over to her legal pad. 'And whom?' A list of names were scribbled on it, but I couldn't quite read them. 'Do I need to review the events with you?'

My eyes squinted, and I pulled the photograph closer to my face so that I could be sure it was his. In the photo, he was resting in a hospital bed, gaunt and metallic. A collection of wires bridged his cheek to the mouth. One eye was swollen shut with shades of indigo. Yellow clumps of hardened pus collected at the tear duct, and broken capillaries completed the shattered facial bouquet.

Marlene didn't feel the need to wait an obligatory five minutes to permit me comfort before reining me in without the courtesy of introductions. No doubt she had more important meetings to attend. In that, I respected her for her efficiency, her veracity.

'Good,' she said. 'I'm glad I've got your attention.'

Though it wasn't exactly Marlene Dixon who occupied my attention, all I could do was connect the image in my hand with the memory still pulsing in my temple; that of the vein throbbing in the forehead of my father just as his hand shifted into the shadowman's face.

'There's more,' she said to me. 'Feel free to look at the next few. Some are profile views, others of the bruising on the chest from internal bleeding.'

I stood from the table and my hands trembled as they pushed against it.

'Sit, Noa,' she sighed, motioning to the chair. Her fingers were long and manicured. 'Please sit.'

'You have exactly one minute to tell me what this is all about and why you have photos of the night—'

'—sit down,' she instructed. 'You don't want to make a scene. Just take a seat again, and I'll tell you everything you need to know.'

I looked to my right and there was a young couple on a first, maybe second date. Then I looked to my left and it appeared to be nothing more than a business meeting.

'Nobody is following you, if that's what you're concerned about.' She paused, sipped from her coffee, and then continued. 'Please sit.'

On cue, I acquiesced, and she took back her photo.

'Is he okay?' I asked.

'This man is my employee. I hired him to follow your father around, and unfortunately, you seem to have gotten in the middle of things outside of Dive Bar—'

'—Bar Dive—'

'—Dive Bar, and, for that, I'm terribly sorry—'

'—Is he okay?' I asked again.

'—you saw, probably, what you should have seen, but nevertheless—'

'—Is he okay?'

Sounds from the minions finally made their way to her, and she stopped for a moment, and listened.

'He was hurt. He's fine now, but he was hurt, and this is where we are.'

'And where exactly is that?' I asked.

I looked around and could have sworn that someone else was listening to our conversation, possibly following me around the same way the shadowman was trailing me outside Bar Dive.

'You paid criminals to follow my father around,' I said, probably a bit louder than I should have. Marlene's pupils shifted momentarily. 'Why?'

She looked again at her legal pad.

'Listen, Noa, we have something in common, and that's why I called you.'

'I don't think we have anything in common, Mrs. Dixon.'

She smiled abruptly as if the movement were a facial tic, pedantic and virile. 'We have absolutely nothing in common, Marlene Dixon, Esquire,' I recited. 'Senior Partner at Adams, Steinberg, and Coleson, LLP. Phi Beta Kappa Princeton University. Summa cum laude Harvard Law School. Head of Trusts and Estates in the Philadelphia Branch. Travels frequently to Tokyo and Hong Kong. I've done my research, too. You think I'm going to show up at a diner for someone who I know nothing about?'

'All right then,' she said, continuing to smirk, almost as if patronizing me was too simple, too pedestrian for her style.

Instead, she pulled out another photograph from her briefcase and dropped it on the table facing me. An inhibited-looking girl, no older than me, stared unhappily out from a portrait studio with a pointed jaw, pearls, and perfectly straight teeth.

'This is my daughter, Sarah,' she declared. 'Sarah, her father, and I are coming to the end of what we like to call the da Gama period.'

'As in Vasco da Gama?'

She moved an errant lock of hair out of her face, and from what I could tell, it was the only aspect of this woman's entire image that was even remotely out of place.

'I'm glad you can read an encyclopedia, Noa. I can see that at least that half a year at Penn didn't slip through your fingers.' She wet the corners of her lips before continuing. 'Now, I'm here because my daughter is coming to the end of her own mini-exploratory period, her period of sailing the intellectual world, if you will. I had hoped she'd use this time to study and take the LSAT or the MCAT or at least by this point be in graduate school. But instead, she is floundering around, spending all of her time with your father and what is barely a job.'

I drank some water and started chewing on a crushed piece of ice.

'I'm not following.'

There were no waiters nearby. We had been seated for minutes, and absolutely nobody had ambled to our corner to offer me a drink, bread, olives, anything. All that was before me on the table was the glass that was sitting at the table when I arrived, sweating as nervously as I was in receipt of Marlene's continued oration.

'Your father is seeing my daughter, and, quite frankly, it's a relationship that neither one of us wants to exist.'

My fingers curled around the glass and slipped down its corrugated torso. He wasn't dating anyone, as far as I was concerned.

'I'm sorry?' I asked.

In hindsight, it might have been more of a declaration than a question. A skip on a compact disc, or an accidental splice in a film that replayed the same frame twice.

'I'm sorry?' I said again.

'It looks like dropping out of college was the worst thing you could have done. You seem to have lost all powers of deduction.'

'Exactly how much research have you done on me?'

'Listen clearly: my daughter is seeing your father,' she said. 'That is a relationship that cannot be. Are we clear?'

'So what?'

'Noa,' she said, calmly, as if her voice were reaching out to mine.

'You want me to be offended that my father is dating someone half his age. My age, right?' I paused, still piecing together the narrative. 'To be honest, I couldn't care less about your daughter's inability to find herself, despite having a moderately rich patron.'

'Don't humor me with your denial,' she said, pulling the photo back.

'I don't care if your daughter is seeing my father. He's nothing to me. He really is nothing to me,' I continued. 'I've known him for all of five minutes.'

'And yet here we are discussing him.'

She picked up her legal pad and turned to a new page. I felt a little embarrassed at my behavior. It wasn't my place to be so obstinate to a woman I'd just met with a longer pedigree than my entire high school's administration's put together. Then again, it wasn't her place to presume that any emotion I felt for my father was basking in the envy of her daughter.

'How do you know I dropped out of college?'

She didn't respond. Instead, her eyes traveled to my exposed wrist. A flash of surprise and she quirked an eyebrow.

'That's quite a nice bracelet, Ms. Singleton.'

I quickly pulled down my sleeves.

'Do you think if you sell it, you'll have enough money to pay your rent? Or go back to school? That is what you want, isn't it?'

My nose itched and the pressure behind my sinuses crept upon me. He told me he wasn't seeing anyone. He told me he didn't have time in his life for anyone. I blew my nose on a cloth napkin, placed it in my lap, and then looked back to her. I never told her I dropped out of college.

'Have you been having someone follow me, too?'

'Look, Noa, you're not fooling anyone,' she said, locking my gaze for the first time.

'How long has it been going on?' I asked. I don't know if I was asking about Sarah or the private investigator. Both, maybe. Neither.

She unraveled her scarf for air to prepare for negotiations. 'Too long.'

'How long, Marlene? A month? Two months?'

'At least eight months. Maybe nine, I can't be sure.'

'Almost a year?' I asked, in shock. Half of Marlene's mouth curled. No doubt, this was the reaction she'd been hoping for.

'This relationship cannot be comfortable for you,' she said, picking up momentum. She was too glib to humor me, no matter the message, when all that mattered was what wasn't said. 'I cannot imagine how you would feel.'

'First of all, it's not at all uncomfortable as I didn't know it existed before now, and second, I couldn't care less who my father or nonfather, if you will, chooses to be with. He did it to my mother and probably about three hundred other women since then. Hasn't impacted my life one bit.'

'Noa, you wanted to find your father. You found your father. And now you've lost your father. It's a pretty simple story.'

'Not really.'

'Did you or did you not come to Philadelphia to find your father?'

'I did not,' I lobbied, taking a sip of my own water.

'Did you or did you not find your father here in Philadelphia?' she asked again.

'He found me, if you must know.'

'Right,' Marlene said. 'And how did he explain his decades-long absence?'

'I didn't care.'

'If you say so,' she said, looking back to her legal pad, before continuing her cross-examination. 'Where did he tell you he was before Philadelphia? Did he explain his three-year stint in a correctional facility outside Louisville, Kentucky?'

I looked around for the waiter again, but none showed. My hand still gripped the water. Waves of perspiration dripped over my fingers.

'What about the time he served in Ohio? I presume you know about California twenty-three years ago, and what brought him back here.'

'Look, Marlene, I'm sorry, but I really don't know what you want from me. So your daughter's dating my father. So they're together. Okay. So you and I may be related one day. So my father was in prison. You're not telling me anything I don't already know. If you don't want your daughter dating my father, that's your problem. Not mine.'

Marlene took the photographs and put them back into her briefcase, only to pull out another envelope to hand me.

'Don't bother counting it. There are ten thousand dollars

in there. I need you to do what you need to do to break up that relationship.'

I laughed. 'You're kidding, right?'

She didn't budge.

'Seriously, you're kidding.'

'I am not.'

I continued laughing.

'Do it yourself.'

She placed both of her hands on the table, neatly woven together at the knuckles as five delicate blood knots.

'If I do anything connected to that man; if I so much as speak with him alone, Sarah will know it was me,' she said, her voice crisp and low. 'That is not an option.'

I couldn't help myself. She was sitting across from me, fetid and poised in her tailored suit and gold locket as if she were royalty, deigning to speak with the likes of me; no, supplicating the likes of me, for help.

'If you say so. Still, get someone else.'

She shook her head slowly.

'There's no one else.'

'There's always someone else,' I said.

She unhooked her fingers from one another, crushed them into a fist, and waited. Then she picked up her pen, dabbed it on her lower lip, and flipped to a new page of her legal pad. She opened a menu stuck together with syrupy residue. She cleared her throat. She tapped her fingernails in a round against the table, all without looking my way. It was as if she knew it took only one minute at most for people to change their minds to hers, as if all she needed to do was sit before someone, threatening to take away her presence, to make that person care. That was something my mother never mastered. If she threatened to remove herself from me, she removed herself from me.

'Why on earth is it me?' I finally asked.

'Because he's your father,' she answered, 'and like it or not, that matters.'

'It doesn't. Not with him. Not any more. Sorry.'

Marlene patted her eyebags and licked her lips.

'This relationship hurts you just as much as it hurts me. And if it doesn't today, it will tomorrow. If it doesn't tomorrow, I promise you, one day in the near future, you will wake up wondering where the father you've so longed for is living, and you'll remember this conversation. You'll remember that, once again, he left you. Only this time, it wasn't for someone different. It was for someone just like you.'

'Someone just like me?' I asked. 'I get that this lunch date has been rather intimate, but I can't imagine I'm anything like your daughter.'

'Your father is not just with someone half his age, he's with someone your age, who went to school with you. And that, Noa, is going to slowly eat at you as you meet new people, as you date, as you want to introduce boyfriends to your parents – one an ex-con in multiple jurisdictions across the continental United States, and another, a failed community theater actress. We both know that's precisely why you're going to help me break up this embarrassing excuse for a relationship,' she said, as if concluding a lecture. 'Now, did you order your tea?'

I shook my head no.

I never even told her I drink tea.

'Do you still want some?'

I shrugged, looking over to the legal pad. Her handwriting was illegible, as if she had been writing out prescriptions all day. As if she were mad herself, a self-appointed Don Quixote. Or maybe she was relegating that role to me.

'How much money did you really bring with you?' I asked. I hadn't paid rent in over a month.

She pushed the envelope toward me.

'You can count it. There are ten thousand dollars in there,' she looked back to my wrist. 'Easier money than selling that bracelet. It could probably help you get back in school, if you really wanted it to.'

My hands escaped back into my jacket sleeves.

'Don't you want to know a little bit more about me first?'

She folded her arms.

'Like my favorite color?' I asked. 'Or what sort of music I listen to? Or, say, my favorite food? Clearly you've done the basic biological research. Absent father, according to you because of criminal tendencies. Blasé mother. Do you know I have a baby brother? He works in porn in North Hollywood. Is that just like your daughter?'

And then quickly unfolded them, unamused.

'I know everything I need to know,' she said.

A spill of laughter fell out of me so slight even I didn't believe it.

'You don't have to believe me, but will you help me?' she concluded. 'At the very least, you can find out a little bit more about him.'

'I know all I need to know about him,' I said, looking back to the stack bedded within the envelope. It seemed to be multiplying the longer I stared at it. Perhaps that's why my father was keeping her from me.

'Where does she live?'

'In a high-rise near Rittenhouse on Walnut Street.'

She stood partially from her seat to move the envelope closer to me. I could tell at that point that she was a bit overweight, but only if I stared at her hips. (Hence, the pantsuits, no doubt.) Inside, I could see just exactly how much was inside. Enough to pay my bills for nearly six months.

'I'm gathering from our conversation that you didn't know anything about this. I'm sorry to be the one to break the news to you, but your father has a predilection toward fabrication.'

She pulled out the photograph of the shadowman again.

'I can't have my daughter with a man who does this for fun. If our roles were reversed, Noa, you'd do the same.'

His jaw was bruised and his eyebrow split in two in a way that looked glued in a permanent state of disorientation.

'If not for the curiosity or familial pull, then at least for the money,' she said, handing me the heavier envelope.

The thing is, the quest that Marlene had given me was sensational at best, but it was a job no less. And it had been nearly five years since anyone had asked me to do anything meaningful, despite the motivation behind it. The quest toward a windmill is more fulfilling than an empty stroll, sometimes, even if the windmill isn't real.

Chapter 12

THE FIRST TIME I SAW SARAH WALKING OUT OF HER apartment in Rittenhouse, she was wearing a misplaced business suit that suggested anything but power. From a distance, I imagine she looked a little bit like what I would have looked like if I were a virgin. Hair tightly pulled back by at least nine clips, eyes bulging out from her head, oversized baggy clothes covering what could be either (a) bulimia or (b) blistering insecurity set off by that one night in college when she was told by a third of the B-string lacrosse team that she was a dull tease.

She strolled down to Broad Street to catch a SEPTA train. I followed her but was caught between the untold limbs squirming among one another like worms competing to escape a tackle box, only to see her slip into the river that was SEPTA's Blue Line. I didn't follow her much beyond that.

The second time I saw Sarah was on the track at Penn. It was almost as if a higher power were gifting me this surveillance. God help you if you're not running after someone.

On the track, she seemed different than on the street or in the photos. Initially she came across as plain, with dirty blonde hair that struggled to find a structured identity between curls and limp strings. It was as if her hair reflected everything on the inside – did she have curly hair or straight? Greasy or clean? Was she tall or short? Pretty or average? She was wearing blue basketball shorts and a black sports bra with an oversized white T-shirt draped on top like a flag. There was a Penn logo on the outside, dirtied with a few signatures from perhaps teammates? Friends, even? If it hadn't been for the T-shirt, she would never have stood out.

She stopped ten, maybe fifteen feet before me on the track and bent over with one hand pushing down on her lower back. Her T-shirt stuck to her body, perspiration revealing every inch of it save the thin straps of her sports bra underneath. Her birdlike arms wrapped themselves around her waist as if they were capable of being tied in three knots below her belly button, and then she began to jog slowly. I watched from the sidelines as she picked up some speed, passing an elderly couple as she turned the corner. Her face grimaced with discomfort each time her body touched the ground, almost as if it were painful to tread through her own life. She was panting even during the slower laps. Then, contrary to what the prosecution claims, I just started running behind her on the track because I was ready to start running again. I didn't stalk her. I didn't pick her out as my victim from the moment we met. It would have been impossible based on their theory – yet another inconsistency in my trial.

The third time I saw her was in her place of employment. She was a curator in training, which according to Marlene was barely a job, as the role of assistant (despite its expected upward movement) didn't require graduate school training. She was one of two assistants to the head curator at the Philadelphia Museum of Art and did everything from liaise with art students to liaise with estates of dead artists to liaise with janitors. She seemed to enjoy her job on rare occasion, despite the fact that she got to climb the Rocky stairs every day on her way in and stare at the works of Thomas Eakins and Georgia O'Keeffe at lunch, if she was so inclined.

When I watched her wander from the American painters to the costumes every so often, she would stop and lock eyes with a subject as if they were sharing a secret. And for that brief moment, Sarah Dixon seemed comfortable. Her shoulders elevated with strength, her feet rested in fifth position, and her hands gathered around her chin as if posing for a photograph. She didn't realize the mounds of visitors jutting around her, the loud kids, the field trips with no more than the one forty-something-year-old exhausted teacher who looked at least fifty, the European vacationers stripping the space to her right and to her left, holding hands. All that she knew was the safety of living in a frame. Something beautiful, painted with the color choice of another, with the artistic intent of that same other, designed for a purpose – to wear an expensive and mightily elaborate coat and be seen in the right place for thousands to ogle on their day off. In that, I could never understand the secret she shared with the Degas ballerinas on loan from the Louvre or the Rubenesque women staring at mirrors.

In all my visits to the museum, never once did I see my father step foot in the Philadelphia Museum of Art to meet her for lunch, to pick her up after work, or drop her off before. If he even knew where the museum was located, he was probably outside on the front steps, impersonating his matinee idol, running up and down, no doubt inadvertently bumping into tourists. I never waited around to see one way or another. From what I could gather, this relationship that Marlene Dixon so proclaimed was one that could not exist, did not exist.

I was moments away from calling Marlene and letting her know that there was nothing to worry about – at least nothing where my father was concerned – when I decided to follow Sarah after work to see if she was going to Bar Dive or some other establishment in North Philly. It was 6 p.m., and she walked out the side door of the museum with a heavy back-pack on her shoulders instead of the leather briefcase that she carried most days. She wasn't walking toward the subway or across the river to go home. Instead, she was meandering across Ben Franklin Parkway, walking east until she reached

Market, turning to cross the river, and continuing block after block, when any other person would have hopped into a cab, until she hit the Penn campus. Somewhere around Drexel, she removed her backpack from her right side, stretched her shoulders, replaced it on the left side, and continued until she reached the library.

I hesitated. I hadn't stepped foot near anything related to Van Pelt Library in five years. But I continued, placing one nervous foot in front of the other until she opened the door. Twenty feet of cement bore the river between us, and it was navigated by dozens of anxious college students preparing for their midterm exams. Before she opened the door, she turned toward me as if she recognized me – from the track? From the park? From the museum? – before disappearing inside.

I walked toward the front doors as just another student eking my way one inch closer to a college degree, until I tripped on a piece of cement sticking out from the ground like an ocean wave. In once-wet cement, there it was, staring at me in submerged cursive: 'Beware the Bloody Mistress of Van Pelt 4.'

I didn't look up to see if Sarah saw me. I didn't continue in after her. I didn't want to see the stacks in the *N*s of History or revisit the multiple interpretations of the French Revolution. Floods of neologisms, neophytes, nepotists, and necrophiliacs washed over me and carried me home alone.

I refused to follow Sarah Dixon for another three weeks.

* * *

Six weeks into my Marlene-funded surveillance of Sarah Dixon, I learned about the Pat's Pub murders. I was outside Sarah's apartment eating a chocolate crepe from my favorite food truck while waiting for her to come home after work, when I stepped in a three-inch pile of dog shit.

A young family ambled by with an expensive stroller, snickering callously, their fingers pointed at me, reminding me of how little I fit in, in Rittenhouse. I looked around for the closest garbage can. Puffs of old ice cream cones, deli paper, and shredded napkins poked out of it like a bouquet of rubbish. I had no choice. I wasn't going to move from my location. I had found the perfect spot: close enough to see everyone come and go, but far enough that I would blend in with the park crowd.

I grabbed the first semiclean newspaper from the garbage I could find and wiped the bottom of my shoe clean. Streaks of black snuck their way into the wavy grooves making it impossible to clean entirely. Still, it worked for the time being. I put my shoe back on and held the contaminated newspaper between two fingers as if it were radioactive waste, and then dropped it back into the can with the rest of the daily rubbish.

As my lens tightened, little black letters from the newspaper illuminated through the brown smears. Peering out at me from behind the pixilated black-and-white copy was a mug shot of my future row mate. The headline just above her photo read, GOALIE PULLED ON THIS LOVE MATCH WITH NO TIME REMAINING. Unfortunately, the journalist writing the piece not only mixed metaphors, but mixed so many sports in this headline that even I hadn't a clue what the Pat's Pub assailant was guilty of, apart from wanting to play better soccer, or perhaps tennis. I plucked the newspaper out of the trash to read on, but got only as far as SPORTS BAR MURDERESS WANTED A SLURPEE TOO MANY when I heard my father's voice calling to me.

'Noa? Is that you?'

I shoved the newspaper back into the trashcan and looked up to see him walking toward me carrying a handful of white Gerber daisies.

'It *is* you!' he cheered, looking behind him for a brief moment, before walking over to me. My arms went limp as I allowed him to hug me. 'How have you been? Where have you been?'

I nodded, emotionless, just staring at the perfect little petals on the daisies in his grip.

'What are you doing here, dollface? You haven't returned any of my calls. I've been so worried about you.'

'I'm just having a crepe,' I muttered, pointing to my discarded food in the trashcan. 'They have the best crepe truck in the city, so I came here for a crepe.'

He shoved his hands before me in playful surrender.

'Just askin',' he sighed, 'just askin', that's all. Doesn't hurt a father to inquire about his only daughter.'

His eyes darted back and forth between me and the front of one of the high-rise apartment buildings.

'Are those for Sarah?' I asked, motioning to the flowers.

Folds of skin instantly dropped around his eyes and mouth. He reached out to me.

'Noa . . .'

'Don't "Noa" me, Dad,' I said, puncturing the patrimonial word. 'What do you think you're doing? She's my age, for Christ's sake.'

He glanced away momentarily.

'How do you know Sarah?'

'I know things,' I said. A breeze plucked a handful of leaves from a neighboring tree.

'Come on, dollface. Doesn't your old pop get a second chance at love?'

My chest started dancing. 'Love? Please.'

'Yes, love,' he insisted.

'Isn't that what you left in Los Angeles, oh, I don't know, twenty-three years ago?'

Again, he displayed those ridiculous jazz hands signaling faux surrender. It was enough to make me want to snap them off.

'That hurt,' he said, pretending to back off. 'But I can take it. I can take it. I'm a tough man, but I've been told worse.'

'You're becoming a caricature of yourself the more you talk.' I motioned over to the building. 'How did you even meet someone like her? She lives in Rittenhouse, for Christ's sake.'

He didn't respond.

'She's my age, Caleb. It's like you're fucking your own daughter.'

'You don't have to speak that way to me.' He jumped.

'Don't I? I'll ask you again, how did you meet her?'

He sat down on a nearby bench. In fact, when I think back to it, it might have been the same bench near the fountain from months earlier.

'Honestly?'

'That would be nice.'

'I was looking for you when we first met. I could have sworn that she was you, before—'

'—are you kidding me? Are you fucking kidding me?'

'Let me finish,' he pleaded.

'I can't even begin to count the ways that is disgusting. I'll try. In fact, I'll go alphabetically.'

'Noa.'

'Arrogant. Beastly. Criminal. Devilish. Empty and evil.' My chest climbed up and down with breath. 'There's two for *E*, because it's so exceptionally, egregiously, egotistically erroneous.'

'Let me just explain.'

'Felonious. Grotesque.'

'Noa!' he shouted, quickly calming himself. 'Please. It was a really hard time for me.'

'Yeah, Dad, it was a really hard time for all of us. What's your point?'

'Please,' he said, struggling. 'This is really hard for me to say.'

'Really?' I laughed. 'Harder than everything else you've told me?'

'Fair enough,' he said in concession. Again those damned hands flipped up in surrender or passivity or perhaps his habitual submission of arrest. 'I was just really nervous all the time. I had just bought the bar and was still getting my life together so I could get in touch with you.'

'Right, four years after learning about me, but go on.'

'I wanted to look for you, Noa,' he pleaded. 'I did. But I still wasn't ready. Then, everything was so crazy. People were thinking about changes to make, amends, that sort of thing. I started thinking about my life, too, you know, and what I should be, and what I promised to myself after my mom died, and I knew it was time to get in touch.'

'Get to the point,' I said.

'I was working out, running, sprinting up and down the Rocky steps, and that's when I saw her, walking out the front door wearing a T-shirt from Penn and a baseball cap, and getting ready for a run. And I knew from your mother and from those letters that you ran track in high school, and so I thought, hey, maybe it could potentially be you, without me even looking for you. You would have just shown up magically for me,' he laughed. 'But as it turns out,' he said, settling into a calmness, 'it was her, and the rest, as they say . . .'

'Don't go there,' I insisted.

'Well, you asked. There it is.'

'How charming. Love almost lost on a case of mistaken identity.'

He rolled his eyes, confused, and then continued with his story.

'You don't even look alike, that's the funny part.'

'Hilarious, Caleb.'

He looked around from right to left, and then back down to the daisies that were starting to wilt in his hands.

'We've been together since December.'

'December?' I asked quietly, as if it were news. 'We didn't meet until February. You didn't even call me until February.'

He accepted this earnestly. No contest, no pantomiming forgiveness. I didn't push it any further.

'Why didn't you tell me about her?'

He breathed in deeply, as if he were trying to think about a plausible response that would enable our relationship to continue, but he couldn't. I couldn't bear to see him continue struggling or listen to whatever response he'd provide.

'Does she know who I am?'

'Yes,' he said, nodding. 'Well, sort of.'

'What is it? Yes or no. It's a simple question.'

'Yes, she knows about you. I told her about you on that first day.'

'—at least your story is somewhat consistent—'

'—and it's really because of her that I built up the courage to call.'

On instinct, I looked away.

'Think about it,' he said, reaching his hand out to me – the one that didn't grasp the Gerber daisies. 'Up until her, I didn't think I would be good enough for you. But if I was good enough for her—'

'—don't finish that sentence,' I asked, placing one hand before my face. 'Please don't finish that sentence.'

The only recourse was simply to remove him from my line of vision.

'You asked,' he said, in earnest.

'Fine,' I replied, equally so, before changing tactics. 'Now I know how you met. What's it gonna take for you to end it?'

He nearly dropped the bouquet on the ground.

'I'm not ending anything with her,' he said. 'You have absolutely no right to dictate how I run my life or who I do it with.'

'I get it.'

'I don't think you do.'

'No, really,' I insisted. 'I get it.'

He looked down at his watch, and then directly back at me.

'There is nothing I wouldn't do for the people I love,' he paused. 'Nothing. You know that.'

He was bouncing on his toes so heavily, it was as if a chain were pulling him to the ground.

'Go,' I said. 'You obviously have somewhere else you'd rather be.'

'No, I want to be here,' he said, swallowing some saliva stuck at the base of his throat. He looked again at his watch. 'But I do have somewhere I have to be. Can you meet me later? So we can keep talking?'

The manure smeared on the soles of my shoe traveled up to my nose.

He asked again calmly, 'Can you meet me later?'

'No, I'm sorry,' I said, shaking my head. 'No.'

Shortly after we spoke, my father vanished into the vortex of a neighboring high-rise building and didn't come out until nearly three hours later. I waited the entire time, chewing on my fingernails and cuticles until they bled. When he finally did emerge, he was alone and glowing with what Andy Hoskins called his 'cigarette recovery.' He held up his hand and with the aplomb of a heart surgeon, called the first available taxi to his side. I hailed a cab just behind him and followed as he rode east a few blocks toward the river, until we arrived at Fourth and Locust, a fifteen-minute walk from the park, and then again disappeared into a corner gift shop. I gave him a good thirty to forty seconds before exiting my own taxi so he wouldn't notice.

He wasn't hard to follow. For starters, my tracking skills had improved from nonexistent to intermediate in the previous few weeks, having watched Sarah Dixon from her apartment, the track, the museum, her Tuesday evening book club, and even when she took the train to go home to the

Main Line. My father was somewhat inconspicuous. That is to say, his average build didn't quite burn into the memories of passersby, but his facial tics and voice and face made him relatively easy to identify.

A few minutes later, he walked out of the store with a bottle of water. Then he strolled along Locust Street, casually pausing to look in store windows, killing time. He stopped at a corner store, picked up a single sunflower, had it wrapped in paper, and continued on until he arrived at his destination – a bluish-modern building sticking out from the architecture of the city like a mole. I looked up at the sign. It was Planned Parenthood.

He grinned with the exuberance of a first-time father and waited. As soon as Sarah arrived, he licked that pea-pod scar over his lip and smiled at her. She pulled my father's hand to her lower back, pushing it in as if massaging out the same cramp she's had for months, and then stretched for a few moments, bending in half so low that her head nearly touched the ground. That was when I first noticed how fragile she was. Through the distance and the oversized clothing, little bones poked out from her vertebrae like pointy pyramids. Somehow, I missed that on the track.

'Hi, dollface,' I heard him say. She blushed, and together, they held hands and walked inside.

Chapter 13

SHE SAYS IT TO ME AT LEAST ONCE A WEEK THESE DAYS.

I'm scared.

Through the bars and putrid space in between our cells, through the apathetic watch guards who wish they were working with the Greyhounds or drug lords, through the darkened hours that have no identity to separate them from the daylight, through the throngs of a morning sun shifting into my cell, I hear Patsmith trembling.

I'm scared.

I know she's not speaking just to me. I know she's not speaking to anyone in particular, but I feel like maybe I can help her become less paranoid or petrified, at the very least, if I answer her once in a while. I mean, she's not alone. Not alone-alone, as long as I've been here. That much I know.

Last week, just after her hourly triumvirate of, 'Pat, I love you, Pat! I need you, Pat! I miss you, Pat!' she spoke directly to me for only the third time in the nearly five years we've resided next to each other.

'Are you awake, P?' she asked at precisely twenty-one past some hour in the middle of the day.

'Yeah,' I said. My voice cracked from dormancy when I tried to answer her.

Footsteps snaked around the corner like columns of black smoke. I was sure it was Nancy Rae. A different Nancy Rae. The behind-the-scenes Nancy Rae who didn't feel the need to unroll her eyes and flip up her gums when lawyers and parents were in the visitor's booth.

'Do you think that lawyer of yours will take on my case?' she asked.

Her voice slipped into my cell like a nightlight under the crack of a door.

'I don't know. I can't imagine Marlene Dixon is taking on any new clients.'

As much as I wanted to give Patsmith a few final months of possibility, Marlene Dixon didn't care about human rights. Not really. Her longstanding heart, to which she finally claimed she's grown into, was clearly targeted at me. Selective advocacy, preferred pro bono, self-righteous rationalization – whatever you want to call it.

'Don't you already have a lawyer?' I asked. 'Don't you have like five? You're always out in the visitor's booth.'

'Yeah,' she said. The word just sort of dribbled out in multiple syllables. 'But not for lawyers. Just visitors.'

'That's got to be nice, though,' I said, and it shocked me that not even one word was sputtered acrimoniously. 'My lawyers only visit about once a month. And before Ollie, other than journalists, I can't remember the last person who even came to see me.'

'Ollie is the young one?' she said, sort of half-inquisitive, half-declarative. 'The boy? Always parts his hair. Looks like he went to college.'

I smiled. 'I would hope he at least went to college.'

'Yeah, him,' she said. 'Think he'll take my case?'

Footsteps filled the nearby cell. I didn't know what to say. I spent years doing or saying the wrong thing on instinct. I didn't want to do that to someone who has only a few weeks left. Days, even. No matter what she did, she deserves at least a little bit of honesty at this point.

'I lost my last appeal,' she finally said. Years of age seemed to congeal around her voice, as if in the course of a ten-second conversation, she jumped from forty to eighty. 'I have two weeks. I don't have enough time left to see my daughter. I need a lawyer to get me time with my daughter.'

My head dropped to my chest. Nancy Rae walked through the cells, spearing us with her gaze.

'How old is she?'

'Thirteen,' she said, laughing nervously. 'She was only one when I was arrested.'

I waited again before responding. It takes time and quite a bit of practice to learn how to hold your tongue. Even here.

'She's only thirteen,' Patsmith said again. 'Thirteen. Almost fourteen.'

'I'm sorry,' I finally said. 'I'm really sorry.'

If Marlene were here, she'd hardly recognize me.

But I didn't put Patsmith in here. She did. She may not understand it now, but at some point, she'll realize that she's here for a reason. She did something wrong. She needs to be here. She'll realize it. She will realize it.

Still, I just wanted to hold her hand.

And I wasn't lying to her.

'Her father refuses to acknowledge me,' she said, 'but my daughter wanted to know me about eight years ago. Someone in her class told her it would be important. Her stepmother, who she calls "Mom", also thought it would be good. They said it would heal her or something like that.'

'So she was only one when,' I stalled again, looking for the right words. I wish they told you that upon admission to prison, you'd lose vocabulary as quickly as you lost friends. 'She was only one when—'

'—when I did my crime?' she said, finishing the sentence for me. 'Less.'

'I see,' I said to her. I didn't know what else to say. I'd only so much as looked at Patsmith from a distance, through bars or glass or a school of big-boned prison guards with necks as thick as goalposts. And again, 'I'm sorry.'

She didn't respond at first. I've garnered from the nightly ritual of blessing the Father, the Son, and the Holy Spirit that her priest probably told her she'd be going straight to hell if executed. (He probably should have told her that upon execution of her crime, but that's another story altogether.) No wonder she lived in fear.

'You know,' I told her, 'there's nothing to be afraid of. When it happens, it happens. We all go at some point. Might as well make it mean something. You killed someone. An eye for an eye, right?'

'One of my lawyers tried to get me to convince my judge that I was crazy,' she said. 'That I didn't know what I was doing. That it was some sort of postpartum defense, but it didn't take.'

'It's not going to ever take,' I said, rather jumpy.

I didn't mean for it to come across harsh or anything. Again, that's another chapter that should be put in a 'Welcome to Prison' pamphlet. Your not-so-subtle subtleties rise up out of your vocal cadence like punches on at least each occasion you're allowed to interact with another. I cleared my throat.

'I just don't think it'll work. It didn't work already, right?'

'I know,' she sighed. 'I know that. It's just . . . I want to see my daughter one more time.'

'Nothing's gonna happen in two weeks' time that hasn't already been cleared up. You aren't crazy. You know that. And even if you were—'

'I didn't realize what I was doing in that convenience store, P. You gotta believe me. I didn't know.'

Again, I smiled, as if she could see through the walls. I didn't mean it in a condescending lilt. I meant it in a solid embrace of solidarity. I felt pity for her. Like she still believed something happened to her instead of the other way around.

I don't know.

Maybe in retrospect, it was really envy. She still believed in herself, at least.

'Listen,' I said to her. 'Did you know that some guy from Arkansas decided to shoot a couple of people in three days on a killing spree? He turned himself in and then, in the process, tried to shoot the cop arresting him. Idiot shot himself in the head, essentially self-lobotomizing whatever brain was there in the first place. You see what I'm saying. Clearly this guy was crazy or incompetent or whatever they want to call it, but from the point he shot himself, he certainly was an idiot. Couldn't tie his shoes or tell anyone his birth date. And still, he was given a death sentence. They didn't allow the insanity defense at all and allowed him to be executed.'

She was quiet. Or asleep. Or praying.

'He was given his last meal and asked his last words. Know what they were?' I continued. '"I'm saving the dessert for later."'

'I wonder if they saved it,' she said, after contemplating this far too long.

Visions of Patsmith slinked through our shared wall in a prism of surgary desserts.

'Why don't you try to focus on all the visitors you have coming to see you before you go,' I said, changing the subject. 'Think about it. Imagine if you knew when you were going to die on the outside, how amazing it would be to see how people felt before. When it actually counts, you know? It looks like you've got that already. That's actually pretty nice.'

She didn't know.

'So, who are all the people visiting you?'

'My family,' she said. 'My pastor. My parents.'

Nancy Rae next stopped at my cell. I looked up to her just as she opened her mouth. Her bottom lip was filled with congealed tobacco. Little specs of blackened hairs seemed to crawl into the pink wedges between her teeth, holding tight in their new home.

'That's really great,' I finally said. 'Try to think about that.'

Nancy Rae fumbled around with her keys, looking for the one to my cell. When she finally found it, a smudge of pasty tobacco slipped out of her mouth and splattered on the floor.

'Singleton, you've got a visitor.'

Chapter 14

'Cheetos or Doritos?'

Oliver stood across from me with a handful of quarters and a lined forehead. We had already met a handful of times since this whole clemency mess began and he'd only just discovered the vending machines. No doubt had one of Patsmith's myriad visitors been in his stead, I would have been feasting on a three-course meal of Frito-Lay-Twizzler-Kisses.

'I'm sorry that I can't offer anything else, but that's all that's left. Do you want Cheetos or Doritos or a really old bag of pretzels that I think might have been in there when you were still part of the British Empire?'

Visitors don't get to personally hand over the snacks they purchase for us when popping into the Row for a quickie. Instead, they purchase delicacies from the patisserie of Frito-Lay or Coca-Cola to serve as a consolation prize for freedom. And since we get these little caloric goodies (which,

I'll admit, do sometimes make an inmate's week worthwhile), veteran guardess Nancy Rae must accompany them to the vending machines, take out the candy bar from the machine, place it in a brown paper bag, and deliver it to us, without their ever having placed a handprint on it. Contraband, they'd call it, if such an event were to transpire.

'Can you see if they have any chocolate?' I asked him. 'I'd like a Three Musketeers bar.'

He calculated the change in his hand methodically, counting aloud. *One quarter, two quarters, three quarters, four.* As he left, Marlene's face took his place. Of course she was wearing the black pantsuit from her previous visit and her omnipresent monotone frown.

'I think it's time we discuss what happened,' Marlene said to me before even sitting down. 'Enough dawdling.'

There was no lead-in, no exposition, no leisurely weighing of options as I considered whether to speak. It probably would have been easier if, instead of Oliver, she were here from the beginning, trying to uncover whatever it is she was trying to uncover with this ridiculous clemency petition. But like all demigods, she sent her underlings to do her work. Patsmith couldn't have had this problem.

'Did you hear me?' Marlene repeated. Her face was rubbery, like she'd had plastic surgery in the previous few years and I'd only just noticed it. I looked back to her, hoping to see Oliver, but he was still at the vending machines. It was certainly easier to talk about my father to him than to Marlene, who, let's be honest, had ulterior motives grander than *the statistics of execu-tions that have been turned down at this level* that Oliver indicated to me on practically each and every visit.

'I'm trying to have a conversation with you,' she demanded.

Oliver snuck back to our little booth. 'All taken care of,' he smiled. 'The food will be out to you shortly.'

I imagined that he was wearing a black tuxedo with a pleated shirt beneath, slightly creased where he had forgotten to iron it. But instead of serving me like a diner at a fancy restaurant, Mr. Oliver Rupert Stansted was offering me my requested meal of Three Musketeers.

'Oliver, if you'll just wait a moment, Noa and I are in the middle of a conversation.'

'No we're not,' I said.

'Sit down, Mr. Stansted,' Marlene demanded. 'I'd like to go back to New Year's Day,' Marlene said, turning her attention back to me.

I sighed. 'Fine.'

'What were you doing that morning before you broke into her apartment?'

'Shopping for beverages.'

'And . . . ?'

'And . . . what?' I asked, the timbre in my voice hinting upwards.

'Shopping for beverages and what else?'

But before I could think, Nancy Rae knocked on my door and handed me the brown paper bag.

'Thanks,' I told her and also mouthed to Oliver. He nodded to me, graciously.

'Noa, please focus on that morning,' Marlene said.

I picked up the Three Musketeers bar and sliced it open from one of the serrated zigzags at the top, so that only a small desert of sepia appeared. I was starving. The dark brown shell peeked out from the wrapper, like the head of a banana climbing out from its peel. Next, I bit the hard chocolate, grabbing an inch-long piece of the candy bar in my mouth. It sat flat on my tongue for a cool ten seconds, melting against my body's heat and vanishing between the invisible taste buds of my tongue. I hadn't wanted food this badly since . . .

'Noa!' Marlene commanded, banging on the partition.

. . . since . . .

'This is ridiculous. I don't need to waste my time on this today.'

But I skinned another wall of the candy bar, this time chomping down on the hardened chocolate.

'Oliver, do something!'

. . . since that time.

'We need to talk to you,' Oliver said.

'Noa!'

The banging was loud on the Plexiglas. I almost dropped the receiver to stop them.

'This is a complete waste of time,' she yelled at Oliver. 'Do your job! Do your job if you want to keep it.'

But the banging continued, plangent and percussive, like the whelps of a police baton.

By the time I finished the candy bar, I no longer saw Oliver or Marlene across from me. Instead, I was back in the police station, locked in a tiny office with no glass wall separating me from an empty desk. My hands were cuffed, facing each other like confused children outside the principal's office. Red slices of my skin ran beneath the silver bracelets, which covered my favorite tennis bracelet, another cruel foreshadowing of my future. And my right sleeve was soaked in blood, hidden safely under my coat. I don't think anyone noticed.

The door creaked.

My heart jumped.

A middle-aged man with a goatee walked into the room wearing jeans and a button-down shirt. He had no badge, no name tag, and he was wearing sporty sunglasses on his head as if he had just come from the beach, despite the fact that it was winter and the middle of the night and we were in Philadelphia.

'Noa Singleton?'

I hesitated before nodding.

'I'm Officer Woodstock. I'm the detective assigned to this case. Do you understand that?'

My eyes pickpocketed the room. There was a glass mirror and a tiny black bulb at the corner of the ceiling. It was inside there that everything I said, everything I did, every move I made, every menacing gaze I gave would be recorded. As of that moment, no red dot accompanied it. That, I'm sure of.

'I'd like an attorney,' I told him. 'I have the right to an attorney.'

'All right, if that's what you want.'

Officer Woodstock then stood up from his chair and left me alone in the room. It was another five hours before he returned.

I waited.

I waited patiently.

I waited for my attorney to arrive – any attorney – state appointed, dollar-store ilk, high-rise firm.

I waited to make my one call, which I eventually used on my mother.

I waited for her to arrive that night, as well, but it took her nearly a week to buy a plane ticket to see me. She was terrified of flying. She was sure a cross-country flight would be hijacked. It had been over a year at that point since 9/11 and my mother refused to fly cross-country, having traveled only in the air from Burbank to Ontario for a shampoo commercial audition.

And, of course, I waited for both Bobby and the guy from Lorenzo's, who I later learned refused to acknowledge me from that point until the trial. Bobby learned about what happened first and commiserated with the guy from Lorenzo's over beer and free pizza. I didn't even know that they knew about each other at the time. I guess I underestimated Bobby. I guess I underestimated his colleagues on the police force, too. I guess I overestimated the quid pro quo from Lorenzo's.

The second hand of the clock in the interrogation room ticked along so slowly, I could count each stroke. My arms shuddered, bruising the skin ever so delicately under the cuffs. I thought of my little brother. I thought of my mother. I thought of Sarah and her last glance at me as she refused that cup of tea.

Footsteps filled the hallway outside my room. At times, I heard the white noise of gossip. It terrified me. My bladder burst, spilling liquid panic down my legs. I hadn't eaten in twelve hours. My underwear reeked from nitrous-rich moisture. The water they had given me five hours earlier abruptly made its way down my urethra from my bladder and onto the seat upon which I was sitting. Some of it even dripped onto the floor below.

By the time Officer Woodstock returned, it had nearly dried, but the stench still remained. And another officer was with him.

'This is Sergeant Egan. For the record, I'm Officer Woodstock. It's five in the morning and I'm going to read you your rights. Do you understand?'

It looked like four men were standing to my side. There couldn't have been more than three feet by three feet of space. Suffocation of inordinate discomfort spilled over me.

Sergeant Egan pulled out a laminated card from his pocket.

He was practically my age. You would think that perhaps we went to the same high school until he started speaking.

'You have the right to remain silent and refuse to answer questions.' He said the word 'right,' with a small-town country twang. *You have the raaght to remayn sahhlent.* It made me lose my concentration. 'Do you understand?'

I nodded. Yes.

'Speak up. We need this on the record.'

My throat tickled as I cleared it.

'Yes.'

'Anything you say may be used against you in a court of law. Do you understand?'

Again, I nodded yes.

'Was that a yes?'

I nodded. 'Uh-huh.'

'Yes?'

'Yes.'

'You have the right to consult an attorney before speaking to the police and to have an attorney present during questioning now or in the future. Do you understand?'

Yes, yes, I understand.

'If you cannot afford an attorney, one will be appointed for you before any questioning if you wish. Do you understand?'

Fuck yes, of course yes.

'If you decide to answer questions now without an attorney present, you will still have the right to stop answering at any time until you talk to an attorney. Do you understand?'

Yes, yes, yes. I fucking know my fucking rights. I read newspapers. I don't rely on television to know my rights.

According to the video transcript played later at my trial, I said yes to almost everything, handing over my rights with a glazed look and virginal shock. According to the video, I relinquished my rights. I didn't ask for an attorney. I didn't ask to stop speaking. I didn't do anything. Suddenly, it was like that first interview with Officer Woodstock never existed. As if Officer Woodstock never came in on his own to ask me whether I wanted an attorney present and as if I wasn't completely ignored when I said, yes. Yes, I want an attorney present. Yes, I want to stop talking. Yes, I fucking know my fucking rights. But nobody ever heard those. It's strange, isn't it? How things can go so differently in your head than the way they appear to others.

Officer Woodstock informed me that I was sitting in that room for upwards of five hours before he'd returned to me. Later at my trial, he said on the stand that the reason was because they were transporting the body to the morgue and properly preserving the crime scene. They had a few other people to question first, as well, and didn't want to backtrack.

'Your name is Noa Singleton?' Sergeant Egan asked.

'Noa P. Singleton,' I corrected.

'What does the P. stand for?'

'P.'

'Don't play games with us.'

'P,' I repeated.

He kicked the front left leg of my chair, causing it to skid on the floor.

'We can find out in five minutes. Just make it easier on us.'

'Then find out in five minutes,' I said. 'Do your research.'

They looked at each other. I knew they wouldn't follow up. Nobody ever did.

'Do you know why you're here?'

'Because there was a break-in at Sarah Dixon's apartment.'

'A break-in?'

'Yeah, that's why we're here. I called the police. There was a break-in. I heard shots. Sarah was hit. I was hit. And you didn't get there in time.'

'Let's talk about Sarah,' Officer Woodstock continued.

'Did you see Sarah get shot?' Sergeant Egan asked.

I nodded.

'Did you see Sarah get shot, Noa?'

I nodded again, refusing to speak.

'We need a vocal response for the record. Yes or no.'

'Okay,' I said.

'Did you see Sarah get shot?'

'Yes.'

'Did you shoot her?'

I shook my head. 'No.'

They continued asking questions without pause.

'Let's talk about what happened. Can you talk about it?'

'I can talk about it.'

'What was the first thing you remember doing yesterday morning?'

'I woke up, brushed my teeth, called my brother to wish him a happy new year.'

'Where does he live?'

'In Los Angeles.'

'California?'

'Yes, Los Angeles, California. What other Los Angeles would it be?'

'Did you reach him?' They didn't skip a beat.

'No.'

'Did you leave a message for him?'

'No.'

'Does he know that you tried to reach him?'

'I don't know. You'll have to ask him that. Or subpoena the damn phone records.'

A little red light started blinking on the black bulb in the ceiling.

'What did you do next?'

'I showered, ate some fruit and cereal for breakfast, and left.'

'Where did you go?'

'I went to a drugstore.'

'What drugstore?'

'Just a drugstore.'

Woodstock and Egan shared a glance.

'Noa, again, we can find out all of this information within five minutes. Just make it easy on us and it will be easier for you.'

'What do you want me to say? An apothecary? A fucking drugstore, okay.'

Egan scribbled something down in his pad.

'Are we talking a small local pharmacy or are we talking CVS, Duane Reade, Rite Aid?'

'It was a CVS,' I decided to tell them.

'What did you buy at CVS?' Woodstock continued.

'Some tea. Sleeping pills. Apple juice.'

'Tea?'

I nodded.

'Ms. Singleton, for the record . . .' Egan nodded again to the black lightbulb.

'Yes,' I said, nodding again.

'. . . I bought tea. It calms me after a night out, like New Year's Eve, for example. Okay?'

'What did you end up doing on New Year's Eve, then?'

'Nothing,' I said, after a long enough pause.

'Okay. What kind of tea did you buy then on New Year's Day?'

'Lemon Zinger. It's the only thing I ever drink.'

'Anything else?'

'Huh?'

'Did you buy anything else?'

'That was it.'

'Were you by yourself?'

'As far as I know.'

'Were you followed at all?'

'How the fuck should I know?'

He leaned back in his chair.

'That's why I'm asking you. Were you alone? Followed?'

I shrugged. 'I. Don't. Know.'

'Okay,' he said, moving on. 'How did you pay?'

'What?'

'How did you pay for the tea and juice? Check? Credit? Cash?'

'Cash.'

'What did you do next?'

I looked back to the red blinking light. My fingers tapped along with it, counting out loud. One blink. Two blinks. Three blinks. Four.

'I left. I just walked around the parade.'

'Did you see anyone you knew?'

'No.'

Woodstock and Egan exchanged another glance. This was becoming both menacing and annoying at the same time.

'Look, my arm is really hurting me,' I said. 'I need to get to a hospital, or don't you care about human rights?'

'Ms. Singleton . . .'

'You think I'm kidding?'

'A woman is dead. We are not joking,' Woodstock said.

'Does it look like I'm joking? I was shot, too.'

Woodstock and Egan looked to each other and then to the two-way mirror.

I tried to lift my arm to show them that blood was still seeping through the gauze wrapped around it, but was unsuccessful. It was the same dressing from hours earlier, placed by the same medic who carried Sarah out of her apartment on a gurney with a blanket covering her face. Now the white gauze was burnt dark with dried blood, waves of color peeking through the porous wrapping, materializing on my shirt in various geometric shapes.

'Your arm was barely grazed,' Woodstock said.

'And don't I have the right to get medical attention for that?' I said, pointing to the new spots.

'You've had medical attention.'

Egan used this moment to take the reins.

'Ms. Singleton, let's talk about what happened after the parade. We know what happened. We just want to give you a chance to help yourself here. That's all this is. A chance to come clean. Get yourself right with God.'

'Are you kidding me?' I asked him, cupping my hand around the flesh wound on my shoulder. 'You're actually sitting there bringing God into this?'

'Well, this is a capital offense.'

In that instant, the red light in the bulb seemed to freeze. The mechanics of the camera twisted, an extended hand crunching into a fist. A director was inside searching for my close-up. And he was getting it in a way that would be replayed at my trial over and over and over again, regardless of my lawyers' running objection.

'Capital?'

'She was pregnant. That's a capital offense. Two deaths,' Officer Woodstock said to me.

'You also broke into Sarah's home,' Sergeant Egan added. 'Burglary is a felony. And Sarah was killed in the process of that burglary. Felony murder. Either way you look at it, capital offense.'

The red light struck my eye like a dart.

'Noa,' Officer Woodstock said to me. 'You're only hurting yourself here. You're in trouble. You messed up. Just fess up, and we can see what sort of punishment we can get for you.'

'I didn't break in. It was a mummer. There was a burglar.'

'We know you didn't live there. A person named Marlene Dixon owns the place and only Sarah Dixon is on the papers.'

'I don't know what you're talking about. I didn't mess up.'

'Sarah's dead, Noa. You killed her. We know you killed her. You might as well fess up now.'

My throat swelled like I was swallowing sawdust. My arms started shaking, and I could see nothing but the red blinking light of the camera expanding in girth, wider and wider, like a mutating starburst, until all that remained were red splashes of light, covering my eyes in miniature gunshots. Blood rushed from my face, my limbs, and fingertips to the lights of the camera.

Red bursts of bullets.

I dropped to the ground where my face rubbed against the urine rich floor. My eyes rolled behind my head. In the corner of my eyes I saw the silver wrapper of the Three Musketeers bar resting so peacefully on the floor.

Vomit was rushing up my body. I wanted to run to the bathroom but was shackled to the table, which was nailed to the floor. I was stuck. My body bent in half, heaving air for up to thirty seconds. After the dryness closed my throat, ribbons of chocolate and remnants of cinnamon bread from the night before traveled up the canal until they joined the puddle on the floor.

'She's faking it,' Woodstock whined, as my body shook on the floor. 'She's faking it.'

'We've got to stop now,' Sergeant Egan said. 'She's bleeding. Get her to the hospital.'

'For a bullet graze?'

My pulse raced along with my pounding temples.

'She's faking, Don. Just let her come to, and then we'll continue.'

'Take her back to the holding cell,' Officer Woodstock ordered. 'And call the medic.'

And then . . .

. . . and then . . .

I can't remember.

In all honesty, I can't remember how the interrogation ended.

The first thing I remembered after that was knocking on

the linoleum floor. Incessant, irritating, brain-curling knocking. High-heeled shoes, tight black ones with the toe peeking out, running into the jail, sprinting, despite a faulty gait. A voice accompanied it, just as excruciating, just as memorializing.

'Is it true? Tell me it's not true. Tell me it's not true!'

It was Marlene. Her speech was slovenly and drenched. She was hysterical. Her fists banged against the door of the interrogation room as I was transported out.

'You didn't do this, Noa. You didn't. Tell me you didn't!'

Although her words were muffled, she was angry. And she was terrified and emotional for once in her life in a way that other people could witness.

'Where is she, Noa? Why did you do this? Why? Why?' she cried, the words dribbling down her chin along with her foamy spittle. 'Why, Noa?' A few officers crowded around her, drawing her away. 'Why?'

I looked up. Her eyes twitched and her hair was wet around the scalp. It was already beginning to fall out, and she looked angrier and more pitiful than any human being I'd ever seen. My own mother included. Sarah included, even at her death. She knew at that point, and almost like a cartoon balloon unplugged from its air source, she deflated.

I never answered her question, even to this date. I'm not sure what changed between that encounter, my trial, and nearly three months ago when she and Oliver walked into my life.

'Where did Marlene go?' I asked him. Ollie was the only visitor on the other side of the Plexiglas. He looked away from me as if he was upset I'd been ignoring him all this time. 'You're not going to answer my question, are you?'

I looked down to the Three Musketeers wrapper in my grip. There was no chocolate left.

'Ollie?'

He didn't reply. Instead, he sat quietly in the chair, brushed his fingers through his hair, and collected his thoughts.

'Ollie?'

He looked directly at me.

'I think there's something more we can do besides clemency.'

August

Dearest Sarah,

You were born during the rain. Did I ever tell you that? I used to hate the rain, and funnily enough, it was during the rain when you were born. Your father was nowhere to be seen when one of the associates had to rush me to the hospital. Thirteen hours later, you were in my arms. Your father arrived around hour six of labor, so he was sufficiently present to claim that he had a large part in your delivery, but you and I both know that's hardly the truth. It's our little secret. We'll share it until I'm with you.

Do you see him? Do you talk to him? There are just so many questions I have for you. I wish I had asked you some when you were alive, but I'll spend the rest of my life trying. I write these little notes to you – questions, really – that are my way of trying to know you. I slip them between cracks at the cemetery as if it were one great Western Wall. Part of me thinks you read them. Somehow you pluck one of the two-by-five-inch torn papers from their stones, and you find unique and mystical ways of answering them.

For example, two years ago when I started MAD, I read books and articles and visited prisons to speak with some inmates, who, in between the cacophonous pleas for help, were able to answer questions about guilt, about responsibility, about their own narratives with such eloquence, such musicality that it brought me to visit Noa. Of course, I couldn't walk inside the prison walls that day, but those few *conversations with inmates (both guilty and, I'm sure, some not) helped me get to the next stage, which was this: I wondered if you wanted to be a mother. I mean really wanted to be a mother when everything started, regardless of what I told you. So I wrote it down on a little blue piece of paper and slipped it behind your gravestone. Two days later, I bumped into your gynecologist at a food truck by City Hall. She hugged me, just as she did at the trial, and eventually gave me the sonogram photos. Although the only copies I thought in existence were part of the trial record in evidence, she had evidently saved another set. She didn't know why she had saved them, she told me, but when we saw each other, she just knew.*

Another time, I wrote a little note asking if green was really your favorite color. I never asked. I never knew. What kind of mother doesn't even know her own child's favorite color? One week later, it rained so hard that all of Philadelphia woke up to an emerald city. Not a single burnt leaf hung in a tree. Not a single aging weed clogged the manicured lawns of the parks. It was at that point that my hatred toward rain melted. You'd think it would have been on the day you were born, but it wasn't. It was the day the wizard actually answered my questions in Oz.

Some time later, I wrote to you asking what you would have wanted to do with your life if I hadn't pushed you into the college of my choosing and toward grad school, or if I had put no dictums on your da Gama period and let you enjoy the museum. On my way out from visiting you, I bumped into an artist doing a watercolor of the gravestones. He smiled at me. He was missing a tooth but didn't seem to notice or even care. The next day, I woke up, and one of my colleagues had placed two tickets to the ballet on my desk. His wife didn't want them, and he said he knew that you had always loved to dance. He thought I might like them. Did you want to be an artist? A painter? A dancer? Both? Were you caught living in an adolescent fantasy that never matured because I never let it grow? I thought you might have wanted to be a painter, because the following day, I received a package in the mail, a thin poster tube, stuffed with bubble wrap and newspapers. There was no return address, but when I opened it, I found the watercolor covered with raindrops from the old toothless man at the cemetery. The date of the crumpled newspaper was your birthday.

You understand what I'm saying, don't you? These things don't just happen. They simply don't.

Yours always,
Mom

THREE MONTHS

BEFORE

X-DAY

Chapter 15

JURY TRIALS ARE REALLY NOTHING MORE THAN POORLY written stage plays. You've got two authors writing opposing narratives and a director who is paid not to care about either outcome. Hired actors sit on either end of the stage, while unwitting audience members strive to remain quiet. No applause should be rendered, no gasps of glory. Witnesses sit agape with fury as they stumble across their rehearsed lines. If only they had practiced just once more. If only they had more time or a dress rehearsal, then they would recite their packaged words with such eloquent delivery that the critics in the jury box would believe only them.

On his most recent visit, Oliver bequeathed to me a clean copy of my trial transcript – all twelve volumes, as if I would read through them and inexplicably be able to tell him about all the testimony that never came in and show him all the evidence that was deemed inadmissible by *Herr Direktor*. He seemed to need some sort of tangible reason for involvement that he could take home to his girlfriend or mother and show purpose of trade. After all these months, he still didn't realize that my memory has become as foggy as an old shadow. As watered down as community theater.

For a childhood spent in the wings of the theater watching my mother traipse across stage to stage, singing that she could do everything better than me, I would say my trial was one of the few comforting episodes of this entire ordeal. Even if I was declared guilty upon arrest, invariably my life was serene sitting on stage right with the director all in black and the stagehands adorned in blue and gold. The audience was, well, the audience – comprised of film crews and journalists, and family, friends, and professional partners of Sarah and Marlene Dixon. The only problem, of course, the only hiccup of human nature in the entire production, rested with the jury: twelve individuals and an alternate selected by the authors of opposing narratives all generating theatrics to get someone to see the story their way. It's the same each time, and yet trial after trial produces the same predicament.

Without fault and without fail in nearly every trial, the judge directs the jury to disregard a statement just accidentally uttered by one of the witnesses. And when they pollute the simple cognition of twelve sedentary jurors, the judge presumes that they will simply ignore it.

'I will instruct you now to disregard the witness's last statement,' the judge says. Ad nauseam. Ad infinitum. Ad . . .

well, you get what I'm saying, at least one time too many per trial.

How a system that delights with impeccable and acerbic precision can employ such a gelatinous technique astounds me, even today. Please disregard what I said when I mentioned my mother dropped me as a baby. Or erase from the appellate record of your cerebral cortex that once upon a time I lied to Oliver Stansted. Or Marlene Dixon. Or that I cried myself to sleep for three years straight after Persephone Riga moved away. Or that I used to fuck the guy down at Lorenzo's for a slice of free pizza every other Tuesday. They have nothing to do with what happened on January 1, 2003.

I instruct you to disregard the witness's statement.

The poetry of the line is almost comical. Nowhere else in life can a person of power instruct another to ignore a statement or observation and ensure its pragmatic compliance. Observation is inherently pliable. In life, we witness movement and emotion and sensation dissimilarly from everyone else. Once spoken, words will never be ignored, no matter how many judges instruct us to do so, no matter how many appellate courts confirm this to be true. People will never forget. Memory simply doesn't work that way.

Madison McCall told me later on (during my first appeal) that the law simply presumes that the jury complies with this judicial order. I guess we on the Row aren't the only bobble heads in the chorus of players after all.

I can't remember exactly how many times my judge

actually instructed my jury to ignore statements made by unwilling witnesses, but it had to be well into the double digits. That many serendipitous errors have to be planned. Or at least cause for a do-over. At the parade of pretrial motions – the government's most expensive dress rehearsal – Madison McCall tried unsuccessfully to throw out my interrogation, but only after an intestinal road of paperwork throwing around words like *Miranda* and *police misconduct*. Even with the interrogation transcript admissible, I would not testify to rebut it, or repeat the offense in phase two, the segment that would bring in the death sentence.

Chapter 16

PLEASE DISREGARD THAT LAST CHAPTER.

Chapter 17

JURY SELECTION FOR MY TRIAL TOOK NEARLY THREE weeks. The county dragged in over three hundred and fifty spiteful antiestablishment cronies who refused to accept their civic duty to sit in judgment of me. Their excuses rained like biblical plagues – entertaining, but time-consuming narratives nevertheless.

'My father's a lawyer. I can't be impartial.'

The constant, omnipresent, ever popular excuse.

'My mother's a policewoman. I can't possibly be impartial either.'

Slightly less popular, but frequently used.

'My daughter went to Penn.'

Eh . . .

'My sister works as an art historian.'

Even more eh . . .

'I'm a teacher, and my students are having their AP examinations.'

Perhaps, if they'll all flunk because you can't stick a sheet of paper into a Scantron grader.

'I'm having back surgery in one week. My doctor can't reschedule. Will this be finished by then?'

Maybe, but likely not.

'My mother was the victim of a violent crime, so I don't think I can be on this jury.'

You're probably right.

'I don't believe in the death penalty.'

I do.

'I had a hysterectomy last year.'

And I care because . . .

'I hate authority.'

I have no idea what to do with you, and neither do the lawyers.

'Kill 'er, I don't care! I believe in the death penalty.'

Hello prosecution!

'I'm a police officer. I see these cases all the time.'

Hello prosecution, again.

'I mean, I could follow the law if I was told to, but I don't know that I could follow the law if I was told to. You know what I mean?'

I don't. I really don't.

'Let each and every one of them fry. Fry like bacon.'

Now you're getting dramatic.

'I'm partial to women.'

So . . .

'I'm partial to men.'

Again, so . . .

'Fry like deep-fried bacon sitting in a batter of butter.'

Now you're just getting sloppy.

'My fibromyalgia will flare up if I'm seated for longer than three hours. I have a doctor's note with me.'

Please . . .

'I also teach science.'

Fair enough.

'I mean, if the judge told me that all the evidence led to one verdict, I would have to follow it. But I couldn't follow it, you know? You know what I mean, counselor?'

I still don't.

'I also have hemorrhoids.'

Good times.

'Let them fry like hot butter.'

I'm laughing at you now.

'With hemorrhoids, if I sit in one place for longer than forty-five minutes, I'll have a bulging pain in my rectum, so I can't be on this jury.'

That sounds fair to me.

'I'm getting married next week.'

Vaya con dios.

'You see what I mean, judge. I mean, with my hemorrhoids, it would literally be a pain in my ass to be on this jury.'

Hilarious.

'Okay, so I could follow the law, yes. If the law says the death penalty is okay, then it's okay. But would I believe that? I don't know. I don't. No, I couldn't. Yes, yes I do. It's okay. I could. I could follow the law. Yes. Yes, I would follow the law.'

Too pliable. Sorry, defense.

'I'm a member of the Church of the Savior of our Father. We do not believe in executions.'

Good-bye.

'No, I'm sorry, counselor. I don't think I could follow the law after all. Is that okay?'

No.

'I used to be a sniper for the military.'

Yikes.

'My mother is sick and I take care of her every afternoon.'

Impressive. And excused.

'I'm going to India next week on vacation. I'll lose a lot of money if I can't go.'

I don't feel sorry for you one bit.

'Please, I . . . I . . . have a heart condition. And I recognize the prosecutor from Wawa yesterday. And I think I went to school with the court reporter. Kindergarten, fifty years ago, maybe in West Philadelphia. And I'm Mormon. We don't believe in the death penalty. Well, that was twelve years ago. Now I'm a Catholic. No, I'm a Jew. An Orthodox Jew. You understand, right? There's no way I can be impartial.'

Of course. Of course, it's perfectly clear.
Judge?

I watched from the defendant's table during every clumsy excuse. Melodious sacraments to my dissonant entr'acte, perpetuating a system that works more often than it does not.

The final few left us with a jury that seemed less like my peers than I could have anticipated. Their names stay with me, even today: Ronaldo Martinez, forty-five at the time. Construction worker. Originally from Kansas. Moved to Philadelphia one year earlier to start anew after his bitter divorce. Beverly DeBeers, forty-three, no relation to the jewelry company. Stay-at-home mom of, like, six humanoids. Wants to move back to the Main Line, especially after being summoned for this case. Nancy Garmond, fifty. Said she was allergic to peanuts during *voir dire*. Owns a company producing jelly preserves and marmalade. No joke. Charlie Levi, sixty-two. Retired schoolteacher. Taught physics, poetry, and pottery to inner-city kids. Amir Ansari, thirty-five. Taxi driver from Turkey. Came to America seven years ago and became a citizen only two. Lakeisha Fontaine, forty-two. Works for the DMV. I could have sworn that I'd seen her before. She might have been the one who let me take my license photo over a few times until my smile wasn't crooked, but I can't be certain (and clearly she couldn't either). Russell Bryan, twenty-one. Recent college graduate. Drexel. Isn't sure what he wants to do with his life. Has a cool ambidextrous name. Lavonne Owens, thirty-eight, corporate lawyer. Loves her job. Likes to wear the glistening fruits of her labors around her neck, fingers, and wrists. Shanaya Portsmith, twenty-six, hairdresser. Wears a different style almost every day. Was blonde, redheaded, and back to blonde during the course of my trial. Vincent Hanger, fifty-eight. Artist. Teacher. Sold a few paintings in a gallery in New Hope recently. Felipe Almuerzo, forty-three, kindergarten teacher. Entirely too happy to be on a jury. Melissa Silva, thirty-six, journalist, hungry for blood. She later wrote a self-published memoir about her experience on this case that made it to the top ten thousand books on Amazon. And of course Samuel Stahl, seventy-four, our trusty alternate. Devastatingly old to be on a jury, particularly one for which he would never even have a vote.

There they were – twenty-six eyes serrating my every blink, the rising cadence of my chest, the unconscious flinch in my face when I unexpectedly sneezed. Thirteen individuals, marinating in the enclosed jury box like a carton of dried-out fruit.

By the time we finally made it to trial, I had been in jail for nearly sixteen months. My roots were halfway down my raggedy mane, and I had no more access to contact lenses. Madison McCall managed to procure an old suit from a thrift store for the trial, and consequently, I looked like a fashion victim caught in the mid-80s. I'm fairly certain I lost a vote or two based purely on the way I looked. Perhaps

Lavonne and Felipe would have focused on me and the facts of the case a little more if I looked better. Or perhaps not. The coquettish concern they displayed with the details of each other's bashful smiles reached me all the way on the other side of the courtroom. (I can't resent them, though. They did thank me later by sending me a wedding photo, which is now taped to my wall.)

But regardless of how I see it, these were the people looking at me. Sitting in judgment of me. Watching me hour upon hour upon hour. Asked repeatedly by Madison McCall and Tom Davies if they could actually stand in judgment of another person – of this woman, Noa P. Singleton. Every single one of them hesitated through their response: yes, yes they could. They thought they could. Of course they could. Yes, really, it would be their duty. Their civic duty. And then they were sworn in.

Chapter 18

TOM DAVIES WAS A SUAVE AUSTRALIAN FROM SYDNEY who had tried at least three other capital cases before landing mine.

The first was a felony murder. Twenty-three-year-old Dean Johnson robbed a liquor store down by Penn's Landing, shooting the clerk between the eyes three times, just before grabbing two hundred dollars from the cash register and a pocket-sized bottle of whiskey and jumping into the Delaware River. When the cops arrived, they found a trio of bullets connecting the liquor store clerk's unibrow from eye to eye so that he looked like a dead Cyclops instead of the former chief of medicine of Mumbai's third-largest hospital. They found Dean dog-paddling from Philadelphia to Jersey on a gimp leg, leaving a fluorescent trail of blood adulterating the water on the way. He confessed that night and almost pled guilty to avoid a trial. At the last minute, he got a newly appointed lawyer who persuaded him to fight the charge, only to meet the needle eight short years to the date of his guilty verdict. His jury deliberated for only twenty minutes.

The second capital case for Mr. Tom Davies was a quadruple homicide plucked from a B-rated Hollywood movie editing floor. Three dead-end guys, construction workers, decided to free their boss of a few ounces of cocaine while he was out screwing his wife's sister. No harm to a quality guy, they thought. So they waited until his car was missing from its spot at his office in North Philly, presumed him gone, and then proceeded to knock on the door. (I never said that they were bright, which is part of what made the case so easy for Tom Davies to win.) A random answered the door with his wife or girlfriend or hooker (quite frankly, I'm not sure who), and the three dead-end guys forced their way in on him, turning the apartment every which way to find the coke. Unfortunately, one of the guns accidently went off in the process, injuring said random's girlfriend or wife or hooker. Shortly thereafter, their boss and his mistress and wife came home, and having no choice but to eliminate all witnesses, they shot each individual point-blank with a 35 mm handgun (but not before the wife cracked a bottle of Corona over the girlfriend's head, leaving her as the only surviving witness of the bunch). The recoil flipped the gun out of one of their hands and was left like a glimmering pot of gold (along with the unconscious but very much alive boss's girlfriend) when the police answered an anonymous call less than an hour later. The three guys were apprehended somewhere on I-76 trying to head to Altoona. Tom Davies tried dead-end guy #1, who is still waiting on a decent lawyer to help with his fifth appeal. Dead-end guy #2 got life. Dead-end guy #3 killed himself awaiting trial.

In my trial, Tom Davies spared no props or theatricality. An Aussie to the core, he spoke with that impeccable fusion of the Queen's English and enough country swagger to make him feel approachable, middle-class, friendly (to which Stewart Harris actually objected on the basis of jury bias). He wore a three-piece suit almost every day, and flip-flopped between chunky plastic lenses, square around the eyes, frameless eyewear, and nothing at all. When he wore his contacts, his face was as naked as a cadaver. You couldn't help but stare at him when his thick black lashes closed in around his salty-blue eyes. I'm pretty sure he knew I had a crush on him, from jury selection to verdict.

It was May and blisteringly hot in Philadelphia the day my trial began. It's possible that the air-conditioning was broken in the courthouse, but I know that's just my memory embellishing history. Humidity puffed out of Tom Davies's mouth along with each of his words, so much so that you could see the sweat slipping from his pores from ten feet away. Hell, you could see the sweat dripping from the pores of the wooden desk behind which I was shackled. (The shackling, of course, was another point of contention that my attorneys lost. But I digress.)

'Ladies and gentlemen of the jury,' Tom Davies began, as I'm sure he began every trial – from driving while intoxicated to double homicide. He could have had a second career reading Charles Dickens to the blind, he was so charismatic with such banality of daily life. 'It is New Year's Day. Snow is on the ground and covering the rooftops. On this special day across the globe, lovers are kissing one another, parents are hugging their children, and in one apartment in Center City, a young woman in the prime of her life is being murdered, slowly and meticulously, according to a plan designed by a woman with lies, revenge, and jealousy on her mind.'

The last time I played in the snow was four years earlier on South Street during an unexpected nor'easter. The time before that was when Persephone and I pretended it was snowing in the ice skating rink at a mall in the San Fernando Valley when we were twelve. But Tom Davies didn't know that. He didn't know a lot about me, but he continued with his little story anyway.

'Sarah Dixon had fallen in love with a local entrepreneur, a man a few years her senior, who proudly owned a small restaurant in North Philadelphia. They dated for months, taking trips around the city, visiting the Philadelphia Museum of Art, and even skiing in Vermont one weekend. Soon, Sarah learned that she was pregnant. This exceptional news was one of the greatest moments of her life. Unfortunately for her, it was also the reason she was targeted by the defendant. You see, ladies and gentlemen, you'll hear testimony that these two women had something in common. Sarah Dixon's boyfriend and the father of her unborn child was also the father of the defendant. And that is not the only similarity you'll see in this trial. You'll see how the defendant and the victim were also classmates at the University of Pennsylvania. You'll learn that as soon as the defendant discovered what her father was doing with Sarah Dixon, she became jealous and envious. You see, ladies and gentlemen, Sarah Dixon came from a family in which she had two loving parents. The defendant was raised by only her mother. You'll hear evidence of how she came to Philadelphia not just to attend the University of Pennsylvania, but also to find that missing piece in her life: her father. And as soon as she found him, the minute she established a relationship with the one man she longed for, she lost him to Sarah Dixon.' Tom Davies was on fire. Tom Davies was a feverish storyteller. Tom Davies was, after all, a modern-day Dickens. 'When Sarah Dixon became pregnant, the defendant knew she had lost her father forever. And she snapped.'

Tom Davies pulled a remote control from his jacket pocket and punched its red button, demonstrably presenting Sarah to the jury: a woman he couldn't properly describe with words. It was his visual sucker punch, his beloved bushwhack, and it worked better than I could have imagined.

'This is Sarah Dixon,' he announced, as all twelve jurors turned their attention to a life-sized photograph of Sarah that appeared on a screen just between the jury and the witness box. 'Just twenty-five years old. Trusting, bright, with her entire future ahead of her. Perhaps you know someone like her. Perhaps you yourself remember that time when anything and everything seemed possible. You can see the joy so clearly.'

Sarah was smiling a gargantuan jack-o'-lantern smile so wide that you could see the pink flesh residing rather unattractively above her teeth. Her hair was pulled back into two braids, each cascading down her bony shoulders, wisps flying out from the bands like unyielding weeds. She was wearing, as usual, her Penn T-shirt and was holding out a bottle of water to the camera – to my father, actually – though I know neither Tom Davies nor Marlene Dixon knew that when Marlene gave him the photograph. I knew that, of course, because I saw him take it when they were running circles around each other on a track two miles from Rittenhouse.

'Jealousy. Envy. The green monster that has been the source of so much hatred and violence from the Bible to today was breathing loudly in that apartment, and Sarah Dixon paid the price. She was caring. She was bright. She was generous. And she was pregnant. It is this final factor that makes this case so important, so serious, and so devastating. I want you all to think about that as I speak and as Mr. McCall speaks to you and as the trial progresses. You will hear witnesses talk about how the defendant couldn't have children. You will hear evidence about how the defendant consistently lies – about her jobs, her friends, her family, and most important, about this murder. You will hear testimony from the officer who arrested her, who questioned her about the murders she claimed were by a masked intruder – a mummer from the parade. You will hear witnesses tell about the defendant's estranged relationship with her father, who was Sarah Dixon's boyfriend and the father of her unborn child. You will hear so many different stories all leading to the same conclusion that the painting you start to see will be so clear, it might as well be a photograph. And in that photograph, you'll see the defendant, jealous and enraged, forcing her way into Sarah Dixon's home with a gun, shooting her execution style, ending not only a vibrant young life but also the life of her unborn child.'

I sat back watching Tom Davies create his fictional narrative for Shanaya and Beverly and Lavonne and the rest of them, and tried not to laugh. It was almost embarrassing the way he was turning my trial into a Lifetime movie. Women don't actually act that way. Between the four lawyers trying my case, only one of them was a woman, and she was sitting second chair to Tom Davies. She had to have been fresh out of law school and barely even rose from her chair the entire week we were in court. No doubt had she been first-chairing the trial, the state's theory would have been different.

'Ladies and gentlemen of the jury,' he concluded. 'The defendant will give you only one way to vote to stop her unconscionable rage once and for all. Not even a prison society would be suitable for her. She killed Sarah Dixon and her child in a depraved and heinous act, and you will see, after the evidence has been presented and the testimony has been given, that the only decision you could possibly reach will be guilty. Thank you.'

If the jury members listened to Tom Davies's opening statement with more detail, they would have picked up on the diminutive inconsistencies and blatant fallacies. But they were distracted. They were distracted by the heat. They were distracted by each other, particularly Lavonne and Felipe. They were distracted by the team of Dixon supporters and their moans in triplicate, scatting sighs in a round of confused emotion. Mostly, though, they were distracted by Marlene's balding head, shining in the center of the room like a fluorescent disco ball. Marlene had a wig, despite her presentation to the jury. I know she had a wig. A woman like that would never be seen in public without presenting her absolute most confident and powerful image to the rest of the world. But no doubt, she removed it each time she stepped foot in the courtroom so that the pathos she so seamlessly, so effortlessly evoked among the twelve individuals sitting in judgment of me, fell slanted to her like crisp fall leaves. I couldn't blame her. I probably would have done the same thing. After all, they were sitting in judgment of Marlene and Sarah, too, even if they didn't realize it.

'Mr. McCall?' the judge called, shortly after Tom Davies took his seat.

Madison McCall nodded, tapping his shoes on the floor three short times (almost like a weak drum roll), and stood up without looking my way.

'Thank you, Your Honor,' he said.

He was the only person not to try and lock eyes with me before his next move. He walked over to the jury box and stood two feet from the wooden bar.

The tag at the top of my shirt was tickling the skin behind my neck and it itched. I scratched my neck with my index finger and could hear the scrape inside the courtroom as the sides changed. Marlene tilted her head over to me when I moved. All twelve jurors and the soporific alternate glanced my way, too. Everything I did, from sneezing to clearing my throat to scratching an itch, would be memorialized in thirteen different ways.

'Ladies and gentlemen of the jury, I am not here to try to persuade you that my client is perfect. I am not even here to persuade you that she has suffered a traumatic life that should give you cause to understand her actions. No. I am here to introduce you to a woman with a name beyond "defendant".'

He looked over to me for the first time and held out his hand, as if presenting me to society in a swollen white dress made of tulle.

'Please stand,' he instructed.

I stood from the defense table while the dozens of individuals in the courtroom ogled.

'This is Noa Singleton. She has already worked with the police and the district attorney and all investigators to facilitate the progress of this case. She has not done any of this in great opposition or in vocal protest. She has done all of it because she is not guilty of this crime. She was simply in the wrong place at the wrong time. Please look at her. Is this a woman who the prosecution will have you believe is a cold-blooded, calculating killing machine? A woman who, given the chance, would do so again? That is simply not the case. She is a normal girl. She did well in school, participated in many extracurricular activities, was a friend and a girlfriend and a sister with just a normal upbringing. Nothing in her history will lead you to the result that Ms. Singleton would kill Sarah Dixon, and nothing that the state will present will illustrate a motive.'

McCall motioned for me to sit down. I acquiesced.

'The state will be unable to present any evidence of what transpired that day,' he continued. 'They are only able to argue one story that has very little evidence. But I can tell you the evidence that you will see. You'll see evidence of a terrified woman, shocked and catatonic, convulsing on the floor of a police station as she lay bleeding. You will see a woman held by the police for hours beyond their capacity. You will see a woman who lost a sibling that day. That woman is my client, Noa Singleton. You'll hear evidence of how the police arrested her and left her without food and water and how they withheld legal representation and medical attention as she bled from a bullet injury for hours. Because you see, ladies and gentlemen, my client was also a victim of the same murderer who killed Sarah Dixon.'

'Objection,' Tom Davies said. 'Relevance.'

The judge agreed.

Madison McCall looked annoyed, but continued.

'The prosecution was right about one thing. My client indeed developed a new relationship with her father when she moved to Philadelphia. However, that relationship was not severed because of Sarah Dixon. It was severed long before. Nevertheless, my client still cared about her father and did what she could to help him. She checked up on his pregnant girlfriend when she called looking for him. Unfortunately for my client, she didn't know what apartment she was walking into.'

I looked over to Marlene who held her gaze with Madison McCall the entire time, nodding with his comments every so often, twisting her neck to disagree with others. But as Madison McCall stumbled through his opening, painfully flogging each sentence so strangely, I was sure even Tom Davies would have done a better job on my behalf. His words didn't flow, his logic was flawed, and at times, I wasn't even sure he believed what he was saying. It was at that point, for the first time since I pulled the trigger, that I realized that there was a strong possibility I might be sentenced to death. It was at that point that I started questioning my decisions in life, notably with respect to Marlene Dixon.

Even during his hapless opening, I contemplated telling them what Marlene's part had been, but I didn't. Sitting there delusional in her power and bald as a ninety-year-old man, she was suffering enough. Nothing I said would change that.

'This case isn't as complicated as the prosecution would have you believe,' he concluded. 'It is about a solitary, introverted girl who sadly never lived up to her expectations. None of this means that she is a killer. She was in the wrong place at the wrong time when an intruder entered the apartment, shooting them both.'

He stepped closer to the jury box, and I don't think they appreciated it. He had neither the looks nor charisma of a Tom Davies.

'Now, you are here for one reason only. You have been groomed, you have been filtered and ultimately selected because of your interest or your religious tendencies or your past relationship with law and order, or because of that little voice inside of you that says that executions are okay.'

The tag at the top of my neck was still irritating me. And my feet began to swell. And my nose itched.

'You are here for no other reason than to gawk at Ms. Singleton's entire past so that you can judge each of her choices in life from birth through . . . well, through today, to find a motive that doesn't exist. You have no other role to play and no other decision to make. Guilt or innocence. It's not an easy task, but you have all been selected to complete it, and you will do so with a conscience. And because the state cannot prove that my client, Ms. Singleton, shot Sarah Dixon in cold blood, you'll have no choice but to find her "not guilty".'

When he was finished, Madison McCall sat down beside me, unbuttoned his blazer, crossed his legs, and watched Tom Davies call his first witness. He never once turned my way. I think that if he looked at me, he'd have to admit that he was sleeping through the trial. He'd have to lock eyes with me and realize that my life literally was held in his hands. Who knows how he might feel when he got nervous and it just slipped out.

Chapter 19

IT'S A FUNNY PHENOMENON. YOU CAN NEVER VISIT YOUR own funeral, but if you want to see how people feel about you, commit a crime. The parade of personalities that intersects with yours over the years is a voyeuristic thrill that few people experience. And it usually begins with the earliest chapters.

For example, Andy Hoskins was flown in from California and asked about our relationship. He said that I never lived up to my potential. He claimed that I was always trying to get him to do things that broke the rules. Most important, he testified that I never told him about the baby – the first instance, they claimed, in my long and malignant line of deception. They got Andy to say things I never knew he was capable of verbalizing, let alone even thinking.

'I . . . I . . . I loved her,' he sputtered, wiping his eyes with the backs of his hands. He kept glancing over to me while he said that, as if he were apologizing for my actions. 'I have five kids now. I would have loved to have had another one. I just never knew. She never told me about the baby.'

The baby. The damned baby came up at nearly every turn.

A psychologist got on the stand and testified that I had borderline personality disorder – not psychopathy as Tom Davies speculated earlier. She argued that I was a pathological liar who felt strength and superiority from telling things that weren't wholly true. She used examples like the fact that I told a few people that I ran a marathon instead of a half marathon, or the fact that my boss from the School District of Philadelphia thought I graduated from Penn when I only went for a few months – that sort of thing, spuriously focusing on the irrelevant minutiae of my fabricated past. She also claimed that I slept with any man in my path because it was the only way I could feel whole. She testified that, while I didn't want Sarah dead, I also didn't want her to have the baby. It was the baby, after all, that led to the disintegration of my relationship with my father. It was the baby, after all, that separated me from him. That made our relationship – the first real one for me – broken. This and the lies led seamlessly to the Psychologist-Approved Theory in the flesh.

My court-appointed psychologist got on the stand and claimed that it was also the baby that changed me – just not Sarah's. She argued that I had been suffering from a persistent case of posttraumatic stress disorder ever since the incident in Van Pelt Library and that I never came to terms with the loss of my baby, my femininity, or the future I'd never have. It was this, however, that caused my Jekyll personality to form. It was the trauma from losing my baby that led me to believe that Sarah, my father's new partner, could not have one either, as it would create a fallacy of identity. Sarah, after all, was the 'phantom me,' and this set me off into a rage. And there we were, face-to-face with the Cain and Abel Theory.

My obstetrician got on the stand, too, telling Lavonne, Felipe, Amir, Shanaya, Samuel, Lakeisha, Russell, Nancy, Charlie, Beverly, Ronaldo, Melissa, and Vincent about the Van Pelt incident freshman year. He talked about how painful it could be and how the type of emergency hysterectomy I survived usually strikes older women, or at least women without children. Ahh, my beloved Victim Theory. All theories presuming I did it intentionally, just trying to explain it away. Mitigate the circumstances, despite the fact that I had not yet been found guilty.

Sarah's OB from Planned Parenthood also took the stand, explaining that she was proceeding well at nine weeks at the time of death. Not only did her baby have fingers and toes, but bones and cartilage were even starting to form. Eyelids, too, and the tip of the nose. She looked straight at me when she said that, as if I could see into Sarah's belly the one time I came face-to-face with her. But the girl was bulimic. She ran. She wore baggy clothes and spent half of her time behind a desk and the other half with an aging alcoholic who owned a bar, carried guns, and spent a majority of his adult life in prison. Most people didn't even know she was pregnant. I didn't know how pregnant she really was. But her obstetrician argued otherwise. She was nine weeks along. She had examined Sarah just a week earlier, and her beta hCG levels were on point with healthy fetal development. Her ultrasound was strong, and the fetus was moving around appropriately in utero. Sarah was gaining weight commensurate with the growth of her child.

The county pathologist testified with an excruciatingly high amount of autopsy photos from the location of the gunshot wound to bolster his testimony so that the pathos of Lavonne and company would align with the prosecution. (Clearly, he and Marlene Dixon had the same tactic, and it worked.) Stewart Harris kept questioning him on the cause of death. 'The indictment says gunshot wound to the chest, but it didn't talk about the baby or whether Sarah died from the gunshot wound.'

But it was a gunshot wound to her chest, and the prosecution found no discernible alternative to the killing based on its location. Stewart Harris left that one alone, too, along with the information in the autopsy report about Sarah's heart. No theory extrapolating why Sarah suffered from cardiac arrest was properly brought to the jury, even though it was the only evidence to ascertain. Shoddy research on both sides, if you ask me. Still, it took the pathologist another thirty colored photographs to show the wound with Sarah's skin pulled back. It took him another twelve close-ups of her torso flipped open with the vestigial heart no longer beating, so that you could see her corrosive stomach, bloated and full of blackened coffee.

'No, I can't be conclusively certain that it was the gunshot that killed her,' the pathologist continued, pointing to State's Exhibit Number 78, yet another photograph of her body laying flat on its back, hands spread wide open, palms up like she was meditating at the end of a yoga class, 'because her heart was not normal. She appeared to be suffering from a cardiac arrest, as well. And her lungs were destroyed.'

'Is it possible that the gunshot wound could have sparked a cardiac arrest?'

'Yes, it's possible.'

Tom Davies followed up. 'Based on your training and experience, doctor, do you see many gunshot wounds to the chest that are accidental shootings?'

'Objection, speculation.'

'No,' the pathologist said anyway.

'Sustained,' the judge said at the same time.

I looked over to Harris, who, once again, stood from his chair.

'Motion to strike, your honor.'

Although the judge agreed and instructed the jury to ignore the last question-and-answer interchange, of course, they'd already heard it, so on they moved.

The police officer that showed up first on scene next tore through his police report on the stand, unable to remember anything that transpired on that memorable New Year's Day without his paperwork crutch.

'The door was open when I got there. But there were splinters sticking out from the lock as if there was a break-in.'

A forensics expert testified later that blood on the door was a match with my own.

'It was just a slight smear, but enough to connect the defendant to the break-in.'

The paramedic who arrived first on the scene testified next.

'Ms. Dixon was dead upon arrival, and there was nothing we could do for her. Ms. Singleton, on the other hand, was suffering from severe trauma. She was sweating, her arms were shaking, and she also was bleeding from her left fore-finger and right shoulder.'

'Could you elaborate?'

'Her fingernail on her left forefinger was torn off, right from the bed. From my perspective, it appeared to be an injury from a struggle.'

'And the shoulder?'

'She was bleeding from her shoulder due to a gunshot wound that merely grazed her skin. We tended to it on the spot.'

The librarian who found me in the stacks of Van Pelt took the stand just to prove that the Van Pelt incident actually occurred. The principal at one of my schools in West Philadelphia took the stand to prove that I was in fact a substitute science teacher. The guy from Lorenzo's took the stand to prove that I liked to eat pizza. Bobby even took the stand to prove that I was indeed found by my father a little less than a year before the murder. He also took the stand to prove, not that it was my father with whom I was developing a relationship during the time in which my personality started rusting, but just to prove that I was a liar. That I lied about that call and the meetings and everything else in our relationship. None of it was relevant, and yet Madison McCall and Stewart Harris just sat there at the table, refusing to rise, refusing to object. Nobody should have heard any of this, but they did, and in it went along with those hundreds of photographs from Sarah's autopsy and Marlene Dixon's proselytizing. I suppose I could have spoken up again at that point, but that would have required my taking the stand, which Stewart Harris adamantly counseled me against doing, and to be honest, I didn't entirely disagree.

Bobby shot me a look of such hatred from the stand when he was talking about our relationship. I know that after my arrest, he was ridiculed to the point that he left the department and was only able to pursue employment as a security guard at jewelry stores and fancy boutiques on Walnut Street. (That wasn't entirely my fault, despite what he believes.) Still, nobody ever took the stand to talk about the gun and where it came from. Nobody took the stand to talk about my own victimization. Nobody took the stand to talk about Marlene and her hatred toward my father. Marlene didn't even take the stand until my penalty hearing, which is why she was allowed to watch the whole spectacle. It was as if a news story was formed without any of the necessary details, without any merit. I wanted to talk to a friend. I wanted to talk to Persephone Riga or my brother, but neither one was at my trial.

My father did take the stand, but did so without having spoken with me once since Sarah died. He testified to his relationship with Sarah and his relationship with me. He talked about his twelve steps to sanity or whatever he wanted to call it. He spoke about my mother and about his bar and my lost childhood. He testified that he told me Sarah was pregnant and that he saw me outside of Planned Parenthood. He spoke about pretty much everything, never once looking my way while on the stand. And when he talked about reconnecting, it was as if he wanted to both hold me and hurt me at the same time. When Tom Davies pushed him question after question after question about his relationship with Sarah, his eyes were connected with Marlene Dixon the entire time. He seemed almost apologetic about it.

'I . . . I don't know what to say,' he said, finally looking toward me.

It was nearly a full day of questioning before he bothered to glance my way. I could see water forming in his eyes, and he kept touching his scar.

'Do you believe Noa is capable of killing?'

'Objection,' Stewart barked. 'Speculation.'

'Sustained.'

My father looked confused, his face wandering about the room.

'How did you feel when you found out Sarah and your unborn son were dead?'

'Objection, relevance,' Stewart said again.

'Overruled,' the judge said. 'Answer the question.'

He looked again over to Marlene.

'I was devastated. I felt at once like I had lost all my children at the same time.' He paused, thinking. 'I did lose all my children at the same time.'

'What did you know about Noa's actions at the time of Sarah's death?'

'I knew she was following Sarah around. She wanted us to break up.'

The lines that Mother Nature had carved across his face were deeper now, each fold reflecting a new decade of erosion. It was as if something else was taking hold of him, corroding the skin and everything beneath, and he seemed old for the first time.

'I'm just so sorry about everything that's happened.' He looked away from me and back again to Marlene. 'And I'll never be the same.'

I don't even remember the closing statements. All I remember is that the jury didn't take long to walk back into their box after deliberating for some four hours.

Marlene was sitting behind Tom Davies's seat, holding a disintegrating handkerchief below her nose, when the judge asked if the jury had made a decision. Still draped in black, her left arm was locked inside her husband's, and she had to unhook it in order to remain focused. She wore the same large gold locket sitting outside of her blazer even then. It lay flat between her metastasized breasts as a badge of courage.

Several of the jury members periodically glanced over to her as Vincent stood to announce my verdict. The rest of them sat quietly and tried as they might to avoid eye contact with me, as if they were just so very sorry. I remember Vincent opening his little piece of paper because he didn't know how to memorize the word *Guilty* . . . and then . . . just white . . .

Chapter 20

For two days, Tom Davies proceeded to call up members of my former life before the judge in order to reveal a carnival of savagery that would rival Lizzie Borden. My mother was called to the stand early in the hearing. Tom Davies subpoenaed her, and even though Madison McCall tried to sway her to my side, she was unable to perform at the requisite caliber. Her acting skills failed me in the one performance that mattered most.

'I blame myself,' she kept saying, like she actually meant it. 'If I was around more. If . . . if . . .'

Tom Davies handed her a tissue, and she patted the bottom of her nose with it, shamelessly flirting with him while under oath. She never cried once when I was arrested or when she visited me in jail (only the one time early on in my arrest). As soon as all her money ran out, she found me just as guilty as the rest. And not once during the entire prosecution – guilt or innocence, or punishment – did she bring up my missing father in a bathtub and a knife, or all those times she was late to pick me up from Persephone's house because of a commercial audition for Tide or Clorox or some other laundry detergent. Or the time she left me to my woes to romance Paramedic One. Or caught me in bed with Andy Hoskins and almost gave me a medal. She left the stand without once saying that she loved me.

One of the earlier witnesses called by the prosecution was Officer Woodstock. He held up his right hand to the Bible and swore to tell the whole truth, so help him God. Dressed in his freshly ironed suit, he would be taken as seriously as any other person in a position of authority. Tom Davies questioned Officer Woodstock about my attitude upon arrest. He claimed that I was contentious. He used that word so many times in his testimony, you would think he was following a script written by a playwright with an achingly limited vocabulary. 'She didn't want to comply with our interrogation. She was,' he paused, 'contentious.'

'Can you explain what you mean by that?'

He folded his hands together and then breathed in very loudly so that, against the microphone, it almost sounded like a plane was taking off.

'At first, she kept trying to question us. And then, when we pushed her further, she pretended to pass out so we would stop questioning her. I've seen that before. It's an attempt at undermining our procedure, to try and circumvent the natural order of things. By policy, we must stop questioning the witness and issue medical attention. In reality, it retards the process.'

But McCall never questioned Woodstock on cross about my attitude. Instead, McCall just kept examining him about holding me unlawfully in a cell for half the night, ignoring the very purpose of the penalty hearing itself – a circus in which to turn my picture of Dorian Gray into the blackened canvas in which it lay. He talked about giving me water and a Three Musketeers bar as my only nourishment for twelve hours of interrogation, despite the wound to my shoulder.

They next called in the guard assigned to my wing to testify as to my perfunctory performance in jail. He claimed that he had to move me three times to avoid altercations within the walls because I was so contentious. I don't think he looked that word up, because I was clearly anything but. He enunciated each letter in that word – even the silent ones. *Con. Ten. Shus.* Evidently he had the same thesaurus as Woodstock.

Davies also called in an expert on prison society. In order to keep me from a life sentence without the possibility of parole, the state needed to prove that I would be a continuing threat to society, that I would be a future danger to all those who inhabited the Camelot of incarceration. According to him (and later the jury), my industriousness, my anger, and my long-standing apathy toward human behavior were all directed at my inability to cohabitate even within the prison walls.

The kid I beat up behind the bleachers in fifth grade took the stand claiming he had nightmares for weeks because of my fist. Tom Davies convinced the judge that it illustrated depravity of heart and was essential in the jury's determination of future dangerousness. So in it went, along with every bad act I had ever done, regardless of proof, conviction, or bias.

'She terrified me, even then,' the man cried.

'She's a pathological liar,' a girl I knew from middle school said on the stand. 'She told me her mother was a doctor. I didn't know that her mother was waiting tables while putting on dinner theater at night.'

'She used me to turn in fake homework,' another classmate said. I didn't even recognize this girl's name or face.

Again, Bobby was called in to show my manipulative tendencies. 'She used me to get background information on people.'

'She used me for free pizza,' testified the guy from Lorenzo's.

'She told me she graduated from college,' said the principal at one of the schools where I worked.

'She never told me she was ever pregnant,' Bobby said again. 'She made me use condoms as if we needed them. And then she lied about her father.'

'I was scared of her when I first met her. I don't know. It was just something about the way she spoke. The way she looked at me. Like I knew I could be her next victim,' said my freshman year roommate, who lived with me for all of five minutes before moving out. 'She said she was pre-med, but I never saw her study or anything. Everyone I knew who was pre-med spent all their time in the library, if you know what I mean,' she said. But how could she know what I did or did not do? I hadn't lived with anyone since high school, and this one requested a room transfer within a day of living with me. Maybe she saw early what even I tried to cover for years. Or maybe she just wanted a single bedroom, barely remembered me, and was eager for her fifteen minutes.

Even Paramedic One was subpoenaed. He was asked about my predilection for getting my baby brother in trouble when I was a kid. He sat up there and claimed that I was the one who ran him out of the house. That it was my fault he left my mother, stranded with two young children, and not the stewardess he was screwing three nights a week in Burbank.

Even the arresting officer from my five-year-old shoplifting misdemeanor was flown in to testify to the sole demerit on my rap sheet. 'She stole a pack of gum and a bra from a department store,' he said. 'Stuffed them in her purse and tried to walk out the front door as if nothing was wrong.'

The very existence of that rap sheet, however, was one of the larger weights the state used to prove my predilection for a life of crime – specifically those of so-called moral turpitude. I had done it before and would do so again if given the chance.

At one point, between all the witnesses from California

and Pennsylvania, I think I saw the accountant's face. In an instant, the Xerox machine flashed over my body while I sat at the defense table, as it did all those years ago over the breakfast table. So many people were there, and clearly, since my back was facing them, I couldn't count the number nor discern familiar faces. But for a brief moment, I thought I saw him, the caterpillar 'stache, the accountant, the second man with whom my mother tried to run off. His glasses had changed to a more modern style – plastic, squarelike, and still meaty – and he had shaved his mustache (at least mostly). In its stead was a thin five o'clock shadow dotted all across the lower half of his face like a Seurat painting. He was there only one day and was seated next to a young man, a student perhaps, in jeans and a vest, with his hair parted in the middle. I kept glancing at the two of them together as if they came in a pair.

I had presumed that every individual from my past would be there, from Persephone's family to the valedictorian in my high school class to my favorite pharmacist, Bob, but they didn't show.

The final witness for the prosecution in the penalty hearing was Marlene. During the entire trial, she sat beside her husband with textbook compassion. His name was Blayne Dixon, and every so often, he would glance at me, trying to frown. He had eyelids like meat patties, slight flaps of creamy skin folded over his lids like a blanket tucking his pupils in. He failed miserably at connoting any sort of emotion save pain from old age. I want to say that his eyes were blue, but in all honesty, I could hardly see their color, what with a handful of flimsy white lashes sustaining the folded skin above them. How hard it must have been to see past it; past that roof of old, spotted skin drooping down into his line of vision.

Marlene untucked herself from his loose grip, stood, and walked toward the stand, slowly, as if it were her personal plank of justice. Her smooth head had adjusted to its alopecic display by this point, and she looked less like a cancer victim and more like an aging singer-songwriter at a funeral. The black pantsuit was a bit tight around her waist, and she flaunted the fact that the top half of her blazer flopped loosely without anything to fill it out. That golden locket still dangled between the open spaces of her chest like a rope swing. And in her hands was a canary legal envelope, at least half an inch thick.

'Can you state your name for the record?' Tom Davies requested, kindly, after she sat in the witness stand.

She leaned over to speak softly into the microphone as if this were the first time she'd opened her mouth in court – in public, no less.

'My name is Marlene Dixon.'

'What is your relationship to this case?'

'Sarah Dixon was my daughter. My only child.'

She didn't crack a note. Her voice was as sturdy as if she were in court for any other case in her long litigious career.

She looked over to her husband. With each new statement she uttered, though, he seemed to dissipate. True, he was old, but he was also delicate, the way an old rocking chair is delicate. Push on it too hard, the joints will break, and it'll fall apart into dozens of fragmented limbs.

'You are under no obligation to testify,' Tom Davies continued, 'but you wanted to testify today. Why is that? Why do you feel as though you must take the stand?'

She looked to me and then back to Tom Davies.

'Because I want the jury to know what she took away from me and from the world. She took away a stunning, intelligent, creative, innocent soul, who was just beginning her exploration of this life.' Tom Davies nodded his head, allowing her to continue. 'And we will never recover.' She looked over to the judge. 'She has to know who she took away.'

'Did you bring some photographs with you?' he asked.

She nodded.

'Yes, I did.'

Tom Davies walked back to the witness stand, gently opened its wooden door, and escorted Marlene down the two steps to the courtroom floor. She stood, slowly, and taking his hand with her free hand (the envelope was still in the other), walked around the witness box directly before the jury box. He placed a chair in front of the jury box and helped her sit down.

Hundreds of edges peeked out from the clean fissure of

the envelope when she opened it. She grabbed a handful and spread them out on her lap as if counting a poker hand. First she chose one in faint sepia enlargement. A baby photograph – Sarah, chubby as a troll, with a scrub of fuzz all over her head. Parts of it wilted into curls by her ears. From my angle, though, she looked a bit like a boy. Marlene held it out to the jury like she was beginning story time for kindergartners. Lakeisha smiled. Shanaya cooed. Melissa clutched her chest.

The next photo skipped to Sarah's tenure in the Girl Scouts. Marlene forced her through Brownies and Girl Scouts, enabling her industrious sale of Samoas for three years, just until she would be able to put it on her college applications. Marlene selected a photograph of Sarah, missing one of her front teeth, her tongue pushing through the gap as she grinned widely, saturated with chocolate and charity. Beverly wiped a tear that was rolling down her nose.

In another, Sarah was sitting in a pool with ten other girls, giggling and contorting her face in girlish camaraderie. And another photo was Sarah on her first day at Penn, hair pulled back, wire-rimmed glasses resting on her nose, and her thick backpack weighing down her feeble bones. Yet another of Sarah in her old school uniform from middle school, brown and yellow checks covering the pleated knee-length skirt. And still another of Sarah with Marlene, both swathed in the professional habit: conservative navy suit, eggshell blouse buttoned up to the neck, hair parted ever so slightly to the side and then pulled into a low-reaching bun at the base of the neck. I knew this photo well. Marlene handed it to me when she first initiated our relationship. In it, Marlene was smiling as if she were in front of yet another camera, perhaps for publicity or perhaps for a client. Her lips were spread wide, covered in an opaque collection of rusts and wine colors. Her bleached teeth were glimmering from the flash in perfect synchronicity – but there was nothing behind the eyes. No sense of accomplishment or pride, no expression of joy that was supposed to match the mouth. Simply a woman wearing her designer smile without the ability to fill it out properly. Sarah, on the other hand, was unable to feign joy, which I presume is part of what made my father like her, at least from what I've garnered thus far. Next to Sarah's, Marlene's head looked awkward, like they were two business colleagues forced to share a photograph for a marketing pamphlet.

At first, I wondered why this was the photo of their relationship selected and framed for display. Their heads were turned away from each other and their arms hung primitively to their sides, but when I watched Marlene pass the photograph around from jury member to jury member, allowing their twelve greasy sets of prints to pollute the front, I knew. It must have been the only image of the two of them that existed beyond childhood.

Madison McCall could do nothing but watch in awe as the jury members – one by histrionic one – voted against me in unanimity. He felt it, too, I know. He was equally privy to the daggers within their eyes, their anger and hatred coming to a boil as they were forced to watch Marlene and her silent picture show. In fact, Madison McCall might have gotten even more bitter glares than me. After all, he was the one who chose to represent me. He had a choice in this entire production. Tom Davies was employed by the state and was just doing his job. Marlene played her unwilling part. And I, well, we know why I was there.

By the time Tom Davies asked Marlene more questions, she had returned to her seat at the witness stand. She was adjusting her microphone as she listened to him, ready with her prepackaged answer.

'Why do you think the defendant should be sentenced to death? Why should she be punished without life in prison without the possibility of parole?' It didn't even sound rehearsed.

She bent over to the microphone, and I could hear the manufactured weakness in her voice splinter the quietude like white noise.

'I've known the defendant,' she stalled, no doubt preparing her thoughts. Tom Davies said nothing for the record, though his face read confusion. She quickly corrected herself. 'If it were not for her, then not only would my Sarah still be with us today, but she would be in graduate school, married, with a family. All of those things were taken away from her by a virulent, destructive woman. Nothing will stop her from taking another person as prey. Inside prison or out.'

She looked over to my father and then directly at me when she finished.

'The death penalty is the single most profound form of punishment to grace our nation's system of justice, and one that should be reserved for only the most egregious of crimes and the most horrific of people who could be stopped by no other means than deactivating their path of terror. No person more suitably fits into the suit of a deserving body of that precious designer as does Noa P. Singleton.'

By the time it was my turn to put on a defense of character, only one reluctant witness remained. My father. Not even my brother could be bothered to fly in for the trial. After twenty-five years of childhood, adolescence, straight A's, surgeries, a life without a single speeding ticket or DWI, my father was still the only person who was willing, albeit unsympathetically, to take the stand tearfully on my behalf. Maybe he wanted to do it out of guilt or maybe because it was the right thing to do. I'll never know. All I know is that I refused to let him speak. I refused to offer any mitigating evidence. I refused to put on any defense of character. I was found guilty. There was no point in furthering the charade at that point.

In the recess shortly before he was scheduled to testify, my father visited me. He walked directly into the holding cell and stood silent, his upper lip twitching in syncopation with his blinking eyes.

'You're not going to say anything?' he asked, confused. 'You're not going to put on any defense of your life?'

Impotence was the first word to come to mind. *Sorrow* was the next.

'Why are you here?' I asked. 'You, above all people, should understand why I'm doing this.'

He shrugged. It was as if he had so much he wanted to say, but his tongue had been plucked from his mouth.

'That's it? You're just going to . . . shrug?'

He ran his hands through his hair, which didn't seem to have been placed under water in weeks. There was dirt under his fingernails, and a stain on his jeans. Even when he came to court, the man couldn't be bothered to clean out the dirt from under his fingernails.

'You're not going to fight? We can fight this,' he said, louder. 'We can do it together. I can say something.'

My right hand gripped the metal bars between us. I shrugged.

'Now you're just shrugging?' he asked.

'It's supposed to be this way,' I told him.

'What are you talking about?'

'We both know it's supposed to be this way, Dad. You and I both know that.'

My hands twisted within the handcuffs searching for my diamond bracelet.

'You're not going to appeal?'

I shook my head. 'No.'

'You're really not going to appeal?' he asked again. 'Why?'

'I don't know,' I sighed. 'I guess . . . I don't know. I guess if I fought it, it would seem like she died in vain. You know?'

He was tearing skin off his lower lips, flaring his nostrils, and looking like a caricature of mental instability. I did this to him, too. I didn't need to do anything more, whether he realized it or not.

'I told myself I'd fight the charge through trial. But now it's done. I lost.'

'Done?' he said. 'It's not done, dollface.'

'It's done.'

He started to slip into nervous laughter, but aged tension held it back.

'Okay?'

He nodded, slowly, dropping his hands from the bars and wiping the excess moisture on his jeans. He couldn't even look at me.

'I'm so sorry, Noa.'

I had waited to hear those words since the day I met him. And now I had.

And then, I told him not to testify.

September

Dearest Sarah,

Your father died only a few months after Noa was sentenced. I think his heart couldn't bear your loss. He held out long enough to see justice, and then he simply died in his sleep. I found him in bed on a Friday morning. His bifocals were resting on his nose, and he was in the middle of a Philip Roth novel. I don't even remember which one anymore.

You and I never spoke much about this, and I know you often wondered how I truly felt, but I did love your father very much, even though I spent much of my life running from marriage. At age twenty, when my girlfriends began to get married and don housedresses to baste chickens, I was studying in France. At age twenty-two, when all of those girls puffed out like tetherballs, their cheeks bouncy like play dough, their toes swollen as boiled sausages, I gawked in fear. But at thirty-two, when my friends regained their tight stomachs and spent their mornings sweeping peanut butter onto jelly-drenched sliced bread, I met your father. He was a wonderful man, a beautiful, statuesque professor with one eye that meandered halfway between green and brown, like a graduating color chart. We could see into each other, both parts of each other: the lawyer and also the pitifully insecure old maid.

To you, I'm sure it seems implausible when I talk about this, but it's the truth. To you, it probably sounds impossible that I even wanted children, and at first, I wasn't sure that I did. But those doubts always existed in the attic of my mind, like a latent desire to dye my hair red or move to China – not something that I would ever entertain. Though I can admit it now, part of me was scared to have you because I thought that my life would be over. There would be no more career, no more traveling, no more independence, no more skipping out on my marriage if it no longer served my needs. There would be handcuffs to diaper rash, colic, and the smell of regurgitated milk radiating within my clothes.

Your father resented me because of that. The minute we got married, he wanted you. He wanted to love you, kiss you, spoil you, teach you, and create you in his image. And I let him. The problem is that you were more a facsimile of me than either one of you would have liked.

Shortly before he died, your father and I met with Caleb. It seems odd to write about Noa's father in these letters, doesn't it? But the most influential people in our lives aren't always the most beneficial, and it was Caleb – not any professor, judge, lawyer, or colleague – who made that clear.

I spotted him outside the police station shortly after Noa was arrested. He was sobbing – for Noa, for you, for the baby, for you all – really, I didn't know. Your father and I took one look at him and made the decision together.

Then we waited.

We waited for your funeral.

We waited for the police to begin their investigation.

We waited for the one-month anniversary of your death.

Then we waited for the two-month, and the three. We had only one shot at this, and we knew it had to work.

After spotting him outside the jail three months after you died, we invited him back to our house. At first, he was taken aback by our willingness to engage, but it took no more than five minutes for him to warm to us. After all, he was the key. He lost both you and his unborn child, and also Noa. It would be his testimony that would cement either Noa's death sentence or her freedom or her permanent residence in the open society of a general prison population, where she would be able, if her behavior was good enough, to learn music and sculpture and writing and ceramics. Summer camp for the morally challenged, an ethically virulent gene splice in the correctional system. Quite clearly, we wanted the first alternative.

Once Caleb was in our home, glancing at the smattering of family portraits over the fireplace, we gave him some scotch, a sandwich, and a copy of the same photograph I handed to Noa less than a year earlier.

'This is your work, is it not?' I said to him, just as he opened the envelope.

Scotch nearly spilled from the glass in his hand when he saw the face in a baneful frame, memorialized in stitches from his perfectly engineered fist.

'You don't need to answer me,' I continued, handing him another photograph. 'We both know who it is.'

He didn't reply.

'I would have presumed that you learned how to fight so well while in prison if I didn't already know why you were there in the first place.'

'That was an accident in a—'

'—I don't really care why you beat my investigator or why you beat another man so senselessly that he died in a bar in Ohio. Or that you organized the second-largest cocaine ring in Kentucky, or that you convinced your daughter you were in those wrong places at the wrong time all due to a dormant need to shoplift.'

He swallowed.

'I pled out to manslaughter on that first one. You know that, Mrs. Dixon. I mean, you'd know that if you looked into it. I didn't mean to.'

'—you didn't mean to what? You didn't mean to hurt him? You didn't mean to hurt my investigator, either? You're starting to see a connection, are you not?'

I placed a coaster on the table where Caleb was close to dropping his glass – one of those mother-of-pearl ones you brought us back from Paris on your semester abroad.

'I'm really confused right now.'

Caleb looked over to your father and then back to me, his pupils expanding and contracting along with his labored breath. I handed him another photo – one of the storefront of the Little Gun and Ammo Shop on the Schuylkill.

'This is where you stole your gun, is it not? The one you gave your daughter. The one she used to kill my daughter.'

He took the photo from me and stared at it. Splashes of luminescence began to materialize.

'The owner's name escapes me at the moment, but I have spoken with him and, it's interesting, because he remembers you. You went in a few times to look at a particular gun, and then one week later, that gun was stolen from his shop. And that gun matches the gun that was used to kill my daughter. Not a bad coincidence.'

'I don't understand. I didn't steal any gun.'

'The thing is, you did. We both know you did. The owner can place you in his store a week before the gun was stolen. And with your history and his testimony—'

Caleb tore the photo in half, in quarters, and eighths, and so on.

'I have many more copies of that photo. And a promise from my investigator that he will have no problem testifying who put him in the hospital that night. He remembers it vividly. He remembers you vividly. He remembers the intricate details of Dive Bar vividly. So you can tear this little photo up as much as you want. It won't change the fact that it exists.'

'I didn't steal any gun,' he insisted, leaning down to put his glass on the wood. I picked it up and placed it in the center of the coaster.

'Whether you actually stole a gun or not really is irrelevant at this point. The shop owner will put you at his store. My investigator will place you at your bar when he was attacked. I am sure you are seeing the full picture that will be painted.'

He stumbled into the couch, stuttering. 'What do you want from me?'

Your father and I looked at each other, and while he couldn't understand how we got here, it was he, your father, who nodded to me to proceed. To this day, I don't know why I was so nervous. I'd done this a hundred times before. In front of heads of state. In front of judges and wealthy landowners. In front of my own daughter when she observed me in court.

'You are currently on probation here in Pennsylvania, are you not?'

He nodded. 'Uh-huh.'

'For the crime of manslaughter, correct? Aggravated assault being the first prison sentence served. Aggravated assault being what your lawyers unsuccessfully attempted as a lesser-included charge up in Pittsburgh a few years back? Clearly, they made a mistake letting you out early. In the others, too. Not just Kentucky and Ohio.'

'I . . . I don't . . .'

'You haven't stopped, Caleb.'

He stared at me.

'You beat up my investigator,' I continued, 'and—'

'—Mrs. Dixon.'

'You scratched the numbers off the gun Noa used on my daughter just before you gave it to her.'

'I don't know what you're talking about.'

'Did you or did you not? Let's not play games.'

'I . . . uh . . .'

'Well, did you or didn't you? It's a simple yes-or-no question.'

'Yes,' he mumbled, '. . . yes, I did, but not to use like this. Not to use like this at all. It was for protection. You know this already.' He paused, reiterating his excuse. 'It was for protection. She knew that. I told her that.'

'Protection?' I laughed. 'From what?'

'From . . . from . . .'

'From?'

'From people following me. From . . . from people in Kentucky, you know, anyone who might be trying to hurt her. I wanted her to be safe. Someone was following her,' he said, close to tears.

There was no need to look anywhere else, though. I held strong and continued.

'But you did give Noa the gun, correct?'

'Uh-huh,' he nodded, again without choice.

'And you did steal that gun from . . . ,' I read from a little piece of paper in my hands, 'the Little Gun and Ammo Shop on the Schuylkill?'

Growing rapids of breath swept out of him.

'You stole the gun used to kill my daughter from that store. Correct? I need an answer.'

'Uh . . . Uh-huh.'

'And the police, to this date, have not been able to trace it back to you, have they?'

Paralyzed but for the shifting of his eyes, he glanced over to your father.

'Over here,' I instructed.

His eyes returned to me.

'Have they?'

'No . . . no, ma'am.'

His stilted legs split in two.

'Exactly,' I continued. The couch caught him when he fell. 'Make yourself comfortable. Please.'

Your father sat down, too, across from him. I'd never been more proud of him. They both looked to me to proceed – one brimming with passion and the other terrified of what I might ask. To this day, I don't think your father truly understood what we were doing or what it would do to his heart after the trial ended, but still he went along with it.

Caleb looked to your father and back to me again.

'What we have here is a situation with an easy solution. I won't bring this evidence to the police or to my friends down at the district attorney's office, which not only implicates you in my daughter's death, but will be evidence of your own set of violations, far beyond mere theft.'

'I don't understand.'

I folded my hands and crossed my legs.

'Well, for starters, you were in possession of a stolen firearm, which, if I'm correct, is a violation of your probation. And it could, if I'm correct, which I'm fairly certain I am, send you back to prison in Pennsylvania alone. Now, of course, the other states will learn about this arrest and will likely vie for your extradition, and it's possible Ohio will win because of the whole manslaughter conviction there, but who knows who will actually win your custody? Drug cartels are often more dangerous than accidental bar fights, so Kentucky could get equally greedy, and Pennsylvania won't want to get left out or let go of you, given the whole "we found you, we caught you" state of affairs here. It could get pretty messy.'

He looked again to your father, as if he could help him, though no bonds of gender resided there.

'So I stole a gun,' he protested. 'So I got into a beer brawl that went bad. So what?'

'Well, since you ask, we both know you assaulted my investigator, who your daughter so affectionately refers to as, what was it? A shadowman? Now Caleb, even if we take away the manslaughter conviction, this new assault would add to your other two aggravated assault convictions and would send you to jail for habitual criminal activity for the rest of your life, not necessarily here, but perhaps in Ohio or Kentucky, or maybe there's another state I'm missing entirely when you claim you merely have a history of petty

theft across the country. Do you understand what I'm saying?'

Red clouds puffed across his cheeks.

'Yes, ma'am,' he said. But in reality, I think it was more of a stutter. 'Y . . . yes, m . . . ma'am.'

'Good,' I said, handing him the rest of the photographs. 'We're all settled then. You will do what must be done to ensure a finding of guilt for Noa.'

The blacks of his eyes shrunk like a retarding aperture. He didn't understand a single word I was saying. I was just another lawyer reciting his criminal history for his own edification.

'You can't ask me to—'

'You will be a witness for the state and the defense, no doubt, given your relationship to both Noa and Sarah. In that testimony, they'll ask you about what you knew. And you'll simply tell the truth. That Noa knew my daughter was pregnant. That you told her she was pregnant, that she was angry and hurt and—'

'—she's . . . she's . . .' he stuttered, pleading. 'She's my daughter, Mrs. Dixon.'

'And Sarah was mine,' I said in the same thought. 'I can't imagine you'd want to add perjury to your list of charges.'

No moments to think. No methodology of response. His tools of language got him as far as five prison sentences, two misdemeanors, six felonies, and at least two illegitimate children, so needless to say, he was without choices.

'But . . . but,' he sputtered, confused, 'before? What about before?'

Your father looked at me, confused.

'I don't understand,' he mumbled.

'She may be your daughter,' I said, 'but may I remind you that you lost another child on New Year's Day, due to your own daughter's hands, and in that, we are the same. I'd hate to see you go down for Noa's actions. Wouldn't you?'

'But—'

'Regardless of what transpired before her death, Caleb, Noa is singlehandedly responsible for our Sarah's death. Let us be clear on that.'

Timid nods of yes and no bent from his head simultaneously. Conflicted emotions, to be sure, but he was clearly without the skills to decipher them.

'Do we understand each other?'

'Mrs. Dixon, I can't.'

Dirt was under his fingernails on the hand that clutched the glass so tightly that I was sure it would break.

'I'm not asking you to do anything but tell the truth. You can do that, can you not?'

He didn't move.

'She's my only child,' he pleaded.

'Noa will understand your actions. She wouldn't want her beloved father risking his life on behalf of hers when there is nothing to really save. That's the only way she'll look at it, I promise.' I paused. 'Once she's convicted, you can *say anything you want about her so-called good heart at penalty. I can take over at that point. There's not a judge in this town who I don't know personally. Now, I'll ask you one more time. Do we understand one another?'*

I refilled his glass, and he drank it all before I put the bottle away. I didn't even wait for his answer.

Mom

TWO MONTHS

BEFORE

X-DAY

Chapter 21

OLIVER HASN'T VISITED ME IN WEEKS. NOT SINCE HE left me with stacks of trial transcripts to read as if flipping through the pages were shoddy excuses for hash marks dictating time served. I troll through the documents like they are my very own Genesis, my Tanakh, my personal Book of Mormon, my trusty Koran. Patsmith does it, too. So do all the other inmates, on the Row or off.

When I read over the pages, at first I think of what Ollie wants me to understand. I look back to the testimony of my ninth grade science teacher, my former School District of Philadelphia employer, even of Bobby, and they all seemed to be trying so hard to make me seem normal, as if sifting through the drawers of my past would help explain what happened on January 1. But they couldn't do it. Normal was not something that my lawyers successfully argued on my behalf at my trial nor what the witnesses portrayed, no matter how hard they tried to make it fit. It was like a pregnant woman trying to fit into her grade school jeans, a twin-sized sheet on a king-sized bed, a tape in a CD slot. It just didn't work.

Maybe Ollie disagrees. Maybe he sees something in me. Maybe he sees in me what I see in him. Maybe he's trying to tell me that if I were anything but normal, then my life's story wouldn't die with the three syringes I'm bound to consume in the next couple of months. If I were truly anything but average, then maybe I wouldn't have gotten caught. I wouldn't have gotten convicted. I wouldn't have gotten the sentence I got.

Then again, maybe he just lost interest as quickly as he found it and is leaving me with my pages for, I don't know, redundancy. Because when push comes to shove, I know that I'm just another story for cable television, expected to leave my final words for society to probe.

Only in the last few weeks have I pondered language as furiously as I did when I was eighteen. These trial transcripts will remain public record until I am gone (and long after I go), and news stories about my death will be played for a handful of afternoons and nights. By this time in two months, everyone will have forgotten about me and about Sarah and about what happened New Year's Day all those years ago. But those words, those last thoughts, which I will be expected to bestow upon the public like a defective consolation prize, terrorize me almost more than my own trial. Granted, just like my trial when I didn't have to take the stand, I also don't actually need to proffer any words of wisdom just moments before the gurney.

And yet, I'm torn.

Language stays with us longer than even our crimes themselves. Perhaps that's what Ollie's trying to get me to see. Those words remain always, while papers and evidence eviscerate, peeling into orange curls and blackened petals in the crematorium of dead documents.

In here, our final words are the criminal equivalent of stars on the Hollywood Walk of Fame. Each handprint and footprint is hardened for eternity in the eye of the beholder for people to fit in their palms or ogle from a distance.

You can be simple and delicate, like most of the women in here, telling their babies they love them and will meet them on the other side. Or you can be shocking and scandalous for the very purpose of being shocking and scandalous.

Before he was executed in North Carolina, Ricky Lee Sanderson said, 'I didn't take [the last meal] because I have very strong convictions about abortion and the 33 million babies that have been aborted in this country. Those babies never got a first meal, and that's why I didn't take the last in their memory.' Bobby Atworth decreed, 'If all you know is hatred, if all you know is blood-love, you'll never be satisfied. For everybody out there that is like that and knows nothing but negative, kiss my proud white Irish ass. I'm ready, warden, send me home.' And of course, George Harris so deftly stated, 'Somebody needs to kill my trial attorney.' (I'm sure he's not the only one who thought that, but he's the only one with the guts to admit it.)

You can persistently protest your innocence by declaring it bluntly.

'I am innocent, but was not given the tools at trial, or on appeal, to make my innocence into a legal reality.' Or, more verbosely, 'An innocent man is going to be murdered tonight. When my innocence is proven, I hope Americans will realize the injustice of the death penalty, as all other civilized countries have.'

You can express remorse, and it seems one should do so, not only for what might or might not happen after the gurney, but for the emotional stasis of your victim's family. Your own family, too.

'I want to offer again my most profound and heartfelt apologies to my victims' families. I am truly sorry. I have tried my best to empathize with their grief and devastation, and I hope they come to know of my concerns and prayers for them,' said Arthur Gary Bishop. Or Napoleon Beazley, who claimed, not through oration, but rather through the written word, 'The act I committed to put me here was not just heinous, it was senseless. But the person that committed that act is no longer here – I am.' If it isn't spoken, though, I'm not sure that it carries the same weight. Do you?

Still, I suppose those last words, either through valediction or the pen, can try to provide a drop of understanding for the public, for the government, for the families.

'It was done out of fear, stupidity, and immaturity. It wasn't until I got locked up and saw the newspaper; I saw his face and smile, and I realized I had killed a good man.' Johnathan Moore. Texas. 2007.

You can be fanatical about your crime, God, religion, your innocence, or even your favorite sports team.

'Redskins are going to the Super Bowl!' said Bobby Ramdass, just before his execution in Virginia. 'Go Raiders!' pumped Bobby Charles Comer, executed in Arizona.

And my personal favorite, a hybrid of all archetypes:

'We all got to go sometime, some sooner than others. I'm going to be busy getting the Browns to the Super Bowl. Working magic. I love you guys.'

Of course, the last thing you want to do is complain.

'Please tell the media, I did not get my SpaghettiOs, I got spaghetti. I want the press to know.' Thomas Grasso, executed in Oklahoma on March 20, 1995.

The pressure grows each day. A last-minute stay is a whisper of the past. I am sure of that now. I should have known that when Marlene thrust Oliver upon me four months ago, but I didn't want to believe it. The writ, too, no doubt has run its course. It must have. I would have heard by now. Oliver would have told me. He would have visited me more in the last month rather than just sending me paperwork to review. He would have done more than just a phone call every couple of days to check up on me. I have to accept that my appeal and my final words are nothing more than permanent imprints of my hands in the cement, now dried in their final mutilated form. Language, after all, does have a way of cementing permanence in history, just like those handprints. People can do what they like with it once you're gone.

So on that final day on the gurney – whenever Pennsylvania deems me ready – I don't know what I'm going to say. I'm not 'inhuman and fearless.' I do have fears, and I have no idea how to control them. The main thing that I fear, that one fright that sits above my head like a bony halo, is that once I'm gone and my soulless limbs float through dirt in an anonymous prison cemetery, I'll just be nameless. And then nobody will remember Noa P. Singleton. Not for what she did or what she didn't do. Not for writing an incarcerated memoir or killing a pregnant woman. Not for getting waitlisted at Princeton. Not for helping to raise her little brother, or for coming up three hundredths of a point below the valedictorian in her high school GPA for the title of salutatorian. Not for flying in a 1980s biplane over the coast of San Diego or saving the little league game in third grade. Not for learning to play the piano, or for drinking sixteen Mountain Dews in one sitting. Not for nearly running a full marathon, or for being cast as the understudy for Ophelia in my high school's spring Shakespeare production of 1995. Not for anything.

Look, I'm not protesting my innocence, or my insanity, or my need to live a long and prosperous life on the outside. I have no offspring. I have no family who visits. No spouse desperate for my consortium. No friends who cry for me on the other side of the wall. And that's precisely how I'm going to die.

Maybe my final words should be just as typical as more than 50 percent of the others. 'I'm sorry for what I've done.' 'May God be with me.' 'I'm ready, warden. Let's do it.'

Windmills of words spin around me, tossing out consonants and vowels with each gust of air. I really don't know what I'm going to say. Sometimes I think I've forgotten how to form a cohesive sentence. Sometimes I think I've forgotten how to form even a lucid thought. I haven't used these tools in years, beyond chatting with Oliver and reading over my spider-webbed appeals and eroded transcripts. I suppose I have a little bit longer to craft a skilled speech. But like that day over ten years ago, my mortarboard held on by a bevy of hairpins, a royal blue robe swimming around me in pleated oceanic purity, I'll probably say something insignificant again.

Chapter 22

FOUR MONTHS OF GRINNING FACADES, THREE MUSKETEERS bars, and stale Doritos had passed since Oliver Stansted walked into my life with Mothers Against Drunk Driving tailing him like, well, like the cops tailing a drunk teenager. Four months of found high school report cards and hospital records from my former life; four months of signed affidavits by my mother's dentist and my brother's best friend, claiming that I was, as Oliver once said, 'worth it'. He'd listened for four months, nearly five now, as I emptied the drawers of my past, folded them (sometimes neatly, sometimes not so neatly) and placed a few of them in his briefcase to take home. It had to end soon, regardless of X-day. Four months is usually the time it takes a new couple to fall in love or part ways, for a business deal to be brokered, and the time it took most people to walk away from me, melodramatically or otherwise.

Andy Hoskins was the first to bring this flaw to my attention, having slept in my bed for no more than four months precisely. Every man or woman I befriended from that point on lasted approximately the length of a season, corresponding with the temperature outside no differently than, say, your coat or scarf, or the length of your jeans. There was Paul, who took me to the Ritz during the fall of 2000; Sandra (who went by her surname, Ginter), who was my confidante back in the winter of 1995; and then Ling, who I met at the nail salon on Chestnut Street and subsequently visited for a weekly manicure in the spring of 1999. The only exceptions to this rule were my father, sort of, and, of course, Persephone. And now it would appear to apply to Ollie, too.

On that dreaded four-month mark, I waited for Ollie to show up and break up with me. I listened to the percussive clippety-clop of his expensive European shoes beating against the plastic rollers of his wheelie briefcase as the predictable seasonal friendship was about to come to a close.

'What do you have in there?' I asked, as soon as he settled into the visitor's booth. There was something different this time, and I couldn't quite place it.

'Sarah Dixon's medical records,' he said, sitting down. He bent over and pulled out a single file, fat with stuffing.

'In that slim little folder?'

He cocked his head.

'Don't be coy,' he said.

His voice was dry and to the point, almost as if he were

a Marlene clone. It was Ling's Nails all over again. I folded my arms while he sat forward in his chair and patted the new bags under his eyes. (He probably named them after me.) Only twenty-five, and already he was schlepping sacks around under his eyes like a vagabond.

Within moments of arrival, he began sifting through the file, displaying piles of papers from my trial, medical records, statements given from friends and family members, teachers and doctors on the table we shared between the Plexiglas visiting booth. Then he added stack upon stack of stapled medical documents, as if it was supposed to explain his absence for nearly a month.

'I found someone who I believe can help our case. A pathologist – he's young – but very bright.'

I waited before responding.

'And?'

'And he's taken a preliminary look at the autopsy report and photos and testimony from the cardiologist and seems to have done a lot of work with obstetrics.'

My palms were beginning to drip.

'He believes that Sarah was *not* pregnant when she was killed. This would mean that it would not have been a capital offense. That it would just be murder. Not capital murder. No death penalty.'

A single finger scratched his forehead. Ollie looked back to his legal pad, picked up his pencil and cut a blunted line through about five paragraphs of writing.

'Are you following me?' he said, looking up. His eyes stood still before me.

I stalled.

'Ollie, she was pregnant.'

'But what if she wasn't?' he asked. 'What if she had just miscarried prior to your visit, prior to your defending yourself, and she was so upset that she lost it. What if this new evidence is the key? This isn't something you'd find in the transcript, because it's not there.'

'Then why did you leave me with more copies of it?' I asked, rather abruptly.

'I wanted you to familiarize yourself with it before we continue down this line into the next step. You have to know what's in that record.'

'If there's anything in my life I know well, it's my trial,' I said.

'I think you know what I'm saying, Noa.'

I couldn't control the sequence that followed. A hearty laugh first, followed by little trickles of whitewash – the kind that washes up on shore long after a wave.

'Look, Ollie,' I said, cooling my laughter. 'These fantasies are wonderful, but like we both know, it's not good enough.'

'I'm just waiting on the report from this new expert and then I'll file the writ. The courts have to listen. They have to allow your case to be reopened with this new information. The deadline is soon, but it's all that's left to be done. It's newly discovered evidence. That's one of the reasons they will actually let us hear the case again. You could potentially get a new trial.'

He was as energized as he was four months earlier, looking around from here to there as if he knew something nobody else did.

'How is it working with Marlene, Ollie?' I asked, changing the subject.

'Focus, Noa.'

'I'm serious.'

'So am I. But it's a little difficult, given my blocked view,' I said, pointing to the Tower of Babel between us.

He put down his pen and sat back. I'm sure he must have crossed his feet near the floor, too. The entirety of the thin writing space that seesawed out from the glass divider was full of my quasi-documented life. It was piled so high, I could hardly see Oliver past the stacks. Then, like Moses parting the Dead Sea, he put his hands between the papers and slid them apart so we could see each other.

'Better?' he asked.

I smiled. And so did he.

'There you are.'

'Why are you always so eager to talk about Marlene?' he asked.

I shrugged.

'What is it about her?' he asked.

'I suppose I could ask you the same question?'

I could tell he wanted to interrupt but was beholden to

manners. I think his hairstyle might have changed a bit since I last saw him. A haircut maybe? A new razor that shaved closer to the skin? Contact lenses?

'What do you mean?'

'Why are you even working for her?'

'Because I believe in MAD,' he replied. 'Because I want to do something meaningful with my career. Because I don't believe in the death penalty.'

'Is that it?' I laughed, leaning back in my chair. 'I was hoping for something more original.'

'Noa . . .'

'Did you ever think about what MAD is really doing? I mean, how are your other cases?'

He sat up straight.

'They're okay.'

'Really?'

He cleared his throat.

'What about the garden variety drug charge? When do you think you'll get into a courtroom on your own instead of all the behind-the-scenes stuff?'

'These things take time. I'm not experienced enough to try a case. Besides, I can't talk to you about this,' he said. 'You know that.'

'Like I'm going to tell anyone.'

He didn't reply.

'Is Marlene working on them, too?'

'What? The other cases?'

'Uh-huh.'

'No,' he said.

'Right,' I said, folding my hands together. 'All we've talked about is this writ you're working on. Does that mean we're done with clemency, then? I thought that was the point of this whole last-chance, last-change plea here. That's what Marlene wanted, right? She was feeling guilty about putting me in here.'

'I'm not sure I'd say that.'

'What would you say, then?'

He didn't reply.

'Come on, Ollie.'

'I don't think Marlene feels guilty about putting you in here.'

'Really?' I laughed. 'Did she tell you that when you were chatting over dinner? At the Adams, Steinberg, and Coleson Partners and Associates retreat?'

He didn't humor me.

'She's an overprotective mother. Ever heard of the stereotype? She practically raised her daughter on guilt.' I swallowed. 'You think that Sarah Dixon wasn't cloistered in a little stupid Rapunzel castle? Of course she was. She was miserable. Why else would she have found my father of all people to screw?'

He picked the pen up again and started clicking on its head. Incessantly, as if it would drown me out in its hollow beat. But I continued.

'Marlene's practically perfected the art of the guilt trip.

Why do you think she's so lonely? It's isolating, like a termite scuffling up your innards.'

'Lovely, Noa,' he said, spitting a bit of scoff my way. 'Taking a poetry class via the post?'

'I try, Ollie. I try.'

He stopped clicking and put the pen back down.

'Are you done?'

'I suppose.'

A shaky hand touched his neck, and he spread his fingers across it, clearing his throat. Only this time, he didn't look down to the papers in his hands. Instead, he smiled at me, unwieldy, as if he hadn't been teased in years, as if he hadn't ever been close enough to anyone to have been teased in his life, as if this were some unwritten form of linguistic foreplay that all those men on death row talk about to reel in the lonely Bratislavan women and such. Part of me was ready to play, and part of me wasn't quite sure what he was getting to.

'So what do you feel guilty about?' I asked him. 'Everyone's got something. You cheated on your math test. You slept with your best friend's girlfriend. You lied to your parents about where you were that one night when you totaled the car.'

'Let's get back to the case.'

But he was still grinning.

'Ollie,' I said. 'It's been nearly five months.'

'Marlene didn't put you in here,' he insisted.

'Deflection,' I said. 'I can work with that.'

'Both Marlene and I are working on this case together.' He overenunciated the word *together* so that I heard practically every syllable, every letter.

'Then how come I haven't seen her in months?' I asked. 'And when I do, she only talks about the clemency petition – never the writ that you're working on. Never this other newly discovered evidence you keep talking about. Are you sure this isn't Marlene's way of intentionally throwing the whole case? Clemency's not going to get me a new trial, Ollie. She knows that. Is that your pet project? Because if it is, you're delusional. She's working against you in that. Trust me.'

'This is not a baseball game, Noa. Lawyers don't just "throw" cases. Particularly on appeal.'

'You clearly don't know Marlene very well then.'

He didn't respond.

'Hear me out, Ollie. Nobody reverses her opinion on the death penalty when her child is concerned,' I said. 'Did you ever think about that? Nobody pulls such a huge reversal without having something to prove. Don't you think maybe she feels just a little bit guilty?'

He laughed again. It was clumsy. And exaggerated. And I think a bit of spittle might have even popped out of the corner of his mouth before he covered it up by trying to speak again.

'You know why she's helping you, Noa. She no longer believes in—'

'—oh shit, Ollie,' I said, 'you don't listen.'

He wiped the corner of his mouth.

'Marlene no longer believes that even the worst of the worst deserves to die. If there is any guilt that she feels, it is for cementing your punishment with her testimony. With her words that you've read over and over again in the—'

'—don't go down that soliloquy of self-righteousness with me again,' I said. 'Especially with Marlene. Good lord, why on earth did you even go to law school? And don't say it's because you believe in justice and fairness.'

He dried the moist rings of his eyes with his fingers and forced a smile.

'Because I wanted to help people.'

I laughed.

'It's really quite simple,' he said.

'Stop, Ollie. Just say you wanted to make money. Go corporate. Or do "civil rights" because of the injustice you saw to your beloved aunt who was a single mother or something, but don't get all generic on me. I was actually starting to like you.'

'And I was actually starting to believe you for a moment,' he said, almost as if he were flirting with me. 'I was actually starting to believe you care about what we're doing here.'

'We?' I laughed.

'Mothers Against Death. Me. Marlene,' he insisted.

The moment he spoke, he turned away from me and fiddled with the empty space around his ring finger, like there should have been a band there. I didn't push. I just let him twist the invisible ring clockwise, counterclockwise, and clockwise again until he was ready to speak.

'Fair enough,' he said. 'I do have something for you.'

'I knew it. I knew it!'

His lips curled in half like he was half-smiling, half-frowning.

'It's not so big a deal. It's just that when I was doing my travels here almost a decade ago—'

'—right, your Greyhound bus tour of America—'

'—right,' he said, catching his breath before moving on. 'On the Greyhound America tour, I had a stop in Philadelphia. I should probably preface this by saying that when I left London, I didn't know what I wanted to do with my life. I wanted to work with people, I knew that, but specifically how, I was not yet sure.'

'Ollie . . .'

'Just listen,' he said, struggling. 'When I was here, I thought about going to law school momentarily. It was July of 2004. I was traveling with some school friends who were thinking of going to law school in America, so someone suggested we go down to the courthouse and watch a few trials, see what it was like. And, well, I sort of wandered into a courtroom and saw part of your trial.'

I wanted to tear off my shirt. I wanted a drink of water. I wanted to sprint around a track.

'That was nearly ten years ago,' I finally said.

Oliver waited to respond until I spoke first. Patient, resigned, his voice didn't shake. It was almost as if the instant he confessed, he was a stronger version of himself, like a painted-in stencil.

'And after all this time, you're still interested in my case?'

'I was only there for one day,' he replied, 'but something struck me as odd, and I've thought about it for years. First, I didn't understand why you didn't take the stand, since most of the evidence against you was weak. I mean, all you had to do was go up there and clear your name and explain your side of the story. People don't just give up so easily unless they're lying or covering up for something or someone. It didn't make sense to me then and it doesn't make sense to me now. Second, I was surprised to learn later that your father didn't testify on your behalf at the penalty hearing.'

I nodded, closing my eyes to picture the accountant and his glassy eyewear, only this time, he was sans mustache. I barely recognized him, living life among the free as just another one of my mother's ex-boyfriends. Perhaps he cared about her more than he let on. Or perhaps it was me he cared about all along. Beside him, I can now visualize a skinny aging flight attendant with makeup from the sixties over her eyes. And to his other side was a young boy who barely knew how to shave. Oliver, flourishing in his delayed adolescence.

A new treble clef of lines traced his forehead.

'I'm sorry I didn't tell you before.'

A rush of blood fled to my arms and to my chest.

'It's okay.' I shrugged reluctantly. 'I, uh, didn't realize I was so captivating.'

He smiled. The lines were still there, but fading.

'You are.'

He patted his lips together as if he had just reapplied ChapStick and needed to even out the smear. Though, upon closer glance, I could tell that nothing had touched them in days, weeks even. A pale rough armor covered his mouth like scales from a striated fish. He forced another smile, and his bottom lip split slightly at the center. A thin red line divided it, like a velvet bookmark fastened within a Bible. In that brief moment, I wanted to touch them, put my own lips on them to heal the gap, smooth the scales.

'So,' I said, breaking the silence, 'you're waiting on this new young expert to file his new report, and then what?'

'And then I file. We file,' he said. 'And we wait.'

My teeth couldn't stand to be buried anymore, and so out they came. Straight, white (although slowly yellowing from the lack of dental hygiene) and exposed. It's funny how undressed a smile can make you feel.

Chapter 23

I TOLD MARLENE ABOUT THE PREGNANCY ABOUT ONE week after watching Sarah walk into Planned Parenthood with my father on her arm like an urban accessory. Forty-eight hours later, she insisted we meet again in person.

Unlike our previous rendezvous, I was the first person to stroll into the diner. I sat at a corner table, ordered a Lemon Zinger tea and an everything bagel and waited. A crew of college students walked in and out, nursing their hangovers. A businessman sat on his cell phone for about five minutes until he realized he was in the wrong place. And I'm fairly certain a deal involving the price of an ounce of cocaine was taking place in the booth just ten feet from my own. As for me, I was nearly on my third refill of hot water and picking up crumbs with the cushions of my fingers when Marlene finally walked in.

'I thought we were meeting at 3:00,' I said to her, looking

at the invisible watch on my wrist. 'I've got things to do, people to see.'

She sat down. 'Don't pull that with me today.'

As she inched into the tight plastic booth, something seemed off about her. She was still wearing her habitual black attire, but she moved around in it clumsily, as if nothing quite fit her anymore.

'You all right?'

'Am I supposed to be all right with this news?'

'We haven't even spoken yet and you want to blame me for your mood? I don't have to stay here anymore.'

She rearranged the table décollage and finished getting ready in the booth.

'Sorry,' she said, without looking at me. 'Sorry. Just tell me what you know,' she demanded, weaker than usual.

'Just that she looked happy.'

'No, no, no,' Marlene burst, pushing up her sleeves. 'She's not happy. She's not happy. This is not okay.'

I crossed my legs under the table.

'I know you don't like them together, but such is life, no? What can you do?'

'She can have an abortion is what she can do,' Marlene declared. In hindsight, it probably should have been more of a shock to me at the time.

'Wow,' I laughed. 'And here I was, thinking I got lucky in the parent department.'

Marlene ran her fingers through her hair and pulled out

a rather hefty score on her way down. She tossed them under the table.

'Shit, Marlene, are you okay?'

'I'm fine, Noa,' she said sternly. 'She cannot have this baby.'

'Yeah, you already said that.'

'I want you to help me, Noa. You must help me.'

The words *needy* and *desperate* never previously applied to Marlene. This powerful woman, this sophisticated senior law partner in a major multinational law firm, was in need. She needed to talk and get something off her chest. And she needed that with me. From me. And that's the one morbidly positive thing I learned from what happened with my father. When someone needs something from you, you offer it to that person, even if you can tell it is leading somewhere dark.

'Please, Noa,' she pleaded, holding out a hand with a Band-Aid. I could see a slight bluish bruise beginning to form underneath. 'Please.'

'What could you possibly need from me now?'

A waiter came by and asked Marlene for her order. She was momentarily flustered when she couldn't find the menu and then just ordered a cup of coffee. No, she changed it. She ordered tea. Then she changed it again to just orange juice. And a biscuit with butter on it. Then she looked back at me, adjusting her posture on the plastic bench. 'Sarah won't speak with me anymore.'

'Is that why your hair is falling out?'

I didn't mean that. I didn't mean to say that. I don't know

why I said it. To this day, I don't know why I said a lot of things to her.

'I went over there to talk her out of this relationship,' she continued. 'And that's when I saw the pregnancy books and clothing and everything. I knew about it before I got your message.'

'I'm not giving you the money back.'

Again, I don't know why I kept speaking to her like that. It was as if the screening mechanism that was stripped from my communication skills upon prison acclimation began fading a year earlier.

'We had a huge falling-out, and she kicked me out.'

'I thought it was your apartment. The whole da Gama period and all?'

'Please, Noa,' she pleaded. 'Stop interrupting me. It's hard enough.'

I nodded and the waiter came by with Marlene's orange juice. 'Sorry. Go on.'

Marlene picked up the glass and drank from it. I could almost see the juice travel down as she primped her nascent balding self into talking to me.

'Sarah has a disease called hypertrophic cardiomyopathy. It's a congenital heart defect that can lead to heart attacks, sudden death.' She paused, thinking. 'Every year or so, there is a news story about a healthy active athlete who drops dead in the middle of the basketball court or the football field or track. You've heard of this, certainly. Well, they likely had this disease – unknown or undiagnosed – or something similar.'

'And, let me guess,' I paused, eyes open. 'Pregnancy makes it worse?'

Marlene nodded, her focus back to me. 'Exactly.'

I shied a bit. 'I see your predicament, Marlene, but like I told you before, this is a little above my pay grade.'

'I'll pay you more.'

'It's an expression.'

'I know that. I know that. I just—'

'Exactly what do you think I can do?' I asked, nervously trying to fill the silence. 'I'm pretty much a nobody here. You could have plucked anyone off the street to do the same "job".'

For a change, I decided to use quote marks around my words. I think it actually might have distracted her a bit.

'I just . . .'

She was trying not to appear flustered.

'Look Marlene, I don't know your daughter. I hardly know my dad. You helped me pay my bills for the last few months, so thanks for the job and all, but now this is what it is. I'm not about to break up a relationship with two loving parents who both want a kid.'

'But your father . . .'

'Okay, you're right,' I corrected. 'Maybe *one* loving parent. That's better than none, right?'

'He's . . .'

'Yes, he's a loser. He's a criminal. He's not the brightest. What about him?'

'You have influence over him, and he has influence over her,' she declared, before clutching the inside of her arm. 'I can't imagine you'd want him going back to prison.'

Marlene was speaking to me as if I were sitting in the wings of the theater, a lone patron to her preauthored soliloquy. As if she actually had any control over what happened with my father's future.

'You're wrong,' I told her. 'I have no influence over my father, so don't try to blackmail me with sentiment.'

'Noa, you do have influence over him. You just don't realize it. You have to learn how to use your role. Your strength.'

'So I have influence and power now?' I laughed, 'and you have . . . ?'

She nodded silently.

'Marlene?'

'I have nothing without Sarah. And now I have nothing,' she said. It was angry and pinched with pity in a way that made me want, at the very least, to keep listening. 'She thinks that I want her to have an abortion because your father is not a college graduate. Or because he's older. Or because he has a criminal record.'

'She thinks you think he's beneath her,' I said, confirming aloud what she clearly had difficulty articulating for upper-middle-class guilt or professional embarrassment or some other concoction that people with china patterns endure.

She looked away.

'She does, doesn't she? It's a class issue.'

'This is America. We don't have class issues,' she declared.

I laughed. 'You're kidding, right?'

She didn't join me.

'Seriously, you are kidding. Your shoes probably cost more than one month's rent for me. You drive home to the Main Line or wherever you live in your Mercedes or Lexus or Audi.'

'That's enough.'

'What?'

'I think we both know.'

'What? That my father is beneath your sacred daughter?'

'Stop.'

'You know it's true. I know it's true. Why try to hide it?'

'Enough!'

She looked around to inspect her surroundings. Luckily, nobody cared whether she raised her voice or not.

'Sorry,' I said. Again, it used to be easy to say that word. It used to be easy to apologize for things I hadn't done. It was the things I had that posed the most problems.

'So you'll help me?' she finally said.

I stood and dropped a few dollars on the table to pay for her orange juice.

'It's just not my problem anymore. Sorry.'

Chapter 24

'I NEED YOUR HELP!'

'Who is this?' I said into the phone. 'Hello?'

'You know who this is,' he paused, breathing heavily into the receiver. 'I . . . I need your help, Noa.' The tornado winds of his voice tossed me aside. More than six months absent, and back we were to our original conduit of reconciliation. 'Please. Can you meet me?'

I inhaled with a deep yogi breath.

'Absolutely not,' I said and then I hung up.

But it rang. And it rang. And rang again until I answered it once more.

'I'm going to call the police,' I said answering the phone. 'I don't want to see you. I don't want to get involved with your business. I'm trying to fix my own life here.'

'Noa, sweetheart,' he pleaded. 'I've never asked you for anything in my life—'

'You're joking, right?' I laughed. 'Seriously, Caleb. You can't hear yourself, can you?'

'Please, I . . . I need you. And I haven't asked you for anything—'

'—you constantly asked me to see my apartment, to visit your bar, to forgive you.'

'Hear me out—'

'—and secondly, you've barely been in my life long enough to even make such claims. The few minutes you've been a part of it, all you've done is ask for favors. Do you even hear yourself?'

'Please!' he shouted, quietly, like a muted stage whisper. 'I don't know where else to turn.'

'Not my problem,' I said. 'Good-bye.'

But I didn't hang up. My hand clutched the phone close to my ear, waiting.

'I don't know what to do,' he said eventually, his voice crumbling.

I listened to him. I'm not sure what took over me at that moment. Maybe it was his panting that felt reminiscent of that stray golden retriever. Maybe it was the fact that I could hear him wiping a lip of a semiclean pint glass with a rag that probably hadn't been washed in the better part of the fortnight.

'I don't know what to tell you, Caleb—'

'—she's pregnant,' he finally said. 'She's pregnant, and I don't know what to do about it. You above all people should know how it feels to have a father like me. I shouldn't be a father. I shouldn't . . . I mean . . . I . . . can't . . .'

'Stop stuttering!'

'I'm . . . fr . . . fr . . . freaking out, Noa!'

'You're a grown man. You've made this mistake before. Deal with it the way you've always dealt with it. Run the fuck away.'

He breathed in through his nose, and I could tell he'd been crying. Every breath was clotted with mucus and felt caught behind a fear he so rarely displayed.

'I don't want to run away anymore,' he said. 'Believe it or not, I really have changed.'

I heard him gulp something liquid. Water? Juice? Beer?

'Where are you now?' I asked.

A faint bell dinged nearby.

'I'm at Bar Dive,' he replied. 'Can you meet me here?'

'It's freezing. I'm not leaving my apartment.'

I held the cell phone in my left hand as I bit the skin hanging off the corner of my cuticle on my right thumb. It tore a little beyond its dead root and started bleeding little rivers drifted into the wrinkles on my hand like red tributaries.

'Please,' he said.

'Aren't you preparing for tomorrow's big new year celebration with Sarah or something?'

'Please,' he said again. 'I need you.'

'Come on, Caleb.'

'Please, Noa.'

I don't know that I recognized a crack in his voice or if it was the swivel in his tone, but I thought about it as if it were true that he had no one else but me in the world. I waited a few moments – long enough for him to wipe the sweat from his brow three times – and then I gave in.

'Fine. I'll be right over.'

I grabbed my messenger bag, draped it over my chest like a Girl Scout sash, and covered it with my black down jacket, a red scarf, red gloves, and purple hat – all courtesy of my new income from Marlene. The whole time I was getting ready, feverishly, as if my father's life depended on it, the sound of his phone call rang in my head like a warning. A siren circling my subconscious as if I knew exactly what was going to happen before it did. It's funny how our minds work. Almost like that movie soundtrack with the tremulous violins prescient of our next move. Even though the soundtrack dictates otherwise, we still enter that dark room. Still, we tell our loved ones we'll be right back. Still, we drive home alone when all the power is out in a thunderstorm.

For me, that soundtrack was playing against the telephone ring in my head when I left my apartment. It played when I dropped into the subway stop and traveled all the way to Girard Street, where I exited by the corner where I first saw the shadowman, strolled the few blocks until I arrived at the hanging tennis shoes and Bar Dive. The letters on the marquee were still canary yellow as they were the day I fled all those months earlier.

The door was locked, and the sign in the window read SORRY, WE'RE CLOSED. I knocked on the door and peeked through the slight opening in the window where the blinds were broken. My father was sitting alone in a chair, trembling, his arms wrapped around his torso like he was wearing a straitjacket. He hadn't shaved in what appeared to be days. No hair grew over the pea-pod scar over his lip, and for a moment, he looked almost like a negative of a thin Charlie Chaplin. Scattered images of my mother's elementary-school fetish flashed in my memory.

'Dad?' I yelled through the glass, knocking on the door. 'Hello?' He looked up and rushed to let me in. 'What the hell is going on?'

'Sit. Please sit.'

My eyes skimmed the bar. It was uninhabited as usual, but seemed scarily vacant. I didn't take off my jacket or my bag beneath.

'Come with me,' he said, taking my hand, trying to pull me to his back office.

'No, no, no,' I said. 'I'm not going back there.'

He pulled harder. 'I need to show you something. That's why I called you over.'

'I thought you called me because you needed to get it off your chest how horrible a father you are and that you realize that you're about to make the same mistake again.'

He nodded, running his fingers over his stubble. Still he pressured me to walk into the back room.

'Don't!' I demanded. 'Who knows what other contraband you've got. I'm not about to be a drug mule now.'

A nervous laugh ejected from his mouth like a piece of gum inadvertently falling from his lips.

'You have exactly one minute to tell me why you dragged me out of my warm apartment when it's freezing outside.'

'Okay, okay,' he said, again with those goddamn surrender hands. He walked to the bar and slipped under the wooden door instead of opening it. He grabbed a plastic pint.

'Beer? Coke?'

'Stop stalling!'

'Noa, please,' he pleaded again. 'This helps calm me as I talk about it. Beer, coke? Diet? I have Mountain Dew. I know you like that.'

'Just water,' I said.

He served me a pint of water, walked back under the bar as if it were one great limbo construct, and sat down at a table, his back facing the door. I sat across from him. If anyone were to look in, they'd see only my face, only my hands. They'd never see any identifying feature on my co-conspirator's face.

'I'm freaking out,' he said for what could have been the fiftieth time. He was sweating. Porous beads slipped down his temples and the ridge of his bumpy nose.

'Because of the baby?'

He nodded.

'Really?' I laughed. 'Gonna play mute with me after all this time? Don't give me another story about twelve steps or your mother's death or me changing your life.'

He looked away from me.

'You're kidding, right?'

'Shhhhh,' he begged. 'Please keep your voice down.'

'I can't deal with this,' I said, standing to leave.

'Look, I don't want Sarah to have this baby.'

'Yeah, I gathered that.'

'No, you don't understand, Noa. I can't have this baby. I really have changed, you see. I have this bar. I made amends with you. If she has this child, I have no chance at being a proper father to you.'

'I think we're a little late for that, aren't we?'

'I'm serious.'

He glanced toward his office and looked back to me. Putrid odors spilled from his lips unlike anything I'd smelled. He must have had eight, maybe nine beers.

'Come up with another reason. I saw you two together. I saw you walk into Planned Parenthood with a smile on your face,' I said. 'You both looked happy, actually.'

Caleb scratched his scar. His pupils danced between my eyes as he struggled to focus.

'She was going to end it that day but decided against it. She knew I didn't want it.'

'Try again.'

'It's the truth, Noa,' he said. 'I swear.'

I looked behind him to his office. The heavy wooden door was cracked near its hinges.

'What is it you want from me?' I asked.

He looked around his bar for a moment before standing up. 'Stay right there, I'll be back in a second.'

He walked to his office and returned a few moments later with a plastic baggie in his hand.

'Seriously, you really are a drug mule now?'

He sat down.

'This is RU-486. It's the abortion pill.'

'I know what it is. What are you doing with it? Planning on drugging your girlfriend?'

His expression didn't alter.

'It's not really as simple as that, Noa.'

'I was joking.'

He gave me time to flush the thought from my system, before attempting a sophomoric explanation.

'It really isn't that simple.'

'Did Marlene Dixon put you up to this? Supply you with the drugs?' I asked, hoping it wasn't true.

He didn't respond, and for the first time, I wished he hadn't been so silent. I wished I hadn't been so vocal when I met with her last. I wished for a lot of things in that moment.

'—she did, didn't she?'

'How do you . . . ,' he stumbled, as if a light were just beginning to radiate, a bit too late for him, but finally, it was turning on. 'You know Marlene?'

'You're actually sitting there telling me—'

'—I'm not "telling" you anything.' He stood up. 'Please, just come with me.'

I followed him into the back, where Sarah Dixon was lying, sprawled across the couch, peaceful as a corpse.

'Oh, my god!' I cried, tripping over my feet.

'Shhhhh.'

'Is she . . . is she . . . *dead*?'

I nearly fell to the ground. My heart skipped a beat. My hands shook.

'That's why I needed you here.'

'I don't understand.'

'I gave her the pill—'

'—you actually gave her an abortion pill?' I cried. 'How . . . how on earth? How did you get . . . how did you get this kind of a pill?'

He stared at me, but we never exchanged words. Not that day, not during my trial, not for any moment of my incarceration.

'Holy shit . . .'

'I put it in her drink, but then, after, she sort of passed out. I don't think it has anything to do with the pill, but what . . . what if it does? What if she's sick? What if she had a reaction?'

'Holy shit . . . holy shit . . .' I started pacing. 'Why? Why do you keep bringing me into your business? I don't want to have anything to do with you. Jesus Christ, stop calling me.'

'You're the smartest person I know, Noa,' he said, holding out his hand to meet mine. 'You were valedictorian of your high school.'

'Salutatorian.'

'You went to Penn.'

'For a year,' I corrected, my hands still shivering. 'Less, actually.'

'You teach science. Right?'

'I sub.'

'But you still teach.'

'I sub, Caleb,' I said again. 'I substitute. I'm not real. That's what a fucking substitute is – someone who isn't real.'

'Noa, I know how bright you are,' he insisted. His voice was weak. 'You're the only person I knew to call. I couldn't just leave her here.'

'Of course not!' I yelled, quickly calming myself. 'Take her to the fucking hospital.'

'We both know I can't do that.'

'Do we?'

'They'll want to know about the pill. How she got it,' he said.

I stared at him. 'Then tell them.'

'I can't,' he said, pacing. 'I can't. I didn't know this would happen. I didn't mean for this to happen. I shouldn't have done it.'

'She's not actually going to turn you in,' I said. 'She wouldn't have actually turned you in, you know.'

I walked over to Sarah. Her thin limbs stuck out from the couch. Her mouth was open, her eyes closed, and her stomach was half covered with her two palms as if she was showing everyone in her dreams her unborn child. I know it's strange, but at that point, the only thing I could think of was Liza Minnelli. I pictured her singing *Cabaret*, thinking of her dear friend Elsie, spread across the bed, corpselike as a queen.

My mouth opened.

'How long has she been out like this?'

'I'm not sure . . . Maybe twenty, thirty minutes before I called you.'

'Thirty minutes?'

I took off my gloves and threw them to the floor. Then I sat down beside her and pressed my fingers against her throat to check her pulse. There was a beat, slow but present. The carotid artery bounced off my fingertips enough for me to know she was alive.

But still, the music continued in my head.

'You know that pill isn't supposed to be given by non-medical professionals. Especially in such a high dose.'

'I know, I know.'

'And it's only a part of the process. She needs to follow up with someone. Did you think you could drug her a second time? Because that's what you'd have to do. Godamnit, why do you do these things?'

He held out his hands in prayer.

'What are we gonna do?'

'Again, we aren't going to do anything. You are going to take her to the hospital. She's unconscious but breathing normally, as far as I can tell. I'm not a doctor, Caleb. She needs a doctor.'

As soon as I removed my fingertips from her warm neck, I felt something move on the couch. It set off a wave of fear in my spine that I'd felt only once before. I'm not talking about the fear that overtakes you when you see a shadow moving through your dark home at night, or when that creak in the wooden planks of your floorboard definitely – almost positively, you swear – came from an intruder inside the house. No, I'm talking about the fear of discovery, the scintillating fear that you know you may be doing something wrong, but you can't quite spell *wrong* or understand what *wrong* is.

My father and I locked eyes just as he knew he needed to take her to the hospital. His eyes spread open, wide like the Adriatic, and he started backing away from me. I looked closer at him until fingertips touched my back. Tentacles, as if from a spider, inching along up my spine vertebrae by vertebrae. And the music played in that wretched mellifluous soundtrack.

'Where am I?' I heard her say, and then I turned around back to face Sarah.

October

Dearest Sarah,

When I look through the glass, I see Noa as I saw her that first day, and finally, I can admit it. (I don't want to, but I can.) She possesses a level of attractiveness; not as she is today, but as she was that first day. I'm not going to go into anything about our brief and scattered relationship, if you can even call it that. Only one e-mail binds us, and I deleted that and its fossilized imprint from my computer as soon as it was sent, erased from my hard drive long before Noa was tried. The state never looked into my computer's memory, and the defense never requested it.

So, instead of replaying that conversation and rereading that letter, I come home and look at your photos to remember how you smiled and remind myself of how you wore your hair and how you spoke on the phone and how you signed your name, and I just can't help myself. I'm starting to see you in her. I hate it. I hate that I'm saying it, that I'm seeing it, because there is nothing like you in her — nothing.

But she was your age, sweetheart, and now I think of nothing else. I know she's not the only person who turned thirty-five this year. She's not the only person who would have turned thirty-five this year had circumstances not been what they were. But still, she's your age. Along with a handful of associates at my firm who just made partner. And the new CNN anchor for the midday news. And a recently elected governor somewhere in the rural South.

And I know it's just a number, sweetheart, truly. I do understand that, but when I look at her prison photo and her mug shot and her collection of manipulative grins behind that glass wall whenever a photographer comes to memorialize her alongside a failed journalist, I'm starting to see you.

And I don't know how to turn away.

I know you are gone. I know that. But I don't know that I can look away. I don't know that I can visit her, but I don't know that I can escape.

I close my eyes and try to see your hair, sophisticated and straight, but see only hers — dirty blonde strands that began as a shiny golden mane and now hang in evolutions of a light currish brown, pulled back to the top of her neck with a torn rubber band. She doesn't have bangs anymore. So now, I see you. And her. And you. That confident stance that has slipped into conflict. That mouth that isn't sure when to open. That poignant widow's peak presiding at the heart of your forehead, right where the hairline met the skin — well, now it's starting to appear on Noa's face. It slips down in those pictures smashed in magazines, and it slides between her eyes in person like dripping paint, and when it does, I think her skin will fade and her eyes will lighten and her voice will command the confidence of humility you grasped at the age of thirteen.

And then she speaks, and I know it's not you.

I know she has genes that belong to a high school dropout

with a penchant for violence. I know she's not you because the tip of her hairline comes together in a jagged tear. And her California tan is sullen and scarred. And her light green eyes are starting to sink. And a handful of the sun's remnants line her face around her mouth and her eyes like misplaced punctuation. There is nothing precise about her. Nothing.

And yet with each glance – each blasted glance I take at her – through the glass window in the visitor's booth, through colored photos, black-and-white newspaper clippings, through video recordings of her interrogation – drops of perspiration crack about her brow in a mosaic of you.

Please forgive me for all of this.

Please forgive me, but I don't think I could look in on November 7 and lose you all over again.

Yours always,
Mom

ONE MONTH

UNTIL

X-DAY

Chapter 25

CONFUSED SPEARS OF DARKNESS SPIKED THROUGH THE metal bars, leaving faint shadows on the ground. About six guards marched into our unit like lethargic storm troopers, their boots stepping in unison, their hair slicked back behind their ears.

I was in bed, trying to get some sleep at the time. My right ankle cradled my left. My left hand cradled my head like a canopy, its heavy weight sinking deep into the pillow all the way to the mattress beneath. But my legs awakened to a tremor when the stomping began. Wide heels of rubber slapping the cement floor. A humming from one novice officer. The heartbeats of them all moving together as one machine. I didn't open my eyes. I knew what was happening. It was October. Maybe it was November. It was sometime around Halloween, and it was Patsmith's X-day.

A jingle of keys rustled against a thick leather belt as

breathing continued in a symphonic round. Some sounded like they might have had asthma and refused to carry around their inhalers for fear of losing their virility. Others breathed in pain, as if from years of filterless smoking. I imagine they counted along the beats of their hearts so that at least something made sense to them that night. The only breathing I didn't hear was Patsmith's. She must have been holding it in this whole time as if she just didn't know what to do with it.

Next, I heard the insertion of the key, the twisting of the lock until it clicked open, and the smooth shifting of metal upon metal. Patsmith's door opened, but still, there was no sound from her. No breathing, no crying at twenty-one past the hour, no need to see her daughter one last time. Just silence. Then the simple and expected placement of handcuffs closing, the sequential footsteps of a shackled inmate strutting on the floor like little bird steps between the longer ostrich gait of the guards as they walked forth.

I didn't open my eyes to see her marched off. I didn't get up from my bed to watch. It wasn't my place to ogle her. This was just the next part of the process. Arrest, conviction, incarceration, appeal, execution. And even though I knew this was coming for her – for me, too – knowledge is a different beast entirely from experience.

The footsteps faded as she walked farther away. She never got to see her daughter. At least I don't think she did, and perhaps that's what makes me sad. She didn't feel closure as she walked to the gurney. She wasn't able to see the one person who mattered to her. If I had one person still alive, I would have given her mine.

A few weeks ago, Patsmith abandoned her nightly cry for just one evening. I asked her why she stopped calling out for Pat that night. I was worried I actually might have to give her a new name.

'I dunno,' she said.

'What do you mean, you don't know?'

'It's kind of pointless, right? I've just been thinking, you know, it's kind of pointless to call out for someone who isn't there.'

'I don't know,' I said. 'It shows you care.'

'I don't care, P,' she said. 'Not anymore.'

I didn't respond.

'Maybe I just needed a change in my day. A new routine.'

'Routine?' I laughed. 'Isn't that what prison is all about?'

'Isn't that what life is all about?' she shot back, as if she'd picked up a GED, BA, and master's in philosophy in the course of a thirty second conversation. 'I mean, if we change our routine, then we can sort of feel something again, right?'

I shrugged, thinking back to my mother's living a new life on stage each season in my youth. To my father, who shacked up with a new correctional facility every other year. To Ollie, who was learning something new about himself each day he visited me. They were all living.

'Sure,' I said. 'I guess so.'

At twenty-one past the hour that night, I sat up in bed, hoping to hear her nightly call. 'Pat, I love you, Pat! I need you, Pat. I miss you, Pat!' It's not that I truly expected to hear it. I heard her walked out of her cell. I heard the bars screech as they yawned. I even heard her teeth as they clapped in fear. I knew she was gone. But for nearly ten years, I'd listened as she cried out to her lover.

There is something illuminating in the change of routine, no matter the direction. Wake up. Urinate. Sometimes defecate. Have your wrists cuffed. Feel the butt of a nightstick thrusting you from your cell. Shower. Feel the butt of that nightstick thrusting you back to your cell. Sleep. Listen to the nightly moaning of your neighbor calling out for her beloved victim. Repeat. This is the life of a decade. And now, it's gone.

I want to say I miss it. That I will miss her. Patsmith's routine was the same as her mantra: 'Pat, I love you, Pat! I need you, Pat. I miss you, Pat!' For Marlene, it was career, money, power. For Persephone, it was probably china patterns, tennis, and laughter. For my father, something having to do with sex, drugs, and rock and roll. Or children, love, and freedom. Maybe my new mantra will be: I'm sorry. I'm sorry. I'm sorry. Perhaps Patsmith will hear me and relay the message to the others.

Chapter 26

'THEY TURNED US DOWN.'

Oliver's expression was weak, almost flaccid, as he closed the door to my appeals as easily as, say, he would close the laminated pages of a menu.

'Oh . . .'

That's all I said.

And I said it again.

'Oh.'

Really, in that situation, what are you supposed to say? *Thanks for trying, young chap. I appreciate your effort. You coulda done better? Why didn't you try harder? Go with God? You just killed me. The court was wrong. Et cetera, et cetera.*

There aren't lists of preordained truisms in this situation. So I did the only reasonable thing I could. I acted upset and feigned concern, as if I had actually sat in the passenger seat on his virginal ride to salvation. My head ducked to my chest and without even feeling my muscles move, I gave him one of those smiles you give when you are uncomfortable or when enough years have passed with an old acquaintance that you no longer have to say hello to anymore when you see him on the street. And then I said it again.

'Oh . . .'

There it was – the rule of threes.

It was only then that Ollie felt the requisite imperative reply. He was reading from a printed copy of the Pennsylvania Supreme Court's ruling on his filing without even bothering to look at me.

'I tried everything, Noa. The court said that even if there were jury tampering issues, it would not rise to the level of reversible error. They claimed that, even if there was error with jury deliberation, with respect to Lavonne and Felipe's relationship, the error was harmless in nature. In other words, you would have been found guilty nevertheless, and it wouldn't have impacted how the jury determined your punishment. The same with the Miranda issue. The police read you your rights, and even though I don't believe they stopped questioning you when the Constitution demands, the court found that that error was also harmless in nature.'

He continued reviewing the opinion. Sweat slipped around on his cheeks, and bubbles of saliva jumped out from his lips, a Shakespearean actor on center stage each time he said any word that started with the letter *c*. *Constitution* and *court* and *claim*.

'During your interrogation, you asked for your attorney, and then they continued to question you. Your former appellate lawyers should have argued this on appeal. And again, the Supreme Court claims that Harris and McCall's strategy was deferential and did not rise to the level of ineffectiveness.'

Still, I didn't know how to respond. It wasn't that I didn't understand what he was saying, but simply that I didn't know how to comfort him from his first very serious and very personal professional loss. I wanted to remind him that they did try to appeal the Lavonne and Felipe issue before, but I cautioned them against it. They did also bring up the issue with my Miranda rights, but again, it went nowhere.

'Okay,' I said to him.

'There's nothing more we can do on those issues,' he replied.

His fingers darted to his eyes, and he rubbed them counter-clockwise. Minute scabs framed his nail beds. Heavy bags bulged under his eyes as if they were filled with water, weighing down his youthful face. I take full responsibility for that transformation.

Plagues of seconds sired the silence between us. He was looking at me without actually looking. Perhaps he was just staring at his own reflection in the Plexiglas as he stared my way. But it was clearly my turn to say something.

'What does Marlene say about this?'

He lay down his chin on his free hand and rested on it like a pillow.

'She hasn't had a chance to read it yet.'

I nodded.

'Why not?'

'She's busy working on other cases. And she's preparing for her meeting with the governor for your clemency petition.'

He answered that a little too quickly for my taste.

'But perhaps she would interpret the decision another way,' I added.

He dropped his hands to his side, freeing his chin, and looked directly to me.

'Their message is clear, regardless of interpretation. They are not granting our request.'

'So all that is left now is clemency?' I asked. 'Exactly where we started?'

'But we're making headway with clemency, too. We've gotten a few declarations in from people who have written in support of you. For example, Andrew Hoskins sent in a notarized statement which we can use.'

I wanted to laugh at that point, but something held me back. Respect? Boredom?

'Andy? Really?'

He mouthed the word *yes,* as he looked back to the copy of the opinion in his hand.

'I'm so sorry, Noa,' he said, dropping the paper on the table.

I wanted to put my hand on his shoulder and push up his chin with a little dose of adrenaline. It's not your fault,

I wanted to say. But it was he who failed – not me. I expected this. It wasn't my first appeal to be turned down. After all this time, I had forgotten that it was his.

I hovered for a moment, thinking.

'Well, okay then.'

He wiped his nose and didn't reply, as if he were thinking. Of Andy? Of Marlene?

'So what exactly did the pathologist say in his report? What did you include?'

Ollie opened his mouth to orate in the only way he knew how. Properly. Formally. Legally.

'As we discussed before,' he said, 'the court will reconsider a case if there is some newly discovered evidence that would provide conclusive proof of actual innocence. This doctor, this expert witness, was going to testify about Sarah's condition at her time of death.' He sighed, looking down at the opinion in his hands. 'I knew it was a long shot, but I thought we at least had a chance.'

'Oliver,' I said, gently placing one hand outward. But his hands danced before his face – naked, neurotic, skittish.

'With his opinion, his declaration—'

'—like you said, the court didn't buy it,' I shrugged. 'These things happen.'

He refused to look at me.

'It's okay,' I said again. 'There's not much to work with. The case against Noa P. Singleton is over.'

'I read the record. I saw the evidence. But—'

'—but nothing,' I said. 'It's over. Go home,' I pleaded. 'Go to your family. Go to MAD. Go back to Philadelphia or London or wherever is home to you these days. It was a nice story, but now . . . ,' I started, trailing off.

'What are you hiding from me?' he asked, sitting up in his chair. His voice shifted.

'Nothing, I'm not hiding anything.'

'You've told me about your childhood, Noa. You've told me about your father. And Sarah.' He brought the chair closer to the divider and even muffled by glass, I could hear it squeal. 'What aren't you telling me? I know it's something. I know you're hiding something.'

His lack of experience could only exacerbate his passion for advocacy.

'You didn't break into Sarah's apartment,' he blurted in self-determined epiphany. 'She let you in, didn't she?'

I looked away.

'Noa,' he persisted. 'There's no evidence to claim that you actually broke in. You just have a broken fingernail, which could have come from any number of sources. Both aggravating factors are eliminated, meaning there is no capital murder. No break-in. No baby. Just murder.'

'Just murder?' I laughed. 'And the "newly discovered evidence" for that is where?' I asked. 'Stop, Ollie. You're embarrassing yourself. One failed appeal a case is more than enough for someone as green as you.'

'Fine. Let's say even if she was still pregnant, how could

they prove that you knew she was pregnant? You said it yourself a thousand times, you could barely see it on her.'

'I knew she was pregnant.'

His eyes danced along with his fingers and the veins in his forehead and neck.

'They never found the man who broke into Sarah's apartment and shot her and you.'

Droplets of water collected under my breasts. My skin was moist and itchy. I wanted to scratch my right shoulder, but held back.

'You were placed in the holding cell for nearly twenty hours without counsel, without food or water, and most important—'

'I had water,' I argued.

'—but most important, Noa, you didn't have medical attention.'

I looked away.

'You were sitting in that holding cell bleeding out, and nobody thought to get you to the hospital? They didn't talk about the struggle at Sarah's apartment or your gunshot wound. The only thing they talk about is you faking a fainting spell to get out of an interrogation.'

'That's part of why the state looked so bad in my trial, but it doesn't change anything,' I said to him.

'You told me about your mother dropping you as a baby. Your father's lip wound. I know the bloody details of every episode of your youth. We've known each other long enough now that I think you would have told me about what really happened on January first.'

'You know what happened. It's in the record.'

'Please tell me what really happened to you. Was there a struggle? Was there really an intruder who shot both Sarah and you? Did you really shoot her in self-defense? Did she go after you first? Is that what happened?'

I kicked the divider between us with my left foot, stubbing my toe in an instant. Ollie tried to look in, but Nancy Rae reminded him to sit back in his seat.

'Noa?'

The toes in my left foot started tingling with pain, a subtle electrocution emerging at the toenail.

'Noa?'

'What?'

He inched closer to me. 'There was no intruder, was there? Was it self-defense?' I closed my eyes and thought of the quiet, peaceful things, like old-fashioned lawn chairs with nylon stretching out like a canopy below your seat. A nice silver wristwatch that ticks in your head when you wear it to sleep. Movie theater popcorn drenched in warm butter. The crack of cheap plastic when you twist a soda bottle open. The tuning of an orchestra until it settles onto that simple A major. A mechanical number two pencil.

'Ollie.'

'There's a reason people are declared "guilty" or "not guilty".'

My eyes spun upward.

'Stop, Oliver. You're turning into a cliché.'

'And there's two kinds of innocence, as well. Legal innocence and actual innocence.'

'Please don't go down the actual innocence road with me.'

'As if you didn't actually commit this crime. We're not talking about some sort of legal fiction anymore or loophole in the case law. You didn't actually do this.'

'Ollie, I shot her.'

He gripped his pen tighter. A yellow inch tore from the corner of his pad.

'Legal innocence, then,' he said, skittish. 'Perhaps your bullet didn't cause her death. It wasn't even close to a vital organ.'

'Ollie . . .'

'You don't know that. You're not a doctor.'

'Neither is the Supreme Court, but they rely on good ones nonetheless to make their decisions. Just like what happened here.'

'But that's not what happened here,' he argued. 'Nobody relied on medical experts for the defense. They just stipulated to the state's pathologist. They didn't protest his work. They allowed all those photos of the gunshot, but this new pathologist swears that Sarah was not pregnant when she was shot. He has new theories about her cause of death. The county coroner never even had a cause of death. The police didn't look into the medical records; they just focused on the autopsy. This new doctor focused instead on the hormone levels at pregnancy. The follicle-stimulating hormone. He stated in his supporting statement that those levels are supposed to spike between eight and eleven weeks, right at the time that she died. He compared the blood taken that day with her levels two weeks earlier at Planned Parenthood. They were on track then. They were at 8,500. When she died, they should have been at 25,000 or higher. Much higher. They could have been at almost 300,000, but they weren't. They were less than 7,000. You see what he's saying?'

I wasn't sure if he was finished, so I waited an extra moment or two. Then for the first time that day, he spoke directly to my face without looking down at his little note cards. This was something that needed no practice.

'The police noted all the blood in the apartment that day, but not just from the gunshot. There was blood in the bathroom and on her clothing – her underwear. Your lawyers didn't even cross-examine the medical examiner about that. The police simply carried all the bloody clothes into the court as if they were popcorn for the jury, without explanation. But nobody really bothered to check up on where the blood came from, outside of their simple explanation of immediate effects from her death. Nobody. They just focused on the gunshot. And you. They didn't bother to look around once you were arrested.'

'Please, just leave it alone.'

'The insurmountable evidence of ineffective assistance is staggering. This would never happen in . . .'

'Please, Ollie,' I pleaded. 'Just let it be. Everyone else has, and I'm happier that way.'

He picked up a stack of new papers and scanned the top page. I watched his pupils skim each line, until the desolation in his eyes faded. I, however, twirled a strand of hair around my index finger, listening to a harmony of the so-called theories that I doled out to the press during my trial. The Marxist Theory, the Victim Theory, the Cain and Abel Theory, and so on, until we came to the Kevorkian Theory, which nobody ever deems appropriate – even for trial. It's too hard to prove, I could hear Madison McCall say to me, before I even brought it up.

'It's not over,' he insisted. 'You're innocent of this crime. Your punishment should be commuted.'

'I don't want to go into this again.'

'You're legally innocent of this crime,' he continued. 'I'm sure of it. You aren't guilty of capital murder. It means you'd be off of death row—'

'—Ollie . . .'

'Regardless of the legal procedural flaws, there are evidentiary flaws in the state's case. You had no motivation to do this. Nothing at all. You can't even tell me what it was.'

'You're so young, Ollie,' I smiled.

'So . . . ?'

'Who knows how long you'll be in this country. Don't pretend that the minute you go home to your flat in London, you're not actually going to forget this case.'

His head shook from right to left, slowly, like a mechanical doll.

'Please don't make such presumptions.'

'Ollie, with your boarding school background and Marlene Dixon worship, what else am I to presume?'

'—Noa,' he said, softly, as if he wanted to argue, in part, and concede, in part. 'I'm nothing like Marlene Dixon.'

I smiled.

'Of course you are, Oliver Rupert. You went to Cambridge. You probably were sent off to boarding school to eat crumpets alongside some earl or duke or someone like that.'

Again, he shook his head left and right. 'You don't get it.'

'What?'

'Yes, I went to Cambridge, but I didn't grow up like that.' He laughed, nervously. 'My father was the first person in his family to go to university. He was a pilot for the military first, and my mom never went to university. And then there's me. And I haven't even been home in years.'

I pulled my hair back and tied it at the base of my neck with a rubber band from my wrist. A red indentation remained where it had previously clung, cutting off the circulation.

'Okay, Oliver,' I said to him, raising my hands. 'Mea culpa.'

'It's all right,' he replied instantly. His voice didn't match his words.

Then he looked to me as if he had more to say, but something stopped him. Perhaps it was his Englishness, perhaps it was Marlene, or the guilt from not having visited his parents in years and instead tracking a double murderer sitting in a Pennsylvania prison for the better part of the last decade.

'So, I've been writing some thoughts down,' I said, breaking the silence. 'When you began working with me, I started remembering a few things about what happened, about my childhood – you know, the usual prison memoir crap. Nothing too much, but I want to send it to you.'

'That's . . . ,' he stalled, as the water swelled in his eyes. 'That's wonderful, Noa.'

I gave him a moment before continuing.

'How can I get it to you?'

'You can give it to me now.'

'I'm not finished. I still have a few more weeks left, don't I?'

He nodded. 'Okay, I'll wait for it.'

'Good,' I smiled.

'Does . . . does this mean we are friends now?'

'Sure,' I said. 'We're friends. But just so you know, friendship is nothing more than a polygamist marriage. At least that's what caterpillar 'stache taught me back in the second grade.'

I tried not to laugh.

'Go ahead, laugh.' I winked. 'It's not my theory.'

'Do you miss them? Your friends? Your polygamist "spouses".'

I'm not so adverse to social norms that I had no friends before, but any friends I had, I pushed away, not the other way around. So other than Persephone, I didn't really have anyone to miss – before Sarah or after. Being my friend, Ollie didn't ask further.

'You can send the manuscript to me at the firm,' he finally said.

'Isn't there another way? Can you get me your home address?'

'Send it to Marlene at the firm. Just in case I move, I want to make sure I get it.'

'You sure?'

'Of course,' he said. 'The firm isn't going anywhere.'

I smiled as slowly as a mother does to a daughter she knows is changing clothes the minute she walks out of the house.

'Okay then,' I said. 'Does this mean you're my Russian Romeo?'

He laughed. 'Haven't we been over this before? I'm Welsh, Noa,' he paused. '*Welsh.*'

Chapter 27

EQUALITY IS A MESSY THING. IN HERE, WE ARE SUPPOSED to be equal to one another. A felon is a felon is a felon is a felon. On the Row, we equally have twenty-three hours of incarceration and one hour of recreation, solitary, men chained inside a basketball den in their facility, women walking the circumference of a sullen courtyard at a separate address.

Outside death row, prisoners don't know the criminal acts of their fellow prisoners, unless they offer the details themselves. Cafeteria lines sing in a dissonant choir of petty thieves, sexual assailants, rapists, and murderers. We're a minisociety in here. The teachers, students, poor souls in the corner wearing the dunce caps, sycophantic pedophiles, grade school teachers who slept with their students – all convicts of the same cloth.

Take one step back into normal society – productive,

diligent, respected nonfelonious society – and that word *equality* slips through the cracks. Juries make their decisions based on emotion. White people based on white people. Black people based on black people. Hispanics on Hispanics. Women for women. Jews for Jews. Muslims for Muslims. You get the picture. Capital punishment is no exception.

Now, I know that our system is great. It caught me, after all, along with Jeffrey Dahmer and Aileen Wuornos. It works. It really does. Like most things, it's not perfect nor is it without flaw, but it functions pretty well most of the time. Except when it comes to equality.

The law has created a protected class of individuals. People who, on the basis of their age or status, are more valuable to society. If they are killed – despite the fact that their hearts work the same, their eyes see the same, their bowels empty the same – the party responsible must die. If we kill someone in that precocious class of individuals, then we are sentenced to death based on whatever state we happened to be driving through at the moment. Kill a five-year-old girl, you get the needle. Kill a six-year-old girl, get twenty-five to life. Kill a police officer, get the needle. Kill your husband, get twenty-five to life. Kill a convenience store clerk after purchasing a pack of cigarettes and some gum, get twenty-five to life. Kill a convenience store clerk while stealing that pack of cigarettes and gum, get the needle. A nation that prides itself on equality treats its victims ever so inequitably in ritual.

In Pennsylvania, murder is first-degree murder with intent.

You could plan out your attack for the better part of two years or form that desire on the spot. If the state wants the death penalty, the state wants the death penalty. And unlike Texas or California or many others, if the victim was under twelve, you also die. God help you if the victim was a year and one day shy of his Bar Mitzvah. Some states have gone so far as to codify capital murder, applying the sentence of death somewhat less haphazardly. Murder and capital murder are different crimes in Texas. But in Pennsylvania, far too many factors contribute to its arbitrary application. Aggravating factors, they call it. Like murder can be any more inflamed than, well, what murder already is.

For example, if the murder was especially heinous or depraved, cruel or atrocious. Killing a government worker, killing for money, as part of a gang, during the sale of a controlled substance, against a ransom subject, or if the victim was pregnant. And, of course, if she was in the third trimester of her pregnancy or just if I knew she was pregnant at any stage, as if killing her had I not known she was a hair shy of her third trimester wasn't all that bad. As if killing Persephone would have been worse had I meant to do it.

Chapter 28

LIKE ALL GREAT STORIES, MINE BEGINS WITH CLASSIC Greek lore. With Persephone, the daughter of Zeus, wife of Hades, queen of the underworld, goddess of death, and my closest friend when I was twelve years old.

As children are wont to do, we thrived on habit and routine. Like I said, many of my afternoons were spent at her new house across town eating Thin Mint cookies on crystal platters and drinking lemonade in crystal glasses. I felt like royalty. Every time I drank from a crystal goblet, it would make a sound like a harp. And every time we finished eating and drinking, Persephone would show me some newly bequeathed asset in their newly bequeathed home of treasures, skipping eagerly from room to room. I was a classicist, an archaeologist excavating matter in my very own Greek myth, led to the underworld of the Riga household by my very own oracle.

For example: the sixteen-person china set, resting peacefully behind a glass casket much like the funeral of a beloved monarch – besotted within a cellophane prison, garnished by roses and medals of valor as a queue of mourning subjects paid their final respects. You may look, you may breathe, you may cry – but you must never touch.

'They're hand-painted, Noa,' she said weekly, as if it came as easy to her as breathing.

Other times she led me to a collection of modern paintings scattered amid their home, covered with a single cloth, like a recent victim at a crime scene or a Jewish home in mourning. There was a Miró, a Picasso sketch, even a Modigliani. 'That one's related to Granddad,' she said to me once. But I didn't know which artist she was referring to and why the painting was buried like her granddad if it was so special. Its face covered with a burlap sack, at the time, reminded me of a stack of old laundry. Now I think of it like a corpse waiting to be lowered into the dirt.

She would pull me to corners of her family's home, hidden alleyways that crept upon us like winding streets in Europe. 'I want to show you something,' she would call, and she would show me something every time. A diamond-encrusted tennis bracelet, fused together with white gold prongs, lying beside her mother's bed. 'A gift from Granddad,' she told me. Stacks and stacks of green bills buried somewhere under the foundation of the house, spread evenly, like casualties of war on a battlefield. 'They're sort of our little fishies,' she giggled, though I'm fairly certain she hadn't a clue that sleeping fish were not something like money that you hid beneath floorboards.

'But this,' she cried, 'this is the coolest thing!' She led me to the guest room where I stayed when it was too late to go home or my mother was too busy to come for me. Just behind the antique armoire was a family safe filled with ammunition, firearms, and relics of past skirmishes. 'Check it out,' she grinned, 'they're from World War Two.'

She pulled out one of the three old rifles and pointed it at me. '*Bang, bang!*' she joked, as if she were seven years old. But we were nearly thirteen, practically adults in some religions and cultures. '*Bang!*' she called, and I pretended to be hit. 'Here, try it out!'

She handed it to me and I took it willingly, no differently from how I accepted the lemonade in the two-hundred-dollar crystal glasses or the occasional movie ticket and ride home. They were heirlooms, familial droppings of wealth begat by someone with whom she would have had absolutely no connection other than perhaps a chin dimple or abnormally high cholesterol. The rifle was heavy and cold and felt more like one of the props my mother would use in that community theater production of *Annie Get Your Gun* than an actual rifle used to kill people in wars past.

'Give it,' she commanded. 'I need to put it back.'

She grabbed it from me and put it back into the safe. Hiding beneath the safe was a small wooden drawer, chipped around an old keyhole that looked like it could have been opened with only a toy key to the city.

'What's that?' I asked.

She shrugged and opened it.

'Ooooh!' she cooed. 'That is so cool.'

She looked over at me in pools of deep indigo. Dark black hair hung over those phosphorescent eyes, while her Greek knob of a nose poked through the waterfall of curls. I imagine if she lived to maturity, she could have been one of those models with what they like to call a quasi-ethnic look. Gorgeous and ugly at the same time, and you can't quite tell what she is. To me, though, she was just Persephone. Not Persy or Perse – just Persephone and sometimes P.

She grabbed the hidden jewel and twirled it around her fingers where the trigger lay. At first twist, the barrel was pointed at me.

'Come on, Persephone,' I urged. 'Put it back. Your parents probably don't want you playing with this.'

'I bet this was Granddad's.'

'Put it back,' again, I urged, 'please.'

She continued looking for initials or some form of identifying detail. 'It must be Granddad's. Why else would it be here?'

'Come on, P,' I urged. 'Your parents.'

'They're gone all day. They'll never know.'

'It might be loaded though.'

A giddy chuckle cracked from her chest as if a rib had

broken. It's funny. Sometimes I think that – even at thirteen – she was trapped in a childhood innocence that most thirteen-year-olds surpass before the age of ten. I suppose in some books that might have suggested she was never destined to grow into an adult. A mystical soothsaying countenance to the core.

'Nah,' she said. 'I'm sure it's fine.'

'It doesn't look so old. Maybe it's your parents'? Like for protection from burglars and stuff. Andy's parents have a gun at home, too.'

'I guess,' she sighed, 'but Mom says that this neighborhood's pretty safe.'

She shrugged, looking around the room. The gun was still perched between her fingers like a lollipop.

'Maybe they got it before you moved,' I said.

She shrugged.

'Maybe.'

'So, are you sleeping over tonight?'

I shook my head, no.

'Oh well,' she sighed, walking over to the bed. She fell back onto it and dropped the gun. It lay alone in the whiteness of the sheets and the lacy duvet cover. 'What time is your mom coming over to get you, then?'

I looked at my watch and shrugged.

'I dunno. An hour I guess? Maybe less.'

Persephone shrugged, too.

'Okay.'

'Are you gonna put that gun away?'

She sat up, bored.

'Yeah, I suppose.'

And that's when it happened. There was nothing dramatic leading up to it. No dialogue, no argument, no juvenile games of Russian roulette. No *High Noon* standoff. No motivation on my part or hers. No class distinctions. No begging. No lies. No theme. No theory. No Kevorkian thoughts at the time. No sibling rivalry. No father issues or mother issues or familial issues or internal psychological issues on which to lay blame. No *mens rea* or *actus reus* or affirmative defense or justification. No immaturity, no silliness, no immunity. No latent hatred. Just a simple favor.

'Hey, Noa, will you put it back for me?'

We were both quite bored, I suppose. With the gun? With the house? With each other?

My shoulders slumped. 'Sure,' I said, taking it from her.

The problem was that her fingers were still curled around the metal, her knuckles bent from their hinges, clinging onto the trigger. It was entangled between our fingers as if caught in a braid. There might have been an involuntary struggle as she tried to pull her fingers out of the frame. There might not have been. I can't be certain. What I am certain of is what happened immediately after the untangling of the gun. My heart trilled like the swirling end of a violin solo. My mind circled like whirling dervishes. My eyes dried as if someone were blowing into them. And, languidly, a horizon of smoke settled between me and Persephone. By the time it lifted, no different than the morning haze, the gun was no longer in Persephone's hands, nor was it in the safe. It was in mine.

That's when I saw her limbs, spread out on the bed just as they were when she lay down minutes before, lanky and long, a bit knobby around the elbows and now jiggling from the impact of the bullet. Her legs seemed almost as long as her arms, marionette-like in their resting position. A small black dot mounted her forehead, the crowning jewel of her newly anointed tiara. It was leaking. Dark fluid drained onto the duvet, flowing like lava from the mouth of a volcano. But with all the movement around her, Persephone was still. Her chest wasn't inflating like mine. Her eyes weren't peeled back like mine. Her hands didn't shake like mine. The only movement was near the floor. A slight seesaw of motion tilted my eyes toward her feet, where her flip-flops dangled off the ridge of her now cooling toes, back and forth, back and forth, back and forth, until one of them finally fell to the ground.

'P?' I whispered.

Nothing.

'P . . . P . . . Persephone?'

Still nothing.

My hands dropped to the ground, and the gun instantly slipped out of my grasp, releasing another bullet, which shot the base of the bed at one of its feet. I can't remember hearing the gunshot. I can't even remember hearing the previous gunshot. Or screaming even. I know that they happened, because I was there and I saw the wood splinter. But there was no sound. There was no memory. I found out later that the second gunshot caused the bed to lose footing. Apparently when the police arrived hours later, Persephone was no longer lying flat, comfortable, napping as I saw her last. Instead, she had slid off the silken sheets when the wood began to collapse and was practically sitting on the floor with her back leaning on the mattress and a single fist clutched under her chin in a macabre Rodin tableau.

My mother was scheduled to pick me up at any moment. She'd know what to do. She'd done it before. She told me the story a million times. She told me the story about how she and Paramedic One met – serendipitously, spectacularly lucky, she always said – when she dropped me from the second floor landing of our home in the North Valley. She never knew how well I remembered sounds from my infancy. She never knew that I remembered everything she did with Paramedic One, and caterpillar 'stache the accountant, and Bruce the speed walker. I never told her that I also remembered her breaking down the walls of my crib so that nobody would know what she really did.

A line of blood slipped out of the corner of Persephone's mouth like delinquent drool.

I didn't see the telephone. I hadn't ever dialed 9-1-1 before. This wasn't the time. But it was a break-in, of course. There's nothing else it could be. A break-in. That's why Persephone's parents had the gun, after all. That's why Andy Hoskins's parents had one, too.

The pearl of blood dripped onto the white duvet like a spot of chocolate. Persephone still wasn't moving. She hadn't yet drifted onto the floor. The wooden bed hadn't yet lost its footing.

But, suddenly, the world began to spin around me. Garments moist with sweat cloaked my arms and legs like shrink-wrap. I closed my eyes and imagined days passing as I would sit cuffed to a chair by myself explaining that it wasn't my fault. It wasn't my fault. It wasn't my fault. Can't you understand? It wasn't my fault.

It was five minutes – just five short minutes that I watched Persephone drained of life. Hades in the form of her twelve-year-old friend grabbed her from the fields and ran her to the underworld. The minutes turned into days, which turned into months and years. Blood rushed to my face. I felt it with my shaky hands, only to scream from the burning sensation, like I had placed my hands on the stove, like I burnt a confession directly into them. Those same fingers reached over and touched my feet, which too quickly also filtered the viscous fluid of loss. My bladder was full, my eyes were leaking, my pores were leaking, but none of them could move. My heart beat in my ankles. My hands blistered over, red and white and yellow with blood and pus and mucus. She needs to get to a hospital. She needs to get to a hospital, I thought. She needs to get to a hospital.

And then I heard my mother say it again on the phone to the 9-1-1 operator.

My daughter . . . she's . . . she's fallen. There was an intruder. Please, come help.

Nobody ever followed up that day.

Please, we need help! There's been an intruder!

But nobody checked in on us to see whether they caught the man responsible. My mother was the best actress I knew and perhaps the best actress in California that day. And now it was my turn.

I picked up the gun and wiped my fingerprints from it, putting it back just as Persephone had asked me to. I closed the safe and pushed it into its coffin just as it was designed. Just as Persephone had asked me to five minutes earlier. I walked to the phone to dial 9-1-1 to tell them what happened: an intruder walked in on us while we were playing, while Mr. and Mrs. Riga were out of the house for the day. But I never made it that far.

For the first time in my life, my mother arrived early. She must have pulled into the front and slammed the car horn with her palm. It honked all the way to the back of the house, where I was waiting with my only friend. I started walking toward the front door, one foot in front of the other. Perhaps my mother was there early for a reason. Perhaps she knew what would happen. Perhaps she'd know what to do. Yes, she'd know exactly what to do. She was there to remind me of what I must do. *Anything you can do, I can do better,* I heard her sing. *I can do anything better than you.*

There was an intruder, I heard my mother say to me,

whispering via infancy, insinuating from a honking car no more than fifty feet away. *Say there was an intruder. Just tell them that. You're a good actress. Just like me. Just like me, you're a good little actress, Noa. You can do this. You can do anything better than me.*

I looked around for a phone but couldn't find one. I would have wanted to call and say, 'Yes, there was an intruder. I don't know who it was, but he came in and took some of my jewelry and then left. And . . . and . . . and when he was here – he was wearing a black ski mask, so I didn't catch his face, but that's when it happened. And . . . and she was shot.'

But I didn't. She was never singing to me from the stage. I needed a new tactic.

I ran upstairs and took the nearest item I could find that weighed more than a pound (a vase, maybe? A frame? I can't remember anymore) and tossed it through the glass case that housed the Rigas' china. Little fleurs-de-lis cracked at the intersection of their curves and crosses so that all that remained were twenty thousand pieces of rubble. I ran to the office, where I found the family's Apple IIc sitting on a high burgundy stool and ripped it from its socket, tossing it on the ground. I didn't wait to watch as it cracked in two, its innards spilling onto the frozen wood paneling below like electronic road kill. And then I rushed back to the room – the mausoleum where Persephone lay moments before slipping into her final statuette of a pose. If a burglar had done this to her, then a burglar would have had his own gun, his own weapon. Or worse, he would have found this gun and taken it with him. I shuffled through the drawers in the room, emptying their contents as if I were actually searching for a weapon. Then I grabbed the gun, wrapped it in my sweatshirt, and placed it in my backpack, where it sat until I could think of its next home.

There was only one more thing that I needed in order for it to look authentic. Upstairs, next to Mrs. Riga's night table was a freestanding jewelry box. I remember my mother always telling me she hid her jewelry in her sock drawer because it was foolish to advertise to a burglar where all your valuables lie. I just presumed she said that because she didn't have anything of great worth. But maybe she was right. As my mother's persistent car honked into an enduring recitative, I ran up to the jewelry box, and opened it using my shirt as a makeshift glove. I knew from school that fingerprints are like your soul; nobody knows how to discern them properly, but everyone has a unique design. I picked out the diamond tennis bracelet that Persephone displayed weeks earlier because it looked like the most expensive item in the box, shoved it into my backpack next to the gun, rushed outside, and hopped in my mother's car.

She was busy looking through a month-old edition of *People* magazine. She didn't ask me how my day was, where the Rigas were, or why I took so long to come outside. If she had listened harder, she would have heard my heart beating through my voice as it dictated the direction home.

A day later, my mother came into my room to tell me

about a tragic accident. She had heard about it on the afternoon news. The police didn't know who did it, but evidently the Rigas' house was broken into, and one of the burglars (there were allegedly two) shot and killed Persephone in the process. She was so sorry to be the person to tell me this. She was dreadfully emotional because, as she knew, 'you were just so very close. Two peas in a pod,' she repeated at least four times in that conversation. She showed me the newspaper clipping of the police report. Along with the homicide, 'the burglars took all sorts of money and a diamond tennis bracelet and smashed twenty thousand dollars' worth of hand-painted porcelain china.' I knew then that I could never tell her what I had done. Three days later, I laid the gun to rest beneath an old oak tree hovering above countless hundred-year-old corpses in the nearest cemetery I could find.

My brother, mother, and Bruce the speed walker went to the funeral with me, where we sat three rows behind the Rigas. After the ceremony, I told them how sorry I was for their loss. They had no other children and weren't sure what to do next. They blamed the inheritance for Persephone's death. They blamed the move. They were probably right about that, but still. I hugged them and told them how much I loved Persephone, too, and how sorry I was again and again and again.

'No dear, don't go there,' they said to me, wiping a tear from my nose. 'It's not your fault.'

November

Sarah,

I just learned that, in addition to the clemency petition, Oliver has been working with Noa on a writ of habeas corpus to file with the Pennsylvania Supreme Court for another appeal. Last week when I came to the prison to get some signatures from Noa to release additional school and medical documents from their custodians that I wanted to incorporate into the petition, I put it together. It had been months since I'd been to the prison, and I presumed the same for Oliver. True, I needed him to visit and try and pull out a nugget of truth here and there about what happened on New Year's Day, but it was quickly and clearly becoming a mistake. He was no longer serving his purpose.

Last Saturday, I drove nearly three-and-a-half brutal highway hours to visit the prison, only to be told by the guards that Oliver was already there. Not that I need to even verbalize this, but he was not visiting clients of ours in general population or continuing to work on any of our other cases. Rather, he was chatting with Noa about . . . well, God knows what. Of course I told the prison officials that I had simply mixed up the days. Of course this was Oliver's scheduled appointment, I told them. Of course it must be my age catching up with me, and I tried to pass it off as self-deprecating humor. They laughed, kindly, and then showed me the visitors' log, which I frantically transcribed all in one place for you so that you can see with your own eyes.

June 3, 2012	*Oliver Rupert Stansted, esq., MAD*
June 5, 2012	*Oliver Rupert Stansted, esq., MAD*
June 18, 2012	*Oliver Stansted, esq., MAD*
June 29, 2012	*Oliver Stansted, esq., MAD*
July 3, 2012	*Oliver Rupert Stansted, esq., MAD*
July 26, 2012	*Oliver Stansted, esq., MAD*
July 29, 2012	*Oliver Stansted, esq., MAD*
August 7, 2012	*Oliver Stansted, esq.*
August 15, 2012	*Oliver Rupert Stansted, esq., MAD*
August 26, 2012	*Oliver Stansted, esq., MAD*
August 31, 2012	*Oliver Stansted, esq.*
September 26, 2012	*Oliver Stansted, esq.*
September 28, 2012	*Oliver Stansted, esq.*
October 4, 2012	*Oliver Stansted, esq.*
October 14, 2012	*Oliver Stansted*
October 20, 2012	*Ollie Stansted*

Sixteen times, sweetheart. Sixteen visits. Some consecutive, some not. Some visiting under the guise of Mothers Against Death, and as the weeks continue, never for MAD and perhaps not even as an attorney at all.

Next, I drove all the way to Harrisburg to see if 'Ollie' had actually filed something on his own. Something beyond the clemency petition he was helping me compose. The court clerk handed me all paperwork filed on behalf of Noa P. Singleton or even just 'Noa Singleton' in the previous year, and that is when I discovered it on thick blue cardstock,

typed with simple black Courier typeface: Oliver Rupert
Stansted listed as the attorney of record on yet another futile
writ of habeas corpus with no connection whatsoever to
Mothers Against Death; Adams, Steinberg, and Coleson, LLP;
or Marlene Dixon, esquire.

My eyes skipped around the language, reading furiously
from ground to ground, hoping to find something new,
something that I hadn't previously considered, something for
which I locked her away mistakenly. But there was nothing
new in that writ, thereby nothing cognizable by the courts
at this point for anything. His arguments weren't even sound.
He brought up issues that have long been settled by the courts,
that have long been settled in this case after the previous
appeals. They lacked merit. They lacked intelligence. They
lacked substance. Just a hunch, a silly hunch that you were
not pregnant at the time you died, backed up by a hack who
based all of his theories on blood tests. And that your heart
was the reason you died, not the clear and unquestionable
gunshot wound to the chest, which was the unambiguous cause
of death. Nothing else. A jury of twelve unbiased peers found
that to be true. A lawyer with five minutes of experience
could have shown Oliver that if he had examined Noa's files
with me, if he had done the research properly, if he had
understood the law accurately, if he had had experience in
this sort of procedure, if he had written down each and every
word he shared with Noa with me (as was his only responsibility on this case from day one), then perhaps things would

have turned out differently for him. But what he filed? A waste. A waste of language, of time, and of resources.

'Find out what actually happened. Write down every word she says,' I told Oliver on that first day at the prison nearly six months ago. 'That's your only purpose. Your only goal.'

But after five visits, he stopped reporting their discussions to me, stopped bringing the yellow pads back to me, and I presumed, had also stopped visiting Noa. He claimed people were writing in support of her. He claimed that progress was being made with the clemency petition, and yet he was spending his time doing anything but. Eleven more visits followed. Eleven? Practically a dozen sessions of psychoanalysis. For what? A waste of my time. A waste of his. Of the Supreme Court's. They don't need to review another faulty writ filed by an attorney with barely a perfunctory knowledge of American law, claiming grounds for review that have long been settled for decades.

Instead of following my explicit orders, instead of expressly getting information from her that could elucidate that last moment of your life, Oliver took valuable time away from the matters that actually counted for everyone involved in this case to file another useless appeal. He resorted to his untested, inexperienced foreign legal skills to make everyone a fool on issues that have long been determined. I know this is not what you want to hear, sweetheart, but I just have to get it out. I'm just so angry, I don't know what to hit. I don't know who to take all my anger out on anymore. On Oliver? He doesn't deserve this, and when I think calmly, I know that. I do know that. Yes, I'm angry with him, but he's also only just barely understood the serpentine path of these filings, and I can't possibly fault him for that. Part of me wanted to applaud his innovation and direction, his selfless ambition. Another part wanted to remind him that his absurd sifting of the law was taking away from his one and only goal. But, as is always the case, regardless of my emotional sensibility, the rational part of me regressed to reason and logic, and I knew what had to happen. His initial purpose no longer existed. I know that you could imagine what happened next. You would expect no less, sweetheart.

When I returned home to Philadelphia, I called Oliver to my office. One of my colleagues at the firm had him working on a major case that was set for trial in three weeks, and although I was tempted to inform him of Oliver's extra-extracurricular pro bono activities, I didn't. His modest performance would say everything that needed to be said. The court said everything that needed to be said, and surely he'd read its opinion.

Oliver came into my office about thirty minutes after my request. Initially, I asked him if he had anything to divulge. 'Honesty is far better than misgivings,' I said to him. 'The bar deems so, and I agree.'

He admitted nothing. Instead of coming clean, we stared at each other until I broke the silence and told him what I had recently uncovered. He claimed that he only came to the prison when I specifically sent him there on MAD business. That he only drove out to the prison when he was sent from me with a bulleted list of information to uncover, with conversations to record, with papers to sign. But when I showed him the visitor's logs and the opinion, he broke down. (This is all public record, though. I haven't a clue how he thought his extracurricular activities would be a secret. But still, he broke down like a child whose secret stash of candy had just been found between the couch cushions.) He didn't realize that he'd be caught, or worse, that he actually did something wrong. In his mind, he was doing something right. He wanted to help Noa, he claimed. He wanted to fix the system that is flawed beyond repair, he pled. He thought that we had the same goal.

'How could you possibly fix it if it's really flawed "beyond repair", as you say?' I said to him.

'Isn't that what you preached when I signed up for this? Your change of heart – excuse me – owning up to the heart you've always had. Your belief that executing people is wrong. That punishing them in prison for life is far worse. Isn't that what this is all about? Having statistics for the future so we can see what actually happens with all of these appeals?'

He was fighting back, Sarah. He was fighting for Noa or his job or his moral code or reputation, I wasn't quite sure. It was sort of inspiring and exhausting to watch at the same time.

'You knew exactly what you were getting involved with when you agreed to work on this case,' I said to him.

'I don't know,' he sputtered, shocked, the adrenaline starting to fade. 'I just thought I could fix past errors.'

'Noa's incarceration is not a past error, Oliver.'

He didn't respond.

'Listen to me, Oliver.' My voice was getting louder, and with each new breath, clarity materialized over my thoughts. 'Noa's incarceration is anything but erroneous. Her punishment, on the other hand, might be. Are we clear? Those are two separate and distinct entities. We have been on her case solely due to punishment issues—not innocence.' I paused. 'Punishment.'

His head dodged the answer, but I read past it. This kind of work required emotions that he lacked. His heart was too visible outside his garments, where it resided like lint on a week-old sweater.

'Are we clear?' I said again.

A mere child before me, Oliver nodded reluctantly. I waited a moment for it to sink in, and, again, he nodded.

'She's going to die,' I said to him.

'Yes,' he echoed, nodding his head up and down slowly, 'but . . . if . . .'

I placed a single hand out, stopping him.

'Don't confuse your feelings.'

'What feelings are you talking about?' he said, uncomfortably. 'I'm just following your lead. Your feelings are the ones that I'm concerned with.'

My brow inched higher.

'Do you remember why you hired me in the first place?'
he asked.

'To try and talk to Noa and understand what actually
happened,' I said. 'That's why.'

'Partially.'

'Completely,' I affirmed.

'Partially,' he insisted. 'The other part we never spoke
about, did we?'

His left eye began to twitch.

'And what other part do you suddenly believe I have put
you on the course to do?'

'To exonerate an innocent woman. Clemency is not going
to free her. These letters just talk about her as a child. That's
not going to sway any governor to commute her sentence.
You and I both know that to be true.'

He said it so clearly, so articulately with that accent that
almost made even him believe what he was saying. But he
was wrong. He was wrong. He was absolutely wrong.
Nobody else was responsible for your death but her. It was
Noa and Noa exclusively. Hear me, sweetheart and know
that. Know that as you sleep, as you watch over me, as
you . . . as your eyes remain closed. Know that.

'I may be older than you and I may be your boss,' I said
to him, 'but trust me, I see what's going—'

'—you know,' he stopped me. 'She's a remarkable person,
Mrs. Dixon. I never would have thought that someone like

that would be in prison, let alone on death row. Did you know that she was at the very top of her high school class?'

Salutatorian, I wanted to tell him, but I didn't.

'Helping Noa isn't going to fix your own issues. You left them in England to come here and play Susan B. Anthony.'

Fingers darted to his eyes in half-hearted circles.

'What exactly, then, do you think you're doing with Noa?'

I watched myself turning into a different person, ogling my actions in shock. I no longer recognized myself. As a result, nothing I said or did felt like my own, which in one way liberated me from everything, and in another, brought me closer to Noa.

'I've got a few new theories on what happened with the case that I'm pretty sure were never developed at trial,' he said, breaking the silence. 'And that is what the writ was about. I was just adding to it. To clemency, if possible.'

He pulled out a thin file of papers from his briefcase and handed it to me. 'These are for the petition. But there is just so much more beyond it to be done here.'

I took it and tossed it on my desk.

'Oh?'

His nubby fingers dropped from his face so that I could see it fully, clearly, like a freshly cleaned window, and he stared through me as if he knew.

'For example, her father was lying,' he declared, quite authoritatively. 'In my mind, I know he was covering up for someone while on the stand, and it wasn't Noa.'

'*Is that so?*'

He nodded.

'*Yes, I'm certain of it. I'm very close to figuring out why. I think I'll know shortly, as I've located him but haven't been able to get in touch with him again. He's living in Canada, tending a bar there. It's called Barre Dive, actually. Which is sort of ironic if you look at the facts of the—*'

'*—is that so?*'

I couldn't listen anymore.

'*Yes,*' *he replied, nodding slowly.*

My heart slipped a bit between the bars of my rib cage, locked inside, incarcerated by osteoporotic bones.

'*Mrs. Dixon?*'

Absolutely nothing.

Almost nothing.

'*Thank you for all of your time and your work on this case, Mr. Stansted,*' *I said, instinctively, folding the printed copies of the court's opinion and the visitors' logs from the prison and then placing them inside the folder of his svelte attempt at research. I looked back to him.*

'*You're fired.*'

His face abruptly crystallized.

'*You are also removed from this case. Please do not contact me or Noa about it again. Is that clear? If you do, I will have you deported, and any chance you have of practicing law in this country will be effectively terminated upon contact with her. Don't think I can't contact the bar and inform them of your inefficiencies. Don't think I also can't make a simple call to the office in London letting them know about your actions.'*

'I don't understand,' he said, confused. 'I didn't do anything wrong.'

'I think I was exceedingly clear.'

He stood up with his briefcase tight within his grip, face-to-face with me. We were about the same height when I wore my heels, which I was wearing at the time.

'But you put me on this case to—'

'—this conversation is over.'

'I'm not ready to go back to London, Mrs. Dixon. We haven't even filed the clemency petition. Noa's execution date is in just over a week, and—'

'—I'm not sure you heard me the first time, Oliver. If you'd like to keep your reputation here and in London, you will excuse yourself from my office. We both know you don't want me to continue listing all of the problems you'll encounter if this conversation goes beyond a mere firing, do we?'

'This is a woman's life, Mrs. Dixon.'

'And it is also the rest of yours, Mr. Stansted.'

He looked over my shoulder at the small cemetery of photographs residing, each in a strategically aged wooden frame, on top of the file cabinet next to my desk. In the center is my favorite photo of us – the one you hated, the one that your father took on the first day of your summer internship at the firm. I haven't gone a single day without seeing your smile, forced as it might have been, beside mine.

Oliver didn't respond.

'That is something I know you are unwilling to gamble with, Mr. Stansted. I've got this additional paperwork now, thank you for that. And I'll complete the clemency petition on my own. Do we understand each other?'

His eyes surveyed the rest of the photos – signed snapshots with Fortune 500 CEOs, my wedding portrait with your father, the first time I visited the Supreme Court, the Great Wall of China – and then he settled upon our only photo before turning back to me.

It wasn't necessary for him to speak at that point. He understood. Just like Noa, just like Caleb, Oliver understood exactly what had to happen next. He shook my hand, thanked me for the opportunity and for all he learned from the last five months on the case and from MAD, and walked out of the office. He didn't even seem surprised.

Mom

ONE WEEK

UNTIL

X-DAY

Chapter 29

I'VE HEARD THAT IT'S A CURSE TO BE TOLD THE DATE of your death. I've heard that, in some societies, precognition of that moment has sent people into a fury of mania so corrupt that it has been used both for political gain and territorial acquisition. It has inspired heartbreak, and derailed it moments later. It has been used in lieu of flailing and water-boarding, the coffin torture or the rack.

For most of these phantom blame-seekers with whom I've shared an address for upwards of a decade, it is just that. A punishment far worse than the three-drug cocktail itself. To me, though, it's a gift. The opportunity we are granted is unlike any other. What a blessing – to be able to plan year after year for your death. The food you want, the words you get to bequeath, the attention you will receive. The legacy. Think about it. People have accidents without knowing the time and date of the car that will cut them off on the freeway halfway to a business meeting. They don't know that they won't make it through surgery when there's a power outage during a triple bypass. Heads of state may suspect, but haven't the certainty, if that one assassin really will be stopped. Nobody can properly plan for that date – even if they know it – but us.

It isn't just because of the date that I'm starting to ponder my last words again or my last request for sustenance. I suspect none of them will matter in the long run to anyone of merit. All I have is the knowledge of November 7 at sometime around 7 in the evening. If I had been given that date on New Year's Eve, perhaps things would have turned out differently. I tried to give it to myself on more than one occasion, but that's the problem, isn't it? Gifts are something that must be given by another.

I hadn't heard from my father since I left Bar Dive less than twenty-four hours earlier. Nor had I heard from Sarah. Or the police. I read the newspaper and read online almost hourly to try and see if any news had been posted about a twenty-four-year-old Penn grad found dead or a Main Line daughter reporting an assault. Everywhere I walked – from the grocery store, to the pharmacy, to the bathroom – I looked twice, three times even. Someone was there. Somebody was always there.

The streets were starting to fill with revelers wearing masks and glasses boasting the inauguration of 2003. Girls draped themselves in miniskirts without covering their legs or shoulders with a touch of wool to stave off the winter chill.

I couldn't call Bobby about what happened with my father and Sarah and get him involved. I couldn't call Marlene and tell her that it was because of her desperation, her senselessness, her goddamned stupidity that she put a deadly weapon in the form of a little white pill in the hands of my father. All I could do was watch the ball drop in Times Square on my fourteen-inch TV and hear my neighbors screwing as I waited for the night to end.

For a brief moment, I thought about visiting my mother in California and about visiting my brother back in Encino, or perhaps even tracking down Paramedic One to find out why he left my mother. I spent all of five minutes stuffing my overused shirts and pants and skirts and dresses into an old-fashioned suitcase – the same one I took from my mother when I went to college all those years ago. (It was baby blue and held together by a frayed navy striped belt around the corners. There were no wheels, and the handle was reinforced with packing tape.) But nothing fit.

I took everything out and stuffed a few contents into my backpack, including the Smith & Wesson handgun from my father, from that indignant evening that seemed like years earlier. It was silver and it slipped in the external zipper just like a hairdryer or an extra pair of sandals. The bullets were still packed tightly in their case. I opened it and poured them over my wallet, my cell phone, an empty notepad and pen, into the old canvas pack, which was flayed at the bottom, its edges spread like the blades of a flamenco fan. Charcoal bullets rained, face-first, thundering quietly between everything I'd touched in the last few years.

I picked the gun up again and ran my fingers over its back, on its sides, and its belly. There was something almost exotic in the glossy silkiness, in the way it massaged the backs of my fingers when they slipped inside, in the way it made me feel as helpless and crippled as Sarah at Bar Dive with her wings spread open and limp. It took no more than a mere inspection, drunken with exhaustion and insomnia, when I turned it over and discovered that the serial numbers had been scratched off. I shouldn't even have been surprised.

Because they were sitting so close to the gun, I next picked up one of the bullets. My palm dropped a centimeter or two with the mediocre weight of both the bullet and gun in one hand. First, I put on the safety and dropped the bullet in the barrel. Then I picked up another bullet and loaded it, too. And another, and another and another until all six bullets were safely tucked away in their proper beds.

When I finished loading the gun, I boiled some water on the stove and sat down until the teakettle whistled its A-minor tune. (I timed it on numerous occasions, and it took no less than two minutes and no more than two minutes and fifteen seconds, to be precise, depending on the temperature outside. This time, it took just a hair under two and a quarter.) The teakettle nearly slipped from my hands when I poured the water into two coffee cups. As if my father would show up and explain to me what had just happened.

As if my mother would arrive and talk me out of it.

As if Persephone would return to me and say . . .

. . . and say . . .

I walked to the kitchen and opened the cabinet that contained my spices, rice, and pasta. Miasmas of chutney and saffron sat in the air as cumulous white smoke. My fingers went to my box of tea, and I plucked the final bag of Lemon Zinger, tearing open the top of the packet in a single stab. I used the same tea bag for both cups, submerging its tender skin, from mug to mug, back and forth, leaving a trail of lemon-scented water between them like forensic clues nobody could decipher.

Pathways of citrus aroma found their way to my nose. My fingers selected a single mug, safe and unconsciously pure. The water felt so warm and soothing on its way down, like honey dripping from a cone. Like ice cream from a scoop. Like thick hot chocolate, gooey with melted marshmallows on its veneer. Sweet and idyllic.

The only thing that could make the night bearable would be a bottle of sleeping pills, but sadly my medicine cabinet was empty. My prescription had long since expired. So instead, I popped two acetaminophen and two ibuprofen on my tongue and massaged the pills as they wormed down my esophagus. And without thinking through the consequences,

I walked casually to my bag and picked up the gun. It wouldn't be as clean as pills, but still.

At first, I tried my left hand and held it out before my face so that I could look directly into the barrel. But my hand was too shaky. I could barely hold the gun in front of my face long enough to pull a trigger, let alone align it properly to the space between my eyes. I had never really inherited my father's great gift of violent conservation, no matter how much I believed. No, I wasn't him. I wasn't him at all. He could probably pull the trigger if he wanted to. I knew that if I pulled the trigger, I'd fail and wind up disfiguring or paralyzing myself. But still, I tried it again with my right hand, and when I lifted the gun, my shoulder ached as if it had already been shot. The hand weight shifted something in my joints, driving my memory, forcing it back to the table. I couldn't hold the gun straight. I couldn't lift it without searing arrows puncturing everything beneath the skin, reminding me that I was twelve years old again. That I was ten months old. It was as if the moment my fingers slipped into place, I felt dropped from the stairway of my mother's house again.

I put the gun back on the table. It was practically midnight. I turned on the television to watch the countdown. The tea was cold and my arms were tired. I can't even remember falling asleep at the kitchen table. I suppose looking back on that night, part of me knew it might be the last I'd sleep in my own home.

Chapter 30

IT HAPPENED ON NEW YEAR'S DAY.

I woke up in my kitchen with my right cheek shellacked to the cheap wooden lining of my dinette table. Two coffee mugs were digging tangerine rings on either side. Resting on its back between them, almost like a scared puppy during a thunderstorm, was the gun – my gun by congenital defect – just where I left it when the seconds ticked down to the new year.

I sat up, stretched, yawned, and walked over to the bathroom to brush my teeth. Then, just like any other day, I strolled to my window, placed the back of my palm on its smooth glass surface to test the weather. It was cold, quite cold, but not as cold as I'd grown used to for a January in the Northeast. Frost residue was peeling from the sill in doilies, but no new patterns had collected overnight.

I grabbed my coat, my backpack, scarf, and mittens. The

minute I walked out of my apartment, I heard a faint chanting, almost like I was attending a concert with earplugs. I could hear the joy from the New Year's Day crowds all the way twenty blocks west. It was the Mummers Parade.

Mummers, by definition: 'urban moral squalor,' as Marlene Dixon would say. The poor man's Mardi Gras. A poverty-stricken Carnival. My father's people, if you will. Thousands of pedestrians, crusty and lethargic with hangovers pacing beside them, saturating Washington Avenue all the way from Broad Street to Penn's Landing, marking their territory with nothing other than a six-pack of beer, beads, face paint, and fluorescent polyester, until they arrived before City Hall to be crowned.

I walked toward Center City and thought of my brother. I hadn't heard from him more than three times in the previous year. It was New Year's Day, and what are these contrived holidays if not for starting anew? So I called him. Of course he didn't answer. I left a message wishing him a happy new year. I said I hoped we would see each other more this year. I told him I'd like to meet his girlfriend. I said I was proud of him, even if he had chosen to be a production assistant for the porn industry's biggest director, that sort of thing. I didn't call my mother.

As I walked into Center City, the voices elevated in both volume and pitch. I rubbed shoulders with a mummer in costume, absorbing a piece of face paint on my jacket as a souvenir. By the time I made it all the way to Broad Street,

I was sifting through the thickest crowd yet. Mummers paraded up and down, hoisting their multicolored umbrellas above their heads with one hand and balancing a bottle of Yuengling in the other. I turned the corner onto Bainbridge and started walking east toward the river, where I found my favorite corner store: an old Apothecary Shoppe masquerading as a modern-day CVS or Duane Reade or Rite Aid. (Or perhaps it was the other way around, I can't remember anymore.) Either way, I darted over to the front door, hidden halfway between two burnt-out buildings on either side. It was almost as if the fire that had destroyed the buildings on the block managed to escape this small sliver of wood and brick.

I went in looking for apple juice and some tea and a refill for my sleeping pills. Shards of light clustered on the glassy walls. Dusty shelves of thick medicine bottles, liquid capsules stuffed in bowls, all stopped with a cork. It was a nice touch. I always loved aged authenticity. I selected a nice glass bottle of apple juice, a new carton of Lemon Zinger tea, paid for them both, and then placed them in my backpack. I didn't realize it at first, but when I opened my backpack and moved around my belongings, the cashier began his lethargic flight, backing away from me, one microscopic step at a time.

His name was Bob. Apothecary Bob and I met ages earlier when he walked out of the back room wiping his hands on a white cloth that he had wrapped around his waist as an apron. I was looking for some cough medicine when he pointed it out for me. He filled my prescriptions for two years, checking me out when I needed juice or soda or snacks or condoms or postage stamps or sleeping pills. He belonged in a different era the way he kept his old-fashioned corner drugstore. White hairs clothed his face all the way from his sideburns to his upper lip and even halfway down his neck.

But this morning, just as soon as he gave me my change and put my purchases in the brown paper bag, he backed away from me. I know he was going for the emergency silent alarm because he told me about it three months earlier when he was robbed. ('I didn't get to it in time. I just didn't get there in time. They took ten thousand dollars' worth of inventory.') And now, he was doing the same to me. That's when I realized something was different. I looked at the coarse creamy hairs of his faux beard first, the voluminous patch of his mustache second, and his eyes third. Of course it was the eyes that told me what I already knew. I followed them into my backpack where I saw my father's Smith & Wesson staring back at me, nestled tightly between the new brown paper bag and an extra pair of panties.

'Get out of here!' he yelled, motioning for the button.

I tried to talk, but nothing came out. I don't know how it got there. I don't know why it was in my bag. I don't remember. I must have put it there, but—

'Get out!' he cried. 'Get out before I call the police!'

The red emergency button was already approaching his hand, shaky and tight.

'But—'

'—out!' he shouted.

I grabbed my backpack and rushed out the door. I wasn't watching where I was running. I just followed the sound of the cheers. My ears were my compass, directing me through arms and legs, masks with long pointy noses, flat balloonlike shoes. Noisemakers and shouts, the crash of beer bottles on the cement, and the delicious crunching of metal cans.

In the dense crowds, I spotted someone I thought was my father, hidden within the Blue Brigade of Generals. He was taking photos with a beautiful woman wearing a bodysuit made of feathers. She was posing proudly between him and another costumed drunk, and was allowing them to smile and pantomime fellatio for the camera. I stopped running and stared at him as his swelling tongue thrust through his left cheek. I don't know if he recognized me, but as soon as he looked my way, I started running again. Away from him, away from Apothecary Bob. Away from I don't know. I just ran. I pictured Andy Hoskins jumping over hurdles and sprinting around a crimson track. I pictured Bruce the speed walker sprinting toward my mother and then back away again. I pictured Sarah Dixon on the track those few times I watched her. I ran so quickly that I collided with a mummer wearing a puffy rainbow wig and painted-on red lips that bled out from his own by at least an inch.

My backpack was the first thing to hit the rough cement. I heard the glass from the apple juice mash against the ground, cracking into hundreds of shards, coated in a prism of juice.

'Sorry,' the rainbow clown mummer said, bending down to help me gather my belongings. 'I didn't see you.' He grinned and flecks of rounded teeth peered out from between the red lips. I almost vomited on his outstretched hand.

'It's okay,' I said, pulling myself up to run away from him.

My phone rang as soon as I was on my feet, and I answered it without even looking at the caller ID.

'Dad?' I panted. 'Is that you?'

There was a pause.

'Is this Caleb's daughter?'

I caught my breath.

'Yeah,' I wheezed, letting it out. 'Who's this?'

'Sarah Dixon's apartment,' I said to the doorman fifteen minutes later.

The Cotton Bowl was getting started on his miniature black-and-white TV.

'Hello?' I said again to the distracted doorman. He was wearing a Texas Longhorns jersey under the uniformed blazer. 'I'm here for Sarah Dixon.'

He didn't even look at me. 'Hold on a second.'

That abrasive tone reminded me of Marlene, and for a brief moment, I blanked on the apartment. Numbers and symbols, which usually came to me as easily as my name and age, spun in my head. Had she even told me her apartment number? Had Marlene? Unfortunately for me, the security guard answered the prosecution's prayers that day. Because of that football game, he had no recollection at trial of ever seeing me walk in casually, request an invite, and then calmly enter Sarah's apartment like an invited guest.

'No! NO!' he yelled at his TV. 'Penalty, that's a penalty!'

'Sarah Dixon?'

'Right. 15P,' he mumbled, still infuriated with the Longhorns.

I walked into the elevator and pushed the button for the fifteenth floor, and as the elevator climbed slowly and with each harmonious ding of a passing floor, I imagined what Sarah's apartment looked like. After all, it was the place that my father presumed would have been mine when we first met – not the musky fourth-floor walk-up with the rodent problem. It would have to be immaculate, with light shining on each newly lain tile from one crown molding to the next. Copper pots and pans would be hanging from the ceiling just over the six-burner stove, where she would come home and cook hybrid dishes like beef Wellington and baked Alaska. I suppose, now that I think of it, that was the vision I had of Marlene's kitchen. If Marlene was subsidizing Sarah's da Gama period, then certainly she would have projected her own visions of perfection and consciousness onto her daughter's palace.

I was bitterly wrong. The elevator opened to the fifteenth floor. Apartment 15P was the second one on the right. The door was slightly ajar. I walked over to it and knocked lightly.

'Hello?' I called.

She came straight to the door, without bothering to really open or close it, and just sort of hovered. Hair was matted to her temples, mascara was crumbling beneath her eyes, and a thicket of red lipstick from a previous application mushroomed at the corner of her lips, waxy and covered with morning spittle.

'Sarah?'

'Don't *Sarah* me. You know exactly who I am.'

I loitered about the threshold for an extra few moments.

'Come inside,' she demanded, directing me beyond the hallway and into her small apartment. She closed the door behind me in a frenzy. My eyes toured the grounds. The reality of Sarah's apartment was quite different from my elevator fantasy.

It was small and dusty. An old refrigerator sulked in the corner of the miniature kitchen. No sunny bursts of copper hung from a sterling silver grate on the ceiling. Instead, garbage leaked from a small plastic bag sitting in the corner of the kitchen with malodorous puddles streaming out from it, fjordlike. And waves of heat instantly sank into my skin.

'What happened in here?' I asked, placing my backpack on the ground.

'My window's sealed shut,' she snapped, 'and the heater's broken. It's stuck.'

She was pacing from the front door to the couch in the center of the main room. I hadn't really seen her up close in person before, at least not conscious. Photos and distant observation make for a poor likeness when face-to-face.

'Where is he?' she asked, wasting no time.

'Where is who?'

'Don't who me! Where the hell is he?' she demanded. She had trouble saying the word *hell*. It was both painful and sort of comical to watch.

I did my best to sound calm. 'My father?'

'Of course your father! Why else would I call the Bloody Mistress of Van Pelt 4, for Christ's sake? Where the hell is he?'

It was hot and it was cold in the room. My hands peeled from each other, in part swelling from the heat and in part smooth as ice.

'I was there, you know. I know it was you. I know,' she added, continually emphasizing the word *I* with her hands. She couldn't focus, she couldn't sit. She just paced to and fro, to and fro before the radius of the couch.

'I'm not following,' I said.

'You and I were both working on projects in the library the day you dropped out,' she said. 'You left quite the mark on our class. No pun intended.'

Words slipped away from me. The cool breeze of sweat started kicking away the heat.

'Did you know that people refused to go to that part of

the library for months after?' she continued. 'God, I can't believe you're related to him.'

I tried to change the subject.

'It's really hot in here, Sarah. You look dehydrated. Have you been drinking enough water?'

'Water?'

'You look like you may be sick,' I said to her. 'Should I take you to the hospital? Call a doctor?'

'Of course I'm sick. You slipped me something,' she said. 'I've been spotting since I got home. I don't even know how I got back here. I think,' she choked over her words, slowing down and sinking into the couch. 'I think something may be wrong with my baby.'

My throat closed up. Nothing was coming out, nothing could come out.

'Didn't you go by Noa Persephone Singleton back in school?' she asked, massaging her belly.

'Persephone is just my middle name,' I told her instinctively, as I had every year since I moved away from home, as I had written on every driver's license, school registration, doctor's form, voter card.

She nodded. 'Interesting response.' A few beads dripped from her brow. 'Look, Persephone or Noa or whoever the hell you are, I don't want to go into a history lesson here. I called you because I got your phone number out of Caleb's cell phone a while back. I was debating getting in touch, but decided against it.'

'Uh-huh,' I mumbled, without hearing a word of it. If I tried to say something else, it would come out hoarse, like a seasoned smoker. 'And . . . and now?'

'I just want to know where he is,' she said with a wheeze. 'I can't get in touch with him. He's not returning any of my calls. Nobody's answering at the bar. We were supposed to spend New Year's together. And . . . and all I remember is that I went over to the bar to talk about the baby, and then suddenly, I'm lying on his couch passed out. Then I wake up and see you. The next thing I know, I'm sleeping in my bed back here.'

She wiped the corners of her lips with her fingers before continuing. The day-old lipstick was now smeared on her fingertips.

'That was two days ago. I haven't heard from him once since then and I've been bleeding. And it hurts,' she said in a panic. 'It hurts like—'

'—like someone is carving a turkey in your belly,' I said to her. At least that's exactly what it felt like when I was researching Napoleon for my history class. I remember making the decision weeks later in the hospital that I would never return to the institution where I experienced such pain. Even if it meant I would never get a degree, never become a scientist or a doctor, I would never return. I didn't deserve to go to college in the first place.

She nodded, slowly, chin to chest, chin to chest, three short times.

'Yeah, sort of just like that.'

She looked up at me and for the first time, the wrinkles around her eyes and the lines across her forehead smoothed. I walked over to her and tried to put my arm around her.

'It'll be okay, trust me.'

'Stay away from me,' she said, as if she hadn't just grasped her belly with compassion, as if she forgot what I was doing there in the first place.

'I've been through this before, Sarah,' I insisted. 'It's all going to be okay. I promise. Let's get you to the hospital.'

'Stay the hell away from me.'

'You called me over here, didn't you?' I asked. 'I'm confused.'

'What did you give to me?' she insisted, lowering her voice.

'I didn't give you anything.'

'I saw you there. I saw you.'

'Sarah, you saw me and my father, didn't you? Why don't you think he slipped you something?'

'Forget it. Just leave,' she said after contemplating my last few words. 'This was a mistake. I don't know why I called you. I shouldn't have called you.' Her hands were spread over the incomplete belly that was her womb. 'As you must know already, my mother is quite the superlawyer in town. You better get yourself a good defense attorney right away.'

'For what?'

'For drugging me. And disappearing him,' she cooed, massaging the slight growth around her belly as if something inside was actually kicking her. I could see little goose bumps pop up all over the bare skin of her forearms as she held it.

'You and I both know I didn't do anything to you, Sarah.'

'I'm not so sure about that.'

It was so hot it felt like ants were crawling down my shirt.

'It really is hot in here,' I said. Sarah nodded her head. 'You need to open this window. You'll pass out in your condition. Think about your heart.'

Without waiting for a response, as I clearly wouldn't get one from her in this state of mind, I walked to the large window to the right of the kitchen and took a butter knife and slid it against the bottom of the window, just where the paint had dried, slicing it open like an envelope, breaking the seal as my hand drew from left to right. She needed some cool air. She needed a hospital. She needed a follow-up examination.

Within moments, there was an opening. I pushed open the glass pane all the way to its peak. A cool breeze tunneled into the dank apartment. I stuck my head out the window and within moments, a few winter flurries found their way inside.

'Ahhh,' I sighed. 'See? Much better.'

When I turned back, I spotted a small pool of apple juice bleeding through the cheap skin of my backpack, dripping onto the floor, and Sarah sitting beside it, rummaging through its contents.

I sprinted from the window toward her.

'What are you doing?'

A few pieces of glass fell out of the bag. She continued investigating, as if magically she would find my father inside. This was not the Sarah Dixon I'd tracked for the previous few months. This was not the Sarah Dixon, spawn of Marlene Dixon, who was as weak as ramen noodle. Or strong. Or confused. Quite frankly, it wasn't clear what she was, apart from acting a hair manic, pale and jittery as if she'd just swallowed a coffee shop whole.

'I'm not sure what you expect to find in there, but—'

'—I'm sure you have pills in here. Or powder. Or something illegal. I know I was drugged. I'm sure it was you. I know it was you. I know what you're capable of.'

'Please stop.'

But she wasn't listening. She didn't even seem to care about the broken glass coating the inside of my bag. She was preoccupied with looking for something that didn't exist. I don't know why I didn't rush over and stop her. I don't know why I didn't grab my bag from her and tear away as fast as I did with Persephone.

'Why is there broken glass in here?' she finally asked.

Like a battered woman, I answered quickly.

'I fell.'

But she didn't care. She wasn't even trying to slow down as she emptied the glass shards onto the floor, the tea bags, my wallet. It was as if she were a train whose brakes had failed, until a bony set of fingers traveled to her chest in animated grandeur, and she stopped.

'Sarah?'

I watched slowly as her other set of bony limbs wrapped around the gun – my father's gun – which had been sitting alone in the front pocket like an only child.

'Let me explain,' I said to her.

She dropped the gun back into the bag.

'It's not mine,' I insisted.

She didn't respond. She didn't move. Instead, she locked eyes with the gun as it rested, uncomfortable amidst the mismatched contents of my bag.

'Sarah, please,' I pleaded. 'Your heart. Please don't get excited about this.'

'How do you know about my heart?' she said, looking over to me. 'My heart is fine.'

'I know it's not,' I said. She stood up and immediately fell back down to the ground, surprising even herself. 'Please calm down.'

'Don't tell me to calm down.'

'Stay right there,' I said as I ran to the kitchen to get her a glass of water. I offered it to her, and she took it willingly.

'What did you do to me? What did you do to your father? Where is he?'

'I didn't do anything to my father.'

'Then why is he gone?'

'Because that's what he does,' I told her. Her breathing was becoming increasingly labored. Nervous laughter penetrated her nerves in redundancy. 'Sarah, please calm down. Let me make you some tea.'

'I don't want any of your fucking tea,' she said, violently placing the glass on the coffee table.

'Please, Sarah . . .'

'I know you hate him. He told me you hate him. I know you hate him.'

'I promise you, I didn't,' I said. 'I don't.'

'You . . . you have a gun!'

'It's not my gun.'

'You have a gun,' she repeated.

'It's not my gun,' I repeated. 'It's my father's. It's his gun. He gave it to me for protection. For—'

'—for Persephone Riga?' she said.

Waterfalls of adrenaline flooded my body. My heart skipped a beat.

'What?' I coughed. 'What do you mean . . . for Persephone Riga?'

She stood from me, distant, as if I were pointing the gun at her. But it was still sitting in the bag, touching nothing but the carton of tea bags.

'I know what you did,' she said. 'He told me about what you did to your friend when you were a kid.'

Wisps of cool air swam into the apartment, mixing with the heat, causing the windows to fog over. This must be how urban legends travel – like gas leaks underground, like streptococcus in a kindergarten class, like impatience at the

DMV – quickly and undeniably. There was only one person to whom I confessed. Only one person to whom I needed to connect one night when he was opening up to me about all the reasons he was in prison, about his absolution, his heavy fists and all the damage they caused as he wept that he feared they had spread to me. But he was quiet. He was trustworthy. He was a vault out of which nothing would ever break. *Now you know my secrets,* he said to me. *Tit for tat, Noa. What's the worst thing you've ever done?*

Before I could even hear myself finish the sentence I wished I'd never uttered, I saw myself walking out of her apartment and closing the door behind me, dramatically, theatrically. My mother would have been proud. *Anything you can do, I can do better.* I saw myself walking halfway to the elevator and pushing the Down button, until I realized I hadn't budged. *I can do anything better than you.* I was still standing inside the apartment, across from Sarah Dixon, who might or might not be having a heart attack at my behest.

'My father gave you the abortion pill,' I said to her.

She laughed, sweetly, in a round.

'He called me over after he thought you were dead,' I continued.

'That's impossible,' she laughed. 'He couldn't get drugs like that without a prescription. You, on the other hand. You might be idiotic enough to drop out of an Ivy League school, but you're clever enough to get in. And you're clearly clever enough to cover up for a ten-year-old murder. I know you know how to get things like this. Where did you get it? You do realize that you might have murdered a child. If you killed my baby, you'll be held responsible for that. Mark my words.'

'Your mother blackmailed him to do it.'

'Stop,' she said. 'That's pathetic.'

My hands started shaking. I wanted to be outside the door. I wanted to be in the elevator, descending to street level, and walking away.

I looked directly at her, though, and continued speaking as if this was planned all along, as if someone else knew what I'd say and what I'd do.

'I don't think my father is what your parents had in mind for the da Gama period, that's all.'

Feathered wisps of lashes. Speedy blinking. A silent clearing of her throat.

'How do you know about the da Gama period? I never even told Caleb about that.'

'Your mother told me,' I said. I don't know what came over me. My mouth opened, and I just said it. 'She also asked me to give you that pill. But I refused, and so she blackmailed my father. She gave it to him, and he gave it to you. That's what happened,' I said. 'Is she bright enough to score that kind of a drug?'

A flake of white snow drifted in from the open window. Although Sarah was trembling, I was burning up.

She sat on the floor. 'My chest hurts,' she said. 'My heart's beating really fast.'

Sarah continued rubbing her arms and, in her white shirt, she looked for a split second like an inmate in a midcentury sanitarium. Her head shifted from left to right, left to right, left to right. Her eyes began to bulge, her arms to shake, the shivering shifted up to her lips.

'I think I'm having a heart attack. Call an ambulance.'

I didn't move.

'Dial nine-one-one! I can't breathe,' she panted. 'I can't breathe.'

I ran over to the phone.

'N . . . No . . . Noa,' she tried to say, but all that came out was air, muffled air with the shadow of a voice. Stridorous breath. Sound was no longer an option for her. Her lips opened and shut. 'Help,' I think she was trying to say, though I can't be certain.

'Sarah?'

I stood over her, peering beneath like a mourner at a cemetery.

'Sarah?' I said again.

No response.

'Shit . . . Sarah?'

Nothing.

The glass of water on the table was beginning to cloud from the cold temperatures seeping in from the open window. The phone was sitting off the hook, still waiting to be used.

It had spilled into the monotone operator who was asking me to hang up. That solitary note, no different from the teakettle's call back home or Persephone's simple request to just do her a favor.

If you'd like to make a call, please hang up and dial again.

I couldn't move. The only difference between us, this time, was that I was breathing rapidly. So rapidly that I was about to join Sarah on the floor.

If you'd like to make a call, please hang up and dial again.

Shit, I panted. Fuck. Fuck. Fuck.

If you'd like to make a call—

My index finger crashed down on the receiver, stabbing the nine so forcefully that the nail split in two. Blood poured out from the tear, but I didn't notice the pain. Not just yet.

I tried again. I dialed. I dialed nine. I dialed one. And then I dialed one again. A man answered in less than two rings.

'Nine-one-one. What's your emergency?'

I dropped to Sarah's body, cradling her in my arms. She was still warm.

'Nine-one-one. What's your emergency?' the man repeated.

'Yes,' I managed to say. 'Please send someone right away. My friend. She's twenty-four years old.'

'And?'

I heard my mother say to me. *You were just so very close, sweetheart, I know. Two peas in a pod.* Persephone's eyes opened on the bed, tilted upward at the edges as I pictured the bullet hole. In my memory, it is still there.

'And?' the operator asked again.

'And there's been an accident,' I mumbled.

'What happened, ma'am?' the operator said. 'I need to know what happened to help you.'

Anything you can do, I can do better. I can do anything better than you.

'She's injured.'

'Who was injured? How was she injured?'

Sarah's bangs were falling in sweaty stalks over her eyes, which still stared at the glass of water on the table. *I don't care what you say. I know you did this to me. You're going to be held responsible.*

'—ma'am?' the 911 operator said. 'You said you think someone's injured? How injured? Is she conscious? How did she get injured?'

You better get yourself a good criminal defense attorney because this is all your fault.

But Sarah's belly was only beginning to swell.

'Hello?' the operator asked.

I know about Persephone.

The cameras in the elevator would put me here. The security guard downstairs would recall my entrance. My regular bus driver would put me at Bar Dive two days earlier when she saw me. Apothecary Bob saw me no less than an hour earlier with a gun in my possession.

'Ma'am?'

I thought of my mother's friend of a friend who was serving

a life sentence for accidentally killing her baby. I thought of my father weeping with regret about his time in prison. He was the one who dragged me into this. He was the one who told her. I wanted my sleeping pills. I wanted to close my eyes.

'Ma'am? Are you okay?' the 911 operator asked.

She was going to accuse me of killing her baby. She was going to put me in jail. She was going to make me pay for something I didn't do. She was going to tell everyone about Persephone.

Persephone.

Persephone.

Oh, Persephone . . .

She was going to—

'—are you still there, ma'am? I'm sending an ambulance. Ma'am, please tell me what—'

'—there was an intruder,' I blurted. Yes, there was an intruder. That's what happened. 'I . . . I . . . I don't know who it was, but he came in and took some jewelry and a laptop and then he left.'

'Did you get a look at him?'

'He . . .' I thought desperately back to my mother's performance; to her life's work. To my work. *He was wearing a black ski mask,* she said to the operator. 'He was wearing a mask, so I didn't catch his face,' I reported. 'Sarah started screaming. We were just sitting at the table drinking tea. Drinking water, I mean. I think it was one of the mummers. Shit, it was one of the mummers. That's when it happened.'

'When what happened?' the operator asked.

I walked back to Sarah and stood over her. From that perspective, I was as tall as a beanstalk. I was as tall as the Empire State Building. King Kong and the Eiffel Tower. I didn't bother to bend down to her the way I did two days earlier. I didn't feel her pulse to see if she was alive. I didn't have to. One of her eyelids spread open and looked at me through its tiny windowpane. It looked like she was trying to tell me something, but she was incarcerated. Nothing came out. Tears formed beneath my chest. She knew about Persephone. She knew about Persephone.

That's when I made the decision.

'Ma'am?' the operator asked.

'I . . . I think she's dead,' I said.

Sarah blinked at me, slowly, one eye closing momentarily.

'An ambulance is on its way.'

Sarah's other eye opened. A wave of salt sank to her mouth from her eyes as if she knew. There's no question in my mind that she knew.

'Holy shit,' I continued on the phone. 'I think she's dead!'

'Did the intruder have a weapon?'

My backpack was sitting upright, two feet beyond Sarah. The external zipper had not yet been sealed, and its contents were fully exposed.

'He had a gun,' I cried. 'Oh my god, please come, quickly! I've been shot, too.'

'An ambulance should be there right away. I can stay on the phone with you until they get there, if you—'

I hung up the phone.

Within seconds, it rang again and didn't stop for the next three minutes. I didn't have a lot of time. They'd be here shortly. I lifted Sarah up from the floor and placed her on the chair at the table, closest to the kitchen. It would have to be her face that the intruder would see when he knocked down the door. I didn't bother checking her pulse at this point. I could feel her infrequent breath on my neck the entire time to know she was still alive.

My father's revolver still poked out from my backpack.

I hobbled toward the bag and retrieved the gun. The grooves in the handle were cold, and my fingers slipped into place, just like that, resting against them. I didn't even bother with the safety.

I pivoted back around toward Sarah, narrowed my line of sight so that only my left eye could grasp the target, that thin shadow sitting lifelessly between the metal studs of the Smith & Wesson, and I shot once. The bullet hit her just below the clavicle. I didn't even feel the recoil thrust me back two full steps. It was only an hour later, when the police were searching the apartment, when the wheels of the gurney rolled Sarah out into the blunted winter, that I noticed my skid marks on the wooden panel beneath. Ragged patterns of mountains cyclically twisting in the sole of my sneaker.

Next, just as my mother taught me, just as Persephone

taught me, I proceeded to tear apart one side of the apartment. I opened the door with my torn fingers and jammed the lock into the wood so it would appear as though someone had broken in, and I thrust my body into the door. Wooden ribbons tied around my right arm.

Then I ran to the kitchen and grabbed the butcher's knife, pulling it from its magnetic home in a single plough, and launched it into the cushions on the couch, just like my mother did. Just as I never got to do ten years earlier. But this time, unlike the faulty memory of my mother, it had to look authentic. And as always, there had to be collateral damage.

The gun still rested, loaded and quiet within my hands, between my palms, its safety off. I walked over to Sarah.

'I'm so sorry.'

Then I turned the gun on myself at a perfect level of perpendicularity to my right shoulder. It was hard to focus, to point directly, and for this I am still grateful – even to this day, but I pulled the trigger. And those few moments, as the setting smoked and feathers glided, as flakes of snow drifted inside, and as the phone continued its ring, were the first I remember being able to live my life since she died. The bullet only grazed my right shoulder, an even column of skin removed from muscle, but it was enough to appear caught in the crossfire of a break-in. I wiped my prints from the gun, tossed it out the open window, and waited for the ambulance to arrive.

Chapter 31

THROUGH THE GREASY FINGERPRINTS AND SCRATCHED surface, Sarah's uneven face smiled back at me. She was on the other side of the Plexiglas divider in the visitor's booth, flat and two-dimensional in a two-by-three-inch grade school photograph grasped in Marlene Dixon's wrinkling hands.

'Where's Oliver?' I asked her.

Marlene sat across from me just as she had six months earlier – only, this time, silent. She had pulled out a few pictures from her stack of papers and was thrusting each photo onto the glass divider, one by tarnished one.

'Marlene?' I asked again. 'Where is he?'

She continued to hold the photo toward the glass in my face the same way she did to the jurors during the penalty phase of my trial.

'I have something I want to give to him.'

'Look at the photo,' she commanded.

'Please, Marlene,' I asked. 'How do I get him a letter?'

'Look at the photo.'

So I did. I looked at the photo.

'This is all getting a little too melodramatic for me, Marlene. Why come here in my final week like this?'

'I'm not playing any more games with you,' she dictated. 'What do you see?'

A slight nervous chuckle escaped my lips. Marlene didn't say a word.

'What do you see?' she asked again, with the same monotone timbre, the same inflection, as if she was an old LP on repeat.

Sarah's pale face, highlighted by a bridge of freckles, her eyes slightly caught between green and hazel, her nose, upturned with a slight bump.

'Please tell me what's going on with Oliver,' I asked. 'I'm worried about him. I haven't heard from him in days.'

'This is not about Oliver,' she said, as if not only his name but his entire existence was expectorating from her gut. Her face was just behind the photograph of Sarah, and after ten years, two deaths, and countless other personal tragedies, no doubt, there was no longer any resemblance between the two. Not that there ever was.

'Oliver is back in England,' she said, taking the photograph down.

Part of me believed her, and the other part didn't know how.

'He was looking to get some experience on a real-life death penalty case. Now he's done that. He was needed back in London. It's as simple as that. We don't need him to complete the last of the paperwork.'

In retrospect, I thought about this for a few moments longer than I probably should have.

'When you say "we", who do you mean? I got the impression from Oliver that—'

'—whatever impression you might have received from Oliver Stansted is certainly far from the truth. He has an excellent mind and much greater perspective than the rest of my bleeding-heart advocates, but make no mistake about it, Noa. He is an attorney, a young and inexperienced attorney, and he worked for me.'

'I'm not sure you know what sort of impression you—'

'—do not interrupt me,' she recited, as if it was part of her planned speech. 'Don't be fooled by any relationship you may have developed in here. He is not a lonely soul searching for a wife on death row, and you are far from the match that would suit him.'

You know there are times where the most important thing you must say in your life has arrived. Someone asks you to marry him. An employer wants to hire you. You are on television. You are on the fucking witness stand defending your life. You've arrived at the pearly gates. Well, the smart ones, the people who have tested their intellect, who have practiced running and tennis and violin day in and day out, the ones who actually read a book a week when they say they will, those are the people who, when asked that pivotal question at the most crucial moment, have the ability to spit back a witty comment, a genuine retort that stabs like a thumbtack, or a heart-wrenching soliloquy that could rival Hamlet's. After nearly ten years in here, any extraordinary potential I might have been given was as rusty and dry as a corroded nail.

'Did you submit the clemency petition, Marlene?'

That's all I could muster. A brief and bootless interrogation. A slip of the tongue. She wasn't going to tell me what happened to Oliver. She was never going to explain to me why his calls stopped. Why he no longer visited me when he said he would every day before X-day. Why the letters and packages of food ceased to arrive in my cell. I already knew. He now inhabited the same uncertain terrain as my father.

'Excuse me?' she said, feigning shock.

And those people who have refused to let their minds gather webs and dust balls the size of hail, they never walk out of a room wishing they could have said: *Thank you for all your efforts, Marlene. I appreciate everything you've done for me, Marlene. I know that if our roles were reversed, I would not be so great a person, Marlene. I would not be able to forgive. I would not be able to believe in humanity again.*

But again, all I said was, 'You weren't—'

I regret it, Oliver. I regret it more than you know.

'I think that you had better choose your comments more carefully, Noa.'

'I . . . I . . .'

'Say something,' she interrupted.

Marlene allowed me to struggle, and I'm fairly certain the right corner of her mouth curled as my deficiencies reappeared.

'I know that you are surviving these last few days, unable to eat, alone without the company of any surviving family or friends, because you have none. Your mother and brother are unwilling to look at your face before you go. And I cannot understand how that could make you feel. But Noa, make no mistake about it. I do not care if you are lonely. Or sad. Or hurt.'

'I don't expect you to care,' I said, softly. Maybe my voice cracked. Maybe it didn't. I don't remember.

'Care?' she laughed. 'I have known you far too long not to care about you, Noa.'

Marlene's ability to care about people is why Sarah was dead in the first place. Marlene's ability to care about people only pushed them farther and farther away.

'But there is a spectrum of colors that define the word *care*,' she continued. 'For one,' she added. Her voice was monotone throughout, a bass guitar keeping the beat. 'I care about what you did to my daughter. I care that you claim you didn't mean to do any of what you actually did. I care that we had a dialogue that you took to mean something inexplicable. I care that you were in touch with my daughter beyond your father's relationship with her. I care that you changed your plans. I care that you had a gun on New Year's Day. I care that you've spent ten insufferable years in here. I care that you have the ability to keep secrets locked tight. And I certainly do care if you live or die. You could use that lofty IQ of yours and engineer yourself a noose in that little cell for all I care. You won't be the first person to take the honor and thrill away from the state. But,' she paused, 'you shot my daughter point-blank execution-style, so please, Noa, do not ever claim that I do not care about you.'

My hands began to shake, and my heart beat faster than it did even at the shootings, the trial, the sentencing.

'Do you have any idea why I didn't say a word to anyone all these years about your involvement?'

'I had no involvement in my daughter's death,' she declared. 'Do not insult me. I'm fairly certain that after everything you've put me through and everything I've done for you, you owe me just a little bit of respect.'

'Respect?'

'Ahhh, there it is,' she smiled.

Up close, I noticed that her eyes were slightly mad. And that dirty blonde hair was mixing with her grays as if she had forgotten to dye it. She was locked in a room full of carnival mirrors. I can't imagine she even recognized herself anymore.

'Don't condescend to me, Marlene,' I asked. 'Please.'

She rubbed her nose. I swallowed and continued.

'We both know what happened. And I haven't uttered a word of your involvement to this day to a soul – Oliver included.'

'We both do not know what happened,' she said. 'What I do know, however, is that you did what you did on your own. That I know. That is clear. That changed everything.'

We both know that's not true, I wanted to say to her. But I didn't. I waited for her to catch her breath.

'You know, Marlene, I may be on this side of the division and you on that, but I am still a human being.'

'You're barely a human being.'

'Just tell me,' I whispered. 'Be honest with me. I know you don't owe me that, but did you ever even plan on speaking with the governor? Did you ever plan on filing my clemency petition? I just need to know. I'm sorry for asking, but I just . . . I just need to know that one thing.'

'The fact that I am sitting here across from you should answer that question for you well enough.'

'Does it? I don't know anymore,' I said. 'Were you ever planning on filing anything?'

Again, she refused to speak, but could not look away from me, consuming my breath, my words, my presence into hers, and for a moment, I remembered exactly how she acted on that first meeting all those years ago when she slapped the photo of the shadowman, broken and compliant, before me. Only this time, she refused to look away from me. She just focused, eyes on my face, lips pursed, wrinkles all coming together at her mouth like a plastic grocery bag tied at the center. Her eyes were filling like a man-made lake, structured, controlled, and focused just enough so that they would never overflow.

'Maybe,' I paused. 'Maybe you wish that I was . . .'

But I stopped myself there. Marlene didn't need to hear me say it. I had already taken two of her lives. The third needle, the third jab . . . well, that was for me.

'Nothing,' I finally said.

Marlene nodded her head up and down a few times, and watched the silver bars above her.

Instead of replying, she put the phone receiver down on the table and gathered the remaining photographs in her hand. When they were all together, she stood them up, again tapped them against the table (sending loud shots through the phone to my ear), allowing them to fall in alignment, and then dropped them into her coat pocket.

'I think that we have all we need for your petition, Noa,' she said. 'I'll be in touch over the next few days.'

There was no point in discussing anything more. Like I said, I was the one who pulled the trigger. I was the one who ended Sarah's life. I was the one who ended Persephone's. And, after all, isn't that why I was on trial?

'How can I get my letters to Oliver?' I finally asked, knowing they might never reach him. When I started writing, I also didn't expect them to have a reader in the first place.

'You can send them to me, and I'll forward them on to him,' she said.

Thoughts sometimes do reach their intended audience, regardless of their mired trajectory. It was the one speck of hope I held on to.

With that, she hung up the phone as if placing a golden ring on a finger, careful not to clash the metal with plastic, placed her leather briefcase in one hand, and walked away. That was the last I ever heard from Mothers Against Death and Marlene Dixon.

Chapter 32

I'M SUPPOSED TO GIVE MY ORDER FOR MY FINAL MEAL. My *final* meal. *My* final meal. My final *meal*. No matter how I look at it, pronounce it, emphasize my favorite syllable in it, it sounds almost biblical. Doesn't it?

I'm pondering chicken parmesan, a thick New York strip steak (medium well), or a three-course meal from Le Bec Fin. Yes, if the system worked the way it should – truly granting us a proper last meal – then I would have someone get it for me from Center City Philadelphia. After all, isn't that why we overspend at expensive restaurants? We want to feel good about ourselves, despite the fact that the food we are eating costs no more to make than a tightly sealed plastic carton of drumsticks from your local grocery store. We celebrate events at fancy restaurants; we introduce friends, future spouses, in-laws. We propose in them, we divorce in them. We tell the world that we are pregnant in them. What we don't do in them is request our final meals. I mean, wouldn't we all go back to those special-occasion restaurants if we knew it would be our final meal on the outside? Of course we would. We'd waste no time at KFC or McDonald's; we'd go straight for Stephen Starr and Gordon Ramsay and tea at the Plaza.

It's settled, then. Philadelphia was the city where I met Marlene and Sarah. Philadelphia boasts the Liberty Bell and Independence Hall and a crime rate worth knowing to anyone in here. Philadelphia is proud to host Le Bec Fin, and so, no matter what it costs, they will get some exposure from my request. Just as I would have wanted to tell my mother there that I was graduating from college or getting married or having a baby, I'll at least celebrate this way and tell her good-bye with class.

I think I'll start off with Escargots 'Persillade'. I've never had escargots. To be honest, I think I'm choosing it because I want to watch everyone mispronounce it. The sheriff says, *ass-car-got*, just like a redneck from Arkansas. My new neighbor has never heard of it and prefers to avoid the subject altogether. She's looking forward to having s'mores and a burger. (She used to love campouts. Sadly, that was also where she killed her husband and his lover, but I digress.) Next, I'll move on to Beef Bordelaise, with Crispy Purple Sweet Potato, Mustard Greens, and Wasabi. It might take a while to pronounce, but I will savor each moment. Of course, I'll finish the meal with a Trio of

Sorbet. If only they would let us drink wine with our last meal.

The three most common last requests are: steak, breakfast food, and nothing. Nothing at all. Honestly, I can't for the life of me imagine what sort of final protest this pathetic statement stands for. You're about to die; you might as well enjoy your favorite food for the last few minutes. It's not like suddenly saying no to something is going to change your fate. No warden is going to see you as humility incarnate for refusing to ingest an absurd amount of calories. Nevertheless, many people refuse. Maybe they have no appetite, maybe they can't remember what they used to enjoy. But, good lord, it can't be for lack of hunger. Go force them to find you exactly what you want. One person actually requested sixteen Pepsis with his final meal. Sixteen.

Over the past few weeks, I've learned that one inmate requested steak with A.1. sauce, jalapeño poppers with cream sauce, onion rings, and a salad with cherry tomatoes, ham chunks, shredded cheese, bacon bits, and blue cheese and ranch dressing. Lemon iced tea and coffee to drink and ice cream for dessert. Another wanted four fried pork chops, collard greens with boiled okra and 'boiling meat', fried corn, fried fatback, fried green tomatoes, cornbread, lemonade, one pint of strawberry ice cream, and three glazed donuts. Others in coalescence: four buns with lots of butter, lots of salt, and two slices of banana bread. Nine tacos, nine enchiladas, french fries, a salad with ranch dressing, beef fajitas, a bowl of picante sauce, a bowl of shredded cheese, six jalapeño peppers, a strawberry cake with strawberry frosting, and, there it is, the sixteen Pepsis.

This is my favorite, though. One man, who had no final request, asked that a vegetarian pizza be purchased and donated to a homeless person for his last meal. The prison officials refused.

I have to be honest, though, I have prepared poorly for this moment. The final meal, the final words, the final thoughts. It's all too formulaic. Too contrived. As if it really is a gift to plan for your final moments. I can't imagine Patsmith enjoyed it. She probably ate breakfast food before she died. Knowing her date was anything but a gift, and, in that, the government met its goal. The gift handed to me by Marlene Dixon, however, was wasted. She supplied me with a vehicle to properly prepare for X-day, and I can't even figure out what I'm going to eat. I thought the gift was from her all this time, but perhaps I haven't planned for these final words and this final meal and these final moments because the gift was never from her.

It doesn't really matter in the grand scheme of things, though. I don't want to be one of those brainless clods who refuses, I don't want to order fried chicken or fried okra or fried fries, and you've got to be kidding me if I'm giving up my chance to finally dine at Le Bec Fin so that someone else can enjoy my service. They can fly it in at whatever cost. They spend enough money here. What's a little more? It will be like I'm inviting the entire public into my special dinner out for the most important of all occasions. My mother will know the news I have to share. Hell, anyone who reads the *New York Times* will, too. The only difference for me is that I just won't walk out of the restaurant. That's all.

ONE MONTH

AFTER

X-DAY

Dearest Sarah,

This is my final letter to you. I've bought a nearby plot to yours and am burying these letters, bound together, next to you, with you, so that you may read them. If you can read them. I don't know what else to say.

Please listen to me and try not to be too upset. I'm also burying Noa's papers with them. Before you get angry or proud (quite honestly, I don't think I even know what you'd feel), please listen to what I have to say.

About a week after Noa died on her execution date as scheduled, I received a letter in the mail. It stood out on the floor from the postal sea of bills and advertisements that were thrust through the mail slot like forgotten debris. It was a handwritten envelope. I didn't wait to close the door when I walked in on it. I didn't even bother gathering the remainder of the mail. I simply picked it up and ran my fingers across the return address from Muncy, Pennsylvania, Prisoner number 10271978.

Standing by the door, I slipped my pinky finger under the opening at the corner, tearing the envelope from one end to the other. A diamond tennis bracelet slipped out of it and onto the floor. I dropped to the ground to pick it up, and in my hands, the sallow golden prongs clutching each miniature diamond stabbed at my fingers, which quickly climbed back into the envelope to find some sort of explanation. A reason for her to send her remaining possession to me. A relic of her former life returned just prior to execution. For reparations? For forgiveness? Spite?

Then my fingers found the note.

PLEASE DELIVER TO SUSAN AND GEORG RIGA OF LOS ANGELES, CALIFORNIA.

No greeting or salutation. No apology. No explanation. Just a basic demand for transference of chattel. A selfish task bequeathed to me by virtue of failure. Mine? Hers? Failure to complete a goal, regardless the proprietor, I suppose, looking back. Noa chose to give no final words before she died, and now she expected to get those from me on her behalf? She expected someone else to do her work for her? Absolutely not. It was not my place to publicize her final orders. Nor was it my duty to hand deliver her junk to Susan and Georg Riga.

A name. Two names.

Familiar names.

Names that sit among the stack of useless declarations in my office all with the embossed seal of a notary certifying that someone matching a driver's license made a declaration on the day scribbled at the bottom of the page. Names I'd heard only once before, names that rested inside the chamber of Oliver's research from month one of this failed excuse for retribution. Names that fare no better than my own.

The bracelet slipped between my fingers and slithered onto my night table, where it remained until I decided what to do with it. I placed the note beneath it and lay awake with those names ringing beside my bed every morning for a week, until I allowed myself to return to work. And when I did, I walked into my office with the note in my hand and found Susan and Georg Riga stamped on the list of supporting affidavits, stacked under the graveyard of frames beside my desk. I knew they were there. I put them there the moment Oliver left.

I opened his folder and found an old newspaper clipping from the Los Angeles Times *back from the early '90s, along with a stack of declarations and affidavits from members of Noa's past who wrote in support of clemency. People asking for her life, not for forgiveness – just for existence.*

There was a note from Andrew Hoskins, who claims he regrets his testimony at her trial, who wrote that a first love is something that cannot be killed. He wrote that he believes she should live. That she was a bright person who made a mistake, who thinks that nothing in her past was so heinous and depraved to lead to this sort of an end. Another letter from Officer Robert McManahan, who now sits in a student dormitory in West Philadelphia, monitoring entry passes from students who flow in and out of the building on their way to class. No matter what, he said, scribbled in barely legible penmanship, she is not a person whose body should be found in a prison cemetery. There was also a letter from her mother, blaming herself and apologizing, wrongfully so, that she didn't visit enough. Apologizing for villainizing her daughter while she awaited execution. There was not much more to her letter than that. And a letter from Georg and Susan Riga of Los Angeles, begging the governor, with more ethos than a stranger knew how, to spare this girl's life. They hadn't seen her since she was a child, they wrote, but they never forgot the kindness she showed to their daughter, Persephone. And for that reason alone, they wrote, she should be spared. What use does removing her do, they asked? The victim wouldn't return, regardless of who took her, or how. And then a perforation of official validation stamped the bottom of each page like a presidential signature.

Persephone.

Persephone.

Persephone.

I don't understand what's happening.

I don't understand what is happening anymore.

Sweetheart, I can't read on.

I don't know what this means. I don't know what they mean.

The only thing I know is that each new day, each new day since X-day, a shiny clean thread rolls out from my belly, knitting a web to cover the city, and I can't stop it. At my home, or in my car, I cannot walk another step, because I know that mixed in with my regular paperwork, lurching above the thread and that newspaper clipping, those declarations reside with the perforated affidavit declaring what I cannot bear to read again.

And so I don't. I wash my face and brush my teeth, clean the sheets, slip each leg into pantyhose, each foot into a heel, and dress myself for work. Every day. Every single day I go to my office and look away from Oliver's files and your photos and your father's wedding portrait.

Then, two weeks after she sent me the bracelet, I received a larger package in the mail, fraught with the same telltale signs of bureaucracy. This time, however, the package was sent to the office and was addressed to Oliver Stansted. When the mailroom brought it to me to inquire about his forwarding address, I told them I would simply pass it on. You wouldn't believe the stares I got when it was handed to me. Instantly I knew what it was. I went home with the box still closed and a blunted scissor in my purse, no different from how I stood at the doorway, opening the first envelope.

Before I create a vision for you of your mother tearing into the novel of confessions like a vulture, as I did with her letter, you should know that once I got home, I calmly placed it on the kitchen table beside the bracelet and note. It was already on its first lap of decomposition, clearly stuffed, overflowing with papers and items, and God knows what else. The rectangular box didn't even sit properly on the flat surface. It seesawed from a bulge in the center, struggling to balance on one side. Imperfect postal systems and the single unit of mail allowed for inmates produced this inoperable tumor in the bowels of a silly little package.

So instead of forwarding that package or opening it to read for myself, I stared at it. I watched it slant one way, for seconds, and then I tapped it with two fingers as it tipped to the other side. I wanted to know what was inside. God, I did. I can't tell you the curiosity that shot through my heart. Maybe it contained a manifesto of the sadness she felt prior to dying, or perhaps a golden beanstalk climbing with the humility and penitence she found in her final years, months, days, hours even before being strapped to the gurney. But, you see, the problem is that apologies are really just little weeds that grow over monuments and headstones. They keep coming back, but never stop ruining what lies beneath. If an apology is truly authentic, the pain is supposed to stop. Right?

As the package settled on its bulge in the center of my clean kitchen, my arms reached out to it. I placed a single finger into one of the metaphorical loops of box string, and I couldn't pull.

Sarah, I was scared. I didn't want to be that person. Not again. I didn't want to untie the brown box string. I didn't want to gut the cardboard box revealing the memoirs of a person's life I so desperately wanted to end. You weren't going to return to me. I cannot be with you. I am not with you anymore. I am not in the dirt beside you, no matter how much I may belong. Instead, I remain above ground, dangling from the thread that sways from side to side, as it drops me just far enough from you that I struggle to stand. I struggle to read, to dress myself, to merely hold on to that ropy thread, that strand of diamonds that the police report in the twenty-year-old newspaper clip said was the only thing taken from the burglary that killed Persephone Riga.

I don't want to know anymore what Noa did or didn't do in her life prior to meeting you, prior to taking you away from me, while finding time to pen these hundreds of pages in her cell. Perhaps she wrote it in the darkness or maybe even while sitting on the toilet. But I don't want to know how terrible she felt for taking you away from me. I don't want to answer to Susan and Georg Riga. I don't want to open the wound that is finally beginning to heal. My blood no longer coagulates. I cannot take any more chances. And I won't.

So I'm going to bury her apology or her tears, her retributive last words, her virulent expletives, and all of her potential in the ground with these letters. With you. She put it there, not me. She had the gun, she filled it with bullets, she used it on you. It was never up to me to refuse to speak with the governor. It was never really my choice to abandon her clemency petition. It was never up to me, sweetheart. None of that would have changed your current residence. None of that would have changed what Noa did, *even without me. And no matter what she said, what she wrote, I'm still up here and I'm sitting at my kitchen and I'm staring at that box. And that bracelet.*

That bracelet with a request. A merciless favor for another. That letter addressed to me, but intended for someone else. I think that maybe she's right. I should give them away. I want to give them away. I want to pass the letters and bracelet on to their intended beneficiaries, but I can't. I can't pick up the phone and call Persephone's parents. I can't look in on Noa's words. So instead, I pick up the bracelet and let it drop around my wrist each morning after I wake, struggling to secure the latch with my open hand. Sometimes it closes on the first try and sometimes not. But every day — it is with me when I drive my car, when I go to work, when I climb the stairs to the county courthouse, when I wait in a crowded elevator, when I present at a meeting before forty businesspeople in platinum cufflinks and tailored suits all looking to me for advice — the bracelet is always fastened around my wrist.

Forever yours and only yours,
Mom

ACKNOWLEDGMENTS

My unending gratitude, inspiration, and love go out to the following people:

The incomparable Richard S. Pine, who is a superhero among agents, with a quick wit and dedication to his clients of hurricane proportions, whose name I will forever say before drinking a glass of wine. Christine Kopprasch, a fiercely kind editor, who guided with panache and gentility, provided room to explore, an accompanying compass when necessary, and the beautiful sparks of an early friendship. Molly Stern, an icon of publishing, whose enthusiasm and energy championed this novel in ways I can never fully comprehend – one conversation with you, and I was smitten. Thank-you, in every language on earth, cannot properly express this gratitude.

To the team at InkWell, including Alexis Hurley, Charlie Olsen, Eliza Rothstein; to the team at Crown, including

Maya Mavjee, Rachel Rokicki, Rachel Meier, Jay Sones, and Annsley Rosner, for their creative and inventive marketing and publicity; to Chris Brand, for his brilliant, spot-on jacket, and Lauren Dong, for her exquisite interior design; to Mary Anne Stewart and Patricia Shaw, for their tireless copyediting and production editing; and to Howie Sanders at UTA, for his cinematic support in Noa's latter stages. Thank-you also to Marion Donaldson, Sam Eades, Jo Liddiard at Headline, and Mark Lucas at Lucas Alexander Whitley in the UK for creating a second home market for me, and to all the publishers around the world who have embraced Noa and Marlene.

Many thanks also go out to the Texas Court of Criminal Appeals and the University of Texas School of Law's Capital Punishment Clinic and its outstanding professors, including Rob Owen and Maurie Levin, and my professors at Temple Law, for providing the foundation that enabled me to write this story.

Several chapters would not have been written without generous grants from the folks at Byrdcliffe Artist Colony in Woodstock, New York, and Circle of Misse in the Loire Valley, France, who provided solitude and time to write. Thank-you also to the University of Pennsylvania's English and Creative Writing Departments and the Kelly Writers House for furnishing a creative home for me when I first started writing, and to the University of East Anglia's Creative Writing MA, for cementing that home in the United

Kingdom. And to my writing teachers and mentors over the years, especially Jill Dawson and Lorene Cary.

Of course, none of this would be possible without the support and dear friendship of early readers and outstanding writers: Emily Bullock, Emma Sweeney, Michelle Pakula, Mark Pryor, Saul Nadata, Harriet Levin Millan, and the Austin Fiction Writers Group.

Finally, thank-you to my family. My parents, Charles and Kathi Silver, who instilled in me a passion for the arts, gave me a parental nudge into law school, and a childhood filled with books, for which I am forever grateful. To my in-laws, Etty and Mordechai Moldovan, whose unconditional support has never dimmed. To my siblings – Arielle, Sasha, Yael, and Adrian – whose closest friendships have comforted and defined me. Mostly, thank-you to my partner in life, Amir, who, before I blurted out my secret literary ambitions, told me when we first met that he always wanted to marry a writer. Since then, you have read draft after draft with the same enthusiasm as the first day we met. Quite simply, without you, I'd be lost in the clouds; and for that, I suspect, my parents thank you, too.